8/13

Carl

Kings of the North Way

QUILLMAAT PUBLISHING

The Vikings

This is a fictional work in a historic setting. All the characters portrayed in this book are mythological, imaginary, or historical figures from the Scandinavian countries.

Cover illustrations by Wes James

Distributed by
QUILLMAAT PUBLISHING
P.O. Box 7594
Helena, MT 59604

Printed in the United States of America

The Vikings

The dawn of the ninth century CE brought a terror from the icy realms of the North stretching from the emerald island of Ireland to the Caspian Sea. Even the might of Charlemagne's empire was unable to stem the tide of invaders. Rapine pillage and piracy became hallmarks of the towering barbarians from the untamed northern wilderness.

Time however, would reveal the Norsemen as far more than savage raiders. Traders, merchants and fearless adventurers, they explored a large portion of the known world and beyond, becoming the first to venture across broad expanses of uncharted seas.

Silver coins from Arabia would find their way to the shores of the New World and luxurious furs and sables would grace the nobility of royal courts throughout Europe. The new trade routes would become established roads of commerce.

Although the Vikings were never considered conquerors, they forged a legacy of indelible effects on their southern neighbors. An agrarian economy remained the bulwark of Norse progress, but wealth plundered from foreign nations and neighbors would change the course of history.

To Beth,

2/3/2011

Glossary

Mythology:

Aegir *(Eagor)*: God of the sea, husband of Ran and father of nine daughters -- the waves.

Aesir: Younger of two branches of gods -- the Vanir and Aesir.

Alvis: Dwarf turned to stone after requesting Thor's daughter's hand in marriage.

Andvari: Master craftsman among the dark dwarves. Cursed a golden ring that ruined many lives.

Angrboda *(Angerboda)*: Frost giantess and mistress of Loki. Mother of the wolf *Fenris*, the serpent *Jormungand,* and goddess of the underworld, *Hel.*

Asgard: World, home, and stronghold of the Aesir.

Asynjur: Goddesses of Aesir, twenty-four in all.

Baldur *(Baldr)*: Son of Odin and Frigga. God of justice, loving and gentle. Killed by his blind brother Hodr.

Beowulf: Nephew of the King of the Geats. Hero and slayer of the monster Grendel and his mother.

Bergelmir: Bergelmir and his wife were the only survivors of the flood from Ymir's blood. Founded the realm of Jotunheim, the world of frost giants.

Bifrost: The multi-colored rainbow bridge between Asgard and Midgard, the world of men.

Borr: Son of Buri. Father of Odin, Vili and Ve. Ancient god that lived before the nine worlds were made.

Braggia: Son of Odin and Gunnlod, a female giant. God of eloquence and poetry. Married to Idun.

Brisingamen: Magic, exquisite necklace coveted by Freya, fertility goddess.

Brunhild *(Brynhild)*: Valkyrie who defied Odin. Banished to earth and imprisoned in a ring of fire.

Buri: Ancestor of the gods.

Draupner: Golden ring of wealth possessed by Odin.

Einherjar: Heroic dead. Gathered from the battlefields by Valkrye to live in the glory of Valhalla until Ragnarok.

Fafnir: Son of the powerful magician Hreidmar. Became a dragon to guard the cursed treasure of Andvari.

Farbauti: Cruel 'striker' giant. Father of Loki, the 'deceiver' -- god of fire.

Fenris *(Fenrir)*: Giant wolf and destroyer of Odin. Son of Loki and the frost giantess Angrboda.

Fjalar: One of two brothers who killed the wise man Kvasir. They mixed his blood with honey to make a coveted mead of wisdom.

Forsetti *(Forsite)*: Son of Balder and Nanna. God of justice.

Freyja *(Freya)*: Name means 'Lady'. Daughter of Njord and sister of Freyr. Fertility goddess and member of Vanir.

Freyr *(Frey)*: Name means 'Lord'. God of the wind and sea. Son of Njord.

Frigga: *(Frigg)*: Wife of Odin. Mother of Baldur.

Gerda: Beautiful frost giantess. Daughter of Gymir.

Ginnungagap: The yawning abyss at the beginning of time. Omnipresent and omnipotent, it was the vast, primordial void that pervaded all existence and everything in it.

Groa: Seeress and wife of Aurvandil.

Gungnir: Odin's magic spear.

Heimdall *(Heimdair)*: Son of nine mothers and ever vigilant watchman for Ragnarok.

Hel: Daughter of Loki and Angrboda. Ruler of the netherworld.

Hermod: Son of Odin and Frigga. Divine messenger of the gods.

Hodur *(Hodr)*: Son of Odin and Frigga. Blind, unwitting slayer of the god Baldur.

Ragnarok: Considered the "Doom of the Gods", the final battle between 'good' (the gods, warriors of Einherjar and light elves), and 'evil' (the frost giants, minions of Loki, dark dwarves and residents of Hel).

Surtr: Primordial giant with a flaming sword guarding the world of Muspellsheim.

Skadi: Goddess of winter. A deity of hunters and mountain climbers.

Historical Figures;

Alcuin: (c. 735 – 804) A scholar and ecclesiastic. Born in York, Northunbria, student of Egbert and teacher at the Carolingian court.

Asa Haraldsdotter: Daughter of Harald Granraude, king of Agder and wife of Gudrod the Hunter. Mother of Halfdan the Black.

Bjarni Herjolfsson: (Est. c. 950 – 1000) Made first reported sightings of new lands to the west of Greenland around 985-986 A.D.

Eirik Bloodaxe: (Est. c. 900-952) Second king of Norway, 930-934 A.D. Killed four brothers.

Eric the Red: Born in Jaeren district of Norway in 950 A.D. Moved with his father to Iceland around 960 A.D. and banished for murder when grown. Established first settlements in Greenland around 985 A.D. Died 1001 A.D.

Gudrod the Hunter: Father of Halfdan the Black and son of Halfdan the Mild, of the House of Yngling.

Gunnhild Ossursdotter: Wife of Eirik Bloodaxe. Known as the 'Mother of Kings'. Reputation of being a witch.

Haakon Sigurdsson Jarl: Reigned from 970 – 995 A.D. Died in 995.

Haakon the Good: (c. 920-961) Third king of Norway, 934-961 A.D. Half-brother of Eric Bloodaxe.

Halfdan the Black: (c. 810-860) Father of Harald Fairhair, first king of a united Norway. Early conqueror of numerous realms in southern Norway.

Harald Fairhair: (c. 850-933) First king of Norway, 872-930 A.D.

Harald Greycloak: (Est. c. 925-976) Succeeded Haakon the Good. Reigned from 961-970 A.D.

Harald Sigurdsson (Hardrada): 1015 to 1066 CE, king of Norway from 1047 to 1066. Known as the 'hard ruler'.

Leif Erickson: Son of Erick the Red, born around 982 A.D. Credited with being one of the first foreigners to visit Labrador and Newfoundland. Died 1025 A.D.

Thorvald Asvaldsson: Father of Erick the Red. Son of Asvald Ulfsson and grandson of Ulf Oxna-Porir. His brother, Naddod, is credited with discovery of Iceland. Banished from Norway for murder.

Olaf Tryggvason: (Est. 960-1000 A.D.) King of Norway from 995 to 1000 A.D. Son of Tryggve Olafsson and great grandson of Harald Fairhair. Played a major role in converting Vikings to Christianity.

Chapter 1

Lindisfarne -
Wolves from the North

The tiny flame dancing on the tip of a slender candle wavered momentarily from a cold gust of wind and then resumed its ambivalent efforts. A dim reflection of the light came from the bald pate of an old man sitting at a crude wooden table directly below the candle.

The dark brown robe with faded yellow trim identified the man as an elder monk of the Aidan monastery. Established in 635 AD, the massive rock walls of the structure broke the brooding landscape of the tidal island of Lindisfarne.

Alcuin paused and studied the faded Latin script to his left. Bishop Cuthbert had entrusted the treasured Lindisfarne Gospels to him shortly before his death and the last few months had been spent carefully copying the Gospels of Matthew, Mark, Luke and John. Tapping the quill pen to his lips he pondered the words of the man known as Jesus.

It was the sixth month of the year 793 and winter was slow in releasing its iron grip of the land. A cold wind moved down from the north and rattled the shutters of the cluttered little room. The monk stood from his labors, rubbed his hands together and shuffled to the window. Closing the shutters eliminated the pallid light the room received from a cloud obscured afternoon sun, making it even harder to see in the darkened alcove.

Muttering a small prayer asking forgiveness for not enduring the cold better, he gathered a few shards of firewood and laid them carefully on the glowing coals of the fireplace. He returned to his bench by the little table when a strange, keening wail broke the tranquility.

He knew the mournful howl was not from an animal, but was primordial in the agony it betrayed. A tremor ran the length of his body as he stood in the silence of the study, trying to identify the source.

Distant, indistinguishable sounds began to permeate his senses, just beyond comprehension. By the time the bellowing and screams were discernable, an initiate broke into the room, eyes flashing wildly.

"Father Alcuin! We are under attack! Wild men from the sea are killing everyone!"

The elderly monk stared at the young novice, not comprehending the hysterical plethora of fear flowing from the quivering lips.

"Berwick! Stop screaming and calm down."

He grabbed the young man by the shoulders, trying to steady the terror in the frantic, darting eyes. "Now what is this about wild men?"

Pulling back and spinning away from the older man's grasp, the youth was gesturing toward the door, slurring his words in the terror that enveloped his entire consciousness. "They're . . . bloody axes . . . God help us Father, we're dead men."

The boy dropped to his knees and stared at the doorway, muttering a desperate prayer. Alcuin wasn't sure what was happening, but knew the monastery was under some sort of attack and his mind went to the sacred Gospels on the table behind him.

He hurried to the massive fireplace and removed a large stone in the west side. Grabbing the heavy book, he reverently placed it in the opening behind the granite block and replaced the stone. The carved masonry fit precisely and careful scrutiny would be required to see the cracks around it.

Turning back to the young initiate, he noticed the novice was sitting on the heels of his feet, uncomprehending in the terror that had taken hold of his mind.

"Berwick! We must . . ."

A guttural roar cut the sentence like the falling of a guillotine. The half-open door leading into the small room was shattered with the impact from a blood-splattered mountain of a man. The huge brute was wielding a dripping axe with a wicked, moon-shaped blade. Tendrils of gore hung from a hook at the back of the weapon, flinging strips of crimson across the stacks of sacred books and crude furniture. A gleaming sword dangled in the man's left hand, but it was obvious he preferred the axe.

The titan paused in the doorway, chest heaving, eyes alight with the fire of destruction. A quick survey of the room revealed little of worth and the bearded face became a snarl of disgust. The main prayer hall had been filled with golden artifacts of the Christians, but the small, adjoining rooms provided little in the way of reward.

Growling in frustration, the towering warrior swung the deadly axe in a sweeping arc down upon the kneeling initiate. The blade hit just below the jawbone, splitting the slim body to the sternum. Alcuin would never know if the lad felt anything. The boy never muttered a sound, just toppled over, the blood covered body shuddering with the spasms of death.

Jerking the heavy, curved blade free, the man stepped on the boy's pale arm as he swept into the room. The grizzled warrior gave the old monk a glance before slamming the sword home in a heavy leather sheath. The crimson axe hung loosely at his side as he began ransacking the room for anything of worth.

Alcuin stood frozen in a daze of fear, awe, and fury at the desecration occurring before his eyes. Woodenly, he moved towards the assailant to somehow stop the destruction. He reached out to grasp the wolf's fur covering the man's shoulder and pulled.

The massive shoulders whirled at the touch and a growl emanated from the hairy lips. "Go away old man."

"You cannot . . ."

The monk saw the flat blade of the axe flying towards him in his peripheral vision, but that would be the last thing he would remember. Lights exploded in front of his eyes and the world went dark.

The Viking raised the dripping broadax for a killing blow just as a comrade broke into the room. "Gudrod! There's a chest of coins in the room below with silver vases and golden chalices. The stories are true – these Christian temples are houses of incredible wealth!"

The prostrate abbot was forgotten at the mention of gold and the raiders vanished as quickly as they had appeared. The old man lay as dead for hours. The screams of the dying slowly faded with the setting sun.

It was the darkest part of the night and unbearably cold when Alcuin awoke, realizing he wasn't dead. Touching his scalp gingerly, the blood had dried, leaving a crusty layer on his skin. He struggled into a sitting position and slowly stood, unsteady legs trembling beneath him. Remembering the events immediately prior to being knocked unconscious, he staggered over to the bloody remains of the young initiate. Kneeling, he quietly murmured a prayer for his soul.

Gently laying a worn, faded cloak over the body, he rose and left the room. The smell of sulfur and soiled clothes hit him full in the face as he exited into the cold, crisp night. A sliver of moon and countless sparks in the sky provided a luminous glow, casting ghastly shadows from the proliferation of lifeless corpses. The cloister was filled with bodies, some ravaged beyond recognition, sightless eyes staring up at an indifferent sky.

He moved woodenly to the ramparts of the monastery and stared out across the sea. There were no signs of the boats that had brought the unimaginable terror. A gentle breeze moved against the surf, creating ribbons of shimmering white along the coast.

His mind was vacant, unable to comprehend the atrocities surrounding him. Then he remembered the Gospel of Saint Mark. A cloud moved over the slim crescent in the sky as if adding emphasis to the thought; *'And when ye shall hear of wars and rumors of wars, be ye not troubled: for such things must needs be; but the end shall not be yet.*

'For nation shall rise against nation, and kingdom against kingdom: and there shall be earth quakes in divers places, and there shall be famines and troubles: these are the beginnings of sorrows.'
The beginnings of sorrows.

The thought brought a sadness to the aged monk's heart that could never come from worldly loss. His mind turned to the hundreds of similar monasteries along the shores of his sacred island and the coasts of Europe. He returned to the interior of the monastery and, taking up quill and ink, penned a warning to the civilized world:

`'The heathens poured out the blood of saints around the altar, and trampled on the bodies of saints in the temple of God, like dung in the streets.'`

Word of the atrocities and ferocity of the attack spread quickly across Northumberland. With each telling, the cruelty and barbarity of the invaders increased. Even nature reeled with the foreboding portent of the bloody raid. Gentle breezes were whipped into maelstroms, lightning danced in the skies, and the shadows of dragons flashed through the gloomy clouds.

Chapter 2

Gudrod the Hunter - Birth of a Dynasty

The morning sky morphed into scudding clouds chasing a distant horizon. Five square sails moved over the emerald troughs and frothy whitecaps with an unnatural ease. Mead and songs of conquest had lasted late into the night and the crews went about their work with a practiced indifference.

A tall, heavily built man of middle age was standing in the aft portion of the lead ship, arms crossed, watching the rolling wake disappear in the early morning mist. He turned slightly at a movement behind him. "Sverre. Good morn. Did you sleep well?"

The grizzled white-hair at his shoulder stood quietly staring out across the waves a moment before answering. "I slept fine." The answer was little more than a growl.

Gudrod turned away from the vista and studied the hoary relic at his side. The old man was an enigma. He had found the Norseman wandering aimlessly in the frozen wastelands of the far north the previous summer. The wrinkled visage said the man was ancient, but the fire in his one good eye belied his appearance.

Questions had produced little in the way of satisfaction. The bushy grey eyebrows dipped beneath a furrowed brow when he was asked something as simple as his name. The vagabond was either hiding dark secrets or unable to remember anything about his past.

One thing the Viking chieftain knew for sure; the grumpy wretch was not what he seemed. The stranger had instilled a burning desire in him that grew with each passing day. He knew he would be the forefather of great Norse kings and win the glorious battles that lay ahead.

The mere presence of the lost soul had brought out the warrior in him. Finding he was no longer content to raise crops and children, the clan leader began building ships and gathering men to plunder the wealth of the world. The newcomer could not remember his own name, but seemed to possess wisdom far beyond the grasp of a mortal mind. The name Sverre was agreed upon until the man remembered his real name.

"The raid went well," Gudrod finally said.

One eyelid in the scarred, venerable face hung limply over a vacant socket, sewn shut and healed ages ago. The old Viking tapped the deck impatiently with the oaken rod he always carried. It was as though he could see into the future and waiting for things yet to come was a heavy burden.

"You are of the house of Yngling and therefore a descendent of Frey -- the old gods of Vanir. The pillage of that island was not a glorious battle – but twas a start."

"Aye. It's just that . . ." He let the sentence trail off, unfinished.

The man's grey eye found the clan chieftain and held him fast. "Alfhild is dead. You must accept that and move on. Olaf is a good son and will make a fine warrior."

The mention of his wife brought a pain that was still fresh in his chest and he glared at the grey hair's apparent indifference to his loss. "Twas not your loss Sverre."

The grizzled wretch hacked up a wad of flim and spit it over the railing. "Do not speak to me of loss! You have no idea of what has been lost!"

Gudrod flinched at the power behind the snarling words. The man was extremely old, but there could be no doubt he meant what he said and could back it up.

The soft face of his dead wife held his mind's eye for a moment before turning away from the memory. Heading towards the ship's prow, he began barking commands at the young crew.

There were less than a dozen children and women survivors that would serve as slaves, but the monastery had contained chalices, crosses and relics of considerable worth -- just as the old sage had foretold. The raid would make him a rich and powerful man back in his homeland.

He stood at the ship's prow and glanced at the snarling dragon's head, craved from a single piece of wood, skimming over the waves as though in flight. It was a fierce looking creature, but not as foreboding as the ancient fossil standing aft. Glancing towards the back of the ship, he noticed Sverre had curled up in some tanned hides, apparently asleep.

An eyelid marked with tiny white lines of old scars drooped heavily over the man's good eye, but twitched from the workings of his mind. The dream was a recurring one about the god-of-gods, known throughout the nine worlds as Odin. It always started the same way.

☼☼☼

The land was in a desperate turmoil after three years of endless winter. He walked across the frozen, windswept Vigrid plain with a fatalistic stride that was the culmination of years of dread.

The gut wrenching howl of a monstrous beast long restrained, but at long last freed from the lashings that held it fast, rolled over the terrain. The great wolf Fenris was loose and bent upon a vengeance that would not be denied. Odin knew he was not alone in this final battle, but also knew the outcome. It was as it should be. The gods had failed and deserved to die.

The immense canine broke from the ancient forest into the rolling brown grass and slowed to a trot, huge eyes sweeping the landscape for his nemesis. He broke the easy gait when the black orbs fell upon the supreme god, standing near the middle of the field. There were others around him, but the mind of the wolf was focused on only one thing; the total destruction of the deity known as Odin.

Fenris knew the gods would bleed and die the same as mortals -- from his maiming of Tyr. However, devouring the god's hand gave little satisfaction for the countless years of confinement.

A thundering roar shook the landscape for miles, rumbling from the massive cavern of the animal's chest as he lunged towards the waiting foe.

Odin stood as though carved from an oaken bole. Not from fear, but a quiet resolution to meet the inevitable. The beast had grown to enormous proportions. Ten feet at the shoulder, the animal was a final culmination of the power and evil of its sire.

The ancient deity sidestepped the enraged charge of the mountain of fury and fur, thrusting the fabled spear tip of Gungnir deep into the wolf's side as it passed.

The deadly conflict raged on and the Norse god inflicted countless deadly wounds upon the monster. A dim hope that his visions and foresight were wrong began to glimmer.

Maybe the preparations had been enough. Maybe, just maybe, the gods would be given another chance. He glanced around at the raging field of warring titans.

Thor stuck Jormungand a killing blow with Mjollnir and the leviathan reeled backwards. The flashing blades of Frey and Surtr were sending arcs of fire across the barren plain. The god of the Vanir was holding his own with the fire giant.

Odin cast his heavy shield aside. It was slowing him down. The monstrous wolf was weakening from the loss of blood and a powerful thrust at the base of his neck would finish him.

The lumbering beast charged again. His cavernous maw opening wide as he thundered towards the focus of his hate. Exhausted, Odin set the butt of the spear deep into the ground and braced for the impact. Fenris leaped into the air twenty paces away and came down upon foe and spear with a shuddering crash.

The wind was crushed from the god's chest and for a moment, he lay gasping for breath. He pushed against the hairy body lying on him and it moved! The huge wolf slowly stood, chest heaving, with blood streaming from the shaft driven deep into its body.

Odin pushed himself up on one elbow and the world spun into chaos. The impossible had happened -- Gungnir was deeply embedded in Fenris' chest, but the indestructible shaft was broken.

He was staring at the ragged end of the bloody spear when the huge jaws descended upon him. His mind moved to a calm acceptance as his body was torn asunder by the cruel fangs.

☼☼☼

Sverre awoke with a start. The dream was so real the smell of blood and hate still reeked in his nostrils. It was not the first time the nightmare had consumed his slumber, but there was nothing to explain the origin. His mind was a blank page prior to awakening at the base of a receding glacier the previous year and wandering south.

Looking around him, the recent events came rushing back. The Lindisfarne monastery and the raid. There had been little in the way of resistance, but the gold it brought would lay the groundwork for greater things ahead. Something going to his very core knew there was a majesty in mankind that only blossomed in the heat of battle.

He struggled into a sitting position and rubbed a tired face, glancing upwards. Grey clouds the color of an unpolished iron blade tumbled in a slow progression across the sky. His thoughts flashed back to the dream.

According to legend, Odin, the supreme god of Asgard, would die in the battle of Ragnarok. The flaming sword of the fire giant Surtr would cleanse the nine worlds in a conflagration consuming good and evil alike. A new world would spring up from the ashes and . . .

Sverre shook his head. He couldn't remember the first time he heard the story of Odin, Thor, and Valhallah, but he knew every detail of their lives. Life seemed somehow surreal; he slept, but was never rested, ate, but was never filled. Who he was and where he came from was a mystery. Did he have relatives somewhere, searching for him?

Pushing the question from his mind, he tossed the fur covered hides aside and stood with a quiet reflection. He believed in destiny and fate. Perhaps the Norns had set him upon this journey to . . . what? Scowling at the unanswered questions, he turned into the biting wind, savoring the salty spray in his face.

Two days later they arrived at Vestfold, Norway, amidst the cheering and shouting of the local populace. Beaching the shallow-drafted crafts was an easy chore and soon accomplished.

Gudrod gathered up shield and spear, espying his mother and son approaching through the crowd. Liv was the daughter of Dags, a mighty warrior long dead, and the wife of his deceased father. Life was hard in the northern reaches of their world and the lines in her face portrayed a map of that existence.

"Mother. How is Olaf?"

The tired, wrinkled face broke into a toothless grin as she hefted the blue-eyed boy. The child's features were somewhat dark, like his father's. The man ran a beefy hand through the mahogany locks and took the boy from his grandmother.

The old woman watched as the toddler hugged the hairy neck and snuggled comfortably in the ample crook of the man's arm. Her son was a hard man, but a good father. She looked from father to son and spoke what was on her mind. "You're a good man Gudrod, but the boy needs a mother." She paused before adding, "And many brothers."

The unspoken words about the chances of a single son surviving to become a man's heir were irrefutable in the old woman's eyes as she turned away.

A day's ride to the north a man would enter into Agder, the realm of King Harald Granraude. The monarch had several sons, but only one daughter. After mulling the thought over for several days, Gudrod sent an envoy to the king, proposing marriage to his daughter and thus an alliance between the two kingdoms.

The girl was barely in her teens, but fair to look upon. The Vestfold chieftain had seen her several years prior. A shy child, she had remained hidden behind her father for most of the visit. Gudrod pursed his lips at the thought of bedding the girl. She would probably be no better than the dozens of women he had known, but she had one thing they did not; a royal blood line.

His envoy to King Granraude returned with utmost haste and the captain of the troop, a Wulfstag Eddleson, indignantly informed his lord that the northern king had not only failed to show proper respect for visiting dignitaries, he laughed at the proposal and had the envoy thrown from his great hall.

Gudrod sat quietly listening to the controlled rage buffeting the man's words. At the conclusion of the report, Wulfstag dropped to one knee and remained silent. The Viking warlord had been uncertain as to the king's response, but he had not expected an outright rebuff.

Surprise gave way to a seething rage. He would retaliate, but the Agder region was formidable and a rash act could be his undoing. Pondering the appropriate action late into the night, he heard a faint knock at the door. He made his way to the heavy wooden beams granting entrance to his study and pulled the latch back.

The door swung open and Sverre stood in the faint light of the hallway.

"What do you want?" He growled.

The deep-set grey eye held him fast for a moment as though weighing his worth. Finally, a bony hand reached up and clawed through a wispy beard. "Kill him," were the only words spoken before the venerable mage turned away and faded into the gloom of late summer.

Gudrod stood staring at the receding back. The old relic was certainly a mystery. There was no reason he should take the advice of a stranger but the demeanor of the man and the certainty in his ways left little room for doubt. He found himself nodding in agreement. That was the right answer, the only answer. He just needed someone to say it.

With a force of two-hundred warriors, he attacked the distant stronghold three days hence. The sun dropped below the horizon for a few hours, but total darkness never came this time of year.

The fighting was fierce, brutal and short. Taken by surprise, King Granraude's troops were quickly decimated. In constant retreat, the monarch made a last stand with his sons in the great hall. The slaughter on both sides was without mercy.

By the time Gudrod reached the scene, three of the monarch's sons were dead, sprawled amidst a pile of quivering corpses. Harald was still standing, brandishing a bloody sword with a broken spear shaft protruding from his side. When the King of Agder saw the tribal chieftain enter, his eyes flared and a bloody froth broke from the bearded lips, but the words were unintelligible.

The sovereign dropped to his knees, dark blue orbs still fixed on Gudrod, but starting to glaze over. The gilded crown spilled from the graying temple as he crashed forward into the dirt of the floor. Warriors from both sides, with heaving chests, paused momentarily to show respect for a well-earned death.

The chieftain quickly surveyed the carnage and realized one or two of the heirs had escaped and the daughter was nowhere to be found. Asa became the center of a hut-to-hut search and a piercing scream betrayed her location.

Gudrod's men had been none too gentle in removing her from underneath a slop trough in the pig sty. She was naked. Whether it was the work of his men or due to the surprise attack, he really didn't care.

Anger and terror were waging a war in the flashing green orbs and the anger won out. She straightened to her full five feet four inches and glared at the killer of her family. "So the mighty Gudrod the Hunter attacks women and children. My father was right in throwing out the trash you sent to ask for my hand."

A killing rage was on Gudrod and he was in no mood for a cat spitting in his face. He backhanded the small jaw and the girl spun away to collapse in the dirt. He told one of his men to tie her to a horse and by the time the wan circle of a sun began to emerge, they were on their way home.

The girl was bathed none too gently when they reached Vestfold and Gudrod took her to his bed – again none too gently. The screaming and fighting soon gave way to a brooding acceptance and a year after the raid, a small, dark wail broke the still of the morning mist.

Chapter 3

Halfdan the Black - King of Agder

Halfdan the Black was the offspring of a girl still in her teens who hated the father with a passion that only the young can know. Before the boy's second birthday, Gudrod would experience the slow burning vengeance of the child's mother.

The tribal chieftain had come a long way in a short time. Lindisfarne had provided the wealth necessary to buy loyalty from warriors and respect from earls -- the foundation of kingdoms. With the realms of Vestfold and Agder both under his flag, Gudrod now assumed the title of King and began enjoying the privileges due him.

Asa continued her wifely duties after the birth of Halfdan, but discarded her melancholy soon after the child arrived. She became quite pleasant and disarming with the charm she exuded. Servants no longer avoided her and the womenfolk came to accept her as one of their own.

Deep within however, the hate burning in her breast had turned a laughing and gentle heart into a frigid block of black ice.

As a gesture of appreciation for her pleasant demeanor, she was given a slave of her own. Marcus, a dark-haired youth among the captives brought back from the Lindisfarne monastery soon came to adore his new mistress.

Sharing the common bond of having been torn from home and family, a secret alliance was soon formed between the two. The lad was a couple of years older than Asa, but still little more than a boy.

Evenings would find them alone on a rocky promontory overlooking the fjords of southern Norway. Marcus had spent far too many evenings in silence, watching Asa. Tonight, he decided to speak his mind.

"Mistress, may I . . . tell you something?"

"Of course Marcus. We are alone."

"I think I may have fallen in love with you."

"Marcus! You must never say such a thing. What if someone heard you?"

"But you said we are alone."

"Yes, but we . . . you cannot say such things aloud."

The boy paused at the statement. "You said we. Does that mean . . ."

"It means I do not want to see your lungs splayed upon your back in a blood eagle."

Marcus boldly moved closer and took Asa's hand. "I would gladly endure the torture if I could be more than just your servant."

"You are more, much more, you are my friend."

"I can no longer bear to be just your friend."

"There is no other choice."

"There is always a choice."

"What do you mean?"

"I watch each day as you laugh and smile at those around you and yet inside, your heart is drowning in tears." He released her hand and gently lifted her chin. "Say the word and I will rid the world of that demon you call husband."

Asa gasped. "No! You must never attempt such a foolish thing." She pulled away from the gentle touch, trying to hide the glistening tears. "The gods have decided this is my punishment for being a vain and proud child." Letting out a shuddering sigh, she added, "I will endure for as long as necessary."

The distant bellow of Gudrod broke the tender interlude and Asa jumped to her feet. "I have to go. He must never see us together like this."

Marcus shook his head sadly, but remained silent as she hurried away. Rubbing the fuzz covering his jaw, he reached out to retrieve a blue flower streaked with white veins. The odor was faint but pleasant and for a moment he tried to remember the name of the plant. It escaped him as the beauty of the vista below changed slowly with the movement of the moon.

He lay back against the verdant growth in the rocks and stared at the night sky. Life is such a mystery when you're young. He wondered if things made more sense when you grew older. People cursed the gods when tragedy or anguish filled their lives and praised them when things were going well. Countless good and bad things happened to thousands of people every day. Were the gods really responsible? Closing his eyes, Asa's face filled his mind and he smiled. Things would work out somehow – they just had to. Wrapped in the warm cloak of young love, he never felt the bone chilling hand of the northern night move across the land.

A vision of Asa running across an open meadow, laughing and reaching for him, was broken by the soft light of a wane sun reflected from the ever rolling ocean. Sitting up and rubbing his eyes, he realized he had fallen asleep, absent from the village the entire night. If anyone noticed, he would receive a severe beating and go without food for a couple of days.

He jumped up and raced along the ridge of the fjord and down into the edge of Vestfold. Slowing to a walk, he noticed people were just beginning to stir and paid him no attention. The small hut he lived in with several other slaves was a stone's throw from the Great Hall and he paused a moment at the doorway, staring at the stately prison Asa called home.

It was not right that she should have to live thus. Pushing back the heavy hide that served as a doorway, he stopped at the sound of a faint noise in the distance. The groan was so low he wasn't sure he had actually heard anything.

He stepped back from the doorway and listened intently. There it was again, barely audible - someone moaning in pain.

Following the pathetic sounds led him around to the side of the Great Hall and there, in the tall rushes surrounding the building, lay the bruised body of a young woman. Heart pounding, Marcus rushed to girl's side and gasped when he recognized the inert form.

"Asa! What in Frey's name . . .?"

He dropped to his knees, gently lifted the girl, and cradled her in his arms. "Asa. What happened?"

Pallid eyelids fluttered to open and the blood dried lips attempted a smile. "Marcus. . . I still haven't learned my place."

"Gudrod! That animal did this?"

The dark blue eyes rolled up as Asa passed out.

Fury burned out of control in Marcus' chest as he lifted the slim form and headed for his hut.

"Marcus!"

The call was from Liv, Gudrod's mother, and he froze. Turning to meet his fate, he quickly realized the matron must have been searching for Asa. She did not seem surprised at the queen's condition, but summoned another male servant to take her from Marcus and left, saying nothing more.

He had never felt so helpless. Even when the heathens had dragged him from his home in Northumbria, he clung to tiny shreds of hope that someday he could escape or help would come. The rescue never came and that morning, the desperate flicker of love in his chest became a raging inferno of hate. He could no longer stand by and watch as the rapture of his world was beaten and torn, again and again.

Silent tears coursed down the square jaw, aimlessly falling into the abyss between him and the ground. Life now how only one purpose -- kill Gudrod, or die trying.

Marcus held his peace the next few days, watching for an opportunity to assassinate the object of a burning hatred. The king however, was constantly surrounded by warriors and friends, never providing an opening to strike.

Desperation finally overtook reason as the young slave slipped silently from his tiny hut in the darkness of a moonless night. Searching the compound, he found a spear leaning against a wooden barricade and, knowing death was the penalty for possessing a weapon, eagerly grabbed the oaken shaft.

Cold wisps from a restless night breeze moved through the village and softly ruffled his long hair. A shiver ran down his spine at the thought of actually taking a life, but it had to be done.

Making his way to the Great Hall, he paused beneath one of the high windows, wondering if his pounding heart could be heard by those within. Gudrod's voice drifted out the window with a twisting tendril of smoke.

"I'll only be gone a few days. Besides, people will expect their king to be at the feast."

"Where is Stiflesund my lord?"

It was the first time Marcus had heard Asa's voice since the morning he found her and his heart leaped in his chest at the sound.

"Tis on the jutting peninsula of the Danes you ignorant wench. Have you learned nothing since you came here?"

Silence followed the cutting remark and Marcus waited in the quiet that followed. The hours passed and finally, the sound of soft snoring drifted from the small square cut into the side of the towering wall. Smiling grimly, he crawled around to the massive doors of the hall, dragging the heavy spear alongside.

He rose in the shadows from a spatter of stars and grasped the heavy wooden stub protruding through the door. Attempting to push the handle upwards was to no avail and he realized the door was locked from within. He released his grip, silently cursing his stupidity. Of course it would be locked – and he had never even considered the possibility. He was a foolish boy who would die on a fool's errand. There was no way to scale the walls of the hall without waking those within. Biting off words of self-incrimination, he sullenly walked back to his hut. Hiding the spear in his bedding, he lay for hours, staring into the darkness of the interior.

Just as he was about to drift off, it hit him! The feast at Stiflesund! He could hide aboard Gudrod's ship and when the opportunity arose -- it might be his only chance.

Three days later, with cramped muscles complaining from the abuse, Marcus pushed the canopy of heavy hides back and peered around the deck of the empty ship. Long shadows from the twilight rays were reaching from starboard to port, searching for anything out of place.

He retrieved the hidden spear and crouched in the darkness beneath the ship's railing. The hours dragged by but all too soon, the sounds of drunken warriors moved from a distant point to the huddled form in the shadows. Thudding footsteps on the gangplank told him that the crew was returning and Gudrod would be among them.

The first mate staggered up the long, wooden planks and fell in his attempt to step down to the deck. Crashing to the oaken flooring, he began cursing as men helped him to his feet. "Ja see that? Somethin grabbed my foot! Twas a demon by Sif's hair!"

Men were laughing at the wild gestures. "You tripped on the tie-down you drunken oaf!"

"Me drung? Gudrod drang all of the mead at our table. Ja see the way he was . . ."

The sentence was cut off with a bellow from the king. "Oldam! Ready my bunk!"

The wild pounding of Marcus' heart slowed to a steady beat and he found himself in a calm world of his own, removed from the drunken chaos surrounding him. Striding through the cluster of warriors like a vaporous wraith, he jumped up on the railing at the end of the gangplank and stood face-to-face with the man he hated more than anything else in the world.

Suddenly removed from the body he had known all his life, he was watching the scene unfold. No longer a participant, but a spectator, suspended in the air off to the side of the gangplank. He calmly watched as his slim, muscular form rammed the heavy spear point into the king's gut. The vision was broken by the grunt of the monarch and he glanced down at the spear still in his grasp. Unable to free the shaft for another thrust, he released his grip. Gudrod stared at him uncomprehending for a moment before toppling from the wooden planks.

The splash of the body hitting the water broke the spell on a mesmerized crew. Roaring in fury, they fell upon the boy with the ferocity of wounded animals bent upon vengeance.

Gudrod's body was quickly retrieved and hauled up the blood-drenched gangplank. The boy was dead before he hit the water, but the king spent several hours in agony before he was finally released to the realm of Hel.

The king's corpse was burned upon a huge pyre, with all honors due a monarch. The warriors wanted to kill Asa and add her body to the flames, but Liv and Sverre intervened. The elder queen and sage had watched silently as the king abused the power acquired by wealth. Now, the man no longer ruled. Upon the ancient Viking's advice, Liv made a pronouncement that the teen-aged queen was free to return to Agder and take Prince Halfdan with her.

The people of Vestfold simply shook their heads when word of the king's murder passed from hamlet to village. The leader had always been a hard man, but admired. The kidnapping and treatment of the young princess had turned many in the realm against him.

Sverre was now considered a sorcerer or warlock by many of the townspeople due to his wisdom and knowledge of runes. His words were given careful consideration. He had once told them that men could endure hardship and depravation with varying amounts of honor and grace, but to know the true nature of a man, you must give him power.

Asa took the child and returned to her former home in Agder and raised him there. Sverre requested and was granted permission to accompany them to the southernmost coastal realm. Liv remained in Vestfold as the co-ruler with Olaf.

Time passed and the venerable Viking warrior, with no family or past, became Halfdan's mentor and the only father he would ever know. Sverre had taken an immediate liking to the boy and instead of the gruff indifference he had for most children, he took the lad under this wing, beginning his instruction at an early age.

The boy was about five, watching his adopted father fashion a toy sword from a branch of pine, when he became quite serious. "Sverre, where did the world come from?"

A period of silence followed the question, interrupted only by the sounds of a knife shaving slivers of wood from the wooden shaft. The child was used to the quiet reminiscing of the old man and sat waiting patiently.

Finally, the patriarch placed the hand holding the knife on his knee and looked down at the bright face. The wrinkled, scarred old visage held no fear for the boy as he grinned with affection.

"Well now, what made you start wondering about something like that?"

At a shrug from the small shoulders, the grey hair rubbed a large nose with the back of his hand as though considering the question. "To start with lad, nobody was alive then, so no one really knows."

"But the stories . . ."

"Ah yes, the stories. Well, the way I remember the tale, before there was thought or memory, neither this world nor any other existed."

The hard, grey eye looked inward, as though staring back in time thousands of years. "In the beginning, there was nothing but an empty black void, vast beyond imagining, called Gunnungagap. An unending realm of ice and cold existed at one edge of the yawning abyss, known as Niflheim, and the fires of a cosmic furnace raged at the opposite side; Muspellsheim.

"In time, heat from the distant flames started to melt the ice of Niflheim and the twelve great streams of Elivagar flowed into the abyss. From those seething waters emerged the first forms of life; a gigantic frost giant called Ymir and the first god, Buri.

"Buri's son Borr married the giantess Bestla. This union produced three gods named Odin, Vili and Ve. The gods and frost giants became mortal enemies and the gods destroyed the titan Ymir, creating nine different worlds from his body."

Dark blue eyes peered up through a shock of black hair. "Is this one of those worlds Sverre?"

"I'm not sure. It would be Midgard if it is."

"Where are the other worlds?"

"That is a long story for another time."

"What about the cow?"

The old sage chuckled at the comment. A rare response indeed, for the grey-beard seldom smiled, much less showed any form of mirth. "You've heard this story before haven't you?"

The boy nodded, wide-eyed, expecting an answer.

"Well, Audhumla represented the nourishment necessary for any new life. You know how much we depend upon our cows don't you?"

Again, the nod.

"That's the reason there had to be a cow there."

"Oh."

Sverre mussed the dark shock of hair and stood up to stretch when a vision flashed before his eyes. A man with a fair complexion and a mane of long, tangled hair was standing in front of a large group of cheering warriors. Covered in blood, he was thrusting a gleaming blade into the air shouting, 'tis done! – we are one!' The sword looked familiar and the vision sent a tremor through the old frame.

The man was as yet unborn, but would be the son of the boy at his feet. Frozen in that spot, Sverre strained to see what lay beyond the celebration, but an opaque veil closed over the scene and it was gone.

His heart hammered with excitement at the glimpse and he knew at that moment Gudrod's son would be the beginning of a Norse Dynasty. The rumble of an African lion stirring from its slumber issued from his chest as he walked away.

The visual premonition made him realize he possessed a unique ability – a blessing and a curse. The more he tried, the more often the visions came. Tumbling, hazy glimpses of something that might occur, or simply a warning of a fork in the road ahead.

The years passed but he still could not see clearly into the future. His young protégé was not considered handsome, but was smart and hard as iron. Dark in countenance, he became a fearsome warrior, not cruel, but pragmatic. Whatever was required to attain a goal was done. It was that simple.

Halfdan learned early in life that a weak king is short-lived and acted accordingly. By the age of eighteen, he was the undisputed King of Agder and had proven himself in hand-to-hand fighting a score of times.

There was one exception to that practical nature. Rather than move in and simply take Vestfold, he divided the region with his half-brother Olaf Gerstad-Alf. Many said it was out of respect for his long-dead father.

Through negotiation and conquest, he added one realm after another to his kingdom. Some large, some small, but in time, most of the southern reaches of what would become Norway and Sweden were under his control.

The first to fall was Raumarike, a petty kingdom northeast of Oslo in southeastern Norway. The tribe was known as the *Heado-Reamas*, or battling Reamas for good reason, reaching the pinnacle of expansion in the seventh century. Sigtryg Eysteinsson ruled the land with an iron hand and a sharp sword. The thin chieftain was grey with age, but stood straight as an oaken rod, unbending even to the ravages of time.

Sigtryg's younger brother, Eystein, was named after their father. Short and stout with a ruddy complexion, the only semblance between the siblings was a square jaw and long nose. Unaffected by the demands placed upon a ruler, the younger brother was easy-going and somewhat inclined to be irresponsible.

The strong bond between the brothers had been forged through the years -- playing with toy swords as children, hunting together as young men, fighting shoulder-to-shoulder against a common enemy and hushed discussions about maidens of the court.

Warning of the rising power of a warlord named Halfdan the Black in the lands to the southwest reached them long before word of an actual attack. The spring snows were barely gone when a messenger from Hedmark came thundering up the grassy vale leading to the village. He leaped from the sweating mount and began yelling about an approaching army.

The brothers had not been idly waiting for the attack. Every able-bodied man in the village had received some amount of training with a spear and sword, with varying amounts of success.

The approaching army was not a well disciplined regiment of uniformed troops, but a rag-tag array of warriors dedicated to their leader. Tales of an arcane wizard who served as the young up-start's mentor had grown to enormous proportions. Supposedly, the wizened sage possessed magic beyond comprehension – the real power behind the brazen warlord.

Sigtryg dismissed the stories with an angry wave of his hand. The victor of any battle was the man with the strongest arm and sharpest sword. Childish prevarications about magic and sorcerers were for whelps and bards.

He helped Eystein into the heavy hauberk and nodded in approval when the younger man strapped a gleaming broadsword to his waist.

Both men swung into the saddle at the same time and with a signal to his troops, the chieftain headed towards the waiting enemy.

Men in both armies knew the victor would show no mercy to their families or homes. There is a natural savageness in man that has free reign in battle and the barbaric ferocity of the encounter broke all bounds of human compassion.

Several warriors stripped naked in their invincibility, screaming and slashing with a strength and agility that alluded to possession by a supernatural force. To a combatant fighting these madmen and still in control of his wits, it would seem the minions of Hel were upon him.

Though the two armies were similar in number, the berserkers and reckless abandon of Halfdan's army cut the fighting men of Sigtryg down like a scythe through winter wheat. The field was strewn with broken bodies, bloody and ragged. Sightless eyes stared upward, to Valhallah and the glory that awaited a good death.

Halfdan spotted the king of Raumarike mid-day and methodically started working towards him. The last few yards of warriors cleared a path when Sigtryg yelled at his men to allow the young attacker to him. Men from opposing armies formed a circle around the sparring leaders.

Both combatants were still mounted, broken spears discarded and wielding heavy broadswords. The adrenalin in Halfdan's blood gave him the advantage of power and speed. But for the older man's skill and experience, it would have been a brief encounter.

Time and again, Sigtryg parried the savage blows, saving his strength and waiting for his young antagonist to make a mistake. Halfdan sensed desperation in the weakening deflections of his opponent and increased the force of the blows. The older man tottered, as though he was about to fall from the saddle.

Seeing an opening, Halfdan lunged. Too late, he saw through the illusion of the feint, but couldn't stop his momentum. Sigtryg twisted quickly to the side, the heavy blade sliding harmlessly over the chainmail on his thigh. Snarling in reprisal, he swung his sword in a sweeping arc that would hit his opponent in the head or neck, it mattered not which.

Halfdan jerked back, but knew all was lost. He gritted his teeth for the impact. It didn't come. A few inches from his neck, the shimmering blade clanged as though striking an anvil and glanced to the side. Both men stared at the ringing blade, momentarily forgetting the battle and each other.

The younger man regained his wits first. Retrieving the gleaming blade and lunging again, he felt the weapon strike deep. The venerable chieftain stared at him in wonder. The expression on the tired visage changed little as Halfdan withdrew the blade, allowing Sigtryg to slump from the saddle and fall to the ground.

The men surrounding the encounter could not believe their eyes; somehow Halfdan had deflected what appeared to be a fatal blow and killed Sigtryg. No one noticed the lone figure in a dusty blue robe standing on a hillock at the valley's rim.

Sigtryg's men stared in disbelief at the bloody body sprawled on the grassy sward. One man and then another tossed their weapons to the ground before walking to kneel at the feet of the dead monarch. There was no honor in killing unarmed men, so Halfdan's warriors turned to the task of finding the king's brother.

Eystein saw his brother fall and rather than wasting his life in a fruitless attempt at revenge, called to his closest retainers and fled the battlefield. The escape was to the dismay and frustration of the young conqueror. He had hoped to make a clean sweep that day. Killing Sigtryg changed only one thing; Eystein was now King of Raumarike.

The man was a king in exile however, and finally the shame of leaving his brother and hiding like a cur could no longer be tolerated. Sending a currier with a challenge to his brother's killer, he met Halfdan on the same battlefield in a fight that would continue until one or the other, was dead.

Eystein was not a coward, but had neither the skill nor experience of his older brother and the fight with Halfdan was short and fierce. Although the exiled king was a few years older than his antagonist, the dark warrior fought with a fury and passion that quickly destroyed the best defense he could provide.

Halfdan did not toy with his opponent, but quickly beat him down and ran him through. The unexpected part was the expression in Eystein's face when the dark warrior made the fatal thrust. The pain and hate that usually filled dying men's eyes was not there – instead, a look of acceptance and . . . forgiveness!

That one look affected Halfdan more than all the battles, glory and wealth filling the balance of his life. Sverre had drilled the importance of strength, valor and courage into every fiber of his being. Never backing down and never giving in. But in that instant, Eystein had shown him the concept of humanity.

The following spring found his army in the region of Sogn, ruled by King Harald Gulskeg, a man with a beard of gold. Early reconnaissance reports told of a wealthy kingdom, but also of a maiden of rare beauty. Ragnhild was the king's only daughter and had just celebrated her twentieth birthday.

Halfdan no longer held any doubts about the ability of his army to defeat any foe, but stories of the princess fascinated him and he decided to pay the monarch a friendly visit.

The young king's features were dark and fierce -- he had never paid much attention to how people viewed his countenance. The heavy black eyebrows framed eyes of such a dark hue they appeared to be spheres of obsidian.

His reputation preceded his arrival as evidenced by the cowering courtesans and officials sent to greet him and his entourage. He strode the length of Gulskeg's Great Hall, stopping at the base of the pedestal used as a 'throne'.

The structure was little more than an elevated platform holding a large, ornately carved chair. The King of Sogn remained seated and nodded slightly at the young conqueror standing before him. Halfdan studied the king's eyes. That's where the truth could always be found. The grey-blue orbs held no fear, only curiosity. Interesting.

"My lord, I ask your hospitality for myself and my men for a fortnight. We have traveled far in search of friends and allies."

The king stood and stepped down from the platform, obviously studying his guest as well. Extending an arm in welcome, he said, "Friends are always welcome in the hall of Gulskeg. You and your warriors are welcome to stay as long as you see fit."

That night when Halfdan and his warriors congregated in the Great Hall for supper, Ragnhild accompanied her father, sitting to his left. Two sons occupied the positions to the right, the eldest at his father's side.

One glance told Ragnhild the guest of honor was interested in her and she demurely dropped her eyes. The man was not handsome, but piqued her curiosity. The dark gaze surveying the room found her and quickly looked away.

She lifted her eyes and began quietly watching Halfdan, hands clasped under her chin. "My father tells me you are a mighty warrior." Dropping her hands, she tilted her head slightly to the side. "But are you a good man?"

The elder king's head snapped sideways at the strange question. His daughter had always been a direct child, but to question a guest's honor in his presence was unacceptable. "Ragnhild! Watch your tongue."

He glanced at Halfdan to see how the question had been received. Instead of anger twisting the scarred face, the man seemed to be seriously considering the question.

Finally, he raised his head and stared directly at the king's daughter. "No. I am not a good man. For much of my life I did not know what a 'good' man was." He glanced at Sverre to see how his mentor would take the statement, but the grey eye was fixed on Ragnhild.

"I had the best of teachers in the elements of warfare and combat, but . . ." The sentence trailed off when he noticed the intensity of the grey-beard's stare.

"Sverre. You seem to have an unusual interest in the daughter of our host. May I ask your fascination?"

"Tis not the daughter." Standing up, the old man pointed a bony finger at her chest. "Where did you get that necklace?"

The question was almost a growl and Gulskeg took it as an accusation. The king slowly stood, leaned forward and placed knuckled fists on the heavy table. "If you've something to say old man, spit it out."

Sverre didn't respond, but stepped back over the bench and made his way around the throng to the princess' side. Ragnhild turned to face him and drew back slightly when he pushed the long, flowing hair from her shoulders.

No man was allowed to touch the king's daughter unbidden and the audacity stunned everyone in the room. The old relic seemed indifferent to the snarls of outrage as he slowly reached for the necklace.

There was something about the man's bearing that made Ragnhild throw up a hand. "Hold! Tis all right." She glanced up at Sverre and down at the filigree of gold and jewels. "Let him satisfy his curiosity."

The princess felt a strange tingle from the necklace when the weathered fingers gently lifted it from her neck. She straightened slightly as a shiver ran down her spine, unfamiliar, but somehow warming, like her first taste of mead.

"Brisingamen." The aged, bony hands were trembling. "Tis not possible." The bushy eyebrows lowered over a grey eye flashing with memories. Memories of a god long-dead.

Gulskeg tensed at the statement. "The necklace of legend? What are you saying?"

Sverre was still holding the exquisite jewelry when he turned to the king. "Where did you get it?"

Halfdan sensed things were about to get ugly and leaped to intervene. "Sverre! We are this man's guests! Need I remind you that . . ."

The sage whirled on his protégé. "No! You need remind me of nothing!" He turned back to the king, letting the necklace slide from his grasp. "I apologize for my rude behavior, lord. When a man is a guest, he should act as such, no matter the . . . circumstances."

The abrupt change in demeanor seemed to have the desired effect on the bristling king and the wizened sage assumed the character of a curious old man. "But, begging the king's indulgence, may I be so bold as to ask where you 'found' the necklace?"

Gulskeg studied Sverre for a moment and saw through the mask, but realized the ancient reprobate was trying to be courteous. He glanced around the huge table and seated attendants. "Bellisson, where did you get it?"

A large man with a heavy yellow beard and numerous scars across his face wiped a hairy arm across his mouth, belching loudly. "We took that from the isles to the south. Remember the realm of King Raedwulf of Mercia?" He glanced at a comrade. "His wife was wearing it was she not?"

"Until her head fell off," the man responded.

A growl from the king cut the raucous laughter short. "Enough!" Turning back, he snapped, "Does that answer your question?"

Sverre shook his head, as though trying to mentally put the pieces of a puzzle together. "Aye, it does. But does not answer the real question."

"Which is?" The king's curiosity won over his anger.

"Where did the queen get it?"

"Does it matter?"

Sverre's gaze met the king's and held it fast. "I don't know."

Halfdan moved next to his mentor and grasped him gently by the arm. "What is this all about? Why would a necklace bring such concern?"

The grey eye met the young Viking's gaze and paused. "Tis a long story lad. Not one that I'll be boring an entire room with."

Several men at the table heard the comment and began banging the table with various utensils like small children. "Story! Story! Tell us the tale of the necklace!"

Sverre slowly surveyed the room. Touching the necklace had brought back his memory. Memories of a god that had been dead for eight centuries. It wasn't possible but . . . He pushed the whirling thoughts from his mind.

These warriors were his disciples, or would have been at one point in time. They wanted the spell of the bard cast upon them. Very well, they would have their wish.

He raised a hand to silence the room and stood staring at the bearded faces watching him. Young and old, the countenances were those of children in many ways. Excitement and passion burned in each visage. Tomorrow was an adventure, just waiting for them alone. The world was theirs for the taking.

The mage moved his hands as though parting a gossamer veil and stared into the past.

"In a time long forgotten, the world of Asgard was filled with trees heavy with fruit, the paths were lined with flowers of every imaginable kind and the forests had an abundance of deer, wild boar and game.

"Gods were powerful and true in the Golden Age of the Aesir. Evil had not yet stained the purity of their beings." Sverre's voice lowered slightly. "But evil was there. Tis always lurking in the shadowy, unkempt corners of life.

"The dark elves, known as dwarves to inhabitants of Midgard, were creatures of foulest evil, but also were the supreme craftsmen of this long lost age.

"Every Norseman has heard the tales of the goddess Freyja and her beauty. But few knew or understood the lust that burned within her breast. Her desire for objects of beauty was unquenchable."

The memory pulled at his heart as the glistening grey orb dropped from the unfolding scene. Men began pounding on the long table again. "Go on! Finish the tale!"

He motioned for silence and sat down upon the crude bench. Scratching a long, wispy beard, he peered once again into the mists of the past.

"Freyja's beauty was that of the old gods. The Vanir were a fair and gentle race protecting the flowers and animals of a world that was ancient when men first appeared in Midgard. The Aesir were new gods. Created from the cosmic collision of fire and ice, they were powerful and fierce, only the strongest survived.

"Representing the calm beneficence of nature versus the power of storms, the two races of gods inevitably came to blows. To avoid total destruction of both, a truce was struck. Freyja came to live with the Aesir, with her father and brother, as symbols of trust. Hoenir and Mimir went to reside in Vanaheim, the realm of the Vanir.

"Time passed and the worlds of the old and new gods settled into routines of peaceful harmony. From idleness springs a restless heart, not only to men, but to gods as well. Freyja passionately embraced her new home, but her longing for beautiful possessions knew no bounds.

"The inability to control desire is the crack in our armor that evil permeates first. Heat from passion and desire are necessary to forge weapons of strength and power – but they must be controlled!"

Several men sitting close to Sverre drew back from the power emanating from the white-haired storyteller. The ringing statements were incongruous with the frail, old frame. The grey eye turned to granite as he continued.

"The goddess heard of a fabulous necklace, crafted by four hideous and malformed dwarves. They resembled miniature trolls in their grotesque features. But clever, oh, they were ever so devious. They knew the power to control the goddess lay in beauty. And the most beautiful object in the nine worlds was made by those twisted hands.

"Through dark arts, they gave her a glimpse of the fabulous necklace in the dancing flames of the massive stone hearth of Folkvang. Immediately drawn to the exquisite adornment, she sent ferrets to every corner of the nine worlds to locate the necklace.

"In time, she discovered the coveted object lay in the world of Nidavellir, the world of the dwarves. The dark, forbidding realm of twisted tunnels and caverns beneath the land of Midgard.

"Her desire would not be denied, regardless of the cost. She changed into a falcon to search the endless, damp corridors, finally locating the jeweled creation in the deepest recesses of the underground kingdom of Svart-alfa-heim.

"To her dismay, she discovered the necklace had been crafted through the skills of the four hideous dwarves. Their names cannot be pronounced in the tongue of the Norseman, but they were known as lust, greed, envy and pride. The price demanded for the twisted gold and glittering gems was nothing less than Freyja's favor for the night.

"She paid without hesitation and wore Brisingamen constantly ever after."

Once again Sverre paused. The expression on the old man's face gave the impression the story was not a bard's tale, but the recall of a faded memory. He blinked his good eye as though remembering where he was. Scowling at the enraptured audience, he blew a wad out of his left nostril and abruptly finished the tale.

"Many of the gods thought the price too high, but her craving would not be denied." Looking back at the circle of faces, he added, "desire comes from within, and from there it must be controlled."

Sverre sat staring at the table a moment before giving a final glance at the necklace. He struggled to his feet and stepped back over the bench. Starting to leave, he stopped and turned back toward the princess. "Tis an old bard's tale lass, nothing more."

Halfdan watched as his friend and counselor pushed the heavy doors open at the end of the hall and disappeared into the darkness beyond. For a long interlude, the hall was wrapped in silence. Finally, Gulskeg spoke. "I've heard the story many times, but never that way."

The comment seemed to break the spell of enchantment and men began discussing the tale – each with a different conclusion. The mindless chatter and laughter began wearing on Halfdan's nerves and he excused himself from the merriment.

Stepping into the cool darkness of the night, he walked a short distance to one of several large stones encircling a massive fire pit. Warm, glowing coals gave proof of the roaring fire that had earlier cooked the pork and venison spread across the groaning tables.

The russet glow from the embers faded against the backdrop of a sky splattered with countless stars. The Viking sat staring up at the domain of the gods, and marveled at the incomprehensible grandeur of their home. Lost in the mystery of the vast expanse, the voice over his shoulder seemed to come from that endless abyss.

"Tis a beautiful night."

The warrior's senses flared in alarm at the sudden sound and he whirled, his hand going for the hilt of his sword. The realization that he didn't have a sword at his side and the words were harmless hit him at the same time.

He paused, feeling somewhat foolish at having jumped in alarm at the quiet comment. Smiling in embarrassment, he stood and offered his stone for a seat. "Ragnhild. I'm afraid you caught me with my mind adrift. I must apologize for startling you in return."

The princess smiled broadly, accepted the proffered seat. "No tis I who should apologize for approaching you so quietly. I live with warriors and know better."

The simple statement made Halfdan feel like he had known this woman his entire life. He settled on the next boulder and was quietly studying her when she spoke again.

"I hope I'm not intruding on your privacy."

"No, not at all. I'm glad you came."

"Why?"

The question was sincere and unexpected. Halfdan thought about it before answering. "I was hoping to get a chance to talk to you."

"Oh? Why was that?"

"Well, at first twas curiosity. The fame of your beauty is widespread."

Ragnhild frowned at the comment. She was not vain and considered the remark commonplace. "Has your curiosity been satisfied?

The change in tone told the young man compliments would serve no purpose with the lady. "I meant no offense."

The visage reflecting the radiance of the night softened. "I understand. Tis just that all my life that is all I have heard. The flowers of the field would tire of the same adulation if the words never changed."

Halfdan smiled and nodded in understanding. He picked up some small twigs from the ground and tossed them onto the glowing embers of the fire pit. The slender shafts curled from the heat before bursting into tiny flames and snapping with the release.

"All my life, people have seen a warrior when I walk by, and nothing else. A leader of men, fearless, and so on." He laid his hands on his thighs and let out a long sigh. "Sometimes I think they're right. That's all I am."

The princess reached over and touched his forearm. "Right now, I see much more than a warrior. I see a man who uses his mind as well as his sword. A rare thing these days."

Halfdan placed his hand on top of hers, and from that moment on, knew his life would belong to no other. "Ragnhild, I . . . that is, would you . . .?"

"Yes."

The young couple spent the balance of the night talking, laughing, reminiscing and bathing in the warmth of a new, budding love. They separated with the faint glow of dawn, enraptured with the possibilities that lay ahead.

Sunrise found Halfdan standing at the foot of Sverre's cot, staring at the recumbent form. The patriarch sensed his presence. "Can't you see I'm asleep? Go away."

"Sverre. What is love?"

The comment broke the steady breathing and for a moment, the white-hair remained motionless. Abruptly, he turned his head to stare at Halfdan. "What?"

"Ragnhild. I think I love her."

The sleepy old wretch swung his feet from the cot, rubbing his face and shaking his head. "No, no, no. Get that idea out of your head, or you'll be no good to anybody."

Halfdan sat on the edge of the cot and clasped his hands, staring at the dirt floor of the hut. "I never felt this way before."

Sverre slowly turned toward the dark haired youth at his side. Many times he had seen the man decapitating enemies and screaming blasphemies that would make any god of war proud, but now appeared to be . . . This wouldn't do at all.

"Love is like fire and smoke lad. You know tis real, but try and hold it too close and it'll burn you. The smoke gets in your eyes at the most inopportune times.

"Whatever you do, don't fall into that abyss. Enjoy the warmth of the flames and smell of the smoke, but don't stand too close or inhale too much."

The young Viking chieftain was shaking his head, but the old man's words were like vapor, swirling around his head and fading away. "I asked her to be my wife."

"Well, that was the purpose in coming here, but not to fall in love with her."

Sverre's expression of surprise slumped to dismay and finally, acceptance, as he studied his disciple. His protégé. He silently wondered which of the Norns was behind this unexpected turn of events.

"Bye the way lad, my memory has returned."

The casual comment brought the swirling thoughts in Halfdan's mind to an abrupt halt. He knew the man was far more than he seemed, but never expected to know the full extent of his past.

"That is great news Sverre. Who are you? From whence do you come?"

Sverre looked at Halfdan and suddenly realized that if he told him the entire truth; the king would think him mad. "Ah, well . . . my family and relatives are all dead. I am the only one left."

"What is your given name?"

"I am . . . Wotun."

"And your father's name?"

Wotun paused before answering. "It was . . . Barr."

The small lie seemed to satisfy Halfdan. Standing and smiling broadly, he clasped the old man on the shoulder. "May I tell the others?"

"It will do no harm."

The wedding was held the next day, prayers and sacrifices to the gods completed, and the feasting commenced. The commonplace world was lost to the young couple, caught up in the wonderland of lovers. That enchanted place that only exists for those drunk with the intoxicating mead of passion.

Summer turned to fall all too soon and the iron hand of winter fell upon the land, bringing a thick blanket of cold, heavy snow and ice. Once again, Skadi, the goddess of winter, donned slender skis and commenced her treks across the boundless northern reaches.

The long, dark winter months watched as Ragnhild grew great with child. Long, frozen ribbons of ice were turning to cold, clear streams when the wail of new life broke the pristine stillness of the forests.

Halfdan came out of the smoke filled hut holding a small bundle, grinning like a child with a new toy. "Tis a boy!"

He held the child aloft to the crashing of spears against shields. The baby began to cry with the rough handling and clanging noise. Wotun placed a hand on Halfdan's arm. "Tis not a chieftain's head lad. Quit tossing it around as such."

The new father looked somewhat abashed and quickly retrieved the bundle. "Sorry Wotun, tis just that . . . isn't he great?"

"Aye, tis the makings of a fine warrior you have there. How shall he be called?"

Halfdan paused only a moment before responding. "Harald – after Ragnhild's father."

The patriarch pushed the furry wrap back a little to see the boy's face. Yellow locks framed the red features. "I see he has his mother's hair. The boy will be fair in complexion."

"All the better."

The following years passed in relative peace, much to the chagrin of Odin's personification. The men were growing fat and lazy and the women passing their time in idle pleasures. At least that was the way it appeared to Wotun. Actually, the days were filled with work in the fields and huts. Crops were grown and harvested, cloth woven and sewn and new homes built.

All of this was fine and well, if you were put on this earth to hoe and sew. But it was not a plowed field that would grow a crop of valiant warriors or great kings.

A petty kingdom to the east known as Vingulmark, ruled by King Gandalf provided the seeds of unrest Wotun had been looking for. The king had three sons; Hysing, Helsing and Hake, thirsting for lands of their own.

The brothers knew the strength of Agder lay in the strong arm of Halfdan and began laying plans to assassinate the young monarch. They knew the king enjoyed hunting the forests between Vestfold and Agder and spent most of his leisure time pursuing the stags and boars roaming the leafy glades.

It was late in the fall, on one of those rare days of the north when a soft breeze moved through the riot of colors still clinging to the rolling vista. The bright violet of the tysbast was long gone, but the beautiful bells of the fagerklokke and pale hued blossoms of mjodurt were still in abundance.

The hunters passed over the daisy-like prestekrage and lldsveve of the lowlands, climbing to the violet skogstorkenebb, yellow sveve and rosenrot of the mountain meadows.

A large stag bolted from the edge of the meadow into the protection of the forest and the hounds began straining at the leashes, baying in protest at the restraints. Halfdan pulled his horse to a halt and motioned to the handlers to stop. "Olaus, make sure they don't release the dogs until the count of one hundred." The man flashed a smile at the unspoken words and waved his lord on.

Olaus had been friends with Halfdan since they were boys and although a year older, looked to the monarch with an admiration bordering on worship. The king treated him as an equal and he spent every waking moment trying to live up to the honor.

Halfdan returned the grin and spurred his mount into a gallop, racing across the meadow and into the trees. He was familiar with the terrain and soon found the game trail he was searching for. Thundering along the worn path through the pine and fir, he reached his destination and swung from the saddle.

Moving a short distance from the trail, he carefully placed the notch of an arrow onto the string of his heavy tamarack bow and waited. The sun was breaking through the trees in several places, creating shimmering shafts of light reflected from the minutia particles in the air.

A small pond intercepted the game trail a stone's throw ahead.

The distant baying of the hounds increased in volume and he tensed slightly. The buck should break into the small opening in front of him at any moment.

Sunlight from the broken clouds produced a shimmering edge to the reeds and watercress lining the water hole. A frog croaked in the solitude and provided a faint plop as it entered the water.

The faint snapping of a twig betrayed the animal's hurried approach and Halfdan drew the bow, breathing steadily. The stag flew into the small opening on the far side of the pond, searching frantically for signs of danger. The roan colored hide was streaked with shades of dun along the flanks and neck.

Too late it heard the twang of the bowstring and noticed a slight movement on the opposite side of the water. There was no immediate pain from the deadly shaft, but the animal's instincts told it something was terribly wrong.

Long, slender legs refused to obey the command to run as it slowed to a staggering gait and dropped. The dark brown eyes were wide with terror as the two-legged animal approached it and drew something across its neck. The pounding heart increased the speed at which the surroundings were beginning to fade.

It would not see or feel the pack of hounds fall upon it in the warm morning sun. Halfdan allowed the dogs a brief victory over the slain quarry and then tethered them to nearby trees.

He offered a silent prayer of thanks for the bounty and turned to dressing the animal. The summer sun was fully upon the clearing when he finished and straightened. Glancing around, he absently wondered where Olaus and the handlers were.

The impact of something hitting him high in the shoulder brought the idyllic scene to an abrupt end.

The sound and feeling of the arrow's strike were familiar and he rolled over the deer's carcass into the reeds bordering the pond to avoid a second shaft. Still grasping the bloody belt knife, he silently cursed at the lack of a sword.

Movement to his left was the first indication the attempted assassination wasn't over. Halfdan rose slowly from behind the body of the deer as two young men moved from the trees. One carried a bow and the other was wielding a sword.

Halfdan recognized the man with the bow as the eldest son of

Gandalf, a petty kingdom to the east. The similarity in the faces told him the two were brothers. "You are a long way from your father's land Hysing. I hope the arrow was an accident."

The man drew another arrow from his quiver and slowly strung it. "I'm afraid not, 'Your Majesty'."

"I might have known a cur would hide safely behind the distance of a bow." Halfdan growled.

The older brother glanced at his sibling. Killing an enemy with a bow was considered the act of a coward and they all knew it. He tossed the bow down and slowly drew his sword, watching his brother to ensure he was ready.

Halfdan glanced at the six-inch blade of his knife and the drawn swords of the assassins as they spread out to encircle him. Several of the hounds sensed the tension of their master and began barking at the newcomers.

He rushed to the dogs and began slashing the tethers to release them. The area became a maelstrom of chaos. The dogs attacked the strangers with an abandon that resulted in the deaths of several faithful hounds, but it bought Halfdan precious time.

The distant shouts of his hunting group brought the two princes whirling about in the realization that the attempted murder had failed. Flailing at the snapping canines and cursing obscenities, they fled into the dense forest.

Halfdan stood staring at the dark vegetation where the men disappeared. He slowly sheathed his knife and patted the heads of the surviving hounds.

He knew that allowing the attack to go unpunished would result in another attempt and the next time, they might succeed. A wave of nausea passed over him from the pain of the arrow and he plopped down in the lush vegetation surrounding the pond. The remaining dogs were taking turns licking his face, reassuring him that everything was all right now.

Olaus was the first to come charging into the little opening provided by the pond. Flying from the still running horse, he crashed to the ground in a tangle of reeds and vines. He leaped to his feet, embarrassment, excitement and worry all vying for control of his face. "Halfdan! We heard the dogs. What . . ."

He fell silent upon sight of the protruding arrow. Hurrying to his master's side, he knelt down and carefully examined the shaft. "I don't recognize the fletching. Tis not one of ours."

Halfdan flinched at the pain and let out a long sigh. "No, it belongs to the eldest son of Gandalf." To the questioning look of Olaus, he added, "The King of Vingulmark."

Olaus studied the face of his lord. The muscles in the square jaw were flexing. "This explains the other 'accident'"

"Accident? What are you talking about?"

"One of the handlers was struck by an arrow as we were leaving the meadow. The bowman eluded us in the woods. We thought it an errant shot from a hunter."

"Gandalf's third son."

"Aye."

The two men were sitting in silence when the rest of the hunting party arrived.

Removing the arrow brought an excruciating pain and the release of oblivion before it was complete. When Halfdan awoke, a craggy, white-haired visage was hovering above him. "Bout time. You been out most of the night lad."

Although no longer a boy, the grizzled fossil still referred to him as such.

"Wotun." Halfdan rubbed a hairy face and realized his hands were covered in dried blood. The events of the preceding day came rushing back. Swinging his feet from the edge of the bed, he paused as a wave of nausea and dizziness spun the room into a swirl of color.

"Easy there. You'll open up all that fine stitching if you're not careful."

"They tried to kill me."

"Figured as much."

"I can't allow it to stand."

"No, you cannot."

Wotun crossed arms spotted with age and studied his disciple. It looked like he would have his war, but it had almost cost him the life of Halfdan. Something about the whole thing made him feel uneasy. For eight hundred years he had been idle, frozen in the endless wastelands of the north. He was being given a second chance, but . . .

He pushed the nagging voice from his mind and turned back to the man who had become the foundation of renewed hopes and dreams. A world filled with warriors, battle and the glory of victory. Without war, there was no way for a man to know the adrenalin filled rush of hand-to-hand combat. No way to experience the sounds, smells and feel of a battlefield. No way for a man to know his mettle.

Before the first heavy snow, Halfdan moved against the kingdom of Vingulmark with an army of vengeance. His son, Prince Harald, was twelve and considered himself a warrior, but his father adamantly refused to allow him to participate in the attack.

"When you're older," was the only response the boy received to the desperate pleas.

The army fell upon the kingdom at sunrise. The morning sun's brilliance held back the chill of winter, but the crisp feeling of late fall was in the air. Gandalf, Hysing and Helsing were killed within the first few hours, but Hake managed to escape with a handful of warriors.

The youngest prince had a cunning few realized and rather than flee the country, he circled Halfdan's army to attack his undefended homeland. Most of the able bodied men of Vestfold and Agder had joined in the war against Vingulmark and Hake's handful of soldiers wreaked havoc across the defenseless realms.

With a daring of desperation, Hake decided to kidnap the Queen of Asgard and hold Ragnhild as a hostage. Halfdan had left a handful of personal guards for the queen and the fight to capture her was short and brutal. In a matter of minutes, the only people left standing in the great hall of Agder were the queen and the marauding prince.

The young man slowly lowered his bloody sword to the turf covered floor and watched as Ragnhild stared defiantly at her captor. Chest heaving, he wiped the back of a bloody gauntlet on a closely trimmed beard. "One way or another, you are coming with me."

The queen pulled a small knife from the belt at her waist and in so doing gave him an answer. The prince nodded in understanding and raised the crimson blade, walking towards her with slow, deliberate strides.

"Stop!"

The sudden sound brought the assassin whirling around. A sigh of relief escaped tense lips when he saw the source. A boy of no more than twelve was brandishing a large sword with both hands.

The lad was fair in complexion, but Hake immediately knew he was Halfdan's son. Snarling in anger, he rushed the child with the full intent of killing him as quickly as possible.

"No!" The scream of Ragnhild went unheeded.

To Hake's surprise, the prince knew how to handle a sword and although backing up, managed to deflect the savage blows. Frustration brought the killer's anger to unreasoning fury and he soon had the boy backed into a corner.

He was so absorbed in finishing off his young antagonist he forgot about the queen, until he felt the knife blade slide between his ribs. Whirling around at the searing pain, he jerked the knife from Ragnhild's hand. He knew he would probably die from the wound, but not before . . .

Snarling in pain and rage, he shoved her back and grabbed the hilt of his broadsword with both hands for a killing blow. The stroke was never completed. His arms refused to obey as he stared uncomprehendingly at the glistening blade protruding from his chest. The boy. An ironic smile twitched at the corner of his mouth as he dropped to his knees.

Blue-green eyes were glazing over by the time he toppled forward. The last heir of the Vingulmark Dynasty jerked in the final spasms of death and lay still.

Ragnhild stepped over the quivering form to grasp her son. Harald was staring at the body with the realization he had killed his first man. It wasn't the glorious, exciting feeling he thought it would be. He felt sick to his stomach.

"I think I may throw up."

"Tis best you do so outside."

Dropping the heavy blade, the boy rushed for the heavy, oaken doors of the great hall. The Queen of Agder watched her son with a mixture of pride, loss and sadness. Never again would he play in the fields of childhood.

The valor of Halfdan's son would become the source of many a bard's tale. A story the father would never hear. Through an ironic twist of fate, returning home, the victorious king would fall through the weakened ice of beautiful Lake Randsfjorden. Horse and rider struggled in a vain attempt to regain solid ice, but the shattered, glistening surface broke each time the horse gained a foothold. A score of elite warriors reached the area as the swirling black mane and glistening armor were sinking into the emerald depths.

Olaus leaped from his horse and, ignoring the cracking ice, ran towards the ragged circle of open water. If not for the quick action of a half-dozen men, he would have leaped into the freezing water in a futile attempt to save his friend. They all knew that even if there had been some way to pull their lord from the water, the temperature of the man's body would be so low his spirit would have already departed.

Several minutes earlier and furlongs away, moving with the bulk of the army, Wotun pulled horse and sleigh to an abrupt halt. Frozen in that moment of time, he watched as the distant scene unfolded before him. Foresight was both a blessing and a curse as he stared in spellbound silence.

The King of Agder was far ahead of his warriors, looking homeward. Hake's escape had been on his mind constantly and Halfdan made no attempt to hide the worry about his wife and son. Cutting across Lake Randsfjorden would save hours of time and he made the decision without hesitation.

The iron-shod hooves of his horse were cutting deep grooves in the soft ice mid-way across the lake when the first crackling groans gave warning of the danger. Halfdan dismounted immediately and moved ahead on foot, wrapping his hand in the reigns of the nervous horse.

Wotun cried out when the ice collapsed and watched helplessly as his protégé was dragged into the water with the horse. Groping futilely at the distant vision, he vainly summoned powers that were no longer at his command. Rider and mount both floundered among the glistening blocks of ice as warriors leaped from their horses to encircle the scene.

The craggy old face finally relaxed with a forlorn acceptance. The fates always made the final determination. He knew men would bless or curse the gods for the event, but . . . A sad, broken smile formed at the thought. The gods had nothing to do with it.

Chapter 4

Harald Fairhair - First King of Norway

The years passed and the mortal who was once a god had to bide his time. Patience served when all else failed.

Ragnhild's older brother, a man named Guthorm, was a seasoned veteran who had accompanied Halfdan on every skirmish or battle the king encountered since his union with the queen. He was a good warrior, but his real strength was his mind. An incredible tactician, he was far ahead of his time in the elements of warfare.

Young Harald worshipped his uncle and quickly agreed with his mother's recommendation that Guthorm serve as regent until the boy was old enough to rule the growing kingdom. The realms of Agder, Vingulmark, Raumarike and Hedmark were all under the flag of Vestfold when the fair-haired son of Halfdan became king.

Six decades had passed since Alcuin penned his warning to the world, and the wizard known as Wotun seemed to have aged very little. As the years rolled by, people began to believe the ancient sage was a sorcerer and it was only natural he would age no further.

Guthorm recognized the wisdom and subtle powers of the arcane Viking and seized every opportunity to search the hidden mysteries of his mind. The age-old games of chess and henfatafl provided a basis for discussions that often lasted far into the night.

Wotun was a master at the games and seldom lost. On the rare occasions when the regent won he would study the placid old face to see if he was being thrown crumbs. He could never tell.

Setting up the pieces for a new game, Guthorm spoke without looking up. "Harald will make a fine king some day."

"Yes, he will," was the thoughtful reply.

"A king needs wisdom, as well as strength."

The white-hair looked up from the game board; the grey eye's piercing stare locking with the younger man's gaze. "Do you have something to say, or are you just expounding the learning of a child?"

The man was used to Wotun's scathing tongue and ignored the remark. "How can our king become wise?" He suppressed a faint smile when he added, "You ill-tempered old wart hog – and how come you're not dead already?"

Wotun enjoyed the verbal banter and responded quickly. "I still have a lot to do." Adding, "And with the likes of you at the helm, it looks like I've a long way to go."

Guthorm glanced down at the board. "Where did you learn so much about runes? You know words and symbols I have never seen before."

"You pay a price."

"You bought them?"

"In a way."

The regent moved his knight and looked up. "You're being evasive. Why?"

"Knowledge is like everything else, one way or another, you pay for it."

"How did you lose your eye?"

"I'm not Odin, if that's what you're thinking."

Guthorm looked down again. "I've heard many tales of the god's search for wisdom. What's the truth?"

"How should I know?"

The younger man remained silent and finally, Wotun relented. "I can tell you what I know, but it must be under an oath of silence."

"Agreed."

The wizened eye moved from the board to the small, reddish yellow flame waving at the end of a short candle stub. The image of a similar candle burning a millennia before slowly took shape and lit the small room around him.

"The war between the Vanir and Aesir had reached an uneasy truce and the gods of each realm met to determine if a lasting peace could be achieved. The desire to end the fighting came with a realization that the evil forces of the frost giants and minions of Hel were gaining strength and the endless struggle between the gods only served to weaken them.

"A peace was struck and under a blood oath, each of the races of deities was given the right to select three gods from the opposing realm as hostages to ensure an end to the hostilities. Among those chosen by the Vanir was Mimir, the wisest of the Aesir gods. A primordial deity of the ocean, he alone possessed the knowledge of life itself.

"When he refused to share the wealth of his mind, the Vanir slew him in a fit of jealousy. Afterwards, regretting their rash actions, they placed the blood of his body in a sacred spring whose crystal depths preserved all thought and memory. The waters became known as Mimir's well.

"Odin plucked an eye from his skull for a draught and did so gladly. With blood streaming from the ravaged eye socket, he gulped the cool water and licked wet lips as the cruel and beautiful truths of the world rushed into his consciousness. Such was the god's thirst for knowledge."

Wotun stopped here and looked from the candle to Guthorm. "Knowledge is like wine to some men. With a taste, the desire becomes insatiable." He shook his head, the sad voice reaching back centuries. "But at such a price.

"With the knowledge gained from Mimir's well, the God of Warriors learned of a kind and wise mortal traveling the breath of Midgard whose name was Kvasir. The wisdom of the man was unrivaled in the realms of gods and men. Odin's search for the sage ended with the discovery of his treacherous murder by dwarves. Fialar and Galar, two dark elves, heard the savant's teaching and, coveting the wisdom, slew him for his blood.

"They mixed the blood with honey and created mead unlike any other. One drink of the liquor would imbue the beneficiary with a wisdom that even the gods did not possess. Odin knew he had to have it.

"Greed, desire, and coveting are not just human vices; the frost giants also heard of the magical elixir and immediately began scouring the nine worlds in search of it. A titan known as Suttung finally found the dwarves and fabled brew far beneath the fair lands of Midgard. The giant killed both dwarves and took the mead."

Once again, Wotun stopped. A wry smile formed above the wispy beard. "Frost giants were strong, but most were incredibly dumb, and rather than drink the mead, Suttung simply took it home and set it in a corner of his home. He assumed that once he had the mead, he would become wise. It never occurred to him that he had to drink it.

"The giant had a daughter named Gunlod that wasn't as dense as her father and she quickly reasoned that the magic of the liquor would be transferred when consumed. She talked her father into allowing her to guard the mead, telling him their house was not a safe place and she would hide it where no one could ever steal it.

"This made sense to Suttung so he agreed. Gunlod moved the mead to a deep cave and sealed the entrance. She considered drinking the magic fluid, and believed it would make her smart, but she would not be any richer. It would be far better to find a wealthy patron and sell it.

"Time passed and Odin discovered the whereabouts of the mead, but rather than attempting to steal the liquor, decided to woo the guardian. The god could be quite . . . persuasive, and eventually the giantess fell in love with the stranger and willingly, even eagerly, allowed him to taste the treasured store.

"To her astonishment, the man drank all three kegs and vanished! She then realized her ardor had allowed the god to take the only thing he had truly desired. In a furious rage, she told Suttung of her betrayal and the giant set out in pursuit of the thief.

"Discovering her daughter's suitor was none other than Odin did not abate his anger and he pursued the god to the very edge of Asgard, where a host of gods set upon him and he was slain.

"Once again, the god-of-gods placed the acquisition of knowledge above all else. He was disgusted with Freyja for giving her honor to the dwarves for a necklace, but he did the same for the gain of wisdom."

The old man wiped his nose with the back of a faded, worn sleeve and moved a board piece. So many things foretold of the fall of Asgard. If only the gods hadn't given in to desire . . .

He pushed the regret from his mind. What was done could not be changed. Glancing up at Guthorm, he added, "Tis a good life if a man does not weaken."

The regent nodded slowly. Wotun was telling him something, and the meaning lay beneath the words. He moved another board piece, mulling the statement over in his mind. The price of sating desire was too high, regardless of the prize, but the payment for truth, honor and the war against evil must be made, even with life itself.

"Harald will be an honorable king."

"Til he succumbs to desire."

The truth in the old man's statement rang like the pealing of monastery bells. It drowned out the bellows of rage, cries of victory and screams of the dying. When all was said and done, man did what he wanted to do.

"Checkmate." Wotun moved the last piece of the game. Guthorm stared at the board for a moment and then looked up at his opponent. He slowly stood and framed a sad smile. "Thanks Wotun." Patting the enduring sage on the shoulder, he took his leave.

The following year passed quickly and winds of change were in the air. Several petty kingdoms previously conquered by Halfdan were now ruled by rebellious chieftains and various provinces no longer paid tribute to the king's heir.

Guthorm knew re-conquering the minor realms would serve no purpose until Harald was old enough to assume the reins of power, so he held his peace. Every day was spent with his charge, teaching him the art of war and elements of defeating a foe with sword, spear or axe.

Enemies surrounded the kingdom as well. Erick Eymundsson, King of Svearike, the land of the Swedes, was a warrior king bent upon expanding his holdings. When Halfdan held southern Norway, Erick moved north and east to easier pickings. The countries of Finland, Kirjalaland, Courland, Estonia and parts of northern Russia fell to his sword.

Desiring to unite the Scandinavian peninsula from the Baltic Sea to the fjords of Norway, the realms of Varmland, West Gotland, Svinesund, Raumarike and Viken were soon added to Erick's kingdom.

On his sixteenth birthday, Harald learned the Swedish king was in Varmland and he sent word to the chieftain of the province, requesting a meeting. Aki Goddersson was the most powerful man in the province and had served with Harald's father during his early exploits.

The meeting was set for the following summer and Aki began building a new feasting hall. The new structure was far grander than anything else in Varmland, containing relics and treasures of plunder from the British Isles and Europe.

Although Eymundsson was Aki's lord, the chieftain's loyalty lay with Harald, Halfdan's son and heir. When the two kings arrived for the meeting, Harald and his entourage were given lodging in the new hall and the King of Sweden was placed in the old hall. Erick considered himself a man of honor and his sword remained sheathed while in the feasting halls.

Harald had been a small child the last time he saw Aki at his father's side, but remembered him well -- the young monarch and aged warrior embraced like old comrades. The evening transformed into a moonless night with countless stars glittering like shattered crystals of ice. The cold darkness was held at bay by the huge, crackling fire in the center of the lodge. Smoke curled upwards to chase along the massive beams in the ceiling, finally escaping through wood framed holes.

Aki quickly moved to the Swedish king's side when his group entered the new feasting hall, seating him in a place of honor at the high table. After exchanging traditional greetings, he introduced him to Harald. Eymundsson's eyebrow lifted at the 'child' presented to him. The king was a proud old warrior and the idea that the youth received more honor than he, riled him considerably.

Harald was young, but no fool, and as quickly as protocol allowed, he excused himself from Aki's companionship and approached the inveterate king. Guthorm had taught him the value of diplomacy and he reasoned this was as good a time as any to wet his blade.

"Your Majesty, I bid you a good eve." The young king was standing next to a vacant stool, but did not sit.

The older man looked up from a cut of roast pork and studied the boy-king a moment before nodding at the empty chair. The auburn beard was streaked with grey and dripping grease. He wiped both with a large, scarred hand before placing his hands on the edge of the table and giving Harald a hard stare as the youth sat down. "Your father was a good warrior. Admired and feared." The grey-green orbs were trying to see beneath the light blue veil in the younger man's eyes.

"Yes, I miss him."

"Tis my understanding," the king went on, "that you requested this meeting."

He was getting right to the point. Harald liked that. "Yes, Aki and other jarls in this region call you 'lord'. These lands belong to Vestfold, the kingdom of my father."

Erick allowed a faint smile to break the craggy face. The young man minced no words. "These lands did belong to your father . . . long ago. The 'jarls' as you call them, freed themselves from that rule and in so doing declared they were fair game for anyone willing to take control."

He removed his hands from the table and wiped them on his tunic. "Men need laws and protection. In turn, they provide allegiance and tribute."

"To you."

"To me."

Harald had just suffered his first defeat in diplomacy, but it taught him a valuable lesson; play the game in your mind before moving the first piece.

"And if someone else can offer better laws and protection?"

The subtle challenge erased the easy countenance of the seasoned king. He leaned back in the chair, the grey-green eyes turning hard. "No one can."

The blue orbs met the icy glare with a hardness that belied the youth of the lad. Harald rose slowly and nodded in respect to the king. "Til we meet again, Your Majesty."

The old monarch watched the young king move away with the smooth grace of a mountain cat. He felt like the wary hunter surrounded by hungry wolves. But then, he had slain many wolves in his life.

The remainder of the evening he sat in silence, watching Aki and Harald talking late into the night. Aki was his man and as such, should not be showing the enemy such hospitality. He would rectify the slight in the morning.

Harald noticed the sullen glare and realized Eymundsson was barely controlling a simmering rage. Young, but wise beyond his years, he knew this was not the time to provoke his adversary. The Swedish king had as much as told him the Norse lands would not be relinquished without war and he was in no position to start one.

To strengthen the newly formed friendship, Aki proposed that his eldest son, a boy of twelve named Ubbe, return with Harald and become his ward. The opportunity for the subtle alliance could not be refused and the King of Agder quickly accepted.

Besides, he liked the lad. A few years younger than himself, the boy bore a strong resemblance to Aki in appearance and mannerisms. He would be a good man to have at your side in the years that lay ahead.

Harald gave the chieftain a final embrace and fond farewell with the morning sun and set out for home. Guthorm had insisted on remaining in Vestfold, believing that his attendance would weaken the young king's standing with the foreign ruler. He had been right. If Guthorm had been there, Eymundsson would have ignored Harald.

Aki stood at the prominence of a hill watching the entourage until they were out of sight. He had truly enjoyed Harald's company and reminiscing about Halfdan. Smiling to himself, he turned back towards the feasting halls and the Swedish king.

By the time Aki reached the main lodge, Erick was mounted and waiting for him. A dozen warriors and half that many servants were in attendance. He reached up to grasp the king's forearm in parting, but the man held him fast. "Ride with us to the forest. I wish to speak with you."

The request seemed unusual, but was spoken earnestly in fellowship, so Aki agreed. A horse was soon saddled and the group filed out of the stronghold.

Eymundsson and Aki rode in the front of the little caravan, quietly immersed in a conversation that started innocently enough. The king spoke first. "Doesn't look much like his father."

"No, but he has similar qualities. Abilities that make for a good ruler."

"For other men – not for you."

The subtle statement and change in tone brought Aki's head around abruptly. "If you've something to say, say it."

"Whose man are you?"

"I have sworn allegiance to you my lord."

"Tis not what I've seen since coming here."

"If I have offended you, twas not my intent."

The seething anger in Erick exploded. "Not your intent!" Jerking his horse to a stop, he whirled around, eyes flashing. "You put your king in a dirty, ancient hall and that, that stripling, in what should have been my quarters!" Spittle was flying from the snarling visage. "And then spend the entire night groveling for his attentions while . . ."

Rage had rendered the man incapable of coherent speech. Shaking with fury, he let out a long shuddering breath.

"Enough!" The king threw a hand in the air and by the time Aki recognized the significance, a bloody spearhead suddenly appeared below his collarbone. He felt the weight of the heavy shaft, but no pain, just a tingling sensation in his arms. His mouth opened to protest the injustice, but no words came out. The gurgle of crimson bubbles was the only response.

Unable to raise an arm to deflect the cruel blade whirling towards him, the sudden pain in his chest vaporized with the sunlight filtering through the leafy glade overhead. His head was still attached to the torso, but lolling around like a freshly cut melon as he toppled from the horse.

Word of the murder reached Agder with the cool air of late summer and Halfdan's heir began preparing for war.

Wotun had been patiently waiting for the winds of war to once again stir the blood of men and felt the time was right. If Harald was to be the first king to unite the wild and restless realms of the Norsemen, he would need help. The only talisman that promised such a future was the fabled sword of Sigmund Volsung.

Sitting in front of the rock fireplace of his hut, the memories of a god long dead pushed once more into his consciousness. He absently scratched the long white beard and stared back though the misty veils of time. Twas an era when giants stalked the realm of Jotun-heim and great men of valor were forming the legends of generations to come.

Chapter 5

Sigmund Volsungsson

The all-seeing blue-grey eye gazed over the nine worlds from the straight backed *Hlidskialf.* The exalted throne served as a watchtower for the mightiest of the gods.

Odin was watching the world of Midgard. The huge hall of the Volsung clan was filled with revelry and the celebration of a marriage. The smoke wreathed length of the great hall shook with peals of laughter, squeals of women, and the screech of children.

Volsung's only daughter was to wed a man named Siggeir, the King of Gautland -- a wild and remote region bordering the Norse lands to the southeast. The man's face was hard, to the point of being cruel.

Signy, strong-willed and beautiful, had caught the neighboring ruler's eye on a previous visit. Ere long, a bargain was struck between the clan's leader and the Gautland king. Siggeir would protect the Norse lands from the powerful Danes to the south and Volsung would ensure the Gaut that no attack would come from the north.

The bride's younger brother, a lad named Sigmund, was his father's pride, but Signy had been the Volsung's joy since birth. The last male in a string of strapping boys, Sigmund had always been the smallest of the siblings, with the exception of Signy.

A bond formed between the two little 'uns that lasted into adulthood. Whether gathering flowers or chasing butterflies, the two were inseparable as children and the thought of losing Signy was hard to accept.

The happy scene was but one of many across the land, but as must be, the winds of change were stirring.

Odin let out a restless sigh and stepped down from the massive throne. Midgard was becoming far too peaceful. The warriors needed a cause and a champion. Men would never know their mettle unless it was tested.

Huginn and *Muninn*, the two large ravens resting on his shoulders, took wing to land lightly in one of the towering windows lining the walls of Valhalla. The winged manifestations of 'thought' and 'memory' had served the ancient Viking god throughout time.

The god-of-gods walked over to stand in front of a vast array of swords lining the west wall of the Asgard citadel. The styles dated back through the centuries, morphing from the crude, heavy bronze blades of yesteryear to the hard, shimmering iron blades of today.

He stopped in front of a finely worked weapon with an extended handle allowing the use of both hands. The guard was heavy and would withstand the hardest of blows. A grim smile formed in the wrinkled visage. Few knew the true story of the fabled smith Volund and the magic blade crafted during a time of cruel tribulation.

The sword seemed to rise from the wooden pegs of its own accord and float into the waiting hands. Hefting the weapon for balance, the cogent deity grunted with satisfaction and walked across the broad expanse of floor to the east wall of the room.

A massive table of ironwood stood beneath rows of towering windows, creating a somber rectangular shadow in the crisp light of the morning sun.

Odin carefully placed the sword on the table and picked up an innocuous looking quill resting in an empty ink well. Muttering Stygian words obtained from the depths of Mimir's well, he etched mystic runes into the glistening blade with practiced strokes.

The arcane god allowed himself a small smile as he retrieved his creation. This was a weapon that any mortal worthy of his salt would desire. In the hands of the right man, the indestructible sword would slay without mercy and the wielder would never tire. This would be a talisman to make and destroy kings. Empires would rise and fall with the rise of and fall of the blade.

He pulled on the broad brimmed hat and dusty blue cloak he used for his peregrinations and once more, looked towards Midgard.

By this time, the wild revelry of the marriage had slowed somewhat. After two days of nonstop drinking and carousing, with a marriage somewhere in the middle, even the hardiest were stopping to rest.

Signy had cried secretly upon the news of her betrothal, but afterwards, accepted her fate with a brave inevitability. If it was her father's will, it must be the right thing. She watched the festivities with the calm equanimity befitting the daughter of a mighty chieftain.

At the end of the second day, Volsung was sitting quietly holding Signy in his arms, watching the last pulses of gaiety die away with the glowing embers of several fires lining the length of the great hall. Most of the family, friends and guests were now discussing crops, livestock, family and the oncoming winter.

A crackling sound in the still air brought a pause in the muttered conversations. Waiting expectantly, the hall's occupants glanced at each other and then towards Volsung.

Removing himself from his daughter's embrace, he stood up and placed a hand on the hilt of his sword. Magic was not unknown to him and if disciples of the black arts were looking for trouble on this day of celebration, he would not disappoint them.

A small twister appeared near the center of the lodge, swirling miniscule bits of dirt and smoke in an increasing spiral. The Vikings stood in spellbound silence as the whirlwind crackled with slender blue streaks of fire.

The whirlwind died as quickly as it appeared and standing in its wake was an old beggar. The man surveyed the crowd with a look bordering on contempt and removed a magnificent sword from the worn, ragged cloak. The finely woven, dusty blue traveling cloak had vanished with the swirling winds.

"Tis a sorry lot my eye beholds. Far too long have you grown fat and lazy in the warmth of your lodges." The grey-blue eye swept the hall with a cold glare.

The stranger slowly raised the long, glistening blade. "I bring a challenge -- if there is a man among you to meet it."

A huge tree stood in the center of the lodge, supporting the main part of the structure. Six feet in diameter, the ancient hardwood known as 'Branstock' appeared to be as old as the gods.

The 'beggar' moved toward the massive ash tree and, with a strength that belied the frail frame, shoved the shining blade into the thick trunk until the heavy guard crushed the rough bark.

Stepping back from bole, he said, "Whoever pulls the weapon free shall be king of all lands of the northern realms. Rewards and treasure beyond a man's wildest dreams will be yours by following the sword."

Volsung broke the spellbound silence that followed. "Who are you? Speak man, friend or foe?"

"Consider and guard my words well, for I will not repeat them."

The stranger said nothing more, but turned and left the lodge in a quiet that was deafening. If anyone had followed the man outside, they would have wondered at his sudden disappearance.

Siggeir, King of Gautland, was the first to speak into the ensuing hush in the Great Hall. "What is the meaning of this Volsung? What sort of trickery do you play upon your guests?"

The clan leader's gaze moved from the sword to the bridegroom. "Tis no trickery Siggeir. The man was not one of mine."

A voice came from the crowd. "Twas Odin! No mortal could have buried that sword to the hilt."

Once again, the huge hall reverberated in silence. No one could refute the statement. Finally, Volsung walked over to the sword and carefully placed his hand on the hilt, lines of uncertainty were flexing around the large, dark eyes.

"Wait! I claim the right of guest." Siggeir's voice broke the quiet.

Volsung turned a questioning look towards his new son-in-law. "Right of guest? What are you talking about?"

"The right to be first at whatever my host proposes."

"And what am I proposing?"

The man's face broke into a knowing sneer. "You were going to try and pull the sword from the tree. I claim the right to do so."

Understanding spread across the tired, lined visage and Volsung stepped away from the tree, swinging his arm toward the sword as an invitation.

Siggeir raised an eyebrow, but didn't respond. Glancing around as though to test the air, he sniffed and strutted towards the tree like a hoary peacock. He stopped next to the protruding hilt, laying a regal hand upon the heavy, golden handle before turning in a sweeping gesture to the waiting crowd.

"Behold! Whoso pulleth this sword is rightful king of all northern lands. Words uttered by Odin himself!"

There was a smattering of applause from his retainers, but a majority of the hall remained silent.

He sniffed at the apparent snuff, or disbelief, it mattered not. He knew he was rightful king and soon everyone else would know. Waving a hand in dismissal of the watching crowd, he turned to face the tree.

Puffing up like a fat rooster, he grabbed the long, ochre hued handle and pulled. The man seemed genuinely surprised when nothing happened. The silence in the hall had grown to the point everyone was holding their breath.

Glaring at the sword like a disobedient servant, he threw his weight into a strenuous heave, but the blade remained fast.

A high pitched laugh broke from one of the serving wenches and he whirled in anger. "Hold your tongue woman! I'll not be laughed at by any . . ."

The man bit back the last of the lashing, knowing the Gauts were badly outnumbered. He glanced over his shoulder at the mocking handle. "Tis not possible to remove the sword. Odin placed it there, only he can pull it free."

Volsung's eldest son spoke above the muttering filling the room. "You try father."

Volsung made a small wave of his arm, half dismissing the request. A chorus of encouragement broke out from the balance of his sons so he shrugged and stepped towards the embedded sword.

He reached up, firmly grasped the hilt and pulled. The blade refused to budge. Turning toward the crowd and the shouts of encouragement, he threw up his hands.

"Enough! The blade is not mine." Turning to his oldest son, he motioned. "Waldur, come, try."

The strapping lad leaped to his feet and glanced at eight brothers surrounding him. "What say ye?" The brothers laughed, slapping him on the back and shoving him towards their father.

Over six feet tall, the young man was in his mid-twenties and an arm-span across the shoulders. Incredibly strong, but gentle with women and children, he was considered the heir apparent. A broad grin chased across the bearded face briefly before fading into a look of uncertainty.

His large hand closed around the rune embossed, golden handle and paused. He placed the other hand against the rough bark of the tree and, setting his feet, pulled. Muscles bulged under the weathered skin, stretching sinew to the breaking point.

Once again, there was a palatable silence in the Great Hall. Finally, the young titan exhaled and released the hilt of the sword. Crushed bark fell from beneath the callused hand to the dirt floor below, but the sword had not moved a hair's width.

He turned back towards the clan and shrugged. "Tis not mine -- Harak?" He stepped aside and motioned towards the prize.

The second eldest son stepped forward and eagerly grabbed the protruding hilt. One-by-one, the sons of Volsung strained at the obstinate weapon. Each in his turn, failed to budge the magnificent sword.

Youngest of the brood was a boy named Sigmund. Barely in his teens, the lad was quick and bright, but the muscles on the skinny frame were no match for those that had already failed.

He had been summarily dismissed as a waste of time by much of the crowd when Waldur threw up a hand. "Wait! All have not tried. Sigmund, put your back to it!"

The boy started to object, but realizing it would be futile, quickly walked over to the sword and gave a half-hearted yank. It moved!

Jerking his hand back as though he had touched a viper, he stood staring at the glistening edge of the protruding blade. It was impossible. He had watched his older brothers strain at the sword and fail.

Pandemonium broke loose in the hall. "It's him! It's Sigmund – rightful king of all northern lands!"

Siggeir, forgotten in the excitement, roughly shoved his way through the crowd. "Out of my way! If anyone is worthy of the sword, tis I!"

He pushed Sigmund aside and grabbed the weapon, attempting to pull it free. Astonishment crossed his face when the blade would move no further. "This cannot be! The blade twas loose – you all saw it."

Whirling in anger, he glared at the Viking youth next to him. "Tis the black arts the young man uses. No mortal could have freed the blade."

Volsung stepped between the man and his son, thunderclouds marring the rugged visage. "Enough! I'll not stand by while any man slander's my son. Courtesy to guests is a rule to be unbroken, but Siggeir, by the gods you try my patience!"

The smaller man drew back from the controlled fury of his host. Realizing his behavior was inexcusable in Viking eyes, he stepped back, frantically searching for some way to salvage his pride.

"I . . . meant no offense. It's just that . . . the boy is of such a slight stature." He bowed slightly, then turned and walked back to the side of his new bride. Putting a possessive arm around Signy's slender waist, he glared at Volsung, daring him to naysay his claim on the young maiden.

Volsung held the stare until Siggeir dropped his eyes. The old clan leader exhaled through clenched teeth and turned back to his youngest son. "I believe you were in the process of retrieving that exquisite weapon. Please continue."

Sigmund glanced at the Gautland king before turning to the sword. The man seemed on the verge of exploding.

Once again, he placed his hand on the golden hilt, only this time slowly, with considerable trepidation. The touch of the metal was not the cold, hard material he expected. Instead the handle felt alive and . . . warm.

Even before he pulled, he knew the blade would respond to his every command. It was an old friend, returned to renew adventures and the camaraderie of a forgotten era.

In the next few seconds, the only sound in the lodge was the sliding whisper of the long blade. Blue-white light flashed along the shimmering blade as Sigmund hefted it above his head.

The hall became a bedlam of hurrahs and barking cheers. Swords were slammed against shields and lodge poles, creating a cacophony of reverberating noise.

One of the warriors broke into an impromptu chant;

Twas on a fair day, early in the spring,
The god of gods gave us our king,
A son in the hall of Volsung,
The last of nine with the name of Sigmund,
With the sword of Odin and fire of the Valkyries,
Over the land and over the sea,
We will follow our king,
To battle and glory and the mead of Valhalla!

The ballad ended to a chorus of stomping feet, dust and shouts. Even the retainers of Siggeir seemed to be caught up in the excitement of exalting a new ruler – ordained by Odin!

The Gautish king watched the events with a cold, calculating eye. The sword belonged to him, but he would not get it by force. Not here anyway.

The corners of the sneering mouth slowly curled into a small smile. Not here. Not now. He would have to change his tactics. The sword was rightfully his and by Thor's hammer, he would have it.

No one noticed the subtle change in the man's demeanor as he approached the clan leader and his son. The gaiety came to a shuddering halt as the foreign king approached the new King-of-Kings. The first High King of Scandinavia.

Anticipating more trouble, Volsung was at the end of his patience when Siggeir suddenly kneeled before Sigmund. His mouth dropped open when the man doffed a regal cap and spoke to his son.

"Your Majesty, the gods have spoken and I wish to be the first to formally congratulate you and swear obedience and undying support for your reign."

The crowd had expected a snarling outrage and was momentarily stunned by the sudden change. Hushed murmurs flowed through the masses and finally broke into a deafening cheer.

Volsung stepped forward, grabbed Siggeir by the shoulders, hauled him to a standing position and slapped him full on the back. "Well said! We forget ourselves in a moment of anger, but good men do not let hasty words let broken fences lay in disrepair."

Several women rushed the two leaders, offering huge cups overflowing with mead. Both men grabbed the proffered vessels with more than normal enthusiasm, slamming the wooden cups together with a force that spilt most of the contents.

Quaffing the liquor, the Gautish king and clan leader marched arm-in-arm back to the head of the lodge and took the seats of honor. Although the 'king-of-kings' stood in their midst, old habits are hard to break.

Sigmund lowered the precious blade, standing in the middle of the great hall staring in amazement at the transformation in people he had known all his life.

There was a glow of pride and possession in their eyes he had never seen. He was not only the greatest of kings, more importantly, he was theirs. A son of Norway was now rightfully king of all the Scandinavian lands.

Siggeir and Volsung were chatting quietly at the head of the long table splitting the northern part of the lodge. Dropping a greasy chunk of roast ox into the vessel at the tip of his beard, Siggeir patted Volsung's forearm in the manner of true camaraderie.

"Volsung my friend, you must bring your family for a visit upon the first opportunity."

"It would be an honor. The full bloom of summer tis not far away and that would be a boon time for reuniting."

The pact made, the two men resumed celebrating the marriage and making of a High King. Two hearts beating close. One, the heart of a Viking; fierce, proud and honorable. The other, that of a covetous man, filled with treachery. A true son of Loki.

The spring passed quickly and after the salmon runs, it was time for the trip south. The clan loaded two of their best longboats with supplies and tribute. After which, the entire Volsung clan climbed aboard, looking forward to once again seeing their daughter and sister.

Signy had performed wifely duties with an honor bound diligence, but the loathing for her husband increased with each new discovery. When she heard her family was coming to visit, at first she was elated, but further consideration made her realize there must be an ulterior motive for her husband's actions.

She finally discovered Siggeir was planning to kill her family upon their arrival and confronted him in a rage. Rather than denying it, as she expected, he calmly confirmed her worst fears and ordered she be confined to her room.

The next few days passed in slow agony for the prisoner. The queen's only confidant was a cousin who had accompanied her on the move to Gautland. Gudren was a year older than she, a hard worker, fair in complexion – with a soft face constantly adorned with a smile. The most important thing however, was that she was of Volsung blood and could be trusted.

Gudren was allowed to bring Signy food the second day of confinement and the queen quickly explained Siggeir's plot against her family, asking her handmaiden to somehow warn them.

Two days later, tiny sails appeared on the horizon. Gudren was hiding in a grove of trees not far inland, watching the 'welcoming committee' on the beach. She knew the handful of Gauts on the shore were but a false token of the real reception.

Concealed in the edge of the forest was a large contingent of armed warriors, lying in wait. Their orders were to kill everyone but Signy's family. Her relatives were to be brought before the king as prisoners, on their knees.

The beautiful morning morphed into a cloudy afternoon and a stormy evening. By the time the sleek longboats carried the Norwegians ashore, thunder followed long streaks of ragged white lines splitting the sky. A growing wind coming out of the north whipped the whitecaps into foam.

Gudren broke from the trees, waving a long, red shawl. Her yells faded against the crashing waves, unheard. If the men and women in the boats had seen her, they would have assumed she was part of the welcoming crowd.

She realized the boats would be ashore before she could warn the occupants, so she decided on a different tack. It might not work, but she had to try.

Walking brazenly into the middle of the small group, she informed the group's leader that Siggeir had sent her down to ensure that no hostilities broke out before the signal.

The smooth courtier sniffed his disapproval at the unnecessary instruction and glanced in the direction of the heavy woods. He would speak with Siggeir about sending a servant to direct his activities. He was quite capable of dealing with the foreign 'guests' without any direction from a woman.

Dark eyes narrowed in the dim light of the forest, wondering why Signy's handmaiden had rushed into the small group of courtesans assembled on the beach. Siggeir growled in his throat. If the woman tried to warn the Norsemen or got in the way . . . Well, Signy would be looking for a new maid-in-waiting.

The roan beneath him shook its mane, as though in agreement, rattling the chain links on the bit. Blowing snot out in the growing wind, the gelding pawed the ground, showing impatience at the tense waiting. The young animal had only been in a couple of brief battles, but could sense the excitement rippling through the soldiers in the trees.

Back on the beach, one of the king's retainers waded out into the surf to catch a rope tossed from the bow of the nearest craft. Turning and putting his shoulder into the line, he headed back to shore.

Shortly thereafter, the boats were beached with passengers wading the short distance to shore. Volsung's chiseled face brightened when he noticed his niece among the welcoming committee. "Gudren! How have you been child?"

Glancing over the slim shoulder, he added, "Where is Signy?"

His eyes returned to the pale blue orbs framed in a fountain of golden tresses. The look he received spoke volumes – things were not as they seemed, something was terribly wrong.

Gudren wanted to scream at them to run, but knew it would only escalate the king's treacherous plan. She bit back the cry of warning and grabbed the clan leader as though overwhelmed to see him. Embracing him in a crushing grasp, she stood on tiptoe and whispered, "It's a trap."

The Gautish group ignored the childish behavior and dismissed it as something that would soon be addressed. If the lass were killed during the skirmish, it would be no loss.

The smile on Volsung's face faded as he released the young woman and stepped back. Looking her full in the face, his expression changed from surprise, to disappointment, and finally to a quiet resolve. If they wanted a fight, that's what they would get.

He glanced along the beach; there certainly weren't enough men in this bunch to be a threat. The bulk of the force must be in the surrounding trees. Lying in ambush.

Hacking a wad of flim onto the sand, the clan leader pulled his sword loose and let it drop back in the scabbard. The sound brought every Norseman on the beach to an abrupt halt. The gesture might be done a dozen times during the day, but this was different and every man knew it.

Waldur noticed the change in his father's demeanor and casually stepped to his side. "Weather's building up father. Should we be seeking shelter?"

The older man nodded, speaking quietly. "Yes. This is the type of storm that brings out vermin." Studying the surrounding trees he added, "And assassins."

The eldest son glanced in the direction of his father's gaze. The thought of fleeing to the longboats never occurred to either man. Treachery was to be dealt with quickly and without mercy. Besides, Signy was here somewhere.

Volsung glanced at Gudren, and with a slight toss of his head, told her to clear out. She started to refuse then realized she had no weapon and would just be in the way.

The cluster of Gauts noticed the subtle change in the newcomers and began wondering if they suspected the pending betrayal. An uneasy hesitation lasted for a span of five heartbeats.

A huge brute in a blue tunic jerked his sword free, stabbing at the neck of the nearest Norseman. If it had not been for Gudren, the ploy might have worked, but the men from the north were on guard and the clumsy thrust was brushed aside.

The area immediately became a small battleground, with the Gauts taking the worst of it. In a matter of seconds, the last assailant fell to his knees, blood spurting from an artery in his neck.

The victors had no time to celebrate. A savage bellow from the surrounding forest was followed by a small army of soldiers charging out of the trees. Falling like rabid wolves upon the handful of Norsemen, the outcome was a foregone conclusion.

The red beards of the Volsung clan stood out like fire in a wheat field and far too quickly, they were the only ones left standing.

Their long blades were dripping with the crimson life of some two score opponents when a cry from without stopped the battle. The attackers backed away, completely surrounding the Volsung clan, brandishing swords and spears.

"Do not kill them! I want them alive!"

A small, twisted face pushed through the circle to confront Volsung. "Now we will see who is rightful king of all the northlands!"

Volsung stepped towards the little weasel, raising his sword for a killing blow. Siggeir threw up a hand and backed away from the threat.

"Wait! You fool – don't you realize what would happen to your precious Signy if you were to kill me?"

The Gautish king turned slowly with a menacing gesture at the circle of spears before adding, "Or if you were to kill any more of my men?"

The meaning behind the thinly veiled threat was blatant; stop fighting or your daughter dies. The man was below the vilest reprobate he had ever met. There was not the slightest hint of honor anywhere in his character.

Volsung dropped the heavy, gleaming blade to his side. "Put down your arms. We will fight no more."

One by one, the young heirs lowered their swords and tossed them with disgust into the sand. They would have preferred to die here and now given the choice, but the decision was not theirs.

The last to drop his weapon was Sigmund. Releasing the treasured sword was like tearing his arm from its socket. A score of eyes fell upon the long, golden hilt and rune worked blade.

The surrounding horde of soldiers swept over them like an angry swarm of hornets, kicking, cursing and binding them far tighter than necessary. After which they were roughly hauled to their feet.

With the prisoners securely bound, Siggeir felt safe in grabbing the coveted sword. Odin had declared whoever pulled the sword free would be rightful king of all the northern lands. It followed in Siggeir's twisted mind that whoever possessed the sword from that point on deserved the accolade and title.

The captives, feet and hands tightly bound, were tied behind horses and dragged to the fortress the king called home. The leather bindings were replaced with chains in the huge portico and the prisoners were led through the main hall in degradation. A muffled gasp drew their eyes to the top of an elegant, curving staircase.

Signy was being held against the heavy banister by Siggeir, hands tied behind her back. The man's fist was twisted in the long, silken hair, holding it where she had to watch the humiliation and misery of her kin.

Silent tears streamed down the pallid cheeks. Releasing a long, shuddering breath, she said, "Let them live and I will do whatever you ask -- without question or pause."

She felt the painful grip loosen and turned to stare into the dark, hard eyes of her husband. The flinty orbs tightened slightly, trying to see what lay behind the promise.

"Anything, without question?"

"Yes."

The man licked his lips and glanced down at the wretched family. "Take them below and place them in the cells."

Signy could not see into her husband's mind or she would have screamed. His show of leniency was nothing more than a screen to cover his real intent. He would not kill her kin quickly, they would be tortured to death, one-by-one. Meanwhile, his obstinate wife would be gratefully fulfilling his every wish and whim, thinking she was keeping her family alive. What could be better?

Husband and wife watched the stream of prisoners exit the huge hall in silence. After the last of the bound men disappeared, the king's demeanor changed to the smooth, silky nature of the man when things were going his way.

"Now my dear, I'm sorry we had to do things this way, but your family can be quite short-sighted and someone had to take them in hand." He spoke as though she were a small child while releasing her bonds.

The tears were still flowing, but the young woman nodded eagerly in agreement. She would agree to anything if it would save her family.

The smile on the man's face never reached his eyes as he turned away. "Now, there is the matter of that serving wench of yours. She really has been a nuisance through this whole thing."

Gudren had hurried to Signy's room after the short and bloody fight on the beach, hoping her part in the fray went unnoticed. She had risked her life to warn them, but it had been in vain. They were the king's prisoners and the best thing she could do now was stay alive.

The relief on Signy's face changed to concern at the mention of her cousin. The king was a cruel despot and if he got his hands on her . . .

She started to break away and shout a warning, but then remembered her promise to the king. If she did anything to anger him, her father and brothers would die. Wringing her hands in desperation, the battling emotions placed a strain on her face she could not hide.

"Bah." Siggeir pushed her aside and stalked down the long hallway leading to her chambers. Signy slumped against the heavy banister, hoping the woman had the sense to flee and not return to the castle.

The heavy door to the queen's stateroom flew open and crashed into an adjoining dresser. Gudren squeaked and whirled around at the sound. She had been staring out the west window of the room, listening to her heart pound.

"My lord! You startled me. The queen is not here, she . . ."

"Silence!" The king roared. "You treacherous foreign trash. Did you think your villainous acts would go unnoticed?" He paused briefly before adding, "Or unpunished?"

The man reached for the newly acquired sword hanging at his side then paused. No, that would be much too quick and lenient. The treacherous wench needed to feel the bite of the lash and caress of the red, smoking iron before she went to Hel's domain.

He released his grip on the sword hilt and stalked across the room, reaching for a slender arm. Gudren's eyes flew wide as she saw behind the merciless gaze. "NO!"

She twisted away from the clawing fingers and, seeing soldiers blocking the doorway, ran to the window and leaped.

Siggeir's arm went up as though to stop the irrational act, then slowly dropped. He growled low at being deprived of the things running through his mind and moved to the window to look down.

It was between forty and fifty feet below to the embankment sloping away from the castle. Lying facedown about ten paces from the base of the stone wall, the slender body had come to rest against the uphill side of a cluster of wooden debris.

He whirled in frustration. "Go get her!" Slapping the window sill he added, "Maybe she's not dead yet."

He threw up his arms at soldiers that were already gone. Everybody was so incompetent. He started pacing the room and noticed Signy standing in the doorway. "What do you want?"

"Gudren . . . is she . . .?"

"She's in Hel's embrace, or soon will be."

The anger and frustration at the loss of his victim was infuriating. Siggeir stormed across the floor, grabbed the queen's arm, and roughly shoved her into the room. "Look out the window if you want to know what happened to your precious Gudren. The crazy, fool woman jumped out before I could stop her."

Signy threw a hand to her mouth to keep from crying out. She loved her cousin almost as much as her family. The woman had been the kindest, most considerate person she had ever known.

Wrapping her arms around herself, it was hard to breath. She glanced at the sunlight streaming through the tall slit in the west wall and started walking woodenly towards the opening.

A few steps short of the window, her feet stopped and refused to go any farther. To see the broken body of her cousin would be more than her mind could manage right now. She was standing two paces from the wall, breathing heavily, unable to move.

Siggeir watched his wife for a moment before tossing a dismissing wave in her direction. "You're better off without her. Besides, she couldn't be trusted."

By the time the king reached the bottom of the stairs, two of the soldiers had returned. "She's not there Your Majesty. We searched the area below the window and there was no one anywhere around."

"Idiots!" The king barked. "You couldn't find your buttocks with both hands!" Pushing past the two men, he added, "I'll show you imbeciles where the body is, and by Thor's hammer if she's dead, or dics because 'you couldn't find her' . . .

He let the threat hang while charging out of the massive doors leading from the great hall. The two soldiers rushed to follow their sovereign.

It took a few minutes to work around the looming castle walls to a point directly below the queen's stateroom. Siggeir drew up short when he found the pile of debris, but no body.

"What's the meaning of this? What have you done with the girl? I'm in no mood for jokes."

One glance at the surrounding soldiers told him he was not the victim of a prank. The woman's body had disappeared.

The monarch picked up a blood streaked, broken piece of wood from the pile and glared into the dark forest. There were many large carnivores in the surrounding woods. That had to be the explanation. Well, hopefully whatever it was, took its time in devouring her.

"Bah, Hel take her," he said, tossing the stick down and turning back towards the castle entrance.

Signy would never know the agony her father suffered that very night, without crying out. The sons watched as their father endured the blood eagle in silence. The unimaginably cruel ritual left the man dead on the cold stone floor with his lungs draped over the broken ribs of his back.

Siggeir watched the torture with eager anticipation which quickly turned to disappointment at the stoic silence of the victim. He whirled and stalked away in anger before the man was dead. The sons would also die, but their deaths would not be a disappointment.

The surrounding woods were filled with an abomination that only came out at night. A descendent of Fenris, the wolf resembled a hulking thrall during the day, but at night became a ravenous, flesh eating canine.

Several squadrons of soldiers had been sent out to kill the animal when it first began haunting the woods. The result was always the same; they never returned. After a period of time, the locals knew they could not enter the forbidding woods after sunset and live.

Waldur was the first to be chained to a massive tree deep in the forbidding forest. A stranger to the land, he wondered at the nervous glances from the soldiers as they quickly secured his manacles and hurried away before the cloud covered sun dropped into the western horizon.

The Gautish king stood on a balcony overlooking the forest in silent anticipation. He licked his lips as the last rays of the setting sun faded into darkness. The wait should not be long.

Volsung's eldest son struggled against his bonds until his surroundings were little more than vague outlines in the growing darkness. He realized that straining against the heavy chains was useless, but there was little else he could do.

Heavy rain clouds moved across the tree tops, blocking out the faint luminescence provided by the distant stars and sliver of moon.

Waldur stopped pulling at his bonds to steady his breathing, silently cursing the cruelty in men's hearts. His father had been a hard but fair man, teaching him the rights and wrongs of a merciless world. Watching him die was the hardest thing he had ever done.

Pushing the mental image of his father's death from his mind, he froze at an unexpected sound. He heard it before the smell reached his nostrils. The soft, but heavy footsteps reminded him of the tundra bear he had seen back home. A putrid odor, strange and foul to the senses, moved through the heavy underbrush.

His panting from the exertion slowed and he was now holding his breath. Whatever it was, the creature had to be just a few steps away in a cold darkness that held no mercy.

The sound of a huge dog lolling its tongue reached his ears, followed by the sniffing of large nostrils testing the air. The rumbling growl that tumbled forth was something Waldur had never heard before. He was as brave as any man, but his conscious mind was frantically searching for a definition of the threat that hovered in the black void surrounding him.

The heavy clouds broke, allowing a faint shaft of moonlight to move slowly through the dense vegetation. Both carnivore and prey watched the light move towards them. Waldur was still bathed in darkness when the pale, luminous glow fell upon the beast towering over him.

The man had never known fear and looked forward to the day he would die in battle. Now however, the monstrous apparition that appeared before him was something his mind could not fathom and he stared spellbound at the huge, malformed wolf.

Black eyes bore into him, streaked with a red that seemed to pulsate with the beating of his own heart. The hairy jaws opened to expose teeth the size of a small man's fingers. A guttural growl rumbled from the hairy chest as the wolf-man tore the upper portion of Waldur's arm away. The act was accomplished with an ease that betrayed the incredible strength of the abomination.

The wound was so terrible the Norseman felt no pain, only a helpless rage. Screaming in defiance at the creature, he cursed it and challenged it to meet him in Valhalla. The animal seemed to understand him and the slavering maw went for the man's exposed throat.

A league's distance away, the King of Gautland stood on the west balcony of his stronghold, leaning on the stone parapet. The roar of the beast and scream of the man brought a satisfied smile to the cruel features. At last, he had heard a Volsung scream and it was music to his ears.

In the nights that followed, the ghastly ritual was repeated with similar results. Seven more times, a brother was taken out and seven more times, the soldiers returned with a few grizzly remnants as evidence the foul deed was complete.

It was almost with regret that Siggeir sent for the last and youngest, brother. Sigmund had watched his father die and his brothers disappear until only he remained. There was no doubt about his fate as the soldiers ambled down the dark hallway to fetch him.

He prayed to Odin and Thor, but there had been no response and apparently this would be the day he joined the rest of his family in

Valhalla. So be it. He just wished he had been given a chance to take a few more Gauts with him.

The soldiers were rank with the smell of mead, but hard and disciplined, leaving no opportunity to grab a weapon. The young Viking was badly bruised and bleeding from several minor wounds when they finally chained him to the crimson stained tree.

Ragged remnants of clothes strewn around the turf removed all doubt about his brothers. They had died at this tree, just as he was about to do.

The fading twilight was almost gone when the faint rustle of someone or something moving through the surrounding underbrush reached his ears. Holding his breath, he listened intently.

The sound moved to a point directly behind him and paused. The suspense was unbearable. "Kill me and be done with it," he growled.

"I do not wish to kill you my lord."

Sigmund whipped his head around against the rough bark of the tree. The voice was that of a woman -- a voice he recognized.

"Gudred?"

"Yes."

She moved around the tree and her appearance shocked him. Her face was drawn with fatigue and fear. Underneath the layers of dirt and grime were streaks of dried blood and the dark stains of bruises.

"By the eye of Odin lass, what happened to you?"

Although the girl was slightly older than Sigmund, she appeared a small, frightened child. "Oh Sigmund, the man is a monster. He . . . he was going to kill me!" She paused before adding, "Waldur . . . and the rest of your brothers . . . it was . . ."

The young woman became incoherent as she leaned against Sigmund's shoulder, sobbing something about a terrible monster devouring his brothers.

He was unable to wrap his arms around the poor wretch, so he leaned his head against hers and made soothing, reassuring sounds.

"It's going to be all right Gudred. We're not dead and we have each other." The tone in his voice changed slightly. "But if we are to survive, we must use our heads and do it quickly."

The woman sensed the change in Sigmund and took strength from it. Straightening up, she started nodding her head and wiping her eyes. "Yes, yes you are right. What should I do?"

The woman's reaction strengthened his resolve to survive this ordeal, no matter the odds. He glanced around him for anything that might be of use. There was nothing but dirt, grass, brush and trees.

"Look at the chains and see if there is anyway to release the locks or free me."

After a moment, she replied, "The manacles are too tight -- there's no way you can get your hand out, and the chain is solid all the way around the tree."

Sigmund nodded. It was as he suspected. They had taken no chance upon a passing stranger being able to free him. He dropped his head slightly, racking his brain in search of a plan.

Finally, he slowly raised his head. "Find a bee hive and bring me some honey, I have an idea."

Gudred knew there was no time for questions, so without responding, dashed off into the woods. She had spent better than a fortnight in these woods and it didn't take her long to retrieve the requested sweet mass.

The fading light was almost gone by the time she returned, hands coated with the yellow, viscous material.

He glanced at the girl and then the honey. The idea became more ridiculous the longer he thought about it, but nothing else came to mind. It was all he had.

"Smear it in my hair."

When she paused, he snapped. "Do it! We don't have time to waste."

The girl jumped slightly and quickly did as he bid. Stepping back, her face was once more lined with fear and doubt. "Oh Sigmund, what . . .?"

He interrupted. "I don't have time to explain. Just listen." He quickly glanced around before adding, "You must go to Siggeir's stronghold and find something to break or cut the chain."

The girl's eyes filled with terror at the thought of returning to the king's citadel. "There must be some other way."

"NO! There is no other way. NOW GO!" The desperation in Sigmund's voice shook her to the very core of her being.

The girl turned and fled, wondering in her heart if she could find the courage that would be required. A short distance away, she slowed to a walk. It was too dark to see clearly and it would serve no one if she fell and broke a leg.

Her pounding heart steadied as she began working her way through the dense foliage. She stopped short as a thought struck her. What if she were successful in entering the terrible fortress and stealing something to break the chain, only to find a few bloody bones when she returned?

The thought was more than she could bear. Putting a hand to her breast, she clenched her jaw. She had admired Sigmund since they were both children and she would not allow her mind to dwell on 'what ifs'.

Pushing the thoughts aside, she hurried on through the darkness.

Sigmund exhaled slowly as the sounds of the girl dissolved into the surrounding trees. He had not seen her since the day they arrived, but he had been in the dungeons and there would have been no way for them to have met.

From her appearance, she must have fled the castle shortly after their capture. She looked half-starved, and terrified to the point of madness.

The hard facets of the young face softened with sympathy. He would apologize for being so harsh when she returned. She must have been through . . .

The thought was broken by a low, guttural growl to his left. The sound was unlike any he had ever heard. Without seeing the creature, he knew the thing was what had taken the life of his brothers.

Turning his head in the direction of the sound, he stared intently into the darkness between the faint outline of trees. A sliver of moon and starlight were shining through thinning clouds, throwing an iridescent outline on the shrubs.

A black shape resembling a very large wolf or bear moved out of the trees into the small meadow surrounding the large tree. The chained youth stared at the apparition in disbelief. Lycanthropy was a myth to scare children, nothing more.

Pausing at the edge of the grassy opening, the animal stopped and stood up. The beast was over seven feet tall and towered over the chained captive. It walked on heavy hindquarters covered in hair.

Sigmund's every fiber focused on the terrifying creature, trying to determine if there were any weak or vital points he could use to advantage.

The monster moved to within a few feet of him and paused, as if waiting for a certain reaction. The previous men had started screaming challenges or obscenities when he stood before them. This youth remained silent for some reason.

Throwing its head back, a deafening howl, neither human nor animal, roared out of the hairy throat, reverberating through the silent forest.

Instead of the defiant tirade it expected from the young man, the wolf-man watched the youth lower his head, as though in deference to the monster's presence.

The beast was both confused and curious at the strange behavior. Stepping closer, the huge canine's senses were testing everything about the boy. The smell of fear was not present, that was something the animal had not expected.

There was something else. Leaning closer, the brute's brain realized it was smelling honey. Drawing back slightly, he stared at the lowered head.

His meal had somehow managed to get the gooey substance meshed in the dirty tresses of his head. The carnivorous mutant leaned forward again, a rumbling growl issuing unbidden from the massive chest.

The huge muzzle touched the amber-tinged mop of hair and paused. Saliva dripped from the hairy maw as it slowly opened. A rough, pink-hued tongue moved out and across the matted strands of hair.

The tentative strokes increased as the animal cleaned the sticky mess from the long, tangled strands.

Sigmund kept his head down, but his gaze moved up from the animal's chest to the throat. The hairy, exposed neck was only a matter of inches from his face. The rancid smell overpowering.

He would have only one chance. The animal froze as if sensing a change in the bound victim. Too late.

Sigmund lunged at the exposed throat and clamped down on the windpipe. The huge beast jerked back, almost snapping the boy's neck.

Biting deeper, the young Viking held on with a strength born of desperation. A muffled growl vibrated within his jaw as the animal pulled away.

A crimson gusher hit him in the face as the beast tore free. Blood was spurting in rhythm with the monster's beating heart. The animal took a couple of staggering steps back, staring with incomprehension at the young human that had somehow caused this strange sensation.

One of the huge paws reached toward him as the abomination dropped to the ground. The werewolf thrashed savagely for a few seconds, futilely trying to stop the inexorable flow of blood. A gurgling moan was the last sound the strange creature would make. Sigmund watched in stunned silence as the malformed, hairy creature changed into the naked body of a large man.

Blood was still flowing from the torn, mangled neck as Sigmund spit the putrid taste from his mouth. He had heard tales of such a beast, but never believed they existed. Never, until now that is.

The silence was complete when Sigmund slumped forward and dropped his head in exhaustion. His mind and body had been in a constant state of tension since Volsung's surrender and now it left him in the residue of a torrent of washed emotions.

He closed his eyes. Everyone he loved was dead. Not everyone, there was Signy . . . and Gudred. She was such a lovely lass – what if something happened to her?

Too exhausted to consider the girl's plight, he felt his mind slip into a dark oblivion. At least he had been able to avenge his brothers.

Time passed and the sound of a woman's voice came from a distant realm. She was calling his name. He raised his head and rays from an early morning sun hit him full in the face.

"Sigmund! You're still alive. Bless Freyja."

The slim figure was bathed in a soft glow, wavering in the morning sunlight. He blinked his eyes a few times and the vision steadied into an image of Gudred.

"You made it back! I feared greatly for your life."

The young woman stepped closer to him, avoiding the blood covered corpse on the ground. "Tis I that have been worried about you." Their eyes met and she added, "I have seen both forms of the beast and shudder to think what you must have been through."

Sigmund didn't respond but glanced down at the prone body and nodded. Glancing back at Gudred, he noticed she carried a sword – a sword he immediately recognized. "Gram! My sword! How did you get it?"

"I know the castle well. I also know where the king keeps his prized possessions." She glanced down at the long blade. "Once I accepted the fact that you and I would probably both die, it was easy."

She looked up from the gleaming sword. "But tis iron against iron; your blade may not cleave the chain." A look of desperation and pain crossed the pale, blue eyes. "I feared this when I took it, but knew not what else to do."

Sigmund smiled. "You did what no other could have done. Tis no ordinary blade you hold. Strike the chain and behold my words."

A puzzled expression crossed her face as she lifted the heavy weapon and drew back. Holding the sword over her shoulder, she moved around to where there would be no danger of hitting Sigmund and swung at the chain with all her might.

The shimmering blade sliced through the thick iron as though it were made of hemp. Sigmund's arms fell to his sides with the weight of the manacles and chain.

He dragged the clinking bonds to a nearby rock and sat down. The sun was climbing into the eastern sky and he knew it wouldn't be long before the soldiers returned to confirm completion of their grizzly task.

"We must move deeper into the forest. The king's men will be returning and Gram or no, I will not be able to defeat them."

Gudred nodded, not taking her eyes from his face. "Yes, you are right -- but first."

She reached up to the sides of her neck and gently lifted a small golden chain he hadn't noticed before. She lifted it from around her head and a small charm that had been nestled between her breasts appeared.

His eyes fell to the talisman and noticed it was a small, fierce looking dragon. The work was that of a master craftsman.

She moved closer and lowered the pendant over his neck. He looked down and felt power emanating from the amulet.

"I don't understand. What is it?"

"Tis a symbol of the old gods. The magic comes from a belief in those deities."

"Oh Gudred, I couldn't"

"You must. It was given to me as a child and has saved my life countless times. I knew the moment would come when I would give it to someone else. Now is that time."

He said no more, but grasped the tiny icon and dropped it inside his tunic. An archaic voice in the back of his consciousness told him to guard the talisman with his life.

The thought of Siggeir's soldiers catching them before they could escape leaped into his mind and he moved to a jutting rock. Dragging the chain over the granite stone, he motioned Gudred to strike the chains from his manacles.

This completed, he retrieved the fabled sword and led her west, into the dense forest. Afterwards, they lived like outlaws for almost a year before Gudred found herself with child. A little boy was born in the dead of winter to a chorus of wolves howling at the frosted moon.

Gudred named him Sinfjotli; child of the wilderness.

Knowing his life would be forfeit if Siggeir ever discovered his whereabouts; Sigmund began making contact with the local populace, only to discover their lot in life was a sad state of existence.

The king taxed and abused his subjects with a cruel fist. Feared and despised, the despot's depravity knew no bounds. The peasants were brave and hardy, but lacked a leader. Sigmund discovered he had a natural ability to lead men and formed a rag-tag army of rebels.

The thralls and freemen were gallant, but outmatched by trained men with far superior numbers and weapons. In the first major confrontation, Sigmund's forces were decimated. He survived with wounds that would take months to heal and leave his body lined with white scars.

Accepting the fact he could not build an army to defeat Siggeir's forces, he turned his back upon civilization and embraced the wild and savage land that had become his home.

Time passed and the young Sinfjotli grew in his father's footsteps.

Hunting, a necessity for survival, became an obsession. By the time the boy was in his teens, father and son were ranging far and wide, killing anything and everything within bowshot.

The thrill of killing with the bow gave way to the intense sensation of taking an animal's life with a knife. Stabbing and tearing, the feeling of hot, fresh blood streaming over their arms and face became an insatiable need.

Early in the spring of the boy's fifteenth year the duo were feasting upon the bloody carcass of a deer when they were suddenly attacked by a pack of ravenous wolves. The battle that followed was that of animals. All but two of the wolves were slain by the long glistening blades of their adversaries. The survivors fled into the forest, snarling in rage and hunger.

Sinfjotli's left arm was bleeding profusely from the broken teeth of one of the fleeing wolves. The virus infecting the slavering maw was invisible, but deadly to humans. Sigmund quickly wrapped the bloody limb with a poultice of leaves and roots, but could not keep the worry from his face.

The days passed and it appeared the arm would heal, leaving a ragged scar in the boy's forearm. A cycle of the moon was almost complete and the wound was all but forgotten.

Using the darkness of night, father and son were stalking a nervous doe and her fawn when the full moon slid from behind heavy clouds. Sinfjotli stopped and slowly straightened. Staring at his father, the clear eyes glazed over and turned black. The boy was changing from a fair skinned, laughing lad with red hair to a . . . malformed beast.

Stunned, Sigmund stood and watched the transformation in a spellbound awe, recovering only to stab the animal when it attacked him. The wild, feeding frenzy in the dark orbs quickly faded to the pale blue his father had loved through the years.

He dropped the knife and grabbed his son, a howl issuing from his chest that sounded like the wail of a mortally wounded wolf. The hours passed and the reality of his life slowly seeped into his consciousness.

It had been months since he had seen Gudred. The last time he and Sinfjotli were home, she watched the pair warily, as though fearing for her life. They had come so far, and all of it in the wrong direction.

Digging a shallow grave, he covered the boy's body with rocks and turned homeward. The tragic event brought many a harsh reality home. His world had become that of a wild animal. It was little wonder the only person left in his life feared him.

Several days hence found him standing alongside a sparking stream a short distance from the hut he had built a lifetime ago. He looked down into the clear pool at his feet and stared. The reflection was of a man he didn't recognize. The dirty, bearded face was creased with age and lined with scars. It was the face of an old man and the eyes belonged to a stranger – wild and haunted.

Unconsciously brushing the ragged tunic, he walked up hesitantly to the door of hut and paused. It was his home, why should he be so afraid to walk in?

Taking a deep breath, he loosened the latch and stepped inside. He could see Gudred lying on the cot against the west wall in the dim interior. Thinking she was asleep, he crept across the dirt floor and slowly sat down on the other cot.

"Is that you Sigmund?"

"Yes."

After a pause, he spoke again. "I'm sorry I woke you."

He knew the familiar face was smiling from the tone in the words that came back. "I wasn't sleeping. Tis good to hear your voice."

Standing, he hesitated only a moment before hurrying across the room to kneel beside her. "I . . . haven't been myself for some time now. Sinfjotli and I . . . He stopped. How could he tell her he had killed their son?

A warm hand touched the side of his neck. "It's all right Sigmund. I know."

"Know? About Sinfjotli?" His voice broke. "How could you

know?"

He watched the azure eyes focus on him in the faint light and a small, sad smile formed beneath. "I have a confession to make." The small hand dropped to the side of the cot. She inhaled deeply as though gathering strength.

"When I gave you the dragon talisman, it enabled me to see the world through the eyes of your mind. I have been with you every moment since we fled into the woods so many years ago."

Sigmund sat in stunned silence at the revelation. There had been so many things the last few years . . . She had watched and remained silent. How she must loathe him.

"Gudred, I had no idea. You must think . . ."

He stopped at the touch of soft fingers on his lips.

"My love, you brought me happiness I never thought possible. I realized long ago, that everything has its price. That price has now been paid. My only regret is . . ."

Her hand dropped in the silence that followed.

"Gudred?"

He leaned closer and noticed his wife's eyes were closed, encased in dark hollows.

Jumping up, he placed his ear next to her face and realized she wasn't breathing. Strong hands grabbed the slim shoulders and it took all his willpower not to shake the frail body back to life.

Trembling with the realization that the last thing he loved in this world was gone, he clutched her to his chest and, unable to cry out in pain, sucked in wind to keep from drowning in the grief. The hours passed and he finally released the slim torso.

Time froze him in a silent agony as the sun rose and fell. No release and no escape, the price was due and must be paid.

Days passed before he finally stood and woodenly went through the process of digging another pit and placing his world within. Hauling a large number of rocks to cover the shallow grave, he finished by carving runes into the large boulder at the head. '*Here lies Gudred, the core of Sigmund's being*'.

There was nothing left to live for as he gathered the fabled sword from its resting place and headed towards the looming citadel he had avoided since the terrible defeat of his loyal army of followers.

He would look back in the years that followed and only remember vague images of the aftermath of that day. The surprised look on Siggeir's face as he drove the long blade home and spilled entrails on the floor; the hurried kiss he gave his sister before fleeing the castle and glancing back to see the entire stronghold engulfed in flames.

Signy set fire to the prison that had been her home for all of her adult life, ending the torment and memories of a life filled with sadness and tragedy. The spark that had been her soul had died with the realization her sacrifices had not saved her family and there was naught but ashes where her heart had been.

Nothing remained for him in Gautland, so Sigmund returned to his native home of Norway to reclaim the Volsung lands and title. An unbearable loss and unquenchable rage burned in the man's chest and countless men fell under the long blade of Gram. The sword was endowed not only with a powerful magic, but the wrathful arm of a mighty warrior.

Time and again, Sigmund and his followers engaged far superior forces and their leader walked away unscathed, with a dripping blade in his hand and fire in his eyes.

There were countless victories, but no satisfaction. What he was searching for couldn't be found. The years flew by in rage and destruction until a young lass named Hjordi appeared in the royal court, bringing news from clans to the south.

The king was smitten by her uncommon beauty and ere long, the couple was wed. The maiden seemed to fill the black void where Sigmund's heart had been, finally closing the gaping wound inside his chest. The Norse hero hung his sword on the wall and swore never to pick it up in anger again.

For the first time in many years, there was peace in the land.

The parade of memories stopped at the sound of a muffled cough. Wotun's gaze focused on the glowing embers in the fireplace, replacing the image of the ancient sword.

A familiar voice broke the silence. "You seemed to be lost in thought."

"What is it Harald?

"I'm sorry for interrupting, but I wished to speak with you."

"So speak."

"Aki's death must be avenged."

"Yes, but a strong arm needs plenty of iron and the heat of a forge to fashion weapons."

Harald understood the meaning behind the words; war required a following of warriors willing to die for him – and preparation. There was so much he wanted to ask in the quiet that followed, but sensed the time was not right.

Wishing he could see into the wizened enigma's mind, he quietly opened the door and left him with his memories.

The colors of fall set the northern forests ablaze by the time Harald and Guthorm marched south. Erick had returned to Svearike earlier in the year, but scores of Swedish soldiers, jarls, and puppet rulers, remained. Upon them Harald wreaked his vengeance.

Ubbe, the son of Aki, was allowed to accompany the army with directions to stay behind with the cooks and blacksmiths. Like most boys, he obeyed for as long as he could -- which wasn't very long. Many a Swedish soldier fell to an opponent he never saw. The sprite was deadly with a spear and floated around the fluttering skirts of a battle, retrieving and throwing the iron tipped shafts with an unerring aim. Always returning to camp before the time the tired and bloody warriors arrived.

Like corn beneath the sickle, the counties, realms, and petty kingdoms fell to the wrath of Halfdan's heir. With the strong arm and guidance of Guthorm, the warrior king spread terror throughout the entire southeastern region of Norway. Wotun no longer actively participated in the battles, but the omnipresence of his subtle power could always be felt.

With the first snowflakes came the vows of fidelity and caskets of tribute from the rebellious realms. Harald was amazed at the alacrity with which the common populace could switch loyalties. Just a few years ago, the people turned their back on the monarch of Agder and were singing the praises of a Swedish king. Now, they cheered and followed him in the streets.

In time he came to realize people by nature are a greedy and fickle lot. They would promise undying allegiance to whoever appeared most likely to give protection and wealth to them. Weapons, gold and power were the real gods.

The heavy snows of winter covered the land, laying a soft, white blanket over the crimson stained fields and forests. The long, bloody blades were cleaned, oiled and sheathed for the endless, dark nights that lay ahead.

With the winter's respite and days of rest, came preparations for the following summer. Hauberks needed repairs, new swords and spears fashioned. The ring of the hammer in the smithy continued for hours on end. Golden candlesticks, crosses, jewelry and silverware were melted down into coins and bars.

Harald was sitting quietly in the main lodge one afternoon when Ubbe came running in, crashing into a matron with a load of laundry. The boy dodged the switch the woman grabbed and rushed to the king's side. "My lord king, the smithy Woglind sent me to fetch you at once." Rubbing a hand reddened from the cold under a runny nose, he added, "I think tis something important."

The young monarch smiled at the excitement in the boy's face and lowered his fur clad boots from the bench in front of him. He set the sword he had been honing aside and stood up. "Well, I guess we better go see what it is." Swinging a hand towards the door, he motioned the boy to lead the way.

He chuckled as Ubbe rushed out the door, allowing the heavy, iron-bound planks to close behind him. By the time Harald reached the portal, the lad had returned to open the door and apologize profusely.

Although not much older than his charge, Harald acted like a father to the boy and mussed his hair before telling him it was all right and to move out of the doorway.

Nodding with enthusiasm, Ubbe spun around and raced for the smithy through the lightly falling snow. The king arrived on his heels and the heavyset smith turned from the massive anvil at his approach. "G'day lord. Sorry to bring you out on a day such as this, but thought you might want to see this."

"Tis no bother Woglind. The boy seems to be rather excited about something."

The smith smiled at the gangly youth and turned back to the anvil. Reaching into a pocket sewn into the leather apron, he produced a heavy gold ring and laid it upright on the flat surface of the iron. The small circle was tinged with a reddish-gold shimmer from the light of the forge.

Harald crossed his arms as the smith picked up a heavy sledge and studied the ring. Woglind swung the huge hammer fully above his head and brought it down on the gold band with a reverberating bang that shook the sodden turf beneath them.

The king drew back at the savage blow and stared at the slight impression in the anvil. He was pretty sure he had heard a ping upon impact, but there was no sign of the ring. "What happened? Where did it go?"

Ubbe immediately started searching through the hair of the heavy hides hanging either side of the anvil, running long, chapped fingers through the soft fur. "It'll be in one of the hides."

Harald frowned. He had expected to see a flattened piece of gold on the anvil's surface, but whether it was on the anvil or in the cowhide made little difference. "Well, let me know when you find it." He turned to go.

"Wait lord."

The smith held up a beefy hand and joined the boy in his search. Ubbe jumped up on the far side of the anvil, holding the prize in his fingers. "Here tis!"

The king moved over and grasped the golden circle, staring at it in amazement. "What in the nine worlds. Did you miss it?"

"Nay lord. The ring cannot be bent or even dented." He motioned towards the forge, "nor will it melt." Staring at the gold band, he added, "In all my years, I've never seen a metal such as this."

"But tis gold."

"Aye, but gold like I've never touched before."

Harald placed the ring in the palm of his hand and carefully picked it up to see if there were any runes or markings on it. Nothing was visible.

Slipping it on the second finger of his right hand, it fit. Strange warmth flowed from the ring into his hand and up his arm. The sensation was unfamiliar and gave him an uneasy feeling. The simple design and indestructibility appealed to him however and he decided to wear it.

Later, he proudly displayed the ring to Wotun and the action resulted in the only serious quarrel the two men ever had. The sage's eye grew wide at the sight of the simple gold band and he became enraged. "Read the inscription," he kept growling. Harald had already confirmed there were no markings on the ring, but his mentor would not listen.

Finally, in frustration, the young king promised he would place the ring in a small wooden box and not wear it. From that point on, there was tacit agreement the ring would not be discussed. The ageless Viking did his best to avoid Harald for a period of time, trying to fit the pieces of another invisible puzzle together.

Ubbe had met Wotun upon their return to Agder and attached himself to the old man like a leach. The snarling rebuffs of the patriarch had little effect on the urchin and he finally accepted his shadow as some sort of punishment by the fates.

A few weeks after the confrontation over the ring with Harald, Wotun entered the great hall at nightfall, carrying an armload of wood, which he deposited near the rock-lined pit. Shuffling to a nearby bench, he thought about the huge fireplaces of shaped stone in the countries to the south. They knew how to build a hearth.

He sat in silence and watched as an old woman took some of the wood and placed it in the pit. She turned away and added something to a large black pot hanging on a swivel near the fire. A pleasant aroma drifted towards him and he inhaled deeply.

"What ya doin?"

The familiar voice interrupted the moment of pleasure and the old man turned to glare at the boy by his side. "Minding my own business. What is the idea of sneaking up on me and yelling in my ear?"

"I didn't yell and you didn't answer my question."

Wotun let out a long sigh and looked towards the mud packed wattle ceiling. This had to be the work of the Norns – if they still existed. Whatever the punishment, it had to be borne.

"I was just sitting here, enjoying the quiet, and watching the women preparing supper." The one good eye turned a baleful glare at the bright, young face staring up at him. "Really enjoying the quiet I was."

Ubbe ignored the hint and grinned at the craggy old face. "If you were as mean as you acted, you would have got rotten and fell off the tree long ago."

The irony in the simple statement hit the ancient relic like a whack to the side of the head. The grimace softened. "What is it lad?"

Now that he had his idol's attention, the boy grew excited. Long ago, he began to believe there was absolutely nothing the old man didn't know -- the trick was getting him to tell you. "What do you know about the gold of the Rhine Maidens?"

Harald's ring flashed into the old man's mind and he whirled towards the boy, barking more harshly than he intended. "Who told you about the Rhine Maidens?"

Ubbe flinched at the vehemence in the response, somehow sensing he had touched upon a forbidden subject. He blurted, "Logge Udarsson. His uncle knows all about the Rhineland. He's even been to Wiesbaden – trading I suppose, but . . ."

He let the sentence hang, unsure whether to leave or wait and see what happened. As always, curiosity won over fear.

The archaic reprobate waved his hand in disgust. "Bah, men tell stories they have heard other men tell – and then change the parts they don't like. Tis all fable and fantasy lad, best forget it and live life as it unfolds."

Ubbe had sat and listened to the ancient Viking enough to know he had him. The man would tell him what really happened to the gold – if he could just keep from saying something dumb.

The grey eye turned down towards the small blue orbs watching him intently. "Shut your mouth boy, you're gaping like a fish."

Ubbe clamped his mouth shut and remained silent.

Wotun let out a long sigh. There just wasn't any way he was going to get out of this. Rubbing a wrinkled hand covered with age spots down the long, white wispy beard, he started.

☼☼☼☼

"A very long time ago, before the Christians came and the old gods still walked the nine worlds, the Rhine and Danube were the most beautiful rivers in the land of men." The wrinkled face softened with the memory. "Twas a marvelous time."

The image of a long, winding, crystalline river unfolded in the old man's mind. Lush vegetation grew along banks heavy with flowers, melding into forests of spruce, fir, and pine, abounding with game.

Wotun leaned back against the turf padded wall and folded his hands across his stomach. "Spirits that were ancient when the Vanir and Aesir were still at war protected the animals of the rivers, forests and oceans of the worlds. Mankind was a product of the new gods and the arcane spirits at first resented the intrusion, but over time came to accept the strange beings.

"The nine waves of the ocean were the daughters of the oldest of those spirits and the young women had many sisters in the streams of the world. Three of those women lived in the beautiful pools of the Rhine during the long winter months and wandered through the pristine forests during the summer.

"During an age before the memories of men, great mountains of ice receded from the countless valleys and vales of the lands to the north and from the particles of life suspended in those frozen lands evolved the essence of three river sprites known as Flosshilde, Woglinde and Wellgunde.

"The flawless hands of the ancient spirits formed the bodies of the three sprites in the likeness of the most beautiful women to grace the natural elements of Midgard. Whenever any mortal would see them, he would immediately be lost forever in that moment of rapture. The elder spirits forbade the nymphs to ever have contact with humans, but even the power of the antediluvian spirits was subject to the whims of the fates.

"Everything in the nine worlds had something that was valued above all else, and to the primordial spirits, it was the golden sunlight of morning. When humans appeared, they were afraid the new creatures might steal the treasured rays, so they bound them in stone and placed them in the depths of the holy water of the Rhine. The common granite, gneiss and quartz of the gravel beds became the most precious gold on earth.

"The three sisters were given the charge of constant vigilance over the gold, day and night. And for generations, they were successful in guarding the priceless treasure. But, as with all secrets, stories of the fabled golden cache spread throughout the nine worlds. Greedy thieves swarmed in droves along the banks of the timeless river.

"All attempts to steal the gold were easily thwarted by the three maidens, who began to delight in a game they always won. Humans were fools for the most part and giants were just plain dumb."

The patriarch stopped his storytelling when the old woman handed him a bowl of steaming stew. She motioned for Ubbe to get his own. The boy glanced at the vapor rising from the brown liquid and his stomach growled. Dashing to the large, black pot, he quickly scooped up a bowlful and rushed back to the old man's bench, licking the hot soup from his thumb and fingers. "Go on Wotun, please."

The man took a sip of the soup, slurping the hot liquid through his moustache and wiped his mouth with a faded linen sleeve. "Ah yes, now where was I?"

"Giants were dumb."

"Aye, that they were lad, that they were. But back to the story."

He glanced down at the bowl of soup in his lap and then continued with the tale.

"Humans and giants made countless attempts to steal the gold and failed, but the sprites had never dealt with the cunning dwarves."

"They say Odin wanted the gold as well," The boy interrupted.

Wotun glared at the statement. "Who's telling this story, you or me?"

"Sorry."

The old man coughed and looked for a moment like he might get up and walk away. Ubbe remained silent and the pleading eyes got their way. Once again, the tale commenced.

"The black dwarves were hideous creatures, but their dark cunning was unrivaled. Among them, a master craftsman named Andvari, lived deep in the bowels of Midgard. There, in the land of Niflheim, he created some of the most beautiful and powerful talismans the world has ever known.

"Upon hearing of the fabulous golden horde under the protection of the Rhine maidens, he set out to gain the treasure. Traversing the banks of the emerald stream in the soft glow of moonlight, he called to the maidens night after night, to no avail. Finally, learning of their passion for music, he fashioned a magical harp and sat under the stars softly stroking the silken strings.

"Wellgunde, the youngest of the sisters, was the first to be drawn to the magical strains drifting over the rippling surface of the Rhine. Andvari watched as the long, golden tresses slowly emerged from the silver shimmer of reflected moon glow. The stubby fingers forgot the melody for a moment and froze as the young maiden stepped from the water. She was nude except for an exquisite, finely wrought belt of twisted gold, sparkling with tiny sapphires. The ugly dwarf sat spellbound at the sight of the soft, pale curves shimmering against a backdrop of black velvet and crystalline stars.

"The nymph hesitated when he stopped playing and it appeared she was going to turn and dive into the water. Regaining his wits, the dark elf resumed softly strumming the enchanted instrument. Once again, the lovely apparition began moving closer

"Andvari was mesmerized by the beauty approaching him and for a moment, the two young women that followed went unnoticed. The sound of a girl humming came to his hairy ears and he realized the music was coming from the sprite standing a short distance away. Only when two other voices blended with the first did he realize the maiden's sisters had joined her.

"Their mouths were closed and throats still, but the humming turned into a melody older than time itself. Lost in the empyrean gossamer that enveloped his thoughts, he forgot the gold and the ugliness of life, drifting into a realm that exists only in the dreams of gods and lovers."

Once again, the inveterate storyteller paused and took a sip of the soup. It was now barely warm, but he knew his audience was short on patience, so he continued.

"Anything is possible in the mind of a dreamer and in his mind, Andvari was no longer an abominable little troll; he was handsome and brave, dashing through the dreams of women desiring only him.

"His hand dropped from the harp and he gently set the instrument aside. Rising from the stone he had been sitting on, he was staring at the smooth stomach of Wellgunde. He reached out to touch the satin skin and she jumped back, breaking the spell.

'What do you think you are doing?' The beautiful vision snapped.

"The cracking voice shattered the dream and the ugly little creature stood there staring at the three naked women like a confused child. 'I . . . I thought you liked me.'

"The appalled look on the gorgeous faces reflected his ugliness and the young woman's retort was that of an offended child. 'You are an ugly, horrible little man. What makes you think we would like you?'

'Well, at least I thought you liked the music.'

'That is music?' the girl said, pointing at the harp.

'No, that is simply a device for making music. There is no music until it is played.'

'Play it again.'

"Andvari complied, though with a heavy heart. Even dwarves have feelings and the bitterness grew the longer he played. Finally he stopped, and in response to the pleading by the nymphs that he continue, he replied, 'Not without some reward.'

"Flosshilde, the eldest, immediately became suspicious. 'And what would that be?'

'The favors of the lass for the remainder of the night." He was gesturing towards Wellgunde.

"The three sprites flushed crimson at the outrageous demand and, since the dwarf had no control over them, laughed at his brazen request. Taunting his desire, they began chiding the hideous thing, swinging their hips and tossing long flowing curls of auburn and wheat hues. 'We guard the most precious treasure in the nine worlds and the little man wants to bed Wellgunde. Of all the foolish creatures we have met, you are the simplest.'

"Twas then Andvari remembered his initial purpose; the gold beneath the surface of the Rhine. Reaching for the harp, he replied, 'You have no treasure to guard. You're just three silly girls pretending to have something of import to hide.'

"Woglinde shot back with heated indignation. 'You are an ugly little fool. We guard the gold of the heavens in our watery abode. A few ounces of the precious metal formed into a ring would make the possessor the most powerful being in the nine worlds. Like the circle of a golden band, the magic would be without end.'

"Flosshilde snapped at her younger sister. 'Woglinde! Prattle on like a child and we shall all pay the price.'

"Woglinde pushed Wellgunde aside to confront her sibling. Leaning close to Flosshilde's ear, she whispered, 'All love has to be forsaken for the power to be invoked. The little troll is lusting for Wellgunde like a hind in rut.'

"Unknown to the sisters, Andvari had exceptional hearing and allowed himself a grim smile upon learning the secret. Picking up his harp, he made as though to leave. To their pleading for more music, he replied, 'I must return to my home, for the light of day approaches. But tomorrow night I shall return and play until your ears are content.'

"The girls sadly agreed and the following night rushed to the soft strains of music coming from a distance, downstream. Leaving the treasured horde of Rhine gold, they flashed like salmon with the current and quickly found the source. Wading ashore, the nymphs espied the harp leaning against a tree, the strings vibrating as though strummed by invisible fingers.

"The melody was enchanting and before long, a chorus of ephemeral voices was melding with the rise and fall of the ancient tune. Time passed and only Flosshilde wondered where the owner of the harp was. The moon was a quarter of the way to its zenith when she suddenly stopped singing and grabbed Wellgunde by the arm. 'The dwarf! What if this was a trick to get us away from the gold?'

"Swimming with the speed of panic and desperation, they quickly flew back to the golden cache, but it was gone. Their wails of loss and despair gradually changed to a melancholy song that reached the arch of Bifrost."

"Bifrost?" Ubbe interrupted again.

This time Wotun didn't scowl at the boy, but simply responded. "I can't describe it in mortal words. Twas a magical bridge between Asgard and the world of men. The closest thing to resemble it would be the bow of colors you see in the sky after a warm summer rain.

He paused before adding, "All inhabitants of Asgard used it except Thor, for fear of his ponderous footsteps shattering the beautiful span.

"Anyway, when the sad song of the Rhine maidens reached the

gods, they went to discover the reason for the despair. Upon seeing Odin and the heavenly host, the water-sprites implored the deities to recover their lost gold. Instead of offering solace however, Loki, the god of fire and mischief, taunted the maidens with a malice unbefitting a god.

"Angered by the god's treatment of their offspring, the arcane spirits of nature placed a curse upon the gold that would hold until the end of days. Only when returned to the holy waters of the Rhine would the curse be broken.

"Meanwhile, Andvari took the stolen treasure to a deep underground cavern and disguised the entrance with a pristine lake, deep in the forest. He carefully placed the gold in a large crate and set it at the edge of his workbench. Cleaning off the bench, he laid a pair of worn, iron tongs on top of the gold.

"Being a creature of magic, he flinched upon retrieving the tongs, realizing that some type of ancient alchemy had transformed the simple tongs into a tool of power. Thereafter, they were his most prized possession.

"The days passed, and with the skill of a master craftsman, he created bracelets, necklaces and other exquisite pieces of jewelry from the golden rays of heaven. Remembering Woglinde's statement about the potential power of a ring made from the Rhine gold, he set about fashioning a simple, but flawless band of gold. When the ring had cooled, he inscribed runes of enchantment inside the band. 'The power to rule the nine worlds is with the one who wears this ring.'

"The dwarf was unaware of the curse the supernatural beings had placed upon the gold and as he slipped the ring on his finger, the runes transformed into; 'The evils of the worlds will possess the wearer of this ring."

Wotun stopped and the grey eye slowly focused on his surroundings. Remembering the boy at his side, he scowled at the lad. "The person wearing the ring was forever cursed after that."

"But what about . . . ?"

Wotun threw up a hand at the boy's question. "Enough for today. I swear lad, you wear an old man out."

Taking a sip of the cold soup, the white-hair frowned at the bowl before setting it down and standing up. Mussing the boy's hair, he shuffled out of the hut into the cold night air.

The winter passed and spring found Harald looking for new alliances. He was approaching twenty winters and had neither wife nor heir.

Erik Steinheldsson was a jarl of a minor kingdom in the jutting peninsula of the lands to the southeast and on lukewarm terms with the men of the North Way. The Danes were an old and proud race of warriors and the opportunity for a union with the powerful clan leader lay in wedding his eldest daughter, Ragnhilda.

The fact that the woman had a name similar to his mother's was taken as a good omen and Harald sent Guthorm to negotiate the betrothal. The king's lieutenant did as he was bid and presented a chest of gold and jewels to the jarl to seal the bargain. The distant lord was pleased with the arrangement, but the same could not be said of his daughter.

A headstrong young woman, Ragnhilda adamantly refused the proposal, until Guthorm informed her in front of her father that King Harald would not accept the rejection. He would return in anger, killing everyone she loved.

The princess saw the truth in the statement and the logic of accepting, so she relented. The wedding was held that spring in the great hall at Vestfold and less than a year later, an heir was born. Eirik Harraldsson would prove to be one of the most feared monarchs of the northern lands. Spreading a bloody path of conquest and tyranny, the infamy of the king would be told in eddas, sagas and lays for generations to come.

The child was quick, proud and fearless, winning his father's heart the day he tried to heft a large spear leaning against the wall of the lodge. Both child and spear crashed to the ground, but instead of crying, the toddler laughed in glee at the scrapes and bruises.

Harald swept the boy up in his arms, praising the gods for the blessing bestowed upon him. Wotun watched the elation of his king with a heavy heart. *It would often be better if our requests fell on deaf ears.*

The conquests of the past were soon forgotten and the monarch began looking to the north and west. The mountainous terrain of central Norway held little of worth, but the coastal lands to the west were lined with wealthy trading villages. A ragtag collection of minor kings ruled the various provinces and Harald knew a powerful and shrewd warrior could soon rule the entire country.

Once again, the minds and wills of Harald, Guthorm and Wotun were aligned and the king's army moved north. The jarl of the petty kingdom of Hordaland met the invading army at the borders of the realm with a hastily assembled army of merchants, farmers and mercenaries.

Harald rode at the front of a line of mounted warriors, ready to level their spears and break any barrier the enemy could provide. Raising an arm to start the assault, he stopped and held it there. One of the adversaries had long, flowing hair and a slight build.

At first he was bemused they were so desperate as to send women into the fray, but then noticed the gleaming mail link of her armor and finely wrought trappings on the horse. This was no futile, desperate effort of defense. The woman had the bearing of a warrior.

Rather than dropping his arm to start the battle, the young king turned and rode along the front of the ranks telling his men to hold. The woman had piqued his curiosity and if fighting started, it might never be satisfied. Assured his men would not attack, he rode a short distance toward the army of Hordaland and pulled the heavy roan to a stop.

Holding up his spear, sword and shield, he tossed them to the ground. By now, both sides were wondering what could explain the strange behavior, but were waiting patiently. Harald spurred the horse to a trot towards the young female warrior and an older man at her side.

The man was Erick Suddersson, King of Hordaland. Harald pulled back on the reigns and slowed to a walk fifty paces from the aged monarch, but his eyes were on the woman. The two were still side-by-side when he reached them. His gaze moved from the cloudy blue orbs of the woman to the steel in the older man's eyes. The grey-streaked beard and lines in the scarred face betrayed his age, but the king sat straight as a ramrod in the saddle.

Harald raised a hand as a show of respect for an enemy and to express the need to parley. The king steadied his prancing horse and slowly raised his hand, trying to see through the deceit of his young adversary. "You invade my lands, but wish to talk?"

"I will not banter words with you old man. I just wanted to know why you send women into battle."

Dark eyebrows streaked with grey rose at the statement and the flinty eyes moved to the woman at his side. "Gyda has a mind of her own. After her mother died, no one has been able to . . ." He let the statement hang, the stranger had no right to know of the family's personal tragedy.

"She does as she pleases."

Harald realized from the comment that the girl was the king's daughter, making her presence all the more amazing. He pulled off the leather padded iron helmet and pushed the hair back from his face. "May I be so bold as to see the fair countenance of your daughter?"

The language of a courtesan was strange on his tongue and he felt a fool as soon as he said it. The expression on the king's face betrayed his confusion at his opponent's strange behavior. He glanced back at the iron nosepiece covering most of his daughter's face. "As I said, she does what she wants."

The hazy blue-green eyes morphed to a deep green as the woman pulled off a gauntlet and removed her helmet. Straw colored hair glittered in the morning sunshine, tumbling down over and around the mail covered shoulders. Harald remembered his father's ramblings about meeting his mother, but the words never meant anything, until now.

She wasn't what would be termed pretty. Pretty was flowers on a hillside, or embroidery on a skirt. The high cheekbones framed a slender, straight nose leading to full lips – lips pursed with anger. The haughty pose was a mask Harald saw through immediately. The woman was beautiful, but her beauty was a thing to be tolerated, something she had no use for.

The young conqueror knew his next words would determine his destiny with the princess and suddenly felt uneasy. He was never nervous and the sensation was exhilarating. Remembering his silly statement earlier, he nudged his horse closer to the princess and extended his arm. "May you die well."

The pursed lips relaxed and Gyda studied him to see any hint of humor. There was none. She reached out to accept a warrior's wish and grasped his forearm. "And you."

Harald smiled in surprise at the strength in the slender fingers. Squeezing hard as a sign of respect, he released the woman's arm and turned to her father. "Lord, I have no wish to fight this day. Instead, I request the hand of your daughter."

The sudden change of events was tumbling around in the old warrior's mind like leaves in a summer whirlwind. "I . . . Gyda . . . what?"

Harald smiled at the monarch's discomfiture and, remembering the earlier statements about his strong willed daughter, turned to the princess. "Will you be my queen?"

"You already have a wife." The green orbs were snapping with intensity.

"A king needs many wives."

"A High King maybe, but you are no High King."

The exchange had suddenly turned a corner. The princess was telling him her price – in the simplest of terms. Conquer all of Norway and she would be his.

A challenge had been made which deserved an answer. Without hesitating or further thought, Harald's eyes turned to blue shards of ice. "By my father's sword, I'll not cut a hair of my head until every kingdom in Norway pays homage and tribute to one king. And that kingdom shall be mine."

In the silence that followed, he nodded curtly to the King of Hordaland and thundered back to his army. The soldiers were disgruntled at the loss of the anticipated looting, but were quickly relieved to discover more realms to the south were still fair game.

Wotun took the news with the aplomb of an arcane wizard. Nothing surprised him anymore. "King of all the northern lands eh?" He glanced over at Guthorm. "Your liege would be High King. What think you?"

"There has never been a High King of the northern realms." The lieutenant looked thoughtful. "But if there were to be, Harald Halfdansson would be the man."

"I agree. But Odin decreed long ago that by one sword alone, would a single man rule all Norsemen."

Chapter 6

Gram –
Sword of Legend

Guthorm's gaze moved to fall on the white-hair. "The sword of legend? Does such a weapon truly exist?"

"It did at one time. There is no reason to believe it no longer does."

"How do you know this?"

"'Tis enough that I know."

Harald interrupted. "Where would the sword be found?"

Wotun paused before answering. "If, and I say 'if', you are truly destined to be High King, you must seek the fates and ask them. The location of the sword would be known only to the Norns."

"Fair enough, where are the fates to be found?"

The sage shook his head. "I'm afraid the realm of the fates no longer exists. I'm truly sorry Harald, but more than this, I do not know." Moving closer to his young charge, Wotun placed a hand on the mail-covered arm. "This is something you must do alone."

"I understand."

By the time the army returned to Vestfold, Harald had made up his mind. He would leave on a quest for the fates, and the sword. The only advice Wotun could give was to point north.

The days passed and Harald found himself moving through the lands of the Finns. The dark forests of the Lapps watched in silence as he rode the ancient trails ever leading north. A fortnight from home, the weary traveler dismounted with the setting sun and started a small fire.

A small rabbit provided the making of the evening meal. Slowly turning the carcass on a spindle over the fire, Harald wondered for the hundredth time if he was on a fool's errand. He had a vague idea of what he was looking for, but no clue as to where he should look. It was a vast, uncharted land he was wandering in and the hopes of finding the three sisters known as the Norns were fading fast.

The fire wavered with a gust of cold air. It was mid-summer and the chill in the breeze sent a shiver up Harald's spine. Smoke from the fire swirled in a tiny circle and moved around his head. Instinctively, he waved the smoke aside with his hand and felt a slight resistance. He became frozen at the touch and his heart began to hammer with the strange sensation.

It was as though he had pushed a curtain back and a strange and beautiful landscape came into view. A castle of clear stone with the appearance of glass stood in the distance. Tiny creatures were flitting around the ramparts, emitting some kind of iridescent light. The vision was mesmerizing.

His view was no longer from a distance, but moved past the smoky veil, across the lush meadow, and through the looming doors of the citadel. Floating across a broad expanse of gleaming tiles, he found himself turning down a dark stairwell and suddenly in front of three women.

One was ancient to the point of death, the second of middle age and the third not much more than a child. There could be no question; these were the Norns of legend.

"You are the fates?" The voice was his, but from a time long forgotten.

"Do not waste our time asking questions to which you already know the answer."

"I seek the sword of Sigmund, of the Volsung clan."

"So have countless others."

"I will find it, with, or without, your help."

"No, you will not."

The truth in the statement stripped away the façade of bravado and left a desperate mortal standing in the midst of a power he could not comprehend. "You will not help me?"

"We did not say that."

His spirit soared at the statement. There was hope. "Then you will!"

"That was not said either."

The elation crashed to the stone paving of the floor. "I . . . don't understand."

"Recognizing that is the beginning of wisdom."

"Please, tell me what I must do."

Skuld, the youngest of the sisters, was the first to respond. "Valor is the right hand of a High King."

Verdandi spoke next. "Honor being the strong arm of the left."

"Wisdom controls the mind and compassion dwells forever in the heart." Wyrd, the ancient one, quietly added the last comment.

Harald was silently repeating each of the qualities; valor, honor, wisdom . . . when the three sisters began to waver as though made of smoke. "Wait! No, please!"

Grasping desperately for something that was no longer there, he stopped as he realized he was sitting in front of a campfire, swinging his arms wildly about in the swirling smoke. He glanced around to see if anyone had been watching and then remembered he was in the middle of a huge expanse of uncharted forest and the chances of meeting anyone were remote.

Waving the sudden appearance of a large butterfly away, he once again focused on the rabbit. The bottom portion was now little more than charcoal, but the upper part was devoured ravenously. He finished the sparse meal and leaned back against the trunk of a huge oak, the words of the Norns running through his mind.

The beautiful, fluttering insect landed on his arm and he brushed it off. A faint tinkling sound reached his ears. Looking around him, he remained motionless for a moment, trying to hear the sound again.

Barely audible at first, the musical notes moved closer and seemed to be right in front of him. He drew back slightly when he noticed the butterfly, or moth, whatever it was, hovering in front of his face – it was glowing!

His mouth dropped open as he leaned forward for a closer look. It was a tiny woman! The gossamer wings were all but invisible with the rapid movement, but the soft curves and raised eyebrow spoke volumes.

Spellbound, and uncertain as how to react, Harald slowly raised his hand, palm upward. She flashed to within a hand span of his face, as though it were a warning to behave himself. Nodding as though satisfied, she floated down and landed in his hand.

The muttering that followed the contact startled him to the point he almost dropped her. His rapidly beating heart began to hammer at the words that were coming from the miniscule, beautiful creature.

"Always me. They always send me. For once, why couldn't they send someone . . .?"

The pixie's thoughts were interrupted by the towering human. "Are you talking?"

She paused, petite hands going to the band of twisted gold at her hips. "I was, but not to you."

"I'm sorry."

"That's all right. It's just that . . . oh, never mind."

"Where did you come from?"

"You're a slow one aren't you?"

"I'm sorry."

"Quit apologizing. Wyrd sent me to help you find the sword."

"Do you know where it is?"

"No. And even if I did, I couldn't just tell you."

"Why not?"

"Arghh! Why didn't they just shoot me?"

"Shoot you! For what?"

Letting out a long sigh, the miniature fairy made a graceful curtsey. "I am known as Feejar. Think of me as a guide that doesn't know where we're going."

"All right, fair enough."

"That's the first intelligent thing you've said since we met."

"Thank you."

The tiny lips pursed as though considering the worth of the looming giant. "You're welcome. Now, let's get some sleep."

"You sleep?"

"I take back the comment about being intelligent."

"G'night Feejar."

"Good night . . . what's your name anyway?"

"Harald."

"Good night Harald."

Soft rays of an early morning sun crept through the treetops, bringing the promise of a glorious day. Breakfast complete, Harald brushed his tunic off and stared at his new comrade. "Well, which way guide?"

"How do you start a journey when you don't know the destination?"

"One step?"

"Very good! What direction?"

"Does it matter?"

"There's hope for you yet. Now pick up a stick and throw it into the trees as high as you can."

Harald knew better than to ask why and did as directed. The stick disappeared into the high branches above and abruptly fell to the ground. Man and pixie stared at the stick and the direction in which it was pointing. Shrugging, he shouldered his rucksack and headed off. The tinkling sound at his shoulder told him Feejar was humming some archaic tune and he couldn't help but join in with a melody from his childhood.

He felt a slight pinch on the lobe of his ear and Feejar's voice permeated his consciousness. "Hermod's heels Harald. If you're going to make those terrible bellowing noises, please do so with less enthusiasm."

Somewhat chagrined, the king of Vestfold and a score of other realms, began quietly humming. To Feejar, it still sounded like the rumbling of a lion in her ear.

By nightfall, they entered a small village where the populace spoke the language of Norsemen, but with a strange dialect. Feejar nestled in a fold in Harald's tunic and remained silent.

The entire town seemed to be in the grip of some unspeakable terror. A pall of fear permeated the vacant streets like a blanket of doom. People rushed across the openings between buildings as if the alleys were strewn with vipers.

Harald walked into the only inn in the village and stopped inside the doorway. A handful of patrons glanced up from their ale and board games at the appearance of the stranger.

"Close the door." The innkeeper seemed none to friendly for a man seeking business. "What do you want?"

"Some food and a flask of mead."

The man grunted and disappeared into an adjoining room. Harald found one of several empty tables at the edge of the room and sat in a crude, poorly made chair with his back to the wall. Glancing around him, the men seemed a surly lot, but the looks on their faces were haunted and drawn.

A dozen candles flickered around the room, casting long shadows, wavering across the rough, wooden floor. The wan light provided by the tallow tapers chiseled the bearded faces into sharp contrasts of black and pallid hues.

"Here ye be. That'll be two dinar."

Harald glanced down at the steaming bowl of stew and mug of ale. To his surprise, it smelled good. Reaching into a pocket in his tunic, he produced a small leather pouch and handed the portly innkeeper the requested coins.

Small, pig eyes in the heavy face studied him for a moment, and then, giving the silver discs a small toss and deftly grabbing them, he headed back to the heavy, wooden counter that served as a bar.

Taking a sip of the ale and grimacing at the rancid taste, Harald reached for the bowl of stew, but paused as another man approached his table. The lined face was framed in a beard tinged with gray. Hard, iron hued eyes found his and locked. "You're a stranger here. Might I be asking your business?"

"Yes you may. I travel from the lands to the south and west, on a quest."

"A quest? What do you seek?"

The newcomer paused before responding. "A sword."

"You carry a sword. What need have you of another?"

"This is a special sword. The sword of the legendary Sigmund."

The man's right eyebrow rose at the statement. He was obviously talking to a madman, or the stranger was making jest with him.

"I am the Lawkeeper in this realm and we've trouble enough without strangers bringing more. Do we understand each other?"

"We do. I'll cause you no grief."

"Be sure that you don't."

Harald reached for the still steaming bowl of soup as he watched the man's receding back. The stygian interior of the little inn reminded him of the strange nightmare he had as a child. In the darkest part of the night, some terrible creature would steal through his village and the ensuing screams would always wake him with a chill in his bones and sweat on his skin.

The stew was actually quite good and soon gone. Draining the last of the ale, he stood and considered his options. Walking across the small room, he approached the Lawkeeper's table. Two other men were sitting with the man and their conversation stopped as his shadow crossed the table.

"Pardon my interruption, but may I inquire as to how you are called?"

"Olaff Gedesson, and you?"

"I am son of Halfdan the Black, Harald."

Once again, the eyebrow rose. "I've heard of you. King of the southern realms of Norway are you not?"

"The same."

There was a definite change in the man's demeanor. It was obvious he was struggling with whether he was still dealing with a madman, or royalty. He decided to play it safe. Standing and making a slight bow he said, "My lord, how may we be of service?"

The man owed him no allegiance, but courtesy to strangers was an unwritten law throughout the Scandinavian countries, and nobility was to be treated with utmost respect.

"Is there a place where a stranger would be welcome to spend the night?"

Olaff glanced at the two men still seated. "The last house on the left going out of town. An old widow woman keeps overnighters for a single dinar."

"I thank you and bid you good eve."

"Good eve, Your Majesty."

Harald turned to leave, but stopped. He had to know. "Oh, one other thing. There seems to be something in the air that frightens the townspeople. Am I mistaken?"

Muscles in the man's jaw flexed. "I'm sorry lord. I know not of what you speak."

The flinty grey orbs couldn't hide the lie. Everyone was living in fear of something. "My mistake. Good eve."

"Good eve."

Making his way down the deserted street, he found the described house, it was little more than a two-story hut really, but would provide shelter from the cold and rain.

The elderly matron reminded him of everyone's grandmother; grey hair in a bun, blue checkered apron and fussing about this, and tsk, tsking about that. Head bobbing constantly, she reassured him she had a nice room and wanted to know if he had eaten.

He decided to broach the question of fear in the townspeople to the old woman and the results were surprising. She responded without hesitation. "Scared spitless they are. And tis no wonder. That monstrous beast, terrorizing villages for miles around."

Harald was just staring at her, so she elaborated. "Don' tell me you haven't seen it? The thing has kilt every man who stood in its way." She began wringing the wrinkled hands in the worn apron. "Terrible, terrible. And who knows what has happened to the children?"

"Children?"

"Aye. The thing has taken almost all of the children from town."

"What for?"

"I fear the worst, but nobody knows. Every man that went after the beast failed to return."

"Can you describe it?"

"Course I can. Tis a man, but tall as a tree and ugly as a troll. Hideous to look upon and strong enough to smash a house."

"A giant?"

"Aye. A more fearsome creature you've never seen."

Harald stood staring at the woman in silence. He had heard of such beings, but no one believed in their existence. Now however, there was too much evidence to dismiss the tale – the village was being ravaged by a thing of legend.

Climbing the crude, but solid, stairs to his room, he whispered, "Did you hear that Feejar?"

The tinkling sound that followed reminded him she needed to touch him to understand her. Dumping his rucksack on the floor of the small room, he found the only candle and lit it in the faint light provided from the iridescent glow of his butterfly.

"Not all giants are bad you know." The words followed a soft touch at the side of his neck.

"I didn't think such things existed."

"Really? Where do you think the stories came from?"

"Just figured people made them up."

"From what?"

For the first time, it occurred to Harald that even the wildest imagining of people were based upon some real life experience. "Well, when you put it that way, it makes me wonder about all the other impossible tales I heard as a lad."

"As well it should."

"How do you kill a giant?"

"Befriend a bigger giant?"

"You're not helping."

"Sorry." The half-hearted apology was followed by a pause and then; "You're not thinking about actually trying to kill it are you?"

"Well the thought did cross my mind."

"Why?"

"Didn't you hear the old lady? These people are terrified of it, and from the sounds of things, rightly so."

"And this is your problem because . . . .?"

"What do you mean?"

"They are not your people. Would you travel hundreds of miles to help someone you didn't know?"

"Probably not."

"That is what you would be doing."

"It just seems like the right thing to do."

"What if you get yourself killed? You'll never find your sword and become king of all the Norse lands."

The comment made Harald pause. As a ruler, one of the first lessons he learned from both Guthorm and Wotun was the concept of duty to his people. There was no heir old enough to assume the responsibility and civil war would tear the land apart.

"What should I do?"

"That is the right question. A king cannot rule with just his heart or his head, but must use both and maintain a balance. Weigh the input of each and make your decision. But it must be yours, I cannot tell you what to do."

"You know for having such a tiny head, you are a very smart woman."

"Maybe there's hope for you yet. Size is just one of a thousand aspects of any challenge."

"Is that a hint about how to defeat the giant?"

"Could be. Don't really know."

The next morning found him following footprints an arm's length across and two paces long. The marks were embedded in the ground to a depth of a cubit or more in places. It would require an incredible amount of weight to crush the soil thus.

A little more than a furlong into the surrounding woods brought them to a large, broken ravine filled with rock outcroppings and huge boulders. The trail of footprints turned into the floor of a canyon covered with similar markings. Careful scrutiny disclosed they were all made by the same feet.

The depth of the canyon increased as they proceeded and before long, Harald was looking up at looming granite walls on both sides of them. The footprints came to an abrupt halt at the base of the towering escarpment.

Looking around him, it was as though the giant took flight from this point on. "Feejar, the tracks end here."

A tinkling sound rose above his head and faded out of hearing. Pulling on the hilt of his sword, he raised it slightly out of the worn scabbard and allowed it to drop back in place. He whirled around nervously as some small stones bounced down the far wall.

The voice inside his head came unbidden. "What are you doing?

You're going to get yourself killed, and for what?" The self-crimination was interrupted by the familiar touch of a soft hand on his neck.

"The tracks disappear because the giant has been climbing the rock wall to an overhang and cavern about ten paces above you."

"Is he there now?"

"I don't think so, but I heard what sounded like children crying."

Dropping the rucksack to the ground, Harald adjusted his sword and started looking for handholds in the rugged face of the granite. In a matter of minutes, he was peering over the ledge into a dark, deep crevasse in the canyon wall.

Hauling himself up, he stood and warily loosened his sword again before heading into the dark interior. A few paces into the opening, he stopped at the sound of something snapping under his feet. Letting his eyes adjust to the darkened surroundings, he inhaled sharply as the outlines of ashen bones began to appear.

The scattered skulls removed any doubt about the source. They were the remnants of people. But there didn't seem to be any small bones among the grizzly remnants.

As though in response to the realization came the faint cry of a child from the dark recesses of the cleft. Wishing he had some sort of light, Harald stopped suddenly. "Feejar, can you shine any brighter?"

The fluttering firefly touched his ear. "Nope. Sorry, but what you see is all there is."

"Would you check and see if you can find that child?"

"Be right back."

Harald noticed a slightly foul odor and after thinking about it a minute, wondered why it wasn't much worse. The giant had eaten all of the soft parts of the people and most of the bones. There was a gentle breeze from the canyon, moving through the cavern, providing fresh air to the interior.

Almost immediately, the tiny glow reappeared. He held up his hand and Feejar landed with the touch of swan's down. "There are a dozen or more children at the back of the cave. They look half starved and terrified."

"We must get them away from . . ."

The sentence was interrupted by a thundering roar from behind. Glancing rays of the sun disappeared completely, blocked out by some enormous form at the cavern's entrance. With the exception of the iridescent glow, they were immersed in darkness.

Feejar's thoughts hit him like a slap in the face. "You must flee! I will distract him, and when I do, run for your life."

The pixie darted away before he had a chance to respond. The tiny fairy had to literally fly into the giant's face to get its attention. The towering monster swung a massive club at the irritating insect, but it was not enough to distract it from the smell of a man in the area.

One part of Harald's mind was screaming at him to run, take his chances -- jump the thirty feet to the ground and find a hiding place. The other part refused to budge. That was not what he came for, and by the gods, not what he would do.

Jerking his sword free, he screamed Odin's name and rushed the titan. The giant bellowed in rage at the sight of the man and brought the cumbersome club around in a sweeping arc. Harald ducked and rolled under the swinging timber, showered with a deluge of shattered rock and splintered wood.

He leaped to his feet and rushed legs the size of tree trunks, thrusting the sword into the bulging muscles. The raging giant became a maelstrom of fury. Jerking the injured leg away from the sudden pain, he threw the puny human across the broad expanse of granite into a cluster of broken stone.

The king's death grip on the sword was the only thing that kept it in his hand. Hitting hard and crashing into a pile of rock, he felt a sharp pain in his side. He was pretty sure some ribs were broken, but that was the least of his problems at the moment. Leaping aside just in time to avoid a crushing blow of the massive club, he gasped at the excruciating pain.

Panting for breath, he scrambled into a protective crevice and marveled at the power the giant exuded in the mindless rage that possessed him. Finally, the titan began to tire and stopped pounding the opening to the cleft his prey had crawled into.

One huge eye peered into the fissure, trying to better see the puny nuisance that was eluding him. Growling in frustration, the monster attempted to get fingers the size of a man's torso into the small opening.

Edging deeper into the fractured rock, Harald felt a familiar soft touch and voice. "I hope this isn't what you had in mind."

"No Feejar. This isn't what I was planning on."

"Any ideas?"

"No . . . wait. Yes, I do have an idea."

Harald whispered something to Feejar and the response was a

tinkling sound that quickly disappeared. Moments later, the giant grunted and moved away from the crack in the rock. More grunting followed and then slapping sounds.

Inching out of his hide-a-way, Harald peeked out. The giant was standing near the entrance to the looming crevasse, shaking his head. Frowning and slapping his ear, he was growling in frustration. The towering beast began slamming the open palm of his hand against the side of his head with incredible force.

By now, the giant had completely forgotten his victim and was snarling at some unidentified irritation and becoming angrier by the second. Sensing his opportunity, Harald rushed the distracted titan and, swinging his sword in a flashing arc, cut the thick Achilles tendon of the left leg.

The results were cataclysmic. Thirty-some feet of bone and muscle came crashing onto the rock ledge to go tumbling over the edge. Smashing into the trees and boulders below, the gargantuan form came to rest at the bottom of the canyon and lay still.

Holding his side to reduce the pain, Harald clambered down the rock formation and strode to the giant's prone form. Stunned, but far from dead, the beast was breathing steadily. Fluttering eyelids opened to find his nemesis standing over him with a sword at his throat.

"Do it." The words were understandable, but sounded like the rumbling of a dying bear.

"You speak our language. Where are you from?"

"The land of the Sami. I am known as Stallon."

"Why do you terrorize the people of this land?"

The huge face softened and for a moment, almost looked human. **"My daughter died and I wished to replace her. The villagers attacked me when I took their children and . . . and I was hungry."**

The muscles in Harald's jaw flexed. The law of vengeance declared he must make the fatal thrust and be done with it. He pushed on the sword until a small crimson flow appeared on the massive neck. The giant lay as though already dead.

Clinching his teeth, Harald said, "If I allow you to live, will you leave this land and never return?"

"May I take the children with me?"

"No."

A cloud passed over the plate-sized orbs. Life no longer held any meaning for the giant and he knew with the severed tendon, he could no longer have his way by force.

"As you wish. I will leave and never return."

"Swear by all that you hold sacred."

"I swear."

Harald retrieved the sword and stepped from the giant's chest. Sheathing the sword, he suddenly remembered his tiny companion. "Feejar!"

An iridescent butterfly suddenly appeared in front of him and he held up his hand. She was chattering before contact made her words understandable. ". . . and then when he fell off the ledge, well, I thought you did just fine."

"Are you all right?"

"You mean were you successful in trying to get me killed?"

"I'm sorry, but it was the only thing I could think of."

"Well, it worked. Besides it was kind of fun climbing into the giant's ear. At least until he started pounding on it." She stopped and the miniscule face made a frown. "Sort of reminded me when I got stuck in some pie dough. The cook was pounding . . ."

She squeaked as a looming shadow from Stallon stretched out from the gargantuan form. The giant was struggling to regain his feet. "Why didn't you kill him when you had the chance?"

"Did you hear what he said?"

"Unless I am touching someone, it just comes across as rumbling. In his case, it sounded like an avalanche."

"He lost his little girl and was trying to replace her."

"With children from the village?"

"Yes."

"What about the men he killed . . . and ate?"

"He said he was hungry."

"Oh. Well, I guess that makes it all right then?"

"You didn't hear the pain in his words."

"What about the sorrow of the grieving relatives?"

"I just couldn't do it."

Feejar studied the sad, chiseled face. "Not a bad day's effort, all-in-all."

"What do you mean?"

"You have not only shown valor in refusing to run when you had the chance, twas compassion that saved the giant's life."

Valor and compassion, two of the attributes the Norns had identified. The import of the statement was still tumbling around in his mind as Stallon hefted the massive club and swung it over his shoulder.

Giving the little man a rueful glance, the titan hobbled away. King and pixie watched the huge form until it was out of sight. Each wrapped in thoughts known only to them.

Releasing the children filled Harald with an elation he had never known. The small urchins were climbing all over him, tears streaming down the drawn faces. Tiny rows of white teeth flashed through the dirt and grime, expressing a gratitude that words could never convey.

Helping the kids down the escarpment turned into an effort of frivolity and laughter. It was late in the day by the time everyone was safely down and headed for home.

The men killed by the giant were momentarily forgotten when he returned to the village, surrounded by the greatest treasure the townsfolk would ever have.

A celebration quickly formed with Harald as guest of honor. The children had developed an immediate and deep regard for their rescuer and he gave up any hope of privacy.

Knowing the local populace would belabor and argue against his departure, he rose before the sun and, ensuring Feejar was still asleep in his tunic, slipped quietly from the outskirts of town.

The brooding morning sky did little to dampen Harald's spirits as he tromped through the woods, heading he knew not where. Defeating the giant gave him a new confidence in the success of his quest. By mid-afternoon, the grey, scudding clouds began to release a mist which quickly turned to a cold rain.

Seeking shelter under the spreading boughs of a huge pine, Harald started a small fire and huddled against the trunk for warmth. Lost in thought, a soft touch on his neck was followed by the velvet voice he had began to cherish.

"You cold?"

"A little."

"Can you imagine those little flames as a raging bonfire?"

Harald stared at the snapping twigs and concentrated. The fire grew and the heat increased. Holding his reddened hands closer to the leaping flames, the warmth permeated his arms and face. It felt good.

"It works!"

"Only if you think it does."

"Thanks Feejar."

The pair sat in silence as the rain slowed and finally stopped. It was late in the day and both were tired. Wrapping his arms around him, he smiled as Feejar snuggled down in the collar of his tunic and was soon emitting incredibly faint sounds of steady breathing.

Closing his eyes, he could not remember ever being this content. Other than the clothes on his back and the sword at his side, he had little in the way of possessions, but for once in his life, the world seemed right. The leaping flames of his figmental fire provided caressing warmth as he drifted off.

The night passed in a heartbeat and he awoke in a snowstorm. Half covered in snow; he stood up and brushed the glistening crystals from his shoulder. Remembering Feejar, he opened the collar of his tunic and gently nudged the recumbent form. "Hey sleepy head, it's time to get moving."

There was no response! He felt his throat tighten as he lifted the tiny body ever so carefully. "Feejar!" Something was terribly wrong. Wrapping the delicate form in his worn kerchief, he tucked her in a fold of the tunic, grabbed the rucksack and rushed into the blinding snowstorm.

The village he left the previous day was hours away. Something told him his companion did not have that much time. Trusting to luck, he began running east, desperately. He pushed on and on, the snow getting deeper. By the time the cold, white blanket reached his thighs, his lungs were burning.

Topping a slight incline, he came upon a crystalline creek, winding through the pristine forest. He slid down the steep embankment and saw a small cottage with a light in the window. Smoke was coming out of the chimney!

He leaped into the frigid waters and gasped at the shock of the unbelievably cold stream. Wading to the far side, he struggled up the embankment, only to slide down again. He grabbed a handful of willows at the water's edge and froze.

There, mid-stream, a large chunk of ice was being swept along with the current. This was not unusual, but the sword lying on the glistening surface was shining with an unnatural radiance.

Unbidden, he heard himself cry aloud, "Gram!"

He knew it was the sword of legend – within his grasp. Stepping back into the ice strewn swirls, he stopped. Feejar. She might already be dead, but any delay . . .

Turning away from the sword was the hardest thing he had ever done. But the decision was made in a heartbeat and with a wild abandon, he clawed his way up the muddy embankment and rushed to the log hut. Pounding on the door, his voice rang with desperation. "Open up! Please. I need help!"

His fists were bloody from pounding on the heavy door, but the occupants refused to respond. Chest heaving, he stopped beating the rough hewn boards and gently opened his tunic to remove the body of Feejar.

As he unwrapped the tiny frame he felt his entire world crumbling. Shaking with a pain he could not endure, he dropped to his knees. "Feejar, Feejar."

"Harald! Wake up."

The familiar voice came from a distance, but was easy to hear. Harald blinked his eyes and slowly focused on his surroundings. He was lying against the base of a huge pine tree and the first rays of morning were breaking through the overhanging boughs.

"I think you were having a bad dream."

"Feejar!" The wild look in his eyes startled her.

She dodged his desperate grab. The tinkling sound that followed told him she was not happy with him.

Grinning like a drunkard, he was making no sense. He held out his hand and she tentatively landed on it.

"Harald! What's matter with you? You want to break me in half?"

"You're alive!"

"Last time I checked. Why are you acting so strange?"

Letting out a long breath, the grin faded. "I had a terrible dream. You were dead, or so it seemed."

"Figured it was something like that. Tell me about it."

Leaning back against the rough bark, he related every detail that he could remember. When he finished, Feejar sat down in his palm.

Putting a tiny fist under her chin, she said, "This has to mean something, but what? The snowstorm, an icy stream, the sword floating by -- and the cabin occupants that wouldn't let you in."

Standing up, she unconsciously smoothed the satiny, form-fitting garment. "Well, one thing is for sure, we have to go north."

"I agree. That was the coldest place I've ever been."

Picking up his rucksack, he paused. "Feejar. I didn't know whether you were dead or not."

"Meaning?"

"Maybe it would be best to leave well enough alone."

"Meaning?"

"If I abandon the search for the sword, you could return to the

Norns and . . ."

"No! If you fail, it will not be on account of me. I'll hear no more such talk."

The vehemence in her voice told Harald that the discussion was at an end. Blowing out a long breath, he headed north.

Summer passed into fall and the arcane spirits of nature began spreading a glorious riot of color across the rolling landscape. Fording countless rivers and streams, the two companions climbed over one rugged mountain range and then another. The elders in each village related tales of the fabulous sword and its location, each story contradicting the previous.

The chill in the air was caressing the entire day by the time they dropped into a huge bay of an uncharted sea and began following the coastline. Ancient runes were still visible on some of the large, protruding rocks and Harald could read parts of them, but not all. One faded set of ancient markings related a tale about a love betrayed and tragedy beyond human endurance.

Rounding a salient point in the coastline, he climbed the rocky promontory and paused at the summit. There, on the beach directly below, was the wooden head of an ancient dragon ship. The longboat was partially buried in the sand, but had the irrefutable markings of a Viking warship.

He climbed down and, upon closer scrutiny, realized it was the remnants of a funerary pyre. The charred remains of the craft reminded Harald of the burning ships he had seen in his youth. A longboat was only sacrificed when the occupant was a person of wealth or nobility.

Walking along the lapped siding, he noticed the mid-section was broken, charred and aged to the point of being petrified. Intrigued by the discovery, he dug down into the sand to see if anything of interest had been placed in the small hold of the ship.

He stopped abruptly when the sand fell away from a broken bone, bleached to an ashen hue. It was human! Gently uncovering the skeleton, the osseous phalanges of a hand still clutched a small cylinder of some strange material. The canister crumbled at his touch, revealing a roll of ancient vellum.

Carefully removing the scroll, Harald felt a shock in his arm as the man's lifetime flashed by in a parade of memories. Feejar was watching and when he suddenly froze upon touching the relic, she said, "What is it?"

"I don't know."

"What happened?"

"This man . . . this skeleton is . . . was, Sigurd Sigmundsson. The dragon slayer and champion in a score of legends. He really existed."

"So?"

"He was the hero of my childhood – of countless children, but everyone believed his life was a myth, a creation of bards."

Harald sat back on his heels. "I just saw what his life was really like." Looking down at the petrified remnants of bone, he added, "It was not a lifetime filled with adventure and glory. There was nothing but pain, sorrow and loss in the vision."

Feejar heard the sadness of a cherished illusion, now lost, in the words. She fluttered down to the hand holding the scroll.

"What is this?"

In response to the question Harald unrolled the ancient vellum and drew back slightly. It was a map. A heavy, dark line led from the edge of a large body of water north through some strange marking to some sort of structure. The image of a dragon hovered over symbols of a sword and ring.

"Tis a map."

"Leading to the sword?"

"Aye. I believe so." Harald rolled up the scroll and looked at Feejar. "Is this the work of the fates?"

"I don't know."

"Would you tell me if you did?"

"Yes."

The would-be king-of-kings nodded. The revelation of Sigurd's life had shaken him to the very core. Everything he believed in seemed to be built of sand. "I'm not sure I still want the sword."

"What about Gyda?"

"How did you know about Gyda?"

"I am a link to the Norns and they know everything."

Rather than answer the question, Harald hefted the rucksack and began following the line on the map.

The days passed and they left the wooded lands of the south, ever wending northward. Rolling tundra gave way to mountainous glaciers and strange formations resembling frozen giants. Harald reasoned the formations represented the strange markings on his map and concluded they were following in the footsteps of whoever carried the fabulous sword to its final resting place.

A crystalline, multi-hued mountain of ice stood out like a lone sentinel in the distance and that is where they headed. Feejar was unaccustomed to the extreme cold, but remained silent as her tiny limbs began to exhibit evidence of frost-bite.

Trudging through the waist-deep snow, it suddenly occurred to Harald that the ever-present tinkling from his furry wrap was absent. Opening a fold in his tunic, he saw the lovely visage he had come to adore. The pallid appearance of her arms and legs made his heart stop. She was freezing!

The icy citadel was less than a furlong away, but he whirled in the heavy snow and headed south. Gently removing her from the frozen garment, he pushed back the fur-lined hood and placed her next to his neck. The little body felt like a shard of ice against his skin. He cried out to the invisible Norns. "Help me! Feejar is freezing and we are a hundred furlong from warmth."

An increase in the howling wind was the only response. The nightmare of the frozen stream and Feejar's lifeless body flashed through his mind. The blood in his veins began pounding with the strain of pushing through the heavy, wet snow at a pace he knew he could not sustain.

Desperation was turning the snow covered wasteland into a glistening ocean of waving ice. Frozen tears clustered on whey-colored eyelashes, making it difficult to see.

"This is not bad."

The familiar voice pushed through the nightmare. Stumbling and almost falling, he stopped and stood rock still.

"Feejar? Was that you?"

"Why didn't you do this a long time ago? I've been freezing my . . . well, various parts of my anatomy ever since you left the ocean."

For a moment, all he could do was grin like a schoolboy and wave his hands in vague gestures. "Are you all right? I thought . . . well, it looked like . . . say something else."

"You need a bath."

After an extended period of silence, he finally spoke. "Agreed. But first things first. We came to get a very special sword and that's just what we're going to do." Turning back north, he paused. "That is . . . if you're sure you're going to be ok."

"I'll just hold my nose until you get it."

The wan sun remained stationary the last half furlong to the crystalline tower. Time itself seemed to stop in the aura surrounding the crystalline stronghold. As they neared the looming citadel, it became apparent that is was not a man-made structure, but a beautiful rending in ice.

The portal was split by a waterfall, frozen in a solid, cascading sheet of glistening hues. Working their way around the mass of vertical ice, they crossed what resembled a bridge over a ribbon of glistening jewels.

Harald paused at the entrance. The air was filled with an arcane power and he realized the interior was a consecrated area. Kneeling, he offered thanks to Odin, Thor and Frey and prayed for guidance. Feejar had remained silent throughout the trek to the tower of ice, but now he felt her pushing at the hooded cloak to see where they were.

"I've heard the Norns speak of this place, but had never hoped to see it."

"What is it?"

"I'm not sure exactly. The fates live in a real crystalline castle, and I think this is some sort of gateway. Only those with the blood of gods in their veins can actually visit the true home of the Norns."

Harald wandered the hallowed halls, marveling at the relics of history displayed throughout. The huge outline of a dragon adorned the wall above a curved doorway and Harald recognized the similarity to the one on the scroll. Stepping through the doorway, he noticed a small talisman hanging from a finely wrought chain. Moving closer, it was a dragon, no bigger than his thumb.

Reaching out to touch it, his hand passed through the icon and he smiled at the discovery. He knew it was real, but not for him. Crossing the broad expanse of icy floor, he left the room and paused at the sight before him.

In the middle of the largest room he had encountered was a massive tree of ice. He knew immediately the hilt protruding from the base was Sigurd's sword of legend, Gram. Advancing to within a pace of the weapon, he stopped.

Feejar was looking at the sword as well. "Tis the most beautiful thing I have ever seen Harald."

"Aye, but tis not for me."

"What do you mean?"

"I mean I don't want to be High King any longer – for Gyda or anything else."

"Why the sudden change?"

"It's not really sudden. I've been thinking about it ever since we found the remains of Sigurd."

"It's not what you want to do? Be a mighty warrior, a hero and man of legend?"

"No. I want to watch my children grow up without the screams of the dying and blood of the slain haunting their dreams."

"And give men like Erick Eymundsson free reign?"

The comment made Harald pause. Feejar did not need explain what she meant by the comment. For evil to flourish, good men simply needed to turn away. He had a responsibility to more than his family. Living the life he desired would mean walking away from the burden of ruling and service to others.

It was a selfish thought, not befitting a king. "Say no more Feejar."

The thought that the sword might not yield never occurred to him as he grasped the golden hilt and pulled. The long blade seemed to be of the very material it was embedded in. Glistening like a slender shard of ice, the rune-worked blade felt warm to the touch, not cold.

Sliding the fabled icon into the worn scabbard at his side, he wrapped the sword given him by his father in a ragged piece of linen and tied it to the rucksack.

The world was one of silence, snow and wonder as the pair trudged homeward. Heading south, the trip seemed shorter and before long, they were once again passing the remains of a hero long-dead, but never to be forgotten.

Climbing up out of the bay, Harald found a rock outcropping and stopped to wipe the sweat away. At the insistence of Feejar, he had bathed in the frigid waters and was now, once again, soaked in sweat.

"The bath was a waste of time."

"Not at all, you rid yourself of twenty layers of grime and have only replaced it with one."

Looking out over the placid bay, he glanced down at the pixie he now considered a part of his life. "How long am I stuck with you anyway?"

"What do you mean?"

"Well, you said the Norns sent you to help me find the sword and . . ."

He paused as a thought struck him. Feejar noticed the change. "What is it?"

"I thought they said I would have to show valor, honor, wisdom and compassion before I could get the sword."

"You did show those traits. Wisdom in not wanting power and honor in accepting responsibility."

"You really think so?"

"By Thor's hammer my lord, you are the most . . . Anyway. I'm stuck with you until the fates call me back."

"That's all right, guess I can put up with you a while longer."

A fortnight later found them trudging up the hill towards the great hall he called home. "Feejar, better wake up. People will be coming out to greet us and without you, no one is going to believe my story."

Silence followed the statement and he gently opened the fold in his tunic. A few iridescent sparkles were the only evidence his boon companion had ever existed. Not entirely surprised, he smiled sadly and resumed his long stride.

All skepticism vanished when Wotun touched the sword. The grey eye grew misty at the sight and the ancient blade hummed in recognition of the gnarled, bony hands. "Tis indeed the fabled blade. I never thought to see it again."

The statement brought several raised eyebrows, but nobody asked the question.

The years passed and one kingdom after another fell to the conqueror from Vestfold. More allegiances were struck and wives added to his lodge, but the warrior lass from Hordaland held Harald's heart.

With the passing years, the king was true to his word and a blade never touched the long, wheat colored hair. Between battles, he would cleanse, brush and braid the long strands, but when screams and blood filled the air, the wild mane became a symbol of the warrior king known as 'Tanglehair'.

By 882 AD, most of Norway was under the Harald's control, but a handful of realms still remained rebellious. Winds from the south brought word of a gathering of kings for a great battle.

Kjotve the Rich, King of Agder and his son, Thor Haklang, were sailing north with the forces of Sulke and Eirik, kings of Rogaland and Hordaland, respectively.

Two brothers, Hroald Hryg and Haad the Hard, rulers of Thelemark, joined the fleet several leagues south of Stavanger. The quiet bay of Hafersfjord would be witness to one of the most important battles of Norwegian history.

Tanglehair's armada included warriors from the chiefs of Frostatingslag and Gulatingslag. The assemblage of ships rocked quietly in the cold, green waters under a restless sky, waiting. Storm clouds gathered as eager spectators in anticipation of the clash that would determine the future of Norway.

A cry went up from the westernmost dragon ship as the fleet of kings entered the fjord. Thor Haklang was a young man, but huge, powerful, and wrapped in the veil of the berserker. The towering giant was hanging onto the jaw of the carved dragon head, screaming obscenities at the enemy and bellowing for more speed from the bending oars.

He espied Harald's flag in the aggregation of longships and directed the steersman to ignore surrounding flurry of ships. Thor's vessel plowed through the shallow waves, heading straight for the nemesis of the minor kings. Haklang had argued late into the previous night with his father about strategy and finally stalked away, determined to do things his way.

The Viking prince felt the death of Harald would ensure a quick and easy victory and threw everything he had into the wager. The faster, lighter ship hit the heavy longboat of Tanglehair's with a shuddering crunch. Shattered timbers and a web of lines became entangled and the hand-to-hand fighting was savage to the point of insanity.

A broken section of the mast from Thor's ship was spinning wildly over the entangled ships from a braiding of cordage, jagged ends creating havoc among the brawling warriors. The whirling timber caught Harald mid-section in the back and sent him sprawling across the blood soaked deck.

Haklang saw the king go down and leaped over several men, hoping to kill him before he regained his feet. Harald was struggling to gain a handhold on the slippery, crimson coated railing when the arcing streak of a long blade caught his eye. Unable to bring his sword into play, he threw up an arm to deflect the killing blow. It never landed.

His gaze moved from the sanguine streaked blade down the muscled, blood soaked arm to the face of Thor. The man was staring at him with a look of complete bewilderment in his eyes. He dropped to his knees and a rivulet of blood spilled from beneath the auburn mustache.

When he toppled forward across Harald's legs, the grim face of Guthorm came into view. "Twas close my lord."

Grabbing his lieutenant's hand, the king stood. "Aye. Too close."

The brief interlude was immediately broken by the assault of a barrage of new assailants. Thor's entire crew was decimated by the time the balance of attacking kings reached the interlocked ships.

Within an hour, a score of ships were lashed railing-to-railing, fires sprang up and for a time, men were free from the mundane cares of the world in a bloody clash of arms. King Sulke and his brother, Earl Sote, were the next to fall and when the king of Hordaland went down under a flurry of blades, Kjotve fled the carnage.

The act of cowardice split the remaining warriors into two camps; those that fought on to the death and the ones looking for a reason to flee. Many of the Agder men followed the lead of their king, resulting in a crumbling of any serious threat to Harald's forces.

The Battle of Hafrsfjord would be the final nail in the coffin of the warring, petty kings of a divisive Norway. Rebellious realms would tear away during future reigns, and foreign powers would gain control over parts of the Norwegian lands for periods of time, but the mold for a united nation had been formed.

Rogaland and Hordaland were the last strongholds to fall and Harald, no longer a young man, returned to Halogaland to claim the hand of his long-awaited princess. Gyda did not play the coy maiden upon his return, but brazenly walked up to the powerful monarch and, standing on tiptoe, kissed him fully upon the lips at their first meeting.

The union was made amidst a great celebration and the kingdom of Halogaland came under the protection of the King of Vestfold and all of Norway. Gyda's father, Erick, was on the verge of death when Harald finally returned to claim his daughter, but swore allegiance to the powerful monarch and welcomed the union as a surety for his kingdom.

Another celebration and feast were held to crown the first man recognized as king of all Norway. The 'High King' now displayed streaks of gray in the heavy beard, but none of his vigor for life had been lost. The man known as Tanglehair for over a decade cut his hair and became known as Harald the Fairhair, king of all lands west of Sweden.

A Christian bishop was in attendance at the crowning, but the Druids of the old gods ruled the day. The venerable, white-haired men chanted arcane spells of protection and power while Harald sat quietly in the great hall of Vestfold. The Christian emissary frowned at the superannuated actions, sniffing at the swirling smoke and rattling bones, but held his peace. The missionaries were making progress with these pagan peoples, but until the rulers accepted Christ as their personal savior, the messengers of God were powerless to influence the masses.

Wotun had refused to participate in the festivities and Harald knew once the ancient sage made up his mind about something, there was no way to change it. The man had been strangely silent since the fall of Rogaland, and there had been no apparent reason for the reticence.

At the first opportunity to be alone with his mentor, Harald sat quietly for several minutes before finally speaking. "You have not said three words to me since Rogaland. Have I done something to offend you?"

The wrinkled visage was turned downwards as though exhausted, or deep in thought. After a moment, the craggy head slowly shook side to side. "No Harald, you have made me proud."

"Why then do you remain silent?"

Wotun drew in a deep breath and let out a shuddering rasp. Harald had never seen the old mage act this way. It bothered him more than he could have imagined.

"There will be other wars. We will not die the straw death of old men in bed," Harald offered, in hopes of breaking the melancholy.

The grey eye turned towards him and the High King could have sworn he saw the glimmer of a tear at the corner of the orb. He had never seen evidence of compassion in the man, much less . . .

"Wotun, something pains you terribly. What is it?"

"Tis of no matter. This is a time of celebration for you. Do not dampen your spirits talking to a despondent relic of what once was."

"What once was? What do you mean?"

"Nothing. Go, join your beautiful wife and gay companions."

"Not until you talk to me."

After an extended period of silence, Wotun realized he could no longer evade the issue. "Tis the loss of Ubbe."

Harald remembered the lad all to well. He had promised Aki to protect and mentor the boy – which he did until grown. The young man had become a warrior and died well at Rogaland . . .

He suddenly realized Ubbe's death was the reason for the white-hair's reticence. To him, the loss had been hard, like losing a brother. For Wotun, the man's death signified a fork in a destiny no one else could see.

The sage had become unusually attached to the youth as he grew into manhood -- they were inseparable. But then, the old man had mentored countless young men and watched them die a glorious death. Why would this one be different?

"Ubbe died a warrior. I was proud of him. You should be to."

"I know."

Offering nothing more, the mage stood and walked away, refusing to discuss it again. Mulling over his pain, he began to wonder if he were trying to piece together more than one puzzle. Walking the quiet countryside alone, in his mind's eye, he looked back again at the life of the legendary Sigmund.

Stopping abruptly, Wotun stared down the worn path ahead, he had just realized something. His bushy brows furrowed at the memory.

"There was peace in the land -- and Odin didn't like it." He muttered in a low growl. His mind's eye could still see the magnificent Gram – hanging idle on the west wall of Sigmund's Great Hall.

☼☼☼

Memories from the ancient legend changed the old man's surrounding vista to the kingdom of Lyngi, north of the Volsung lands. In the tranquility that followed the union of Sigmund and Hjordi, Odin convinced King Lyngi to attack Sigmund's realm. The results were glorious and terrible. A thousand brave men died that day – filling the halls of Valhalla.

But Odin knew when the battle was done, Sigmund would lay Gram aside once more. The beautiful and terrible sword had not been created to hang on a castle wall.

Taking up arms, the god entered the fray and in a furious hand-to-hand contest with Sigmund, shattered the fabled blade. Sheathing his weapon, Odin walked from the battlefield, leaving his opponent surrounded by enemies with no way to defend himself. Soon thereafter, he was not surprised to learn the fabled Norse King had joined the Einherjar in Valhalla.

Sigmund had died a glorious death and the victors commended the valor by gathering up the body and broken sword, returning everything to Hjordi.

There had been no chance for the queen to tell the fallen hero she was with child. A child that would grow up to slay the terrible dragon Fafnir and take up the burden of Andvari's curse.

Wotun paused as his surroundings came into view once more and a faint smile chased across the rugged visage. Oh, the tales the bards would tell of the mighty Sigurd, son of Sigmund the Great. Pushing the legendary memories from his mind, he returned to the village and the approaching winter.

The gut-wrenching moans of the battle horns fell silent with the first snow and, with the exception of minor skirmishes between warlords, the land of the North Way experienced peace. Harald turned his boundless energy towards building a stronger kingdom.

The enigma known as Wotun often left the realm, disappearing for months at a time. Lost in his own thoughts much of the time, he seemed to be losing touch with the world of men.

The king was approaching seventy winters when a servant named Tora Mosterstrong caught his eye and soon found herself in his bed. With the coming of spring, she was heavy with child, a boy who would become known as Haakon the Good.

No less than two score offspring called Harald 'father' and twelve sons would vie to become heir of the fledgling empire. Brothers and friends growing up, they would become bitter enemies and deadly foes when the hair of manhood covered their chests.

Chapter 7

Eirik Bloodaxe -
Reign of Terror

Eirik was the eldest son of Harald Fairhair and his father's favorite from birth. Fearless and astute, the child grew into a young man believing the world was rightfully his for the taking. Admired and respected by a flurry of younger brothers, the days of their youth were spent hunting, working, and learning the ways of war, side-by-side.

With a thirst for adventure and twenty summers behind him, he took three ships and five score men into northern Russia. The winds of summer, 920 AD, found him sailing north along the coast of Norway to strange lands he had read about in the *Voyage of Ohthere.*

The book recorded the quest of another adventurer; Ohthere of Halogaland, some three decades earlier. According to the testament, the Viking took a small fleet of ships along the northernmost parts of the Scandinavian Peninsula and then sailed south into the White Sea of the Northern Rus.

Stories of fabulous pelts, silver, and plunder reached the prince while growing up and he had no trouble in finding men to accompany him on the trip. Two of his half-brothers, Bjorn and Olaf, stood by his side at the helm of the lead ship, a salty spray covering their faces. The deep fjords and inlets of their father's realm passed along the starboard side with the lengthening days.

Olaf was the youngest of the brothers, and the largest. Although he was just a few years younger than Eirik he outweighed him by five stone. Wiping cold water from his face, he turned toward Bjorn and winked, unnoticed by Eirik. "Bjorn, do you supposed this is another one of our brother's 'misadventures'?"

The elder brother picked up the ruse immediately. "Olaf, you know that remark is unfair and uncalled for." He turned and looked at the oldest brother. "There was no way for him to know the nest still had wasps in it, or that baby badger had a mother nearby, or the bear was wounded, or . . . "

"Ok, ok." Eirik threw up a hand and grinned at the chiding. "So a couple of things haven't gone as planned." The smile faded as he turned to look at the rolling sea ahead of them. "But this is going to be different. I feel it in my gut."

The serious note erased the smiles on the faces of the younger brothers. Eirik had always been the leader and the intensity with which he lived was hard to understand. Highly competitive, if he lost at anything, he would work until he became undefeatable.

"Ohthere wrote of a fabulous treasure he believed to be in a city called **Bolghar**. The god of the Sami holds a bowl of silver and jewels in his lap as large as this ship." Eirik's voice seemed to be coming from a distant place -- a realm visible to only him.

The two younger brothers exchanged knowing glances. Eirik was often lost in a world of his own. Bjorn patted him on the shoulder before turning with Olaf and heading aft.

Few men traveled to the land of the Finns and Lapps and returned. If they weren't slain by the treacherous tribes of the north, they were drowned in the icy waters. But there was no way the brothers were going to let Eirik go alone.

Two more days passed before the land turned east and the ships followed. Another day and a half, they reached an estuary leading inland to the southeast. Following the inlet, it opened into a huge bay that could only be the White Sea described by Ohthere. A score of small islands dotted the surface, as barren and white as the snows of winter.

Traversing the southern edge of the spreading, open body of water, they tried several inlets that led nowhere but finally reached the mouth of a large river. Realizing this was the opening they were searching for, they put their backs to the oars and headed upriver. After traveling a few miles, they came upon a small hamlet and put to shore.

The initial meeting with the local inhabitants was tense and difficult. Slightly smaller in stature, the Sami spoke rapidly in a language none of the Vikings understood. The common tongue of the merchant saved the day however and amber and iron were traded for some of the finest pelts the men had ever seen. Beaver, fox, wolverine and ermine hides with a thick, soft fur surpassing any animals to the south. One beautiful hide of the huge white bear of the far north cost them as much as five bundles of the smaller pelts.

Mead was not unknown to the locals and after the trading had been completed, large fires were started. Native and visitor alike found common elements in the warmth of a fire and mugs of ale. The stars were just becoming visible in the night sky when a ripple of excitement moved through the village. The Vikings soon learned a shaman of some importance had arrived from a town located several leagues to the east.

The man was ushered almost immediately to the circle of Norsemen and to their surprise, he could speak their language. Taller than his kinsmen, the sage appeared to be quite elderly, but still in good health, with a strong body and mind. The long face was creased with lines of age and framed in white hair. The snowy mane was knotted in the back and the long beard carefully braided.

Introductions revealed the man's name was Vearald, a noaide from the eastern provinces. Known as a mediator between mortals and the spirit world, the man was revered to the point of worship. Immediately assaulted with a barrage of questions from the Vikings, he answered, but with some hesitation.

Eirik sensed the reluctance in the responses and tried to reassure the sage they meant no harm. "I must apologize for all of the questions. As you know, we are strangers to your country and are seeking to learn about your ways."

"Strangers come in many forms."

"We are not pirates."

The mage's gaze found Eirik's eyes and held them in a grip of iron. The brownish-grey orbs of the white-hair were unlike any the Viking had ever seen and for a moment, he was spell-bound by the depth.

"I knew that before you spoke." Vearald's eyes released their grip. "However, what is today will change tomorrow."

"We will not be pirates tomorrow." The muscles in Eirik's jaw were flexing.

Bjorn moved over next to his brother and placed a hand on his shoulder. "I don't think he meant to say we would be."

The shaman's face softened. "Your friend is right. I am still foolish enough to hope what I do today will change tomorrow." Spreading his worn robe, he sat on one of the large rocks circling the fire. "Tomorrow will change, with or without me."

Eirik began to wonder if he was talking to a man no longer in possession of his senses. Scowling, he sat back down and remained silent.

Olaf broke the lingering quiet that followed. "Are there many towns to the east?"

Once again, suspicion filled the old man's eyes. "Why?"

"We would like to trade with them."

After a brief period of silence, the response came. "Yes."

Bjorn decided to try a different approach. "What do we need to know to trade with the people along this river?"

The noaide studied the group of Vikings a moment before coming to a decision. Reaching into a small leather bag at his side, he retrieved some green crystals and tossed them into the fire. The flames leaped brightly for a moment and then returned to normal.

"What was that for?" Olaf looked from the crackling fire to the sage.

The man shrugged and nodded towards Eirik.

The oldest brother's eyes were fixed on the fire, mesmerized by something invisible to the others.

"Eirik?"

Olaf moved to shake his brother when the shaman barked. "NO! He will return to us when the journey is complete."

The youngest brother slowly sat back down and looked at Olaf. The elder brother nodded. He didn't like this either, but the mage seemed certain of what he was doing.

Eirik had watched Vearald cast the crystals into the fire the same as everyone present, but the flare of smoke and flames had not dissipated. Instead, a portal opened, enveloping him in a beautiful forest. Standing in the midst of a verdant wonderland, he turned slowly, marveling at the surrounding beauty. Countless shades of flaming color were falling from groves of aspen and oak. The fragrance of a field of wildflowers caressed his face and moved on with the warm breeze.

Shoving large hands in worn pockets, he began wandering aimlessly through the lush vegetation. He topped a small rise and noticed a black castle of obsidian beauty rising above the towering trees in the distance. The allure of the citadel was irresistible and the Viking responded with long, purposeful strides.

A league from the stronghold, he felt a strange presence and reduced his pace. The air around him began to hum, changing from a faint breeze to a gentle wind, ruffling the long hair and braided beard. He stopped in the middle of a meadow surrounded by the dense forest and rubbed his arms against a sudden chill.

The tiny whirlwind moved away to shuffle dead leaves on the ground a few paces away. Eirik stood still, staring at the waving grass and swirling leaves as though in a trance. A wavering image began to form in the midst of the swirling foliage.

As suddenly as it had appeared, the wind was gone and a young woman stood in a circle of leaves and grass. The Norse prince had never seen a woman such as the one that now graced the meadow. Auburn hair flowed down over the soft curves of her shoulders, cascading over full breasts, almost reaching the small waist.

The translucent, gossamer gown was bound with a girdle of golden leaves circling the slim torso -- she was the most beautiful woman Eirik had ever seen.

He slowly closed his mouth as she approached him. A few paces away, the woman stopped and tilted her head slightly as though studying him. "You are not Sami. Why do you enter the world of the Seita?"

"Seita? What are the Seita?"

"We are the . . . keepers of the Sami."

"I wish to learn the ways of the Sami."

"Why?"

"I travel from a land to the southwest, to trade and barter."

The alluring maiden moved next to Eirik and gently touched his face. "You are a man of destiny." Her gaze moved from his face to an unknown realm as though deciphering runes as yet unwritten.

The Viking was enraptured in the moment, realizing he had been holding his breath when she dropped her hand. "I've never met anyone like you."

"And will not again."

"Who are you?"

"To the Sami, I am known as Biejje."

"Are you mortal?"

"Come, there are things you should know."

Saying nothing more, she turned and moved into the dense forest with the supple movements of the willow. Eirik suddenly felt the most important thing in the world was slipping from his grasp and he frantically rushed to catch her.

The lush vegetation swallowed the ethereal vision as though she were nothing more than vapor from a cold winter stream. Thrashing into the trees and underbrush, he called her name with a desperation verging on madness. For the first time in his life he had witnessed what few mortals would ever see and fewer understand.

He searched the rolling countryside for hours, all to no avail. Finally exhausted, he collapsed beside a large pool formed by a cold stream meandering from distant mountains. The sun moved overhead, slowly dropping into the tree rimmed west.

Tossing pebbles into the stream, he stared at wavering visions of the beautiful woman formed in the circle of ripples. He missed her terribly and there was no explanation. With the passing of time he felt rested and stood, dusting his hands off on the worn tunic.

"Good day young man."

Eirik whirled at the stranger's voice. An aged man stood just a few feet away, watching him.

Instinct sent his hand for the sword at his side. He was unarmed, but realized the newcomer meant no harm. "You startled me."

"I apologize."

"Who are you?"

"I am known as Raedie."

"Are you a native?"

The comment brought a wry smile from the craggy face. "Yes. I am of the people who live in this land."

In the silence that followed, Eirik spoke again. "I seek to learn more of your people. What can you tell me?"

"I know why you are here. That is why I have come." The aged stranger studied the Viking a moment before continuing. "Please sit. There is much you must know."

Eirik did as requested and watched as Raedie found a sandy area and also sat. There was no way for the prince to know he was in the presence of the most powerful of the Sami gods. The personification appeared the same as many patriarchs from around the world.

The deity folded his hands and placed them in his lap. "First of all, my people are much like yours. They work hard, pray to their gods, raise children and crops, grow old and die.

"A bountiful land produces an abundance of grain. And therein, lays the difference."

Eirik frowned. "I don't understand."

"The realm of your childhood is harsh and unforgiving. Only the strongest of the crop survives.

"Your blood is tinged with the hue of iron. The road you travel will encounter many forks and the decisions you make along the way will influence the weaving of the Norns.

"A ring of gold and a beautiful maiden lay in your future. Though fair in countenance, the woman is of the dark arts and the ring is possessed of an evil curse. Avoid these and your path will lead to greatness."

"And if I cannot?"

"Without control of one's self, a man is a slave to his desires. Greed, treachery and violence will be his companions. Men will smile and sigh with relief at his death."

"I understand."

"Understanding is an important step to gaining wisdom."

"Is there anything else you can tell me of your people?"

"Do unto them as you would be treated. Show them cruelty or betrayal and they will rise up like the giant Stallon. The wrath of vengeance will sweep through your villages as though Mubpienalmaj were once again walking the world of men."

The deity's voice rose with the concluding statement and Eirik knew it was a warning. "What you say rings true in my ears. It will not go unheeded."

"I wish it were so."

"What do you mean?"

The ancient manifestation did not respond, but stood, dusted off the fine linen tunic, faded to a translucent image, and disappeared.

Eirik sat staring at the spot where the man had vanished. The words were still ringing in his mind when the crackling sounds of a fire reached his ears. Blinking his eyes, it was dark and he was watching the dancing flames of a campfire.

The incident of the mage throwing powder into the fire flashed through his mind, but he could still see the enchanting woman and wizened Sami god.

"Eirik!"

The sound of his name brought him out of the reverie and Olaf's face took form. His brother's face was tight with concern. "Are you all right?"

"Yes. I'm fine." He glanced at Vearald and the magic powder. "Thank you."

The noaide shrugged as though it were nothing. "I did little. What happened was between you and the gods."

With the exception of the snapping embers of the fire, the scene fell silent, each man lost in their own thoughts and dreams.

Bjorn and Olaf pulled their brother aside at the first opportunity and set upon him with a barrage of questions. Eirik explained the strange encounters as best he could, but there was much that could not be put into words.

Finally agreeing that attempts at further explanation would serve no purpose, the brothers turned in for a restless night. They were in a strange land, surrounded by strangers with ways that were hard to understand.

The next day, traveling to the south and east, the Vikings began to see sizeable towns and strongholds along the river. They realized trading was an option as long as the goods held out, but any attempt to take something by force would be foolhardy and doomed to fail.

Far from disappointing, the journey turned out to be profitable not only in terms of trade, but information. Eirik now felt he could convince his father to outfit a raiding party of sufficient strength to return and take what they could not barter for.

The chill of winter was in the air by the time the expedition reached the shores of home. Of all the treasures unloaded, silver coins from a distant realm known as Arabia caused the most excitement. The currency was not unheard of in Scandinavia and the value in commerce was immeasurable.

Harald Fairhair, King of Norway, had passed eighty summers by the time his sons returned and no longer wished to hold the reigns of an empire. The aged monarch made the decision in Eirik's absence and announced it upon his return. His eldest son would now be High King of Norway. Knowing he could not bequeath the entire kingdom to one heir, he distributed the regions amongst his eldest, and favored, sons.

The realms of Vestfold, Ranrike and Vingulmark passed to Bjorn, Guttorm and Olaf respectively. A great celebration was held, marking the beginning of a new dynasty. Wotun returned from one of his countless excursions the eve of the announcement. The ancient relic watched in silence as Harald removed the High King's Crown.

Amidst the cheers and clamor of the crowded hall, the monarch placed the symbol of power on his chosen heir. Twas only a matter of days before the newly made king was also wearing the ring that had caused the angry words between his father and Wotun so many years in the past.

The arcane curse of the ancient spirits rang in Wotun's mind like the pealing of monastery bells. The ancient Viking never prayed, but he fervently hoped Eirik would find love as his father had and never invoke the dark malevolence of the ring.

The fabled sword Gram was given a place of honor in the monarch's stateroom. It was the one thing Harald refused to part with.

Plans for raiding the towns of the Rus and Sami were forgotten in the swirl of changing events -- as was the warning of the Sami god.

Decades earlier, his father had been concerned about a suitable heir and now, the new High King's thoughts turned in the same direction. Careful consideration of the issue brought him to a conclusion -- the Danes were a powerful nation and made formidable allies, or enemies.

Eirik's mother and grandfather had some Danish blood. Therefore, he reasoned the King of Denmark, Gorm the Old, should welcome the union of the new High King of Norway with his daughter, Gunnhild. There was no way for newly crowned monarch to know the girl had been kidnapped some years earlier.

A trip to Jutland soon revealed her father had been unable to find the missing child. With the passing years, the aging monarch had given up any hope of ever reclaiming the laughing, dark-haired lass.

Upon further questioning, Gorm explained it had been over a decade since two Finnish wizards appeared in his court to amaze the royal entourage with feats of magic and skill. Far too quickly he gave them his trust and they disappeared soon thereafter, with his only daughter.

Every summer in the years that followed, he led warriors to the Finnish realm in search of the sorcerers, but to no avail. There was no response to offers of a large reward and envoys returned empty handed and down-hearted. Finally, the grizzled old warrior resigned himself to the fact he would never see his daughter again.

Eirik listened to the sad tale, firmly resolving the king's story would not end there. He stood, drew his sword and cradled the blade in bare hands. Approaching Gorm, he dropped to one knee. "With your blessing, I will find your daughter and return her to your embrace."

There was something in the young suitor's voice and demeanor that made the king believe the man would succeed where so many before had failed. Gripping the blade midway, he responded. "Go with my blessing, and take whatever I possess that you have need of."

Two weeks passed before Eirik set out from Norway with three brothers and a host of warriors. Olaf and Bjorn were at his side as always, but this time they also took Sigrod, another half-brother.

The sleek ships rounded the southern coast of Sweden and headed north into the inland sea of the Baltic. Four days later, the expedition beached their longboats on the eastern shore of the Gulf of Bothnia. The sun was still high in the sky, so they headed inland through scrub brush, climbing into mountainous terrain, heavy with timber.

By nightfall, the company of warriors drew to a halt at the bottom of a vertical abutment. A trail followed the base of the sheer granite wall and they fell into single file, traversing the path until dark.

Eirik threw up a hand, indicating they would camp for the night. Shortly thereafter, several campfires sprang up in the darkness and the soft clatter of preparations for supper filled the night. Muttered conversations permeated the void following the evening meal and finally, an uneasy quiet settled over the recumbent warriors.

Vikings by nature were a hardy lot, adventurous, and true to their codes of honor. Any foe of flesh and blood they would meet with relish, but confronting manifestations of the black arts was something different. Every man in the troop knew that was what they could be facing and it provoked a tremor in the stoutest of hearts.

The darkest part of the night drew over the glowing embers of campfires and the four sentries guarding the points of the compass took turns putting more wood on the scattered mounds of warmth.

All four men froze when a low, eerie wail broke the soft cooing of the night birds. The sound was unlike any the men had ever heard. Eirik and Olaf awoke at the sound and sat upright.

"Did you hear that?"

"What was it?"

"I don't know. Wake Bjorn and Sigrod."

The four brothers were soon surrounded by a host of warriors, shuffling feet and exchanging uneasy glances. Even the normal sounds of night had disappeared with the haunting cry. The silence was unnatural and palatable.

Sigrod folded his arms and shrugged off a shiver. "What should we do?"

"Build up the fires and keep your weapons at hand." Eirik's response came barely above a whisper. Twisting the gold band on his finger, he swallowed rancid bile. Ever since assuming his father's throne, his gut had been in turmoil.

The men were in complete accordance with building up the fires and staying awake until dawn – which took its time in arriving. The faint, gray outlines of trees and cliffs foreshadowed the morning sunrise. Even the bright light of day did not bring the return of the birds or normal forest sounds.

The smell of various stews began to permeate the campsite, and the hushed conversations became light banter with the promise of another day. Breakfast was almost complete when a new odor drifted to the nostrils of the clustered warriors. The stench was familiar. Death.

A faint wind from the northeast provided a direction to the source. With considerable trepidation, the troop loaded up and headed out. There had been no sounds of battle, yet the smell of dead and decaying flesh began to fill the air. High above, ravens circled.

They crossed a grassy ridge and dropped into a wide swale, generally following the alignment of a small stream. A new odor, unfamiliar to the Vikings, began to mingle with the smell of the dead. More foul by far, the strange fetor was enough to make the bile rise in men's throats.

"Hermod's heels, what is that stink?"

"I don't know." Olaf stopped to stare at the mangled remnants of a body hanging from one of the trees. "But that's not it."

Sigrod called from a short distance away. "Eirik, come look at this."

The prince moved towards his younger brother and noticed a strange looking rock protruding in the middle of the small clearing. "What is it?"

"I don't know, but it has some kind of markings all over it."

The eldest brother stopped next to Sigrod and folded his arms. There was a strange feeling in the air and a barely perceptible aura permeating from the stone. "This could be a *sieidis*."

"A sieidis?"

"Yes. The Sami believe there are portals or focal points of magic that serve as gateways to the spirit world. I saw one in the lands to the north of here several years ago." Eirik called back over his shoulder. "Bjorn, Olaf, come over here."

The two brothers approached and studied the rock. "Looks like the one up north, but that doesn't explain what we found over there."

Eirik looked in the direction indicated. "What did you find?"

"Come."

The four brothers walked some thirty paces to the lush grass bordering the stream and stopped. Olaf pointed down and Sigrod gasped. "Looks like a footprint."

Eirik raised an eyebrow and stepped into the print. His foot was large, but barely filled the impression left by one of the toes. "A very big footprint, if that's what it is."

Glancing in the direction the toes were pointing, he added, "If there is one, there should be more."

The search was quickly rewarded with another print. This time made by the left foot some ten to twelve paces across the creek up the far embankment.

By this time, the brothers were joined by the balance of warriors and after the initial exclamations each man grew quiet, watching the surrounding woods with haunted eyes.

Bjorn studied the huge print a few seconds before turning to Eirik. "Stallon -- do you suppose such a being exists?"

"Stallon. Who, or what, is Stallon?" Sigrod interjected before his brother could respond.

"A fearsome giant of the forest. Tis a Sami myth, nothing more."

"I remember father mentioning something about fighting a giant when I was a small child, and these prints are not a myth."

"Aye, they are not."

Olaf glanced in the direction of the tracks. "The monstrous fiend is feasting on the sacrifices." He paused before adding, "Or the hangings were made as an offering to the beast."

"Either way, we best keep our weapons close. It would seem the titan is fond of human flesh" Eirik said, absently patting the hilt at his side. "Tell the men to pack up, we're heading north."

Meanwhile, several leagues to the northeast, dark sanguine streaked eyes were staring into an ancient cauldron hanging over the warm embers of a hearth fire.

"More warriors from lands to the south. These men are tall and fair, unlike their predecessors." The skin of the wrinkled countenance was like brittle parchment. The black orbs moved from the huge pot to the man at his side. "You said they would never return in search of the girl." The words were barely above a whisper.

"Worry is the occupation of small minds, Elika."

"Karhu, what is it?" The young woman's voice brought the hushed conversation to a halt.

"Nothing, go back to your room."

Instead of obeying, the girl pushed her way between the two repulsive creatures. Glancing down into the cauldron, her face tightened. "I do not recognize those men. Who are they?"

The two wizards exchanged glances before answering. "Evil men from the southlands. They come to kill and steal, nothing more."

"Elika, I know when you are lying. Why do you attempt to deceive me?"

Karhu responded. "We do not know why they are here. They may be looking for you." With a repulsive sneer he added, "If so, they will fail, just as all the others."

The girl had not cried in years and the cruel remark fell upon a hardened heart. "The day will come, you abominable old wretch, when the debt of your deeds will come due." Fire flashed in her eyes. "And it cannot be too soon."

Blue sparks flared around her fingertips and the Stygian sorcerer drew back. He was sure their combined strength was more powerful than the girl's, but the last few years had seen a profound change in her.

When they first brought her to the stone keep, deep in the woods of Finland, the days passed in a parade of pain and terror for the child. Crying brought an immediate and harsh response from her captors and was finally abandoned to a sullen and moody existence.

At first, the arcane magic practiced by the two aged wizards was little more than a curiosity. With time however, she realized there was great power in the dark arts and every waking hour was spent learning the chants and ingredients of countless spells and potions.

During the last year, the young woman's knowledge and skill surpassed that of her mentors in many areas, resulting in a subtle change in the relationship. The physical abuse had stopped entirely, but the verbal lashings were as vicious as ever.

"You are strong child, but not that strong." Karhu snarled. "Use care with that tongue."

Black eyes of obsidian locked with emerald shards. Finally, the girl looked away. "The day will come." She pushed past the ancient warlock and walked out of the room.

Wandering down the hallway of the stronghold, she once again wondered how the two sorcerers had come into possession of the citadel. A stone castle in the middle of a vast forest was an enigma she had never solved.

Another mystery was why no one had ever discovered the forbidding keep. Several times after her abduction, Danish warriors had passed within bow shot of her window, without seeing the looming turrets or hearing her cries for help.

The structure was real, about that, she had no doubt. Long ago, she came to understand her rescue lie in solving the riddle of the castle's invisibility. With the passing years, the attempts to discover the secret dwindled and finally disappeared. The need to expose the citadel vanished with the last sightings of her people.

Now, with the possibility of another rescue attempt, Gunnhild's mind turned to the dilemma of a massive stone structure that no other mortal could see. Late into the night she studied the spells of invisibility and enchantment, but found nothing to explain the ability to conceal something as large as the castle.

The days passed and, based upon the direction the Norsemen were traveling; they would pass by the stronghold the afternoon of the following day. That gave her one more night to solve the mystery.

For several hours, she poured over the same spells, discovering nothing new. In exasperation, she slammed the ancient book closed and strode out of the castle.

The summer night's air brushed her face and cooled the raging furnace that burned within. The old reprobates were so smug in their control of her – there had to be an answer. Wandering amidst the surrounding trees, she paused to remove a stone from her sandal.

Leaning against a huge oak for support, she shook the pebble loose and straightened. For the briefest of moments, she felt as though some connection had been broken. Staring at her hand, she placed it on the tree again and felt the tie once again.

Stepping back, she stared at the tree a moment before moving to the next one and touching it. A small smile crept over the tired face. Now she knew.

Nibbling her lower lip, she headed back into the castle. The trees surrounding the keep were imbued with the fumes of an elixir that would render anything of stone, touched by man, invisible. There was no spell to counter the effect – which she knew of.

She paused next to a tall window, deep in thought. Once again, a smile formed in the starlight. The old wizards would finally get their due.

The next day, the Vikings were trudging up a long incline when one of the men called out. "Look! Tis a bow of the rain!"

Several men gasped at the sight. The sky was clear and there had been no rain for several days.

Instinctively, they headed for the multi-hued arch. However, instead of moving away like rainbows do, this vision remained steady.

In a matter of hours, they were standing at the edge of a large meadow with a huge mound of stone in the center. The parallel shafts of color radiated from the granite outcropping as though the rock itself were the source.

Uneasy mutterings ran thought the group of Vikings. Each man knew what they were seeing was not natural, and magic was a thing to be avoided.

"Well, we can see where it comes from. Now let's be rid of this place. It's turning my bones to water."

"Nay, tis wizards we seek, and if this is not the work of a sorcerer, I'd say the gods had a hand in it." Eirik rubbed a sudden chill from his arms. "Either way, we stay and . . ."

The sentence was cut short as the rainbow suddenly vanished and a blue-grey plume erupted from the massive stone megalith. The powder settled on the outcropping, but rather than coating rugged rocks as expected, the dust outlined the ramparts of a castle.

With the appearance of the barbican and battlements, the entire structure appeared – the spell was broken. The warriors stood agape at the forbidding citadel. Most had never seen such a structure and for a period of time, simply stared in silence.

"Eirik! Look!" One of the men pointed upwards toward the highest turret of the stronghold. Silhouetted in the dark rectangle of a window was the outline of a woman. The eldest prince had pulled his sword partially from its scabbard with the revelation of the keep, but now slammed it home and headed for the massive portcullis.

"Come. I think we may have found what we have been searching for."

The band of warriors was halfway across the grassy meadow when a ghastly screech broke the long strides. Inside the massive citadel, the wizards cursed their prodigy with arcane profanity when they realized what she had done.

Calling upon the primordial gods of darkness, Hiisi and Piru, to destroy the intruders, the sorcerers watched as a horde of demons attacked the Vikings. The winged atrocities were flesh and bone manifestations of terror. Wingspans three paces wide were covered with a leathery skin. Claws the size of a man's fingers extended from malformed limbs protruding from the leading edge of the wings,

The head of the creatures resembled a gargoyle with ivory bicuspids hooded by ponderous lips. A torso resembling a starving lion transformed into muscled legs and clawed feet.

A guttural roar from the warriors answered the fiendish howls and the soft grass of the meadow became a chaotic battleground with no quarter.

Several of the warriors fell to the crushing jaws and slashing talons almost immediately. However, rather than moving to the next foe, the demons began feasting upon the slain. This mindless act of the carnivores proved to be their undoing.

Fighting over the bodies of the dead men, they became easy prey for the gleaming swords of the Norsemen. The pristine meadow was soggy with blood, most of it the demon's, by the time the men sheathed their weapons and drew in ragged breaths.

In a killing rage, they charged the citadel. The massive portcullis was sealed with towering doors bound with iron and the attempts to shatter them proved futile.

Bloody swords in hands, the men backed away from the portal, calling insults to those within. The search for something to breach the stronghold was interrupted by the crackle of lighting from inside the stone walls.

Human howls could be heard above a strange hissing sound. The heavy doors groaned and began to open. Not questioning the strange occurrence, they rushed through the gap. Inside, a woman was standing on a parapet on the west side of the castle, facing two men barely visible behind the crenellations on the east side.

The wizards dashed along the walkway, dodging the lashing of a ragged blue flame pursuing them. Flying down a rugged set of steps along the far wall, they rounded a rock face of the oratory and crashed into the Vikings.

"Kill them!"

The woman's voice rang clear and with authority. Without hesitation, the warriors rushed the sorcerers. The feeble and decrepit appearance of the warlocks was deceiving. Sword blades clanged against a transparent shield, ringing the frustration of the wielders across the dusty expanse of bare ground.

An invisible ball of power encircled the two gray-beards, preventing any harm from the slashing blade, but also imprisoning them. The battle was at a stand-off – until a bolt of blue-tinged white light flew from the parapet into their midst.

For a heartbeat, the sorcerers' protection failed. The slaughter that followed was brutal and bloody. Stabbed and slashed countless times, the twisted, torn bodies were barely covered by the shredded tunics.

The hairy mass of men stepped back from the carcasses, chests heaving. As one, they turned to stare at the princess as she descended the broad staircase leading from the parapet. Dressed in rags, the woman still had the bearing of royalty. Long black tresses cascaded down over the full breasts and slim shoulders.

The movements were those of a large cat, flowing and graceful. Long legs flashed under the frayed tunic, muscled, but smooth and contoured. Eirik's gaze moved up from the curved torso and met her eyes. A shiver ran through his body.

She moved to a point in front of the eldest prince without hesitation, stopping to put hands on hips. "Where is my father?"

"Your father?" For a brief moment, Eirik was stunned at the cold beauty of the woman's face.

"Gorm the Old, King of Denmark." Gunnhild seemed slightly perturbed at having to explain who her father was. "Is that not who sent you?"

The haughty manner of the woman was incomprehensible given the fact she had just been rescued from the two abominable creatures lying at his feet. "I . . . I know your father, but he did not send us."

"Then why are you here?"

Eirik's confusion gave way to anger at the woman's condescending demeanor. "I came to find a wife." Stifling a growl, he sheathed his sword, grabbed her arm, and threw her over his shoulder.

Whirling around so fast several men had to jump aside to avoid a collision; he stomped across the stronghold's interior towards the looming portal.

Gunnhild stiffened at the abrupt and rough handling. "Release me or by the gods, I'll . . ."

The sentence was cut short when Eirik unceremoniously dumped her on the ground. Scrambling to her feet, Stygian power formed a pulsating aura around the slim body. The warriors backed away in awe at the strange, fascinating sight.

"Don't move!" Slender fingers were tracing runes in the air. Every man in the courtyard was suddenly frozen as though bound in straps of iron. Even the fury burning within Eirik was insufficient to break the bonds that held him fast.

She pushed through the cluster of Vikings to stand once again in front of her rescuer. Unable to even move his eyes, the prince felt a warm softness briefly touch his subconscious and vanish. His rage was giving way to curiosity. The woman was different than any he had known. Definitely an enigma and he felt strangely attracted to her.

Gunnhild reached up to gently touch the side of his face. "You have found what you seek." A subtle movement of the feline fingers released the iron bands and the men were once again able to move.

Smiling for the first time, she took his hand and walked out of the castle as though it were the most natural thing in the world.

Eirik felt his pulse rise at her touch. She ignited a fire he had not known existed. Not the crackling warmth of a campfire, but the raging consumption of a forest aflame. The darkening of his soul seemed to pull strength from the heat.

With Gorm's blessing and gratitude, the couple was wed immediately upon their return. Never needing an excuse for celebration and inebriation, the mead and ale poured to overflowing, the vows and oaths proclaimed and proper protocol observed.

Bjorn was the first to notice the change in his older brother. Eirik had always been fun-loving and adventurous, but those characteristics assumed a harder edge. The discussions with the young monarch moved from hunting and discovery, to gold and power.

Upon returning home to Vestfold, with Gunnhild and entourage in tow, the prince turned High King introduced his new bride to his aged father and Wotun. Harald was delighted at news of the union, but the brows of the ancient sage turned down at the meeting.

Eirik noticed the scowl. "What troubles you old man?"

"Do you love her?"

Now it was the king's turn to frown. "Love is for women and children. It has no place in a man's life." The question irritated Eirik and his following remark was little more than a growl. "This was a marriage of necessity. You know that."

Wotun slowly nodded his head. "Yes, I know."

There was no point in discussing the curse of the ring. The fates would lay the course of the road ahead. Saying nothing more, the patriarch patted Eirik on the shoulder and left the room.

Returning to his lodge, Wotun's mind was in turmoil. There were so many unexpected and unexplainable turns in the road ahead. The fabled sword and cursed ring, both relics of legend, and now a part of unfolding history. He had a part to play, but he had never been so . . . uncertain of how to proceed.

Eirik was the son of a great warrior and king, as was Sigurd . . . Memories of Sigmund's son and the terrible dragon Fafnir filled Wotun's thoughts as he poured a mug of mead and sat in his favorite chair. The embers of an almost dead fire beckoned the need for fuel.

Was there some connection between the legends of the Volsung clan and the heirs of Harald Fairhair? What if there was a critical event in the ancient saga that would influence the weaving of the fates.

The life of the hero known as Sigurd, none other than the son of Sigmund Volsung, began to play out in the old man's mind.

Chapter 8

Sigurd and the Dragon

Sigurd put numb fingers in the pits of his arms and shivered. It was bitter cold and the light leather tunic was not much help against the arctic wind coming out of the North. His stomach growled with neglect.

He shifted in the saddle and noticed a few sparks of light in the darkness, indicating a hamlet in the distance. With his mother's blessing, he had set out a fortnight ago to make his mark in the world. His father had been the famous warrior and king; Sigmund Volsungsson, and people expected no less of him.

Blowing on his hands, he listened to the crunch of dead leaves beneath the horse's hooves as he rode along the deserted dirt road. Letting out a long sigh, he thought about his mother and the warm fires of home.

Hjordi married a kind old king named Alf a few years after Sigmund died in battle and the aged monarch was the only father Sigurd had ever known. The ruler fought in many wars in his youth, but sadly died a 'straw death' in bed, surrounded by a handful of retainers, a middle-aged wife, and a small, blue-eyed boy of eleven.

That had been six years ago. His mother never remarried and seemed to live in the past. Sigmund had starting asking his mother to go on an 'adventure' when he was twelve and ever year since.

Finally, with grey eyes glistening with sadness, or pride, he couldn't tell which, she consented. Although he was anxious to be on his way, she told him that no warrior was complete without a sword and a horse.

Following the matriarch down to the recesses of the castle, they entered the armory and the youth stared in amazement at the assortment of weapons. Striding across the room, he seized upon a glistening double-edge blade with an ivory carved handle and intricate runes in the base.

"This one mother! May I have this one?"

"That belonged to a brother of Alf's, a jarl. I'm sure he would be pleased that you selected it."

The reflection of a broad smile flashed from the shimmering blade in the dim interior of the cold, stone room. It had been many years since the voice of a young warrior had rang within the gloomy halls.

The excitement in his voice made Hjordi's heart leap in memory of another man. The boy was so like his father, it tugged at her heart. Turning so he wouldn't see the glistening tears, she said, "Come, we must look to a horse."

"Yes mother, I can't believe I'm finally . . ."

The sentence was cut short as he stopped part way across the room. A glistening shard of metal lying in a silver and glass casket caught his eye. Walking over next to the oblong box, he stopped and stared at the contents.

"Mother, is this what I think it is?"

Hjordi stopped, a small hand flying to her mouth as she stood staring at the boy and glittering chest. "Oh. Oh dear . . . I had almost forgotten."

Sigurd glanced towards his mother and noticed the glistening orbs. He had seldom seen his mother cry and the sight unsettled him. He must have done something terrible to cause such pain.

"Mother? What is it? Did I do or say something? I meant no harm."

Her eyes focused on the lad and softened. "What? Oh no Sigmund, it is nothing . . . it's just that it has been so long since . . ."

She let the thought trail off as she walked over next to the small chest and placed a hand gently on the edge.

"When your father was killed, the bodies were stacked to a horse's belly around him. If his sword hadn't shattered . . ."

Pulling her hand back to hold it close to her breast, she turned to her son. "Tis of no matter. With respect and admiration, warriors from the opposing army placed his body upon a shield and carefully gathered up all the pieces of his beloved *Gram*. Sigmund and the shattered remains of the fabulous blade he pulled from the Branstock oak tree were returned with an awe bordering on reverence."

She let her hand drop and expelled a long sigh. "I watched as the flames leaped around his body on a pyre for the trip to Valhalla, but kept the broken blade in remembrance of him."

"It must have been an incredible sword."

"Another time and another place, but in your father's hands, they were without equal."

"I wish father were here."

"If wishes were horses, the beggars would ride."

Sigurd understood what his mother was saying and the trace of a smile played across his face. Women provided an insight that was invisible to men.

Hjordi turned away from the silver and crystal chest, and pushing the thoughts from her mind, gently took Sigurd's arm and started the long ascent. Arm-in-arm, mother and son climbed the stone staircases in silence.

Upon reaching the top of the last stairwell, she turned to face Sigurd. "Now, we were talking about getting you a suitable mount. Best we get on with it."

Sigurd's eye's flashed with excitement at the thought. "Yes! May I choose my horse mother?"

The woman smiled at the enthusiasm and nodded. He was definitely his father's son – everything was an adventure. She had no doubt the young man would make a name for himself in the time that lay ahead.

She stood on the steps and watched him race away towards the verdant rolling pastures and herd of horses. Her smile faded slightly when the appearance of a stranger broke the idyllic scene. It appeared to be an older man, moving slowly and approaching her son in the distance.

Sigurd stopped abruptly when the man stepped from behind a massive oak and walked towards him. There was no way for the lad to know the being within the faded blue cloak and broad hat was none other than the god Odin.

"Good morn Sigurd."

The prince reached for his newly acquired sword, but felt the stranger meant no harm and let his hand drop to his side. "You startled me. What finds you on our lands?"

Strong fingers stroked a long beard tinged with grey. The man had only one eye, but the piercing gaze held him fast. "'Tis my understanding you seek a horse. Perhaps I could be of assistance?"

Sigurd felt a shiver run along his spine. The stranger was unlike any man he had met. He had heard of shamans and wizards and many of the tales were of black magic. "How . . . how did you know that?"

A reassuring smile softened the hard lines in the aged face as the man turned towards the horses. "You will need a mount that never tires, is fearless and intelligent. Can you tell by looking which horse has those qualities?"

The youth slowly closed his mouth and turned to look to stare at the herd. There were a variety of colors and shapes, but they all looked pretty much alike. A horse was a horse.

A broad, knowing smile broke out on the weathered face. It was as though the stranger could read his mind.

"What?"

"Horses are as unique as people my young friend. They are strong or weak, fierce or timid. A few are very smart and some dumber than rocks. The trick is to find one that matches his rider."

"And how do I do that?"

"What do you admire in a person?"

"Strength, courage, intelligence . . . and honesty."

"Well spoken, now go find your horse."

Sigurd understood what the stranger was trying to convey and for some reason it seemed important not to disappoint the man's expectations. Without knowing exactly what he was going to do, he started walking toward the horses.

Then it hit him. The river.

With a war hoop that rocked the area, he charged towards the milling herd, waving his arms and yelling.

Startled at the sudden racket, the horses broke towards the river to escape the madman that had suddenly attacked them. Plowing into the strong current, many of the weaker horses were swept downstream to quieter waters.

The strongest of the horses swam to the far bank and, after climbing the muddy slope, turned and snorted their discontent at the forced departure from their favorite pasture.

Sigurd smiled at the chain of events and glanced at the blue-cloaked grey-beard. The man's face was shaded by the broad-brimmed hat and unreadable. Wiping sweat from his neck, the youth headed up to the ancient, spreading oak tree and plopped down. Leaning against the trunk, he closed his eyes.

After dozing for a couple of hours, he opened his eyes ever so slightly. A small, satisfied smile crept across the tanned face. The horses were back on this side of the river.

Leaping to his feet, once again he went screaming towards the horses, waving his sword as though his only aim was to hew their legs from under them.

Neighing in fear and anger, the horses fled into the river in another attempt to reach the far bank. He continued the routine throughout the day until only two horses remained. Although both animals appeared to be exhausted, he had to know which was best.

Once more he chased the horses into the river and the smaller of the two was finally carried downstream with the strong current. The sole survivor, a large stallion with a coat so black it appeared blue in the river, swam to the far bank and once again climbed to safety.

Sigurd nodded his head in satisfaction. He had found his horse. Now all he had to do was wait. Just as he turned away, he noticed the horse heading back into the river towards him.

This was the first time this had occurred and he stopped to see what was going to happen. To his amazement, the horse swam back across and after wading out on his side of the river, the animal shook his head as though to say; "I'm not done yet. Are you still watching?"

Sigurd answered the unspoken question by nodding and the horse turned away once more to swim the river, this time without any prompting from his young antagonist.

Upon the stallion's return, the lad raced to its side and clasped his arms around the wet neck. The horse snorted in tolerance of the unsolicited affection. The prince was going to take a considerable amount of work to shape into a suitable master.

Mother and son glanced to where the blue-cloaked stranger had been standing. There was nothing but the tall, emerald shaded grass swaying in the wind over the rolling hills to the horizon. The mysterious image had appeared and disappeared with the wind.

Sigurd returned to stroking the long, ebony mane, talking as though they had known each other all their lives. "Well, you will need a suitable name. What shall we call you?" In response, the warm summer breeze carried the word 'Grani' from a land the boy had never heard of.

"Grani?" Grinning at the horse and then his surroundings, he patted the animal once more. "Very well, Grani it is."

Unbidden, the horse followed Sigurd back toward the palace. His wet, black coat glistening like polished obsidian in the afternoon sun. The remainder of the day was spent finding a suitable saddle and accoutrements for his newly acquired mount.

The early summer sun dipped beneath the horizon for a couple of hours and Sigurd begrudged the loss of those hours with inactivity wasted on rest. His mother had insisted and he didn't want to jeopardize the upcoming trip, so he complied.

It was a new day now and hopefully, nothing would prevent his departure. He was up with the first rays of the sun, pacing the cold, stone floor of his room.

Unable to wait longer, he went in search of his mother. Finding her stateroom empty, he headed down the quiet hallway towards the kitchen. Halfway there, a noise in the storage room interrupted his search. He pushed the rough, wooden door open and peered inside. The woman had her back to the door, but he recognized it immediately.

Hjordi stuffed a warm, woolen tunic into a burlap bag and added a smaller sack containing some dried meat, fruit and bread. She turned away from the completed task and glanced around the room to determine what else her son might need.

Her eyes swept past him and quickly returned. "Sigurd! How long have you been standing there?"

"I just now entered mother. Here, that looks heavy, let me carry it."

Taking the sack from his mother, he embraced her with his free arm and felt a sudden charge of adrenaline at the thought of the adventure ahead.

Hjordi returned the embrace and felt as though her heart would break. The boy was the last ember of a fire that had burned so brightly in her youth. There would be nothing left but memories and cold ashes after he left.

"Don't forget your heavy vest. The nights are cold and getting colder." The garment had been made using the time consuming and complicated method of knotting countless tiny loops of the woolen yarn. The nalbinding technique produced a cloth that would never fray.

"Yes mother. I packed everything else last night -- I'll grab the vest."

She nodded as he raced off to retrieve the worn pack that looked so natural on his back. Far too quickly he returned and was bidding her farewell at the palace steps.

The lad's profile was bathed in the bright morning sun as he waved goodbye and turned Grani east. Hjordi kept the smile glued to her face until he was out of sight and then turned to the silence and solitude of the stone castle.

--

Remembering the sublime departure brought the trace of a smile to Sigurd's face as he pulled the leather tunic closer. The reminiscing also brought to mind the heavy vest his mother had insisted he bring with him.

Pulling Grani to a stop, he reached back in the packsaddle and rummaged around until he felt the fleece lined garment. The warm vest put an entirely new face on the growing darkness and he found himself humming a tune he had learned as a child.

Dusk was settling like mist on a pond as he entered the little hamlet. There were only a few lights along the rutted roadway and he noticed one appeared to be coming from a small inn near the end of the street.

He tied the stallion to one of two posts on either side of the entrance and dismounted, checking his sword and money pouch. Both seemed secure so he headed inside.

The innocence of his youth betrayed him as he entered the dim interior. A hard-looking lot stopped their games and drinking long enough to give the newcomer a once-over.

One burly brute, bald with an auburn beard, flashed an ugly smile. "Well, well, well. Me prayers have been answered. Tis a gift from the gods" Winking at his comrades he patted his knee. "Come here my boy and sit on the lap of a real man."

Sigurd ignored him and approached a man in a worn, leather apron who appeared to be the owner of the inn. The man paused in the task of wiping greasy bowls and glanced over at him.

"You wantin somethin boy?"

Sigurd stammered, "Yes . . . I need a place to stay for the night . . . and some food."

The man went back to wiping the mugs. "This ain't no charity house. Best you be movin on."

The boy reached for his money pouch, but before he could respond, the brute behind him guffawed. "Maybe we should send him after the dragon's horde. Then he would have plenty of money."

The inn rocked with raucous laughter at the comment and Sigurd whirled at the insult. Throwing back the dust covered cloak, his hand went to the ivory hilt of his sword. "I have offered no offense and will accept none!"

The sight of the weapon and the youth's cutting remark slammed the room into silence. The voice was that of a young man, but seemed to lack any fear of the hostile surroundings.

The rogue jumped to his feet, sending the crude wooden chair tumbling behind him. "Bark at me you insolent pup! I'll whip you like a cur!"

An old sword, badly chipped and tinged with rust, leaped into a large, scar-laced hand as he pushed patrons out of the way. The boy stood fast, pulling his gleaming sword free and realizing he would probably die in the next few seconds, but so angry he didn't care.

A broad set of shoulders suddenly blocked his view of the approaching threat and when he stepped to the side, the shoulders moved with him.

Turning to look up at the newcomer, Sigurd noticed the man was advanced in years, but not beyond his prime. Grey eyebrows dipped slightly as he winked at the boy behind him. Sigurd drew back in surprise at the sudden intervention and the nonchalant demeanor of the man.

Some enraged brute was about to kill him and this character seemed to be amused by the whole incident.

"Sir, I do not know your purpose in interfering, but that man means to kill me and he may harm you first if you do not get out of the way."

The man threw a "in a minute boy", back over his shoulder and continued to face the attacker.

"Gjordi, he's just a boy, where's the honor in killing sheep?"

The man stopped in front of the newcomer and glared. "He insulted me and for that he's going to taste my blade. Now get out of the way."

The intruder's stance didn't change, but there was a slight shift in the timber of his voice. "Well, if I was going to taste someone's blade, it would be nice if they put a whetstone and touch of oil to it once in a while."

Insulting a man's weapon was like attacking his mother. It just wasn't done. The quiet muttering in the room faded to dead silence as the man's eyes moved from Sigurd to the interloper. "Regin, I've no quarrel with you and you've no cause to insult me." Glancing back at Sigurd, he added, "Now are you going to get out of the way or not?"

In answer, Regin crossed his arms and let out a long breath, but stood firm. Gjordi stared at him for a moment before slamming his sword back in the worn leather sheath, snarling, "You best watch your back Regin. This isn't forgotten, not by a long sight. When you've forgotten and are a thinkin everything is . . ."

Regin cut him off. "That's enough Gjordi. Either pull that excuse for a weapon or go sit down."

The veins in the man's neck were pulsing as he gritted his jaw and turned away. Sigurd was pretty sure he had never seen anyone that angry before.

After the brigand returned to his table and yelled at the barmaid to fetch more ale, Regin turned to the lad behind him and extended a large, callused hand. "Sorry I didn't have a chance to introduce myself, but I am Regin Hreidmasson. I must apologize for the manners of some of the locals, but they don't take kindly to strangers in these parts."

Sigurd grasped the beefy paw and realized the man could easily crush his hand. The boy had never known fear, but realized there was a lot about the world he didn't know and never imagined.

The grip was firm and friendly, but nothing more. Patting the youth on the shoulder, Regin turned to the innkeeper. "Beli, I believe you were about to get this young man some food. Is that correct?"

The innkeeper didn't respond, but disappeared behind a heavy door and returned shortly with a bowlful of steaming stew. Dropping it in front of the boy, he gave Regin a look that betrayed the suspicion behind the tired, grey eyes. "What you up to Regin?"

The mischievous glint returned. "I was bored."

Sigurd marveled at the abrupt change of atmosphere in the room. Somewhat disappointed, the patrons went back to their games and drinking. They were hoping for a little bloodshed, but Regin had put a damper on the whole affair.

He glanced down at the goulash and reached for the leather pouch at his side. "I have money for the stew." Loosening the drawstring, he pulled a couple of coins from within and dropped them on the counter.

The innkeeper raised an eyebrow at the silver and, wiping a greasy hand on his apron, deftly retrieved the coins.

"Best keep that bag out of sight," Regin murmured around a glass of ale he was quaffing. "Several of the 'patrons' in here would slit your throat for half of what you just dropped on the table."

Sigurd glanced down at the paltry sum and knew the man was telling him the truth, but to him it seemed a small amount to argue over, much less kill anyone.

"I believe you and will take your advice."

The older man didn't respond, but nodded before draining his ale.

"When you finish your supper, I want to show you something."

After starting in on the stew, Sigurd remembered how hungry he was and it didn't take long before he was wiping out the interior of the bowl with some pieces of dried bread.

"That was actually quite good, or I was very hungry."

"Hunger adds spice to any food. Come on let's go."

Sigurd studied the man a moment before responding to the invitation. "Why are you treating a stranger with such kindness?"

For the first time since he met the man, a look of uncertainty flashed through the grey orbs. He was considering his answer and Sigurd wasn't sure if this was good or bad.

"Years ago, when I was not much older than you, I had two brothers. The younger was known as Otter and the older was called Fafnir. Otter was a child of nature and Fafnir was . . . hard and strong."

Sigurd spoke into the pause. "Was?"

"Otter died young and Fafnir . . ." He let the sentence trail off unfinished.

"I still don't understand why you have an interest in me."

"When my brothers and I were young, we met a . . . man who had a profound effect on my family. As I've traveled different paths in my life, there have been forks in the road where I had to make a decision. Let's just say I believe this is one of those times."

Sigurd smiled through the puzzled expression on his face. Whether the man wouldn't or couldn't explain his interest in him, it appeared that was the only answer he was going to get.

"Where are we going?"

Regin placed a large hand on the slim shoulder and squeezed gently. "You're going to need a place to sleep and I don't think this inn would be a very good place to stay."

The lad remembered the hulking brute who wanted to kill him and nodded quickly. "You've got a point. What did you have in mind?"

"Come. I'll show you."

It was dark and cold when they stepped outside. The light from countless stars cast a glistening net of silver over the scrubs and trees surrounding the hamlet.

A short distance down a grass lined lane they entered a large, mud and waddle building. Shafts of starlight pierced the darkness through openings in the walls. The sound of flint and steel preceded the eruption of a cheery flame flickering on the end of a candle.

Regin walked around the interior, lighting a series of candles, which when combined, spread a warming glow over the crude structures within.

Sigurd's eyes swept his surroundings. It was a blacksmith's shop. The walls were lined with knives, swords, shields, plows, harness and bridles. In the center of the room, a large set of bellows embraced one of the biggest forges he had ever seen.

He walked over and placed his hand on a large anvil next to the forge and felt the lingering warmth from the softly glowing coals.

"A blacksmith's shop." He glanced over at the smith who was standing with his arms crossed, watching him.

"Aye boy. A man's work. A warrior's friend."

A smile crept onto the young face as the prince turned towards the weapons lining the wall. A few steps brought him alongside and he carefully reached up to touch the cold iron of a long, shimmering blade.

"You are a master craftsmen. These weapons are better than any I have ever seen."

Regin walked over next to Sigurd and pulled one of the swords from the wall. "They are good, but that blade at your side is not the work of a novice."

"It was my uncle's. A gift from my mother."

"Tis a weapon to wear with pride."

Sigurd felt fatigue from the day seeping into his bones and his host must have noticed, for he quickly changed the subject.

"Well, time enough for talking about swords and glorious deeds tomorrow, I'm done in and it looks like you could do with a bit of a rest."

The youth smiled in appreciation and lost the battle with a yawn struggling to freedom. "Yes, if you have some straw . . ."

"Nay lad. I wouldn't bring you here and have you sleep on the ground."

The smithy had an upper platform built into the southern portion of the structure and at the top of the rough stairs, there were three cots lined up in the loft.

"Every once in awhile when I have a few ale with my friends, we all wind up here, sleeping it off. Why don't you take the one on the end?"

Sigurd managed a nod and a 'thank you' Before tumbling onto the soft layers of down and leather.

He awoke to the distant sound of a cock and tiny sparks of light from the minutia dust particles floating in the air. The upper part of the building was actually quite warm and it was the first time he had felt comfortable since leaving home.

The smell of bacon drifted up from below and his stomach responded with a growl. Realizing he had slept in his clothes, he dusted off his trousers and straightened his tunic. The sword was still strapped to his side.

Feeling a little foolish for having fallen asleep like a child, he quickly unbuckled the prized blade and laid it across the bunk. He ran a dirty hand through a long mop of blond hair and hurried down the steps toward the popping sounds of breakfast.

Regin was leaning over a cast iron griddle setting on a rock outcropping next to the forge. The rock abutment was actually a little cubicle with a grill over the top. The small fire underneath cooked whatever was on the grill and the forge would keep it warm for hours.

He glanced up as Sigurd approached and flashed a broad smile at the young man. "Good morn. I was beginning to wonder if I was going to have to eat all of this myself."

The saliva was beginning to brim at the corners of his mouth and Sigurd suddenly felt as though he hadn't eaten in weeks. Catching the teasing in the man's voice he responded. "That would be terribly inconsiderate of me. And even though I'm not sure I have room for a meal, I will force myself to partake of whatever you see fit."

The serious delivery of the statement stopped Regin for a moment until he saw the twinkle in the lad's eyes. "Ah yes, well tis most important I be a gracious host. Therefore I shall not require that you eat more than is desired."

With that, he cut one of the smaller strips of bacon in half and placed it on a large wooden plate. When he handed it to Sigurd the youth accepted it and stared momentarily at the tiny piece of meat.

Popping it onto his tongue, the morsel brought the taste buds in his mouth to a clamoring chorus. "Ah, that was most filling -- and delicious."

He glanced down at the heaping pile of bacon still on the griddle. "Maybe to be a more gracious guest I should . . . eat a little more?"

Regin broke out laughing as he shoveled a large potion of the sizzling strips onto Sigurd's plate. "Tis mighty gracious of you lad. The bards will sing praises of your courteous and brave ways."

Grinning broadly, the boy began stuffing the food into his mouth as he found a nearby bench and plopped down.

Things have a way of occupying the days in a person's life and such was the way with Sigurd and Regin from that point on. The days turned into weeks, the weeks into months and the months into years. Tales of a terrible dragon to the north were rampant in the little hamlet but Sigurd gave them little mind until the last year of his teens. Two years in the blacksmith's shop had taught him a valuable skill and -- he was no longer the skinny boy the locals would taunt and tease. Broad shouldered and incredibly strong, Sigurd was now well liked, and respected, by the villagers.

Late in the afternoon on a particularly fine fall day, a cry from an aged matron brought everyone to the main square. A small boy of about seven had been discovered a short distance from the hamlet.

Badly burned, the boy was delirious for several days, ranting about some monstrous beast coming from the sky and burning his village. On the third day, the child awoke, wide eyed but lucid. Staring at the strangers around him, his eyes were darting left and right, looking for some terror lurking behind or beyond the calm, reassuring faces.

Ali, a village elder, was sitting on the small cot next to the boy. Running a fatherly hand through the matted hair, he spoke soothingly. "There, there lad. You've had quite a bad spell. Now, can you tell Uncle Ali what happened?"

The calm, reassuring voice dispelled the imaginary monsters and for the first time in days, the pale azure eyes glistened with tears. "My home, my family . . . they're all gone. Dead."

The old man nodded as though he understood. "Yes, yes child. Go on."

The small face focused on the cragged visage for a moment then dropped. "We were all so happy before . . . It came from the sky. A terrible flying monster. Killing everything . . . everyone."

The elder glanced at the faces surrounding the child and shot an admonishment at the gasps that followed the statement. Turning back to the boy, he tried to keep his voice steady and low. "And then what?"

The boy didn't look up, but said, "I ran. I ran and ran and ran until I collapsed." After a brief pause, he continued. "After I woke up, I started running again and realized I didn't know where I was going."

He reached up to scrub a dirty face, smearing the tear tracks. "And then, I just walked until I couldn't go anymore."

The simple story tugged at the old man's heart as he reached over to embrace the skinny frame. "Well, you're safe now. No flying monsters would ever dare come near here."

The small eyes widened at the statement. "Really? The thing doesn't frighten you?"

The old man delivered the lie without hesitation. "The demon you saw is afraid of this town and will never come near it."

The tension in the young face relaxed at the reassurance. "That's good. That's a very good thing."

By the time the elder laid the boy down, the child was slipping into a peaceful slumber. Laying a finger to his lips, the man backed away and motioned everyone out of the hut.

Letting the heavy hide drop over the entrance to the cottage, he was immediately surrounded by villagers wanting to know what he was going to do.

The old man waved a weary hand in response. "How many men have we lost to that monstrosity? What would you suggest I do? The beast cannot be killed. All we could do is sacrifice more of our young warriors to it."

The cutting remark silenced most of the clamor, which turned to muttering as the people returned to their homes. The dragon had not been seen for several years. People were hoping it had died. Others, who had never been witness to its atrocities, doubted it existed.

Regin and Sigurd had wandered over and caught the last part of the exchange and stood together silently watching the small crowd disperse.

The young smith glanced over at his mentor and was about to remark on the incident when he noticed the strained expression on his friend's face.

"What is it?"

The question brought Regin out of his rumination and he turned a blank expression to his companion. "What's what?"

"I know you well Regin, and the expression on your face tells me there is much you are not saying."

The older man shook his head as he turned away. "Some things are best left alone. Things that cannot be fixed or ever set right."

Sigurd crossed his arms and stood firm. Too many nights he had heard his friend mumbling in a deep sleep or suddenly awaken covered in sweat.

"Are we friends – or am I just an employee?"

A flash of anger crossed Regin's face and disappeared as quickly as it appeared. "I'm sorry Sigurd. You are the best friend I've ever had.

A truer man I'll never find. It's just that . . ."

"I'm not moving from this spot until you tell me."

The years were beginning to show in the older man with flecks of grey and heavy lines around the eyes. "Very well, but let us sit while I lay the tale at your door."

They both walked a short distance to the circle of rocks built for village bonfires and sat on an old log that had been used for a bench year after year.

They sat in silence a few minutes before Regin began the painful story.

"When we met I told you that I was reminded of my youth and that was no falsehood. For some reason that night brought back the memories of a long forgotten, fateful day like it had been a fortnight before.

"Tis no lie, none other than Odin, Hoenir and Loki walked up to my father's house one morning, carrying the body of my younger brother. My father was a powerful magician and in his anger at the death of Otter, imprisoned the gods then and there.

"His greed for gold won out however and he made a bargain to release them for the vast treasure of Andvari, the dwarf."

The old smith paused to see Sigurd's reaction. There was no hint of mirth or disbelief in the young, chiseled face, so he continued.

"Loki stole the huge golden cache and delivered it to my father. The wealth wrought a terrible change in the old man. For most of his life he had coveted the dwarf's fortune and I lost several brothers in vain attempts to gain the treasure.

"He finally had what had been the focus of his life and everything else was lost to his sight. Even his children became suspect.

"The nights were filled with his nightmares, screams and fear of losing the vast treasure. Many were the long nights Fafnir and I lay awake for fear of being killed in our sleep.

"It was hardest on Fafnir. Next to Otter, he had always been father's favorite. The hurt of being suspect and ignored turned to anger and finally to hate.

"When I realized how much my older brother despised our father, I was not surprised to enter our small home one day and find him standing over the body of the old man with a long, crimson blade dripping life from the tip.

"The wild look in Fafnir's eyes struck terror to my heart and I fled. I know I should have stayed and avenged our father, but he was my brother.

"I returned once, several years later, but the grotesque monster I found guarding the golden treasure no longer resembled the man and sibling I had known.

"That was the last time I saw what had once been my brother. There is no doubt that winged monster is none other than the soft spoken man I once called Fafnir."

Regin stopped, and letting out a long breath, snapped a twig he had been turning in his fingers and let the pieces fall to the ground.

"Now you know a truth that no other living mortal knows. I swore long ago to never divulge the secret of the dragon's origin, but you changed all that."

Sigurd stared into nothingness for an expanded period of time before finally speaking. "So your father's murder has never been avenged."

"No."

"Do you seek vengeance?"

The old smith paused before answering. "There was a time . . . but no, not anymore." Looking directly at Sigurd, he added, "but tis no longer a question of honor – you saw that small boy from the village to the north. The monster must be destroyed."

Standing and dusting his trousers, he threw back over his shoulder in a voice barely audible. "Even if it was once my brother."

Sigurd let the smith walk away. It was apparent Regin needed some time alone. Standing and watching the receding back, he wanted to sort things out in his own mind as well.

The sun was dipping below the horizon by the time the young man had made up his mind. He was going to kill the beast. It had to be done and he might as well be the one to do it.

Shortly thereafter, he divulged his intent to Regin and waited for a reaction. For the first time since Sigurd had known him, the man seemed uncertain of his response. Finally, he laid large, strong hands on the broad shoulders and said, "Let's sleep on it and discuss it in the morn."

The young smith simply smiled in return and patted the older man's arm. He had made up his mind.

The next morning, when the sun was a hand span above the tree line, Regin rolled over in his bunk and sighed at the sight of the empty cot on the other side of the loft. He had tossed and turned through the night -- Sigurd was going to try and kill the terrible beast and he knew there was no way to thwart the attempt.

Resigning himself to once more being alone, he halfheartedly fixed breakfast and fired up the forge for another day's work.

Meanwhile, several furlongs to the north, Sigurd was steadily plodding towards his destiny. Tales of the dragon were common in one respect; the beast protected his horde of gold in the mountains to the north.

He kept asking himself why he was risking his life on this quest. His heart held no desire for treasure or glory. He had no cause to seek vengeance -- it just needed to be done.

Having resolved in his mind that was adequate reason, he stopped to allow Grani a breather and gaze in the distance at the brooding mountain that was the final goal.

He passed the still smoldering ruins of a village in a valley to the west, but kept heading in a straight line for the craggy crest breaking the far horizon.

Evening of the second day brought him to the base of the sheer cliffs. He dismounted and started working along the base. Climbing over broken outcroppings and huge boulders made for slow progress and by the time a foul odor reached his nostrils, the sun was once more dipping into the boughs of distant trees.

He dropped into the shelter of a leafy glade and stretched out on the verdant carpet beneath a canopy still streaked with shafts of the fading sunlight.

A small spring seeped from a mound of cool moss and after drinking his fill he pulled some dried meat from the small leather pouch at his side and tore small strips off with strong teeth.

He leaned back and let the exertions from the last few hours of climbing fade to the peaceful rhythm of his beating heart. His mind drifted back over Regin's story about his brothers and father. The man was an enigma in so many ways. Kind, strong and gentle, but his father and brother were . . .

The full, bright sun was in his face when he suddenly awoke. Cursing his carelessness, he glanced around and his rapidly beating heart began to slow. How could he have been so careless? To fall asleep at the doorstep of a monster?

The foul smell was still in the air but faint.

He stood up and made sure the ivory handled sword was loose in the rune embossed scabbard. A voice in the back of his mind began chiding him. "So you've sparred with Regin a few times. What makes you think you can succeed where so many others have failed? Hardened, experienced warriors. You, my foolish smith, will die just like the others."

Pushing the annoying voice to silence, he moved quietly through the dense vegetation along the base of the towering cliffs. The smell of putrid meat and ash preceded the view of a clearing at the base of the cliffs a short distance ahead.

The dragon's lair. This had to be it. His heart began to pound so loud he stopped and wondered if the beast could hear it. Sucking in several deep breaths, he left the safety of the heavy vegetation and started across the open grassy area in front of a large black hole in the wall of the cliff.

Over his shoulder, he heard a familiar voice. "Brave lad. I know you can do it." He stopped and looked around him, there was no one there, but he knew he had heard the voice before.

He paused at the cave's entrance and realized he didn't have anything in the way of a torch to see where he was going. The voice in the back of his mind chided him again. "Foolish boy on a man's errand. Turn back before you get us killed."

"Flee if you so desire."

That seemed to silence the voice and, flexing the muscles in his jaw; he headed into the black interior. A short distance inside, his feet bumped something in the dirt. Reaching down, he felt a large bone.

Tossing the thing aside, it clattered and he silently cursed himself for the thoughtless act. Maybe he was a foolish boy on a man's errand.

Walking slowly, his vision began to adjust to the darkness and the vague outline of a huge cavern came into view. Phosphorescent veins cast an eerie light over the interior and he gasped at the sight of a huge pile of glistening gems and gold.

Never in his wildest imaginings had he envisioned such wealth. For the span of a heartbeat he felt drawn to the power emanating from the glittering pile.

The rumblings of an unfamiliar sound broke the spell and his eyes searched the balance of the cavern with a frantic haste. Swinging past and then returning to a large object that seemed out of place in the gloomy interior, his heart leaped when he realized he was gazing upon the sleeping form of a huge dragon.

It was impossible to imagine the recumbent monstrosity could have been a man at some point in time. Thick scales gleamed with an unnatural luminosity in the damp darkness. Claws resembling scythes protruded from huge, grey limbs that had once been hands and feet.

Sigurd placed his hand on the hilt of the sword and crept toward the slowly pulsating mass. The stench was overpowering as bile rose in his throat.

He swallowed deeply and stopped to steady his breathing. Once again, his heart was pounding so hard he was sure it would awaken the beast. The glimmer of a small object to his left caught his attention and his eyes turned away from the dragon.

A heavy, golden ring, alone on a granite pedestal, glimmered with an eerie glow. Tiny runes had been worked into the crest and Sigurd thought it was the most beautiful thing he had ever seen. There was no way for him to know it was the same ring Hreidmar had demanded from Loki so many years in the past.

Turning back to watch the behemoth, he quietly stepped sideways to take the ring from its resting place. Dropping it into the pocket of his breeches, he slowly loosened the long blade of his uncle's sword.

The weapon slid silently from the well oiled leather sheath and flashed in the dim light of the cavern.

Feeling the uneven floor of the cave with his feet, he slid, more than walked, toward the sleeping titan. Thanking the gods for his luck, he paused near the head of Fafnir and shook his head in disbelief. The thing was truly hideous, with protrusions resembling horns curving up from the massive head.

Heavy lips bulged from blood streaked teeth the size of a miner's pick. Although the monster's eyelids were closed, Sigurd knew the sight of them would be a reflection from the pools of Hel.

Taking a deep breath, he grasped the two-handed broadsword and raised it over his head. Clenching his jaw, he brought the heavy blade down with all his strength upon the exposed neck of the beast.

The well honed weapon struck the plate-sized scales with a shattering clang that resonated through the vast interior of the cavern.

Sigurd quickly retrieved the blade and stared in disbelief at the ragged edge of the chipped sword. The scale that had adsorbed the brunt of the blow appeared to be deeply scored, but unbroken.

The force of the blow woke the dragon, but sleep was still clouding the ability to focus. The animal might be a dragon, but it had the brain of a man.

Blowing smoke laced with fire from flaring nostrils, the head rolled to the side, much like a man waking from a deep sleep.

Sigurd's heart leaped in his chest at the movement and a flood of adrenaline surged through his veins. Fafnir would waste no time in killing him once he realized he was there.

Throwing the heavy sword in an arc around his shoulders, once again he slammed the sword down with all the strength of a young smith's body. The power of the surging chemicals in his blood gave the corded sinews the force of a sledge on an anvil. There was nothing that could prevent the double-edge weapon from cutting deep into the thickly corded neck.

Nothing, that is, except the shattering of the exquisite blade. Several huge scales were broken from the force of the blow, but the ragged hilt Sigurd held in his hand was useless. He cast the finely wrought handle aside to break and run headlong through the darkness.

Falling and leaping to his feet again and again, he knew the cave's entrance was close when a deafening bellow rocked the interior of the tunnel leading to the cavern.

The rage emanating from the inhuman howl sent a bone-chilling ripple of fear down Sigurd's spine and it seemed his feet were no longer touching the ground.

He broke into the open air and flew as much as ran down the short, open space into the protective vegetation surrounding the mountain. The shuddering roar that followed him into the heavy trees told him Fafnir had espied his flight and would soon be upon him.

The air in his throat was burning and pain in his chest told him the demand placed upon his heart could not continue without paying a heavy debt. Ignoring the pleas of his body, he kept charging through the underbrush, hoping somehow Fafnir would loose his trail.

Gasping for air, he dropped to his knees and sucked in wind, unable to run farther without rest. But there was to be no rest – a huge shadow blocked out the sun and the blast from a giant blowtorch raked the treetops above him.

The area immediately became an inferno and exhaustion gave way to terror as Sigurd leaped to his feet and threw himself through a break in the foliage.

☼☼☼

The man known as Wotun was asleep, but the eye of Odin was looking down from the throne of Hlidskialf. So many of his plans lay in the survival of the young Viking. If Fafnir killed him . . .

Pushing the thought aside, he continued to watch.

✧✧✧

Again and again, the winged demon plummeted from the sky, enveloping his victim in scorching flames. Sigurd realized after the second attack that Fafnir was taunting him, making sure the man understood he could kill him at any time, but was not going to make it quick, or easy.

The fear that had given strength to exhausted limbs was now beginning to wane and a bottomless fatigue was filling every part of his body. He could go no more. Blisters, unheeded, covered his body. He would die here – here and now.

Topping a small rise in the terrain, he smiled faintly as blue irises covering the ground rose to meet him and he toppled forward. Rolling down the gentle incline, his unconscious form cart-wheeled into some heavy brush and disappeared into the dense growth.

The shrubs slowed his descent, but didn't stop the muscled body from careening over a canyon rim to plummet to the raging river below.

A bellow from the gigantic, multi-hued dragon circling overhead was much the same as a cat yowling in frustration at having lost a mouse it had been toying with. Lower and lower Fafnir flew, watching the surface of the quiet pools downstream from the rapids, but nothing surfaced.

Finally convinced his nemesis was dead, and he could torment him no further, the monstrous beast spiraled upward and disappeared. If Fafnir had realized his most prized possession had been stolen from the cave, he would not have given up so easily.

A gentle breeze moved across the bloody, beaten body that washed ashore a furlong downriver. A lesser man would never have survived the ordeal, but the steady beat in his chest refused to stop.

Time passed and Sigurd finally found the strength to drag himself out of the water and drop onto the warm grassy embankment. The warmth from the earth seeped into his cold body and ignited a small flame that crept into his consciousness and told him he must get up, get up and live.

He rolled over onto his back as the slanting rays from the sun caressed his body, coaxing him to struggle on. He had never hurt this badly and for a time, his body was fighting with his mind for permission to quit.

Crying out in pain, he struggled to an upright position and was somewhat amazed to realize he accomplished the simple feat. The cold water had abated the burning on his back a little, but the peeling away of blisters the size of biscuits brought pain that refused to be ignored.

Just sitting and thinking seemed to help as much as anything. He was hungry, in a great deal of pain, and miles from home. But there was nothing broken and he had survived. He glanced up at the sky and ran a callused hand over his face before remembering that even his face had not escaped the blistering heat from the dragon's attack.

He reached down to the soft mud and scraping some loose, began to apply it to the areas he could reach. It might become infected due to the swab, but there was no doubt what would happen if the raw flesh was not covered.

Standing up, he let out a long, shuddering breath and looked homeward. His mind flashed back to his mother and the castle, but that was no longer home. He vision was of a crude building with a forge and old man waiting for him.

Regin was like the father he never knew. He would get back somehow. With a single step, he started out. Finding Grani was the first indication he might actually survive. Unable to mount the horse, he walked alongside, clinging to the saddle.

Sigurd would never remember stumbling into the outskirts of the little hamlet called home. He would not hear the cries of discovery or feel the strong arms of Regin carry him the short distance to the smithy. The exhausted mind that brought him back would not have the strength to retain these simple memories.

Time and again, the old man poured soup past the cracked lips, but most of it ran out and down the blistered chin. The young man was like a son to him and the long nights were passed sitting at his bedside.

A fortnight passed before Regin noticed the eyelids of his patient flutter and Sigurd opened his eyes. The smith pushed some errant strands of hair back from the chiseled face and smiled. "Well, well, well. Decided to join the world of the living eh?"

At first, the image hovering above him was just a blur, an image of something familiar. Sigurd reached up to scrub a callused hand across and stubble covered chin and flinched at the pain. "Oww . . . ahh."

He glanced at his hand to see why it would cause such pain and a flood of memories about the dragon rushed into his consciousness.

Regin drew back at the sudden flash of terror in Sigurd's eyes. "What? What is it boy?"

The young smith's eyes focused on the man leaning over him and the facial muscles began to relax. "I . . . Fafnir . . . for a moment I thought . . ." He let the sentence trail off, with a nervous glance around the loft.

The older smith stood and brushed his hands off on the worn tunic and placed them on his hips. "Let's get some food in you and you can tell me what happened."

Sigurd glanced up, managed a faint smile and nodded. "That would be good . . . Regin. Thank you."

He lay in the cot for a few minutes before sitting up and swinging his feet off the edge of the bunk. The exertion increased his heart rate and he blew out a quick breath. Glancing down at his arms, they were covered with reddened splotches – scores of blisters that had peeled away and were beginning to heal.

The clothes he was wearing were clean and soft. Apparently Regin had removed the ragged, burnt remnants clinging to his body when they found him.

The smell of pork chops and eggs drifted up and his stomach growled in anticipation. He stood up and steadied himself on the cot's frame for a few seconds before working his way down the steep ladder.

"Smells good."

"Come sit."

Sigurd ate in silence and quickly realized that his stomach would not yet tolerate much in the way of solid food. "That's good Regin, but I'm afraid I will have to finish the rest later."

The old smith reached over and slid the tin plate to the side. "That's fine lad. Now, are you up to telling me what happened?"

Sigurd felt his side and realized he was no longer wearing the scabbard his mother had given him. The shattered sword came to mind as he placed his hand back on the table. Looking inward, he licked his lips as the disastrous quest paraded by.

"I found Fafnir in a cave, far to the north, at the base of some cliffs. He is indeed a monstrous dragon. Tis hard to believe the terrible thing could have once been a man.

"As luck was mine, the creature was sound asleep when I ventured into the cave. It was very dark inside and but for the light from some of the stones; I wouldn't have been able to see anything.

"When my eyes became accustomed to the dim light, I espied the beast, asleep in the middle of a vast cavern. It was a terrifying sight, I fool you not Regin."

The older man nodded solemnly and motioned for him to continue.

"Well, I drew my sword and . . ." Sigurd stopped abruptly and looked around the smithy. "My clothes! Where are the clothes I was wearing?"

Regin drew back at the sudden change and intensity in his ward's manner. "What . . . your clothes? Why they're . . ." He paused as if trying to remember what he had done with the rags. "Oh, I tossed them in the corner behind the forge. I was going to burn them, but haven't got around to it."

The old man watched with a perplexed expression as Sigurd jumped to his feet, wobbled unsteadily, and then hurried to find the ragged, burnt remnants.

Searching the pockets of the breeches frantically, he froze as his fingers encountered something inside. Slowly, he pulled his hand from the ragged, torn pocket and walked back to his mentor.

He extended the hand, clutching something, towards the old smith. "Tis yours."

Regin reached out with an open palm, a puzzled expression covering the wrinkled visage, with a small smile playing around his mouth.

The smile vanished when Sigurd dropped a heavy, gold ring into the open palm. "It was lying on a single pedestal in the cavern and I stuffed it in my pocket before . . ." He left the sentence unfinished.

The man slowly retrieved the extended hand. The palm was still open and he was staring intently at the ring. "Tis . . . the ring my father demanded from Loki."

He looked up at Sigurd as though an explanation would follow, but the youth just watched him with delight. He was sure his friend would be pleased with the gift. "Put it on." Grinning broadly, he added, "I didn't kill the dragon or get anything else, but at least it's something."

Regin slowly slid it on the third finger of his right hand. It fit. A shudder ran up his arm as he released the golden band. It was a strange and disquieting sensation. Repulsed at first, he started to remove the ring, but realized Sigurd would be hurt and forced a smile. "Thank you. Tis a gift worth a son's ransom."

He dropped the hand abruptly to his lap. It seemed incredibly heavy. Pulling his thoughts away from the ring, he turned back to the young man hovering over him. "Now, sit and finish your story."

Sigurd plopped down in the opposite chair, grinning with pride and satisfaction. Shortly after sitting down, the expression once again changed to anguish as the memories of the encounter with the dragon tore through his mind.

"There's really not much more to tell. As I said, twas asleep when I found it and when I tried to kill the thing, my blade shattered on the scales." He began shaking his head. "The monster has scales as big as plates and harder than iron – I don't think it can be killed."

"Aye lad. No one has lived to tell the truth of it before, but what you say rings to the source of the demon's power."

The old smithy became enveloped in silence as the two men sat reflecting on past events. Regin was feeling the nascent effects of a dark stain touching his very soul and wishing things could go back to the way they had been. Sigurd, on the other hand, was juggling emotions of delight in delivering the treasure to his friend, and shame at having failed to kill the beast and then fleeing in fear.

He would never admit to anyone the shear terror he had felt when running through the trees with that abomination blasting him with fire from the forges of Hel.

It was something he would have to live with.

"Well Regin, I'm feelin kinda tired. I promise I'll be back at the forge in the morning," Sigurd said, rising slowly and heading for the loft.

"We'll not be worrying about that for a few days – and forget about that monstrous beast. I'll not have you risking your life again on an impossible quest."

Sigurd nodded and smiled sadly. "I should never admit it, but I was hoping you would feel that way." He headed up the rough steps, throwing back over his shoulder. "I truly hope it does not mean I am a coward."

"Tis a fool, not a coward, that throws his life away."

The sincere comment made Sigurd feel better as he collapsed on his bunk.

Late summer saw a shortening of days and subtle changes in the old smith. Sigurd noticed it first in the man's dealings with customers and friends. He was becoming bitter and angry. Little, everyday mishaps threw him into a rage and money became the focus of his every effort.

Somehow Sigurd knew Regin would someday ask him to try and slay the dragon again and the dreaded day finally came. The older smith was mulling over some lukewarm porridge and staring at the gold ring.

"It's just not right lad. The monster will continue to ravage the countryside until it is killed. Tis not enough that my father has never been avenged – we must consider the people of this hamlet and surrounding shires."

The statement brought Sigurd's wandering mind to an abrupt halt. "What are you saying Regin? You're not suggesting I try again?" The Volsung descendent was vainly hoping the old smith would tell him to never go near the dragon again, but instead the man replied, "There is no other choice. The beast must be destroyed."

A tiny glint in the smith's eyes went unnoticed. "And the treasure restored to its rightful owner."

"Its rightful owner?

"Aye."

"But how?"

Regin stood up and this time Sigurd noticed the golden glitter in the older man's eyes.

"Are you ok?"

"Aye lad. But tis time I start work on a suitable sword."

"Sword?"

"A blade that will cut through the iron scales of the world's fiercest dragon."

Sigurd watched in silence at the old smith turned to the forge and the task ahead.

The summer passed and Sigurd regained his youthful stamina and strength. The moon was approaching a second full disc by the time Regin manufactured a 'suitable' sword. Handing the weapon to Sigurd, he nodded at the long, glistening blade. "What do you think?"

Sigurd disapproved of the changes in his mentor, but held his peace. Accepting the weapon, he felt the balance and it was good.

Walking over to the massive anvil that stood in the center of the smithy, he swung the blade in a sweeping arc and brought it down on the shiny, flat surface. The resounding crash of the colliding metal sent hard vibrations up his arm into his torso and shattered the blade.

"What in the world -- what did you do that for?" bellowed Regin. "You can't slam a blade onto an anvil and not destroy it!"

The man was furious, but Sigurd held his ground. "I'll not try again – not without a blade that will withstand such a blow."

The anger in the old man's eyes tore at Sigurd's heart. Regin was a changed man and he didn't know why.

The days passed and sword after sword was shattered against the anvil. Finally, the old smith grabbed a broken hilt from Sigurd and tossed it aside. "I'll not try again. Such a sword cannot be made. You are just using this as an excuse for not facing Fafnir again."

The cruel statement rang the smithy to silence. Sigurd could not deny the accusation. Maybe he was using it as an excuse. Maybe he was a coward.

Clenching his jaw, he spun on his heel and headed out of the smithy. He was done with the old man and his vengeance. If he wanted his brother dead so badly, he could kill him.

He walked for an hour in the woods, his mind in the turmoil of a civil war. He loved that old man, but was he willing to die for him – and gain nothing?

His thoughts turned to the castle of his childhood and his mother. It had been years since he had seen her. He wondered if she was still alive. Maybe he should return. It would be an ignoble homecoming.

The faint trail he had been following through the woods turned a corner and paralleled a downed fir tree. Plopping down on the trunk, he pulled a handful of long grass and began shredding it in his fingers. Life had been so much simpler when he was young.

The rambling thoughts retraced the gift of his uncle's sword and the armory in the castle. Suddenly, an image of the crystal and gold case holding the shattered remnants of his father's sword flashed in his mind and he froze.

There were tales of the sword cutting through anything. No one knew how it was broken, but if half the stories were true . . .

He jumped to his feet and raced back towards the hamlet. It was as though the ebbing fear that had been eating at his manhood was swept away and replaced with a resolution that only gods possessed. Now he knew his destiny.

Regin listened intently as the young smith related the story of the fabulous sword and the broken shards lying in the crystal chest. After Sigurd finished, he said, "Would your mother let you have the pieces? We might be able to forge them together again."

"I'm sure of it. I'll leave immediately."

The afternoon of the seventh day following the discussion, Sigurd topped a small hill and the castle that had been his childhood home came into sight. The excitement of seeing his mother again brought a rush of adrenaline and he spurred Grani into a run.

They covered the short distance to the citadel in record speed and he flew from the hand-worked saddle to race up the steps.
"Mother! Mother I'm home!"

Greigir, the groundskeeper, met him at the door. "Whoa! Hold on there young man, you can't just come charging into . . ." The sentence was interrupted by an old woman coming down the stairs. "Greigir. Never you mind, I'll deal with this. You get back to the garden."

The man nodded, bobbed his head at Sigurd and disappeared. The old matron approached him then drew back suddenly. "Sigurd?"

"Hello Helga. It's been a long time. Where's mother?"

The woman's mouth dropped open and for a moment she was speechless. Then, slowly closing her mouth, the pale blue eyes began to glisten with unshed tears. "Oh Sigurd. Your mother passed away last winter. We didn't know where you were."

The words were like a blow to the stomach. Dead. It had been a long time, but the thought never crossed his mind. He should have come back sooner. He pushed aside the thoughts that were berating his lack of care. "Where is she?"

The old woman didn't answer, but walked through the open, massive doors at the entrance and pointed to the west.

Sigurd followed the length of her arm and at her fingertip in the distance was a large stone, worked with runes. It stood beneath the ancient oak he had played upon as a child.

A warm breeze rustled his long hair as he stood silently over the grave. There were so many things he had learned that he had wanted to share with her. But most of all, he had been looking forward to just holding her in his arms one more time.

The blurry runes provided a simple epitaph; "This stone was raised by Sigurd Sigmundsson for his mother, Hjordi."

He reached down and grabbed a handful of earth and sprinkled it over the slight mound of the gravesite. "And to the earth we return. I will miss you mother."

A little over a week later, he rode into the familiar hamlet that had become his home and stepped down from the saddle. He was tired, but had accepted his mother's death and was once again looking forward to what lay ahead.

The days passed and Regin seldom left the forge; working like a man possessed. Time after time he attempted to meld the shattered blade together and each time, the shards fell apart when the glowing sword was thrust into cold water.

The two blacksmiths were sitting in the little shop one late afternoon after a particularly disappointing failure when a stranger walked into the shop and inquired about a bridle for his horse.

The man appeared to be middle-aged with a large, faded blue hat pulled low over his face and an auburn beard streaked with grey. One lid drooped over a missing eye and the deep voice fairly rumbled with authority and power.

Regin and Sigurd both knew they had met the man before, but held their silence. The man was a stranger to their village, but seemed to be quite familiar with the smithy.

He walked around the interior but said nothing, nodding at this piece of work or that, pausing briefly to run his hand over the broken shards of Sigurd's sword. "Twas a fine weapon at one point in time. It would take great heat and a master's hand to return it to a former glory."

He glanced at Regin with the comment and then turned to Sigurd. "Killing a dragon is a nasty business son. If I were to attempt such a thing, I would go for the belly of the beast."

Regin's eyes narrowed. "What is our business to you?"

The man threw up a hand to respond in silence and turned to walk out of the smithy. Regin tossed the hammer he was holding onto a nearby table and followed him outside. The stranger was not going to get off that easily.

"Now see here . . ."

The old smith's voice trailed off when he realized the visitor had vanished. The ground was level and clear for a stone's throw in all directions, but there was not a soul in sight.

He walked back into the shop and stared at Sigurd. The young man looked out the door over Regin's shoulder without meeting his eyes. "Odin. That was Odin wasn't it?"

"Aye lad, I believe twas."

The old smith walked over to the broken shards of the ancient blade and noticed the soft glow surrounding them slowly fade and disappear. "A great heat."

Sigurd glanced at his mentor. "What was that?"

Regin retrieved a worn leather apron from a spike protruding from a heavy support post and slipped it over his head. "Odin. He said it would take a great heat. I'm sure he was telling us how to meld the sword."

The prince walked over and stared at the forge with his hands on his hips. "How do we get more heat?"

"Air, fuel and hearth. We have to increase each of these."

SIGURD AND REGIN
Repairing the fabled sword

The following night and day were spent rebuilding the old forge. The depth of the hearth was increased and a larger bellow was connected to a new tuyere with an increased diameter to pipe the flow of air into the base of the hearth.

Exhausted, the pair fell asleep on their bunks late the second night and the sun was half a circle above the horizon before they began to stir. After a hasty breakfast, they threw themselves into rebuilding the sword as though their lives depended upon it. In some ways, it did.

Again and again, Regin grasped the red hot pieces with his favorite old tongs and doused them in the slack tub. Water surrounding the blade came to an immediate boil, hissing and sending tendrils of steam upwards into the cool air.

The increased heat caused the shards to meld as never before and the smith began the critical elements of folding, shaping, heating and hardening. The hours fell away and the two men continued without thought of food or rest.

Finally, late the fourth night, Regin held the blade aloft and marveled at the glittering reflection of candles scattered throughout the smithy. "Tis a beautiful blade Sigurd. I've never made one better."

Turning to the young smith, he somberly added, "But it must pass the test."

Sigurd did not reply, but reverently accepted the sword and felt the balance. It was perfect.

Clenching his jaw, he stepped next to the anvil and studied it for a moment. It had destroyed so many of his hopes in the past. Would it do so again?

The thoughts racing through his mind brought a rush of adrenalin and without hesitation he swung the long blade around in a sweeping arc and slashed downward. The resulting sound was not the resounding clang that had accompanied his previous tries. The thunk was the sound of an axe splitting cordwood.

The long blade had not only sheared the massive anvil in twain, the heavy wooden block beneath was neatly split as well. For a heartbeat, Sigurd stood staring at the lowered sword. "We've done it Regin. This is the blade I need."

The old smith moved next to the young man and nodded solemnly. "Aye lad. Forgive me."

The unusual remark brought Sigurd around sharply. "Forgive you? For what?"

The inner turmoil between the life he had lived and the growing evil within was apparent on the older man's face for only a moment. "What? Oh, nothing . . . I was just rambling."

The memory of the pile of gold and jewels laid before his father had been haunting his dreams at night and his thoughts turned constantly to the treasure during the daylight hours. Wealth had meant little to him prior to Sigurd's attempt to slay the dragon. Now it seemed to be everything.

Sigurd raised the gleaming blade and turned it slowly in the flickering candlelight. "It's beautiful Regin. A weapon fit for a king."

The old smith didn't respond, but turned away, lost in thoughts of another time.

Early the next morning, Sigurd tied some food and a packsack on Grani's back, adjusted his sword, and grabbing the pommel, swung into the saddle.

Regin seemed reluctant to talk -- they had said their goodbye's the previous night and there was no point in waiting. Digging his heels into the ebony hide, he leaned into the crisp morning breeze and though he knew he could be riding to his death, it was with great anticipation.

Grani seemed to sense the importance of the mission, reaching out in long strides that quickly ate up the distance.

The sun was long gone by the time the looming cliffs appeared in the pale moonlight. He smiled inwardly. The towering mountain no longer reeked with unimaginable terror. Now, he knew the demon he faced and would not allow rash acts or fear to govern his conduct.

This time it would be different. He would not rush in, sure of victory. Odin's comment kept ringing in his mind; "soft underbelly of the beast." That was the key.

This time he would study his enemy and develop a strategy before waging war. When victory was in his mind, it would be his in truth.

Cold, dried beef and spring water were his dinner in a fireless camp the first night. The next morning he lay quietly in the forest, waiting.

☼☼☼

Wotun awoke, staring at the cold ashes of a fire long dead. The stain from a spilled glass of mead streaked his worn tunic. "Hel's heels Hermod; I'm getting as clumsy as . . ." The realization of who and where he was hit him and he stopped rambling.

Faint light from a bright moon filtered in through the window. Absently wondering what time it was, he reached for the fire-staring flint. Stretching the stiffness out of his back, he watched a tiny flame leap to life, happy with the world. He reached for the jar of mead and poured a mug full. Bubbles in the dark ale reminded him of another time, another place . . .

☼☼☼

By mid-morning Sigurd's patience paid off. The familiar, reeking stench preceded heavy, dragging sounds a short distance away. Crawling on hands and knees, he crept to a small rise and froze at the sight of the huge dragon lumbering down the slight incline in front of the cave.

A stone's throw from the cave's entrance, crystal clear water from a small spring pooled in a small swale and then rushed on down towards the distant sea. Fafnir stopped at the pool's edge and lowering his massive head, drank deeply for several minutes.

Sigurd reached up to his chest to slow a pounding heart and his hand felt the tiny dragon there. Touching his father's talisman gave him reassurance that he would not fail and the hammering subsided.

The next day the dragon repeated the ritual and for two more days, the young smith lay in the foliage and watched the terrible beast drag its massive bulk to the pond and drink.

The fourth night, Sigurd dug a narrow trench in the dragon's path and covered it with limbs, leaves and grass. Lying prostrate in the ditch, he waited.

Bugs and spiders crawled over his body, but he remained motionless and the hours dragged by. Finally, when he wondered if the beast was going to repeat the ritual, the stench of rotten meat and feces swept over him and he swallowed the impulse to gag.

The fabled sword was lying by his side, cold to the touch, but reassuring. The shrouded sunlight disappeared and he knew the moment to strike had arrived. Gripping the long hilt with both hands, he rammed the blade upward through the grass and leaves.

An ear splitting bellow followed the desperate thrust and Sigurd was yanked from the trench, still clinging to the sword. The long blade was completely buried in the soft underbelly of the dragon, but the monster was far from dead.

Spreading enormous wings, Fafnir took to the air, carrying his assailant with him. Twenty feet from the ground, the blade pulled free, cutting a gaping hole in the belly of the demon. Fafnir screamed a deafening roar that could be heard for miles.

He rose into the air and spotted Sigurd splayed on the grassy turf in front of his cave. The dragon was leaving a crimson trail in the air current behind him. The bloody stream twisted in the wind and feathered out into a fan of death.

All reasoning left the monster's brain when he recognized his assailant and dove toward him with eight inch talons exposed. Sigurd rolled under a boulder, barely escaping the mindless assault.

The plummeting dive was uncontrolled and the huge dragon plunged into the rock abutment adjoining the cave's entrance. Rocks and debris crashed down on the hulking mass, but just seemed to further enrage the monster.

Thrashing free of the broken rock and timber, the beast whirled in search of the human that had dared attack him. He spotted Sigurd staggering to his feet less than twenty paces away. Bellowing around the fire spewing from the gaping maw, Fafnir charged.

The young Viking knew he couldn't escape, so he stood his ground, determined to die with valor. Raising his sword, he hoped to get in one good stroke before . . .

The dragon stumbled in the charging rampage and fell. Sigurd waited, expecting the monster to regain its feet and finish the vengeful attack.

Instead, the behemoth struggled in an attempt to stand and collapsed. The youth slowly walked to the dragon's side and realized the belly wound had been fatal. Fafnir was dying.

Without hesitation, he moved to the side of the huge head and quickly swung the sword in a sweeping arc, bringing it down mightily on the exposed neck. The heavy blade almost completely severed the impossibly thick neck, scales and all.

The second stroke sent the plate covered head rolling down the slight incline. A short distance away, it came to rest, sightless eyes staring at an indifferent sky.

Sigmund stood spellbound, unable to take his eyes from the dead beast, trying to assimilate the feat he had just accomplished. For years, the monster had terrorized the countryside, killing and burning for reasons that were beyond comprehension.

A tinge of regret crossed his mind. Although they cursed and feared things they couldn't understand or destroy, people needed them.

They needed the dark shadows of night and the marvelous fairies tending the flowers of the field. Without them, life was mundane and unbearable.

Following a ritual as old as the mountains around him, he built a small fire and cut the heart from the huge chest. Skewering the massive muscle on a green branch, he laid it across the forked braces on either side of the campfire.

The dripping blood sizzled as it dropped into the crackling flames. The young smith absently licked his fingers, staring at the snapping embers and thinking about the last few years. Regin had been his guardian and mentor for a long time. He was the best friend a man could have, but he was changing. The tone of his voice, the look in his eyes – he wasn't the same. But what . . .

"Your thoughts do not deceive you young man."

The strange voice brought Sigurd's heart to this throat as he sprang to his feet. The bloody sword leaped into his hand as he spun around looking for the source.

A gentle breeze moving through the trees was the only sound he could discern. His pounding heart slowed and he listened intently. Nothing.

He slowly returned the long blade to the worn leather scabbard, wondering if his imagination was getting the better of him. Rubbing a hand under his nose he muttered, "Don't start jumping at shadows. Pretty soon you'll be seeing things as well as . . .'

"It's not your imagination Sigurd; you're just not looking in the right direction."

This time he did not jump, but looked up, searching the heavy foliage above him. A large, black feathered bird was sitting on a small branch part way up the towering conifer just to his left. The raven's head turned slightly to the side when their eyes met and Sigurd drew back slightly at the intelligence in the dark eyes.

He glanced around, nervously wiping his hands on the worn tunic. Looking back up, he noticed the bird was still watching him. "Did you say something?"

Feeling foolish as soon as the words left his mouth, he dropped his eyes and started to chide himself again. "Gods above Sigurd, what is the matter . . ."

"Yes I did."

The voice broke his rambling and once more his gaze met that of the raven's. After holding his eyes for a moment, the bird spoke again.

"It would appear you are not accustomed to speaking with the creatures of the forest."

Slowing swinging his head back and forth, he said, "No. And as far as I know, no one else is either."

A sound resembling a chuckle followed. "No one else has slain the terrible Fafnir – and tasted his blood."

Sigurd glanced down at the partially dried blood on his hands. "His blood?"

"Much like the double-edged sword at your side, the arcane knowledge can be used for evil or good. Which will it be?"

Sky blue eyes moved from the large, callused hands to the voice above. "I don't understand."

"When you eat of the dragon's heart, all will become clear as the morning sun. Regin will try and kill you upon your return. The curse of Andvari's ring has poisoned his soul and there is no . . ."

The confusion in his mind flashed to anger at the words and he grabbed a rock, throwing it violently at the raven. "NO!" The bird took flight to avoid the missile and vanished in the dense forest.

Sigurd watched for the bird momentarily and licking his lips, glanced at the roasting heart. Maybe it would be best to cast it into the underbrush and walk away. In his heart, he knew he could never walk away from the unknown again.

Taking the sizzling meat from the fire, he touched the hot surface and licked his fingers to alleviate the scoring heat. Visions of a dead otter and an ugly dwarf flashed through his mind. He knew he was seeing the memories of a monster's twisted mind.

Strong white teeth ripped into the tough meat and tore a piece loose. The muscles in his jaw flexed with more than the exertion as he chewed the flesh. It was just as the raven had said. He could see it clearly as runes on a stone -- Regin would try and kill him when he returned. The man's soul had turned black as the coal of Hel's domain. With or without the treasure, there would be no reasoning with him.

Sigurd stopped chewing as silent tears slid down the facets of the hard face. He loved the man like a father. How could he kill him? The pain in his heart was unbearable. He swallowed the bite and lay the rest of the heart aside. He was so tired.

He couldn't kill Regin, but . . . The sight of Regin turning into a replica of Fafnir crawled into his mind. That would be a fate worse than death. Somehow, he would have to find the strength to do the terrible deed.

Leaning over against the carcass of the dead dragon, he closed his eyes. Maybe he would simply die from the pain in his chest and then he would be free of the impossible burden. The stench of the beast began to fade as darkness consumed one terrible image after another.

In the distance he heard a man's voice. It wasn't Regin, but it was familiar, calling him.

☼☼☼

"Wotun! Tis long past break of day." Eirik's voice broke into the painful dream, bringing him back. Back to a time and destiny which was somehow inexplicable and surreal.

Sitting up, the pains of old age gave him constant reminders of days long past. "What is it lad?"

"I've wanted to talk to you."

The patriarch stretched and ruefully glanced at the cup of mead, still untouched.

"About?"

Eirik stared at the aged Viking for a moment before responding and finally let out a long sigh, sitting on the edge of a worn cot. "I've been having strange dreams at night."

"Strange. How so?"

"It's confusing. There's this hideous dwarf and an old magician in the woods. A lot of gold and a monstrous dragon." Rubbing a tired face, the king dropped his hand. "There are just bits and pieces. It doesn't make any sense."

Wotun stood up, crossed the small room and reached down to grasp Eirik's arm. Lifting it, he placed gnarled fingers on the ring of gold encircling the third finger of the king's right hand.

Both men tensed at the contact and Eirik looked from the ring to the patriarch. "What is it? You know this ring?"

"Aye. Tis the ring giving you the dreams."

"I don't understand. Why would a ring give me such dreams?"

"Tis cursed."

Eirik straightened slightly and stared hard at the old man. "Cursed? By whom?"

"The ring you wear was made by none other than Andvari, the most powerful of the antediluvian dwarves. Twas he who stole the Rhine Maidens gold and from it made the cursed band." Wotun's eye moved from Eirik's face to the ring. "Untold centuries have passed since Loki stole that very ring from the dark elf, and the curse placed on it by the dwarf has caused the downfall of countless souls, starting with the god of mischief."

"Father wore the ring. Why was he unaffected by the curse?"

"Your father wore it briefly before finding a woman that meant the world to him. Harald's heart belonged to her from the moment of their meeting. For the curse to be invoked, the wearer must disavow love."

Eirik knew Wotun referred to Gyda, and not his mother, but he knew his father loved Ragnhild as well and that was what mattered. Pulling his hand back, he grasped the ring, absently twisting it on his finger. "I've seen glimpses of the road ahead and it's a path I'd rather not travel."

"The decisions are ours, but the trails we follow have many forks, twists and turns."

"What if I were to remove the ring?"

"I don't know. But accepting the ring is accepting the curse." The grey eye moved from the golden band back to Eirik. "Do you love Gunnhild?"

The king met the baleful stare with hard eyes. "She is my wife."

"That is not what I asked."

The dark azure eyes finally dropped and the High King of Norway remained silent as he left the hut.

With the passing of time, Harald noticed a change in his eldest son and began to question the wisdom of passing most of the realm to him. Gunnhild overheard the aged king discussing his concern with the second in line; Bjorn, and decided to resolve the issue. The next night, the venerable lion died of a massive heart attack.

The death of his father seemed to erase the last trace of humanity from Eirik. Before the heat had cooled from the raging funerary pyre, he assembled a large war party and headed north – to fulfill a destiny of conquest.

Once again, Bjorn and Olaf accompanied their brother to the reaches of the White Sea and beyond. Sailing down the broad Dvina River, they sacked town after town, each attack becoming more brutal and savage than the last.

It was late in the day when a score of square sails entered the port of the small trading village of Permina. Tales of the Viking's ferocity and barbarity preceded them. Chaos consumed the town upon sight of the ships. Incomprehensible terror rendered many villagers incapable of action.

Those with their wits about them were scrambling to hide valuables and children, in that order, from the marauding invaders. The slaughter that followed was atrocious, even for barbarians. By nightfall, the last of the screams had died away and the entire hamlet was in flames. Eirik came stalking out of one of the larger structures, a handful of amulets and valuables in one hand and a bloody axe in the other.

One of the Viking warriors was standing beside Bjorn watching the leaping flames when the king appeared. "King Eirik of the bloody axe."

"Aye, I think maybe he enjoys this a little too much."

The man looked at Bjorn and raised an eyebrow. Most men would agree with the statement, but none would have ever made it.

The quiet comment was the beginning of the end between the king and his brothers. When they returned to Norway, Bjorn took his leave to become King of Vestfold, Guttorm moved to Ranrike, and Olaf assumed control of the realm of Vingulmark.

For the next few years, the decree of their father was honored and peace existed between the brothers, if not with other nations. The High King of Norway had become known as Eirik Bloodaxe throughout the reaches of the Scandinavian tentacles.

Bjorn met and married a few years after the trip to the land of the Sami and fathered Gudrod Bjornson -- destined to become the great-grandfather of Olaf II of Norway.

The relationship between Eirik and Bjorn deteriorated from a tense parting of the ways to a silent distrust. With the passing of time, the bonds that had bound them tightly as brothers began to unravel and decay. The demand from the High King that he pay scat, or tribute, was the beginning of the end.

Bjorn had earned a reputation as both a seaman and merchant, establishing the trading center of Tonsberg. With success comes wealth and envy. The tax envoy from Eirik was sent packing, with a message that Bloodaxe was not his father and would receive no tribute.

This seemed to be the only excuse needed. The High King of Norway was in the Baltic with a fleet of warships when word of the refusal arrived. In a rage, Eirik sailed to Vestfold to confront his brother. After an angry exchange, he left, only to return under cover of night and slay Bjorn.

Stories of the treachery spread fast and far. Olaf and Sigrod felt compelled to avenge their brother's death, even though at the hand of another brother. The sad moon grew to a full circle thrice by the time the brothers assembled a large force to attack the High King.

The battle of siblings was a civil war. But short and merciless. In a matter of days, Eirik walked away from the bodies of both brothers, bloody and torn, never to rise again. Many would say Eirik's queen, Gunnhild, the Stygian sorceress, was the unseen force breaking shield walls and causing spears to miss their mark. Only the 'Mother of Kings' knew the part she played.

Memories of laughing, teasing brothers plagued Eirik's dreams, but his path was bound by towering walls of granite from which there was no escape.

Wotun's enigmatic foresight led to countless sleepless nights filled with foreboding. This was not what the aged Viking wanted, not what Odin would have wanted. Everything seemed to be spiraling out of control. The thought brought his wandering mind to a halt -- he smiled to think he ever had any kind of control.

Unable to change or accept the course of events, the venerable mystic bid the royal court adieu and left. It would be many years before anyone would see the ancient sage again.

Hakon, the youngest of Fairhair's male offspring, was barely a toddler when Harald had sent him to the royal court of Athelstan in England. The King of Mercia became the foster father of the bright, young child, delighting in the intelligence and kind nature of the boy.

With the passing years, the Norwegian prince became the pride of the English court, surpassing his peers in the reading and writing of runes and swordplay. The lad was an astute student of board games, and over time, Athelstan began to think of the boy as his own.

When word of the siblicide reached the English monarch, he reluctantly told Hakon. There would be no option for the youth but to avenge the death of his brothers. Still in his teens, the youngest of Harald Fairhair's sons received the news with a cool restraint. Reared in a Christian realm, the lessons of his childhood would serve him well in the years to come.

Hakon sailed north with a formidable fleet of warships and the support of a monotheistic world. The shrewd prince avoided direct conflict with his older, half brother, undermining the Norwegian's king local support by promising to remove the taxation invoked by their father.

Eirik's bloody crusade had alienated many powerful jarls and landowners, paving the way for Hakon to promise his way to a position of strength. Word of a new ruler called 'Hakon the Good' spread like chaff in the wind across the realms of Norway and by mid-summer, Eirik's army dwindled to a skeleton of the mighty force it had once been.

Even Gunnhild's conjuring had little effect on her brother-in-law's efforts. Some power greater than hers thwarted every incantation and spell. The High King of Norway was no fool and realizing a war with Hakon would be fatal, fled home and hearth with his eldest son, Haeric, to the Orkney Islands.

Gunnhild returned home to the land of the Danes with a brood of children, unable to accompany the frantic flight of her husband.

The jarldom of Orkney provided the refuge Eirik needed to re-group. Befriending the jarls Arnkel and Erland, he was soon on his way to leading a powerful army once more. Ragnhild, his eldest daughter was betrothed to none other than Arnfinn, the son of Thorfinn Turf-Einarsson and future earl of Orkney.

His days were filled with planning and promise, but the nights; oh the nights were a time to dread. The dreams were becoming voyages of betrayal and tragedy. The age-old tale of Baldur's death at the hand of his brother Hodur played over and over as he tossed in a sweat-soaked bed.

Time and again he had pulled the cursed ring from his finger, casting it aside, only to frantically retrieve and replace it before his heart ceased to beat. It had become a part of him he could not live without.

Hakon's foster father, Athelstan, King of England, died the winter of 939 and his heir, Edmund, was killed in battle, seven years later. This opened the door for Eirik's aspirations in England.

Setting sail for the northern shores of the British Isles with a fleet of sixty ships in the spring of 947, he found little in the way of resistance. Dissatisfaction of the local populace with the weak king Eadred opened the door to Eirik and for a short period of time, they welcomed him as King of York.

Eadred however, lashed back with a terrible retaliation for what he considered treason and the people drew away from Eirik. Without local support, he was forced to flee England, opening the door for Olaf Sihtricsson to assume the throne. Olaf was a friend of Eadred's but a poor ruler and four years later, the populace of Northumbria was up in arms, welcoming Eirik back as their king.

"Once again, the true King of York is on the throne." The

Archbishop made the statement as a simple statement of fact.

Eirik raised an eyebrow at the statement. "Wulfstan, you never cease to amaze me."

"How is that?"

"If memory serves, you were telling Olaf that very same thing only four years ago."

"Times change, seasons change and the wind changes. Such is the nature of man. Four years ago, Olaf was the right man."

"I see."

Wulfstan dipped his head in the form of a bow and stroked the carefully trimmed beard. "You have received the Lord as your personal savior and will be guided by his right and powerful hand in all endeavors."

"What about Eadred?"

"The King of England is in London. As he should be." Sweeping his hands at the surroundings, Wulfstan added, "And I am here. As I should be."

Eirik knew the Archbishop served the Pope and not Eadred, but it was a fine line to walk. "Fair enough."

The King of York walked away from the encounter with a frown wrinkling the heavy brow. He had accepted Christianity as a matter of necessity; you cannot rule a Christian people as a pagan king. The concepts were troubling though. The belief in the long-dead messiah was so strong in some individuals they would die willingly rather than change their belief. It wasn't natural.

He had summoned Gunnhild upon his ascension and she had brought several of his sons with her. Calling each by name, "Gamle, Guttorm and Erling!" he embraced them warmly. "It does my heart good to see you." The reunion was interrupted by the entrance of Haeric, his eldest son and Ragnald, a step-brother.

Gunnhild ran to embrace her favorite son. "Haeric, I have missed you sorely. Have you been well?"

The young man was no longer a child, but blushed at the attention and turned toward his uncle. "Mother, this is Ragnald. I don't think you ever had a chance to meet him." Memories of Eirik's dead brothers flashed through her mind and marred the perfect features for only a moment. "No I haven't. What brings you to the court of my husband?"

Eirik stepped in. "Ragnald has been at my side for the last four years. We have been in several skirmishes together and he saved my life before we realized we both had the same father."

Gunnhild raised one eyebrow slightly. "King Fairhair visited a lot of countries in his younger days."

The men exchanged knowing glances and let the matter stand.

A coronation celebration was held that evening and hundreds of people were in attendance. The high-reeve of Bamburgh, a man named Olsuf Bebbanburg, worked his way through the crowd of dignitaries. A courtesan by nature, his smooth smile and easy manner opened doors with an aplomb that amazed his liege. The steward was one of a handful of men the king felt he could trust.

Eirik worked his way through the Great Hall towards Olsuf, with Gunnhild and Haeric at his side. There was important business to discuss and the matter would not wait for a more opportune time.

"Olsuf, may I have a word with you?"

The smooth face and carefully trimmed beard framed hard eyes the color of slate. "Yes Your Majesty. May I be of some service?"

The king glanced to the young man at Olsuf's side and recognized the steward's son, Maccus.

"Maccus, tis good you could join us this eve."

The youth bowed and flashed a broad smile. "Tis a rare opportunity Your Majesty. I am awed at the power and grandeur of your court."

Eirik acknowledged the deep bow, managing to avoid a smile. The lad was following in the footsteps of his father. "Yes . . . ah, Olsuf. There is a matter of some import I wish to discuss with you."

"Of course."

The two men walked to a small, adjoining room and Olsuf lit several candles in silence before the king finally spoke.

"What I am about to tell you, is known to no other and I must swear you to silence of the subject before I speak further."

The high-reeve knelt before his king. "Upon your sword, Your Majesty."

Eirik pulled the long blade free and held it in the flickering light of the candles.

Olsuf gently grasped the blade and kissed it. "Upon this blade, I lay my life and sworn oath that what you are about to tell me will never pass from my lips."

"So be it. Stand."

The steward stood and remained silent.

The king let out a long sigh and slowly raised his right hand. "The ring upon this hand tis a heavy burden. It possesses great power and . . ." Eirik paused. "corrupts the soul."

Olsuf stared at the heavy, gold band. "Tis beautiful my lord. It does not seem possible such a prize would be a thing of evil."

The king waved the comment away. "Tis what it is." Turning away, he added, "I've had dreams, visions if you will, of a great horde of gold in the isles to the north." He turned back to the steward. "You of all people know how tenuous my hold upon this realm currently is."

The high-reeve did indeed know the king held power simply due to the will of the people, which could change overnight. "Nay my lord, your strength is . . ."

Eirik cut the statement short. "Olsuf! Tis I you speak to. Do not patronize me with reassurances of vapor. I need wealth to buy security. That is the way it has always been."

"Yes Your Majesty. What would you have me do?"

The king placed both hands upon the shoulders of his friend. "Find this treasure and bring it back."

"Aye lord. It will be done."

The next morning, Olsuf and Maccus set sail, bound for the isles of the north. The months passed and Eirik spent every waking hour walking the ramparts of the Great Hold, watching for sails on the horizon. Winter came and went and the King of York finally gave up hope of claiming the treasure of his dreams. His envoys must have perished on the high seas, otherwise, they would have returned with news of their quest.

The longing within him cried out in frustration. He knew with the insight the ring provided; he could find the golden horde in a single passing of the moon. Gunnhild watched her husband change with the passing seasons, but he had never confided the purpose in sending his steward north and she never asked.

She lay in their bed, night after night, as Eirik sat bolt upright in a cold sweat from one terrifying nightmare after another. Finally, her patience at an end, she confronted him. "My lord, you cannot continue jumping up in the middle of the night, crying out in fear, or pain, I know not which. What is it that troubles you so?"

Eirik looked at the faint silhouette of his wife's face. A pale moon cast a soft iridescent into the room, outlining the smooth contours of her still-youthful figure. "Tis nothing my love. I'm sorry I woke you."

Flashes of a Stygian fire ignited in the dark blue eyes. "Eirik, tis no dove of the rafters you speak to. I am your wife and queen. More importantly, your confidant. Do not speak to me of nothing. Tell me what troubles you and tell me now!"

The quiet power behind the voice reminded him that his wife was not of the common mold and would not be treated as such. Nodding slowly, he spoke into the darkness. "I cannot keep the kingdom without wealth and . . . I cannot seek gold and silver without leaving the fold to the wolves."

He wiped a weary hand over a haggard face. "Every way I turn, I see the dead faces of my bothers, the slavering jaws of wolves and blood from a hundred axes drips onto my face from the halls of Valhallah."

Gunnhild's soft features hardened into granite. "Tis the whimpering of a child I hear, not the voice of a warrior and king." She grasped Eirik's hand and held it up. "Send Olsuf back with this ring and he shall not fail!"

"Olsuf is dead."

"By the gods Eirik! If Olsuf were dead, do you not think I would know?" She dropped his hand. "He and Maccus will return with the full moon."

From the iron in her voice, he knew it was true. His steward would return and . . .

The thought of parting with the ring tore at his guts. But there was no choice. Gunnhild was right – she was always right.

Olsuf did return as foretold and with the waning moon, set sail once again. The revulsion he felt when the Stewart slid the golden band on his finger was the foulest excrement his senses had ever known. The fealty sworn upon Eirik's sword was the only thing that kept him from ripping the ring from his hand and casting it away.

The queen was right in her prognostications about the ring and finding the golden treasure. She had told Olsuf to twist the ring upon landing and follow the visions.

The island they encountered in the middle of the northern Atlantic was uncharted and unknown to the travelers. The sandy beaches led upward to forested glens and rugged mountains. The ring tugged at his hand as though someone was leading him and in a matter of hours after landing, they were gazing upon the broken escarpment of a distant tower of granite.

Images of a terrible dragon pursuing a hapless victim brought him up short. The temptation to pull the ring from his hand became overpowering and he found himself tugging at it desperately. Fingers bleeding and swollen, he realized the ring would not come off without taking the finger with it.

Maccus watched his father with a growing concern until he could no longer hold his silence. "Father! What are you doing?"

The man whirled on his son. "What I have to!"

"I don't understand."

"Neither do I." Shaking his head and trying to hold his trembling hands steady, the older man began panting; sweat coursing down the long face. "Maccus, what is happening is beyond our control. We must finish what we have started."

The youth nodded in agreement, but he did not understand.

Olsuf climbed from the wooded surroundings into the cleared area at the base of the cliffs. A dark hole in the granite escarpment marked the entrance of a cave. Somehow, he knew this cave – and the treasure within.

Gasps of amazement came from the crew surrounding him as they gazed at the pile of gold and jewels reflected in the light of a dozen torches. Chest after chest was hurriedly filled with the precious horde and carried to the ships.

The youthful exuberance of Maccus filled to overflowing. "We are rich father! Wealthy beyond our wildest dreams. Why aren't you happy?"

The core of Olsuf's soul was turning black and beginning to decay. His voice betrayed only the slightest hint that something was terribly wrong. "We Maccus?" He made a sweeping gesture of the treasure. "This belongs to our liege and master, Eirik, King of York."

Maccus had never heard the resentment, tinged with scorn, that was in his father's voice. "But surely he will give us our fair share?"

"What is fair to you and 'fair' to our lord 'Bloodaxe' are apt to be two completely different things."

Eirik had forbid the use of the word *Bloodaxe* in reference to him upon his return to the throne and it was the first time Maccus had heard the term in several years.

"What are you saying?"

"I am saying son, that if we want reward for our labors, we must have the cunning of a fox."

"I don't understand."

"King Eadred is the answer to our dilemma."

"He hates King Eirik."

"Exactly."

The man slowly formed a grim smile, staring at his son. "What would happen if Eadred knew of this treasure?"

"He would want it."

"What would he be willing to trade for it?"

"I don't know."

"The kingdom of Northumbria."

"But . . . Eirik would have to be deposed."

"Yes. With these chests of treasure going to the winner, Eadred would raise an army and attack tomorrow."

Olsuf stopped. What if Eirik should somehow win? Gunnhild was a powerful force and the local populace and earls still were strongly in favor of Haraldsson's reign.

There was only one way to ensure victory – the King of York must die, before or during the battle.

When word and evidence of the vast wealth reached the ears of Eadred, an army was raised and began the march upon Northumbria. Five kings assembled with Eirik to meet the threat in the region of Stainmore.

On the eve of the battle, the king known as Eirik Bloodaxe, son and heir of Harald Fairhair would die from a treacherous blade in the dark of night. Maccus did as his father instructed, and would never have a peaceful night again.

Without the will and might of Eirik, the kings were decimated in the battle that followed, but died with valor. Oh, the tales the bards would tell of that fateful day and the reception of the valiant host in the halls of Valhallah.

Once again, Gunnhild fled to the safety of Denmark. Warmly received by her brother and king, Harald Bluetooth, it would not be the last the world would hear from this woman, destined to be the 'Mother of Kings.'

Olsuf did receive the kingdom of Northumbria as agreed upon, but would never again enjoy the hushed beauty of a quiet evening, the gentle strains of music, or the satiation of a great feast. The man's heart had turned to stone and life was simply a series of days through which to exist.

The cursed ring was stolen as he lay on his deathbed by a household servant, not reappearing for many years.

With the passage of time, the sun continued to rise and fall, as did many a petty kingdom. Hakon the Good would reign as king of Norway for a period of years, with subterfuge, betrayal and war lurking in the wings.

There was no land left for the younger heirs of many a king and the Norsemen began looking for unexplored, and unclaimed, lands. An era of exploration and westward expansion was beginning. Furrows for a new breed of Vikings such as Eric the Red had been plowed and with summer rains and sunshine, the crop sprang forward.

Chapter 9

Eric the Red

Dark thunderclouds drew a ragged cloak over the pale sun as the gods rumbled their discontent, sending long streaks of cold fire across an endless sky.

Tiny drops of liquid ice fell on a mounted figure silhouetted against the brooding horizon, slowly at first and then in a steady drizzle.

The cold rain splattered on glistening chain mail, running down a hairy arm covered with scars onto the handle of the battle axe hanging loosely alongside. Dried blood turned crimson and dripped from the edge of the curved blade.

A heavily muscled stallion with a glistening black coat stood quietly looking out across the grey waves below. The animal ignored long cuts streaking the ebony satin of his legs and neck.

The battle rage was gone and an inner calm returned with the incoming tide. White vapor formed around the horse's head when his nostrils flared. Tiny clouds swirled away in the cold mist and like the screams of men dying in some forgotten battle, faded away.

The man's bushy brows were pulled low and streaked with gray. Icy, blue-green eyes stared out across the crashing waves, seeing nothing. Blood trickled unnoticed from a gash in his cheek and muscles flexed under the weathered skin.

He should feel something; exultation, disgust, remorse, something, anything, but his heart was empty. The old gods were dead and there was nothing he could do about it.

Lifting a gauntleted hand to wipe away the rain and blood, he paused as an image began to form on the long, sandy beach below. In his mind's eye, he traveled back to a day in his childhood on a smooth, sandy shore similar to the one stretching out before him. It had been a lifetime ago on a day very much like this one.

☼☼☼

It was late in the afternoon and a grey sky grumbled with restlessness as two young boys ran along the water's edge in the lengthening shadows. The unceasing pulse of water pushed the white, frothy foam farther and farther up the sandy beach, leaving a trail of seaweed containing tiny crabs and seashells.

The older boy appeared to be about nine, with dirty hair the color of rust and eyes blue as a winter sky.

"Hey Wulf, look what I found!"

He held up a pearl colored shell about three inches in diameter which appeared to be unbroken. The younger boy quickly flipped a rock he had been examining into the surf and ran to have a closer look.

"Fenris' fangs Eric! Tis beautiful! I wish I could find one – that wasn't broken."

Eric smiled at his younger brother and reached down to take his hand. He wiped the sand from the newly-acquired prize and placed it in the open palm. "There. You've looked really hard and deserve it."

Wulf's fingers slowly closed around the treasure as his eyes flashed from the shell to his brother and back again. "Oh, I couldn't. Are you sure?"

"I'm sure. Tis yours."

The small shoulders drooped slightly as the boy studied the shell. Hesitantly, he returned the present to his older brother. "Tis ok. You don't need to give me your shell. I'll find one of my own."

Eric stared to protest and then changed his mind, reaching down to accept the opalescent shard. He recognized the invisible battle Wulf had just won and didn't want to deprive him of the victory.

He nodded solemnly and grasped the shell gently. "You will grow into a fine man and mighty warrior someday. I am proud you are my brother."

Wulf nodded in acceptance of the compliment and let out a long sigh. It was nice to have praise, but he really wanted a good, unbroken sea shell.

He brushed wet sand from his hands onto clothes that were little more than rags, forced a smile, and started down the beach again.

Eric slid the shell into the patch his mother had sewn over his trousers to serve as a pocket, and patted Wulf on the shoulder.

Wandering down the beach behind his brother, he decided to try and spot another shell, but figure out a way for the younger boy to 'find' it.

A late summer wind moved in off the ocean and although it wasn't blowing hard, it was cold. The boys didn't have much in the way of warm clothes and Eric decided he had better talk Wulf into heading back or the child would be sick again for sure.

He put a hand to the side of his mouth and called, "Wulf! We better go. Come on, we'll come back tomorrow."

The younger brother had stopped a considerable distance down the shore, staring at the water's edge. He turned and hollered something unintelligible.

Eric waved him back, but Wulf motioned for him to come closer. Letting out an exasperated sigh, the older boy continued walking down the beach.

It only took a few minutes to cover the distance, but to Eric, they were going the wrong way. He walked up within hearing distance and repeated himself. "Wulf, we have to go home. Tis getting colder and mom will tan me if you get sick."

Wulf turned to look at his brother, but instead of saying anything, pointed to a strange mound protruding from the sand.

The older boy moved closer and noticed the hump resembled a little ramp, covered with seaweed and moss. Glancing up and down the sandy beach, he realized there was nothing in the area similar to the protrusion and it obviously did not belong there.

He knelt down next to the mound and started removing the covering of seaweed and debris. As his fingers closed around a clump of stringy moss, he yelped in pain and jerked back.

Grabbing his hand, he saw that he had cut it somehow. The wound did not seem serious and after soaking it in the salty water of the surf for a few minutes, the flow of blood stopped. The cut wasn't that painful, but he had a strange, tingling sensation in his arm.

He walked back to the sandy pile and looking around, spotted a branch of driftwood a little farther up the beach. Wiping the injured hand on his trousers, he quickly retrieved the dried branch.

He used the stick to clear the remaining seaweed from the mysterious object, uncovering the edge of an ancient blade of some weapon.

Caught up in the excitement of the discovery, both boys began digging in a frenzy to expose the object. In a matter of minutes, they were staring at the head of an archaic spear, incredibly sharp and covered with runes. The hardwood handle was made from some type of wood they didn't recognize and was broken off about four feet from the head.

Eric tossed his digging stick aside and reverently lifted the spear. It was heavier than it appeared, with a well honed edge.

"This is the greatest thing we've ever found!"

He glanced over at his little brother, adding, "And you found it Wulf! I wonder who it belonged to?"

The small boy's eyes were gleaming with excitement. "It belongs to us now. We found it, so tis ours."

Eric looked thoughtful a moment before nodding in agreement. "You're right. It does belong to us now."

He suddenly remembered the time and frowned. "We better head back home. Mom will have supper ready."

Wulf flashed a grin at his older brother and took off in a run.

Eric yelled at the receding back. "Hey! Wait for me."

Breaking into a trot, he soon caught up and both boys slowed to a walk. They headed along the beach towards home. Their excited chatter and laughter could have been heard for a considerable distance. That is, if anyone had been listening.

The boys were still expounding upon the glory of their discovery and the accolades they would receive when Eric stopped and grabbed his little brother by the sleeve. "Wait, listen." The faint screams were little more than snippets of indistinguishable sounds at first.

Wulf was grinning with anticipation when he stopped and noticed the change in his brother. "What? What is it?"

The older boy put his finger to his lips. "Quiet! Listen!"

Barely audible over the crashing waves of the ocean, the unmistakable sounds of a battle trickled through their consciousness. The two boys listened intently as they resumed walking down the beach. The muffled sounds became clear and they realized the screams and savage bellows were coming from their village.

Their bare feet were flying down the beach in a matter of moments, the spear in hand, but momentarily forgotten. A hundred paces farther on, they rounded a salient point on the beach; a lonely sentinel of black granite rearing up against the grey sky. They slid to a stop and stared towards home with their mouths agape.

Less than a quarter of a furlong down the beach, they could see the flashing red and yellow of huge flames. The fire was dancing above the tall salt grass lining the beach, lighting up the sky, reaching for the heavens.

The raging flames mirrored in the small, wide eyes burned an indelible image in the minds of both boys. Out of breath and terrified, they stood momentarily frozen on the deserted, windy stretch of beach. Uncertain as what to do, they walked hand-in-hand to within a hundred paces of their home.

There they stopped and dropped to their knees, staring at the conflagration that was consuming their world. Finally, Eric stood up, grabbed Wulf's sleeve and hauled him up the short, sandy incline towards the overhanging salt grass. He put a finger to his lips as he pulled his little brother down next to him. They huddled under the canopy of vegetation, watching the last rays of the pale, autumn evening fade to darkness.

The sounds of metal hitting flesh and bone, followed by shrieks and howls, filled a cold wind clawing its way down the coast. Eric slowly parted the heavy grass and raised his head. His eyes moved along the horizon until they fell on his village. Wulf watched the expression on his brother's face change from fear and curiosity to shock.

When he rose up to have a look, Eric dropped and jerked him back down.

"I want to see. What's happening?"

He started to complain at the mistreatment when he noticed the color had drained from his brother's face.

"What's wrong?"

The older boy was unable to find the words, shaking his head side to side. He rolled over onto his back below the overhanging grass and slowly the rose tint returned to his complexion.

Wulf was lying on his side, watching his brother. By the time the ruddy color had returned to Eric's face, tears were streaming down cheeks covered with a fine layer of sand and dust.

Throughout the remaining twilight, the boys lay in hiding. The intermittent screams of women and horses were heard less and less as the hours dragged by, and finally all was quiet except for the crackling flames.

The stench of sulfur and burning flesh drifted out to sea as a cold, black mantle settled over the somber coastline. The cry of seagulls could be heard overhead as Wulf huddled closer to his brother against the chill.

Numb with fear and exhaustion, the boys finally fell into a fitful night of dozing and nightmares. Movement in the older boy's eyelids betrayed the images that were flashing through his mind.

He was standing at the helm of a Viking longboat and they were plowing through six foot waves a thousand furlongs from home. Straight ahead, the coastline of a familiar landscape came into view. A score of similar ships followed in his wake.

There were dense forests, deer and beaver in abundance. He would settle here and raise his family. There would be no more wars or death. The graceful ships beached on a grassy stretch of shore. A tired but excited crew quickly unloaded a few necessities.

He headed inland. A beautiful woman with hair the color of marigolds walked by his side. The rugged coastline looked the same, but . . .

"Eric? Are you asleep?"

The voice was familiar, pulling him away from the face he loved so deeply.

It sounded like . . . Wulf? Where was he?

The voice came again. "I'm really cold Eric. Can we go home now?"

He blinked a couple of times and moved. Cramped muscles complained vehemently. Rubbing his face only introduced more of the small, abrasive material into eyes that were already red.

"Wulf? Oh, I must have fallen asleep. I dreamed I was . . ."

He stopped in mid-sentence, glancing at the pale face of his little brother and the grass hanging over their heads. The memories from the previous night came crashing into his consciousness.

Staring briefly at Wulf, he slowly raised up on one elbow from his sandy bed. Maybe it was just a nightmare – what he thought he had seen last night was just . . .

He sat up slowly and pushed the grass aside to see a few isolated areas of smoke rising from the remnants of what had been a happy, bustling hamlet only yesterday.

Looking carefully in all directions, he stood up and stared vacantly at the devastation. From this distance, all that appeared to be left were broken piles of black, smoking rubbish.

He brushed unseen sand from his clothes, took hold of Wulf's wrist and walked down the beach to a gentle slope leading up through the vertical embankment.

They climbed up the short incline and the stench of death and burnt flesh hit them full in the face. Eric glanced at Wulf and watched the terror moving into the small orbs. "Don't look. Close your eyes."

The boy was no longer hearing his brother's voice. The screams from the previous night were bursting the seams of his mind.

Eric stepped in front of the younger boy and took him by the shoulders, staring intently at his face. "WULF! Look at me."

He gave the child a violent shake and Wulf's eyes found his. The small mouth began to work soundlessly as tears welled up in the pale blue eyes.

Eric let out a long breath and stopped shaking the slim shoulders. He lowered his voice and spoke as steadily as his trembling body would allow. "We're alive and they're gone. Whoever did this is gone."

He clenched his jaw and pushed a dirty mop of hair back from Wulf's face. "We're going to be all right. There is another village to the south of here. We'll go there and ask for help."

Slowly, his brother's eyes focused on him and Wulf began to nod. He gave the boy a faint smile and turned to the carnage that lay behind them.

Taking hold of Wulf's hand, he walked woodenly though the piles of smoldering debris, dead animals and . . . bodies. Braggia, Valdur, Freyfilis, Gils, Gunna, Thorkell. All dead.

The boys recognized several more of the ashen, staring faces as they staggered through the village. A few bodies were ravaged or burnt to where there was no semblance of a laughing smile or slender finger remaining.

Silent tears streamed down tracks made the previous night. Nothing was said as they made their way towards the small hut that had been their home.

They stopped in front of the smoking heap that had been a source of happiness and security since they were born. A pale, white arm was visible under the blackened end of a ceiling beam. Eric started working his way towards the body.

"Eric! No!" A deep voice rang out.

The sound shattered the deathly silence, causing both brothers to jump and spin in terror. The tall apparition that had suddenly appeared behind them loomed like a menacing giant in the morning gloom. Momentarily frozen in fear, they were unable to move as the man moved towards Wulf.

Eric was frantically searching for anything that could be used as a weapon. He remembered the spear head, but they left that on the beach. A blackened kitchen knife was lying in the dirt a short distance away and he leaped for it. Grabbing the knife, he noticed the handle was nothing but charcoal and crumbled in his grasp. The blade was still solid however, and hot, searing the palm of his hand with an intense heat.

He gritted his teeth against the pain, leaping between the man and his little brother. He grabbed Wulf and pulled him back, turning to meet the stranger. The man stopped and watched as the boy rushed to defend his brother.

The brooding giant let out a long sigh, reaching up to push back the cowl covering his head.

"Eric, tis me. Your father."

The boy's eyes narrowed as he tried to see through the deceit. His father had been gone for over two years and was supposed to be dead. He wanted to believe that the man he had worshiped as a child had returned, but the terror of the night still controlled his mind. The towering figure standing in front of him did resemble the father that had left so long ago.

He glanced at Wulf; the younger boy's eyes were wide with uncertainty. Their eyes met and the small shoulders shrugged.

Turning back towards the man, Eric slowly lowered the knife. "Let me see your forearm, your left forearm."

The man's face broke into a knowing smile as he pulled the heavy sleeve of his tunic up to expose a hairy arm. There, running from a point just below the wrist to the elbow was a long, white line.

Thorvald received the wound in his first battle and had shown it to his wife with pride, burning up with a fever and out of his head. It was before Eric was born, but the boys had seen the scar and heard the tale many times when they were growing up.

The scar ignited a memory in Wulf's mind.

"Father!"

He raced around Eric and was in the man's arms before his brother could react. The huge brute tossed the boy in the air and roared with laughter.

Eric dropped the knife and walked slowly towards the man who had been his idol from as far back as he could remember. The Viking held Wulf with one arm and wrapped the other around Eric as his eldest son hugged father and brother as one.

"That's more like it. I thought you were going to skin me there for a while."

The brothers grinned through dirty, tear stained faces, the carnage and death surrounding them was forgotten for the moment. But only for a moment.

Eric released his father and stepped back, noticing a small cluster of people gathered at the edge of the village, quietly talking and glancing at the father and sons.

"You're not alone."

Thorvald set his youngest son down and glanced over his shoulder. "They're friends and companions. Come, I want you to meet them."

The man took hold of Wulf's hand and noticed Eric once again staring back at the ruins of their home. The hardened old warrior had seen too many villages left just as this one. The thing that made this different was the slender arm still visible under that blackened beam.

He placed a beefy hand on the slim shoulder. "War is a nasty business son. You kill or you die, and there's nothing nice about dying."

The boy glanced up at his father. "But . . . mom wouldn't have hurt anyone. Braggia, Valdur . . . they weren't mean, they didn't even know how to fight."

Thorvald released Wulf's hand and grasped his elder son by both shoulders. "When a battle comes, your enemy will not care if you know how to fight, he will kill you or you will kill him. Tis that simple. You must learn to defend yourself, for no one else will."

The words were callous, and the man's eyes glistened like chips of blue ice as he uttered them. Eric knew his father was telling him a basic, hard truth. The land they lived in was cruel and unforgiving, but the people had always been kind and caring. For the first time, he realized people could be just like the land.

He nodded that he understood and turned towards the strangers.

Once again, Thorvald grasped Wulf's hand and letting out a long sigh, led the boys out of the razed village.

Reaching the small cluster of humanity at the edge of the trees, the man introduced everyone to his sons with obvious pride. Each person in the group shook the small hands and a couple of old timers ruffled Wulf's hair.

There were several women and girls in the group also. The matrons looked disapproving at the rags the two boys were wearing, brushing them off and running fingers through mops of unruly hair. The girls giggled and hid behind their mothers or demurely watched Eric with an air of indifference, depending upon their age.

One battered relic of a man in the group appeared to be on the verge of death. He coughed up a wad of mucus and hacked it off to the side before acknowledging Eric's extended hand.

The boy tried not to stare when he noticed one eyelid hung over an empty socket in the scarred old face.

The old man's hands were large and surprisingly strong. A strange light flashed in his eye and he seemed to freeze when their hands touched.

Eric flinched at the sudden change in pressure. As the ancient Viking slowly released the boy, he kept staring at him intently, as though trying to see inside the boy's mind, or his soul.

"Who's your father, boy?"

The sudden question brought all of the conversations to an abrupt halt. Thorvald whirled around at the question, eyes flaring. "I am, Wotun. I thought I already made that clear!"

The old man glanced at the warrior for just a moment and then back at the boy. "Who's your mother?

Eric quickly looked to his father to see if he was in trouble.

Thorvald walked over to stand between the patriarch and his son. "What's this all about? What does it matter who his mother was?"

The old man did not seem the least bit intimidated by the towering warrior. "Humor me."

The huge Norseman gritted his teeth and growled. "Thjodhild, Thjodhild Thorkenson is . . . was his mother. She is among the dead behind us."

He glanced quickly at Eric and turned back to Wotun. "Now, tell me what this is all about."

The white haired warrior still had the boy frozen with his eye when he replied, "He has a spark of the old gods in him."

He released Eric from an ironbound gaze and looked at Thorvald. "You are a mighty warrior, but you do not have that fire. Where did his mother come from?"

Thorvald threw up his hands in exasperation. "She flew into the village one day and landed on a rock. She was pretty, so I picked her up."

Unperturbed by the outburst, Wotun stood quietly waiting for an answer to his question.

Finally, the boy's father exhaled. "She was brought to our village as a child. My uncle and his brothers had been on a raid and she was too little to 'use' and too big to leave, so they brought her and a few other girls with the livestock."

The withering eye of the old man returned to the boy and narrowed. "So. We have an unknown in our midst. Very interesting."

Thorvald wrinkled his brow at the comment. "Wulf had the same mother as Eric – as far as I know."

The last comment brought a ripple of laughter through the small group, but the old man simply turned to the younger brother. "Give your hand, boy."

The lad looked at his father before responding to the old man. Thorvald swung his massive head towards Wotun, indicating the boy was to comply.

Slowly, and with some trepidation, Wulf took a few steps and extended his hand as though he were placing it in a wolf's mouth. The wrinkled old claws closed around the small hand and held it firmly for only a moment. "Bah. Something is amiss."

The white-haired old wretch turned abruptly and stalked off with the ash branch he used as a cane. He walked a short distance away and sat down on a granite boulder.

Thorvald shook his head in confusion before turning to ask his sons if they had seen any game in the area in the last few days. Eric said he knew of a wooded glade some distance to the south where they occasionally found large rabbits and ground squirrels.

He had just finished telling his father about the rabbits when he remembered the spear.

"The spear! Wulf! We left it on the beach."

Whirling to run back towards the shore, a huge hand of iron grabbed his shoulder. "Whoa, where do you think you're going?"

He quickly looked up and his father was staring at him in surprise.

"The beach, Father. We found a spear yesterday and I want to get it."

Thorvald loosened the grip on his son. "Spear? Where did you find it? Tis probably rusted beyond use."

Wulf interrupted. "Oh no. I found it and tis like new, except the handle is broken."

The huge man crossed his arms, looking down at his two sons. "All right, run and get it, but don't take too long. We need to clean up here and keep moving."

They hurried back through the smoldering remains of the village, trying to avoid touching or looking at the corpses strewn about like abused and abandoned dolls.

They didn't recognize some of the bodies. The boys knew the strangers were part of the marauding band that had struck the village. From the stories they heard growing up; the men that died bravely with a weapon in their hand would go to Valhalla.

Dropping off the short, steep embankment, they ran a short distance back down the beach to the place they had spent the previous night. There it was, lying where they left it.

Eric picked up the spear and then stopped. Turning to Wulf, he handed the weapon to his little brother. "Here, Wulf. You're the one that found it. You should show it to Father."

The younger boy's face lit up as though Eric had just handed him a horse of his very own. Taking the ancient weapon reverently, he looked up at his older brother and solemnly nodded.

They turned back together and ran up the beach to find the little cut in the embankment. Climbing quickly to the top, they were soon standing next to their father once again.

Wulf was panting from the exertion, but his eyes were flashing with pride and excitement as he handed the weapon to Thorvald.

His father's face held a trace of amusement when he reached down for the weapon, but the look quickly changed to consternation when his hands closed around the shaft.

"Where did you say you found this?"

Eric blinked in surprise. He was sure his father would be proud and pleased at the discovery. Instead, he almost sounded angry . . . or afraid.

"About three furlong down the beach, next to the water." He paused briefly before adding, "Did we do wrong, Father?"

The grizzled warrior glanced from the weapon to the eyes of his son and his manner softened. "No. No, of course not son. You did no wrong. The marks, runes on the spear, I just . . ."

Turning his eyes in a sweeping gaze, they came to rest on the old white beard, resting on a rock. "Wotun. What do you make of this?"

He made his way through the little cluster of warriors and women, walking over to stand in front of the old man. He extended the weapon and waited patiently for the old Viking to acknowledge the question.

Wotun's eyes remained downcast when he responded. "I do not need to look. I know what you hold in your hands. Throw it into the deepest waters and never make mention of it again."

Thorvald studied the old man for a moment and exhaled quickly, dropping his shoulders. He knew asking further questions would serve no purpose.

The brothers were listening and when Thorvald turned away from the old man, Eric ran to his father's side. "No father! You can't throw it away! It belongs to Wulf. He found it and tis his now."

The clan leader did not understand why Wotun had told him to throw it away, but there had been no mistake in his intent; the white hair was serious and it must be done.

He pulled away from his son and shook his head. "I'm sorry, but Wotun would not tell me to do so unless there was no choice."

Eric seemed to be more upset than Wulf when he glared at Wotun and went back to comfort his little brother. The old man never looked up, but suddenly stopped wheezing and abruptly inhaled. "Hold! Thorvald wait a minute."

He slowly raised his head and resumed wheezing. "Did either of you boys touch the head of the spear?"

Eric glanced down at the red streak in his hand. Wulf said, "It cut Eric when we found it, but he soaked his hand in the water and tis fine now."

The old man stood upright, raising the staff he had been leaning on. "Gungnir! NOOO! NOOO!"

He slammed the wooden rod into the ground with a ferocity that belied the feeble stature of the man, weaving back and forth in frustration. "Not again! It can not be."

His chest was heaving from the exertion when he finally calmed down and spoke once more to Thorvald. "Do not cast it into the ocean. For a time, we must keep it with us."

He glanced at Eric, the message in the hard, grey eye unreadable as he turned away and started walking to the south.

Thorvald stood watching the receding back of the old man for a few minutes before he slid the spear into his arrow quiver and turned to the small knot of men near him. "We must send the remaining bodies to their rest."

The men began digging through the rubble, methodically pulling bodies from under broken, burnt beams and carrying or dragging them to the smoldering remains of the ships from the village.

By mid-day, several men were clearing debris from the southwestern part of the little town when a faint groan broke the muttering work. Thorvald was standing a short distance away when the men stopped abruptly and called to him. "There's somebody under here – I think they're still alive!"

Everyone in the area rushed to the call and began hurriedly clearing away the ash and remains of a dead horse. The small leg of a child was protruding from underneath the carcass and when they rolled the burnt roan over, a little boy appeared. He wiped a sooty hand across a dirty face and grinned at them. The clan leader stared in amazement at the lack of fear in the smiling face.

"You all right boy?"

The lad nodded quickly, but when he moved, the faint color drained from an already pale face. Glancing down, he noticed his left leg was at an impossible angle and blood was seeping from a compound fracture.

He looked from the leg up to Thorvald, smiled weakly and passed out.

"Hermod's heels, the boy's got a broken leg. Give me a hand lads."

The clan leader pushed debris away from the small body and studied the leg for a moment as several men gathered around him. Eric pushed through the group and stood beside his father.

"Snorrack! Is he alive Father?"

"Yes, but his leg is broken and he's losing blood. That dead horse must have been holding back the flow. We better act fast or he won't live long."

Several men with practiced hands straightened the fractured limb and set the broken bone. They quickly applied and wrapped a compress, followed by splints from nearby shattered boards, and bound the cast tightly.

Eric watched the men in silence and put his arm around Wulf when the younger boy timidly approached and stood next to him. "Is Snorrack going to be ok?"

"He's going to be fine Wulf. Father's friends fixed him up just fine."

The tow haired child nodded in acceptance of the statement and wiped a runny nose on a dirty, ragged sleeve. It was good to see at least one of their friends survived the bloody raid.

Thorvald put one hand on his hip and the other on Eric's shoulder. "The pain made him pass out."

"The boy turned and looked up at his father. "The pain? Oh, maybe, but Snorrack can't stand the sight of blood. He keels over like a chopped cornstalk at the sight of it."

Thorvald stared at his son in disbelief. "A Viking who can't stand the sight of blood? You jest with your father."

"Oh no, he's been that way for as long as I've known him. Even if he sees a cut finger, his face gets all pale and over he goes."

Snorrack's small eyelids fluttered and opened to reveal dusky blue eyes in a mantle of soot and dirt. The shy smile reappeared and Eric jumped to help his friend sit up.

"Eric! They didn't get you. How did you get away?"

"Wulf and I were gone. When we got back it . . . ."

He let the sentence hang unfinished.

Thorvald spoke into the awkward silence. "Snorrack's your name?"

The boy nodded in acknowledgement. "Yes sir, Snorrack Sturlesson."

"You didn't seem to be afraid when we found you. Why was that?"

The youth glanced at Eric before responding. "Well, if you were the terrible men that hurt everyone, you wouldn't have gone to the trouble of digging me out." Pulling some sticky goop from his hair, he added, "And since you did, I figured you were good."

The simple statement brought a slow smile to the craggy face as Thorvald shook his head. If you want the truth, ask a child.

Turning away, the hard, ice-blue eyes surveyed the carnage. "Well, we still have some work to do, let's get on with it."

Several of the men slowly nodded their heads in agreement and turned to the work that lay ahead. It took the better part of the day to find and carry all of the bodies to the charred remains of boats along the beach.

The brothers watched the men at work and wondered at the cold detachment they used in carrying the dead to the remnants of the ships. Some of the bodies were small and Eric turned away to wipe his face with a dirty sleeve. Wulf was still a child and people would understand why he was crying, but Eric was almost a man and it would be frowned upon.

He knew Thorvald had avoided their hut as long as possible, but finally his father threw back the beams with a controlled anger and slowly lifted the seemingly frail body. Muscles rippled beneath weathered hide as he stepped over the rubble and made his way toward the boats. Both boys watched as he carried their mother past them and noticed the lidded orbs were glistening.

Years later, Eric would realize his father cared more deeply than anyone could have imagined, but shared his innermost feelings with no one.

The sun was setting when the last of the bodies and limbs were tossed over the railing and oil from the remaining lamps spread about the ships.

The brothers stood at the water's edge, with the waves gently lapping around their feet when several torches were tossed over the railings. The men stepped back from the leaping flames. Working together, a dozen warriors put their shoulders to the prows and shoved.

The long, somber coffins rocked slightly as they crested the small surf and continued floating out to sea. Invisible arms seemed to surface from beneath the waves and wrap themselves around the entire lengths, pulling them farther away from the people on the bank.

In a matter of minutes, the small flotilla was engulfed in flames, sending broad reddish-orange and yellow fingers clawing towards the darkening sky. Slender, scarlet ribbons scampered across the rolling whitecaps of the ocean.

The entire area was quiet and dark by the time the last glowing ember was snuffed out in the black velvet expanse before them. Thorvald let out a long sigh and, placing a hand on Wulf's shoulder, motioned everyone to move out.

It was far into the night when they finally stopped and built a small fire for camp. A fresh water spring was nearby and the water was sweet. A couple of the men in the group managed to get a half dozen rabbits and some berries for supper.

The brothers sat on a rock outcrop near the crackling warmth, huddled close together, watching the rest of the men and women.

One of the younger warriors, a man named Bjortelm, had just returned with a flagon of water from the spring. As he passed it around and everyone took a swig, the man named Ulfberht wiped off his chin and belched. "That's the sweetest water I've had in many a day. I wonder if that's what the eternal spring tastes like."

Wulf looked at Eric and whispered. "Eternal spring?" The older boy shrugged and was about to say he didn't know what it was when he felt the gentle touch of a hand on his shoulder.

He turned and looked into the bluest eyes he had ever seen. The pale face was framed in a mass of hair the color of the morning sun.

"Tis a magical fountain in a faraway land. A land with tall trees, lots of deer and fruit hanging low on the bough."

Eric blinked and stared at the girl with his mouth hanging open. She resembled the woman in his dream. But was still a child.

He shook his head. His imagination was really getting the better of him. Closing his mouth and clearing his throat, he responded. "Magical fountain?"

"Yes. Tis true. Tis in a land far across the sea. I heard grandfather tell my uncle about it."

Eric glanced over at Thorvald to see if his father was watching the exchange. He was.

When he gave his father a questioning look, the man simply pursed his lips and shrugged. He could neither confirm nor deny the tale. The story of a magical spring was only one of many he had heard growing up. The only thing the warrior knew for sure was that nothing was certain – in this world or the next.

Eric turned back to the girl and attempted an awkward smile. He liked her but wasn't sure if he should, or why.

"I . . . I'm Eric."

"Yes I know. I'm Thorhild. That's my mom over there," she said, pointing across the campfire.

He moved over a little on the rock shelf and the girl hesitated only a moment before sitting down. There was an extended silence before the young pair began a quiet conversation.

Wulf was carving a wooden horse from a piece of driftwood when the old, one-eyed man caught his attention. The relic was sitting by himself at the far edge of the warm glow provided by the campfire. He seemed to be lost in thought, and the boy couldn't tell from the expression on the man's face whether they were pleasant or sad memories.

Mustering his courage, he stood and hesitantly walked towards the old Viking. He still held the stick he had been carving and stopped in front of Wotun, waiting for the man to acknowledge his presence.

After standing quietly for a few minutes, Wulf decided the old man wasn't going to look up, so he turned to go. A gruff, raspy voice stopped him. "What is it you want lad?"

He stopped and turned back towards the man. "I . . . I just wanted to ask . . . you seemed to recognize the spear we found. Do you know where it came from?"

Wotun slowly turned his one eye towards the boy and studied him, as if contemplating the answer. "Yes. Yes boy, I know where it came from."

Wulf's eyes flew wide at the answer. "You do? Where? Whose was it?"

The old man let out a long sigh. "Tis a long, sad story and I'm very tired son. Maybe some other time."

The boy couldn't hide his disappointment, but politely replied, "I understand. Thank you for talking to me."

As he turned to go, Wotun's voice stopped him. "Odin. It belonged to Odin."

Wulf spun around with eyes the size of silver coins. "Odin! The god Odin?"

The cracked old lips curled with a slight smile at the excitement in the boy's voice and the man nodded slowly. It was the first time Wulf had seen him smile and it made the ancient terror seem almost human.

"Tell me more, please."

Wotun glanced over Wulf's shoulder and noticed the boy's brother approaching. The older boy stopped a short distance away, not wanting to interrupt a private conversation.

The old man swung his head indicating he was to join them. Eric smiled in acceptance and walked over to put an arm around his younger brother.

Wulf began chattering excitedly when he recognized the newcomer. "Eric! The spear belonged to Odin, the god Odin! Wotun said he would tell us about it."

Eric drew back in surprise. There were countless stories about the ancient god, each one different than the last. He quickly decided the old relic must be making up a story for his little brother.

Turning a conspiratorial smile towards the white haired patriarch, he said, "I would also like to hear the tale of Odin."

The man's eye met Eric's but did not hold the look of humor he expected. The look was unreadable, like staring into a cold abyss.

The man ran wrinkled fingers with dirty nails resembling claws through the long, white beard cascading down onto his chest before beginning his story.

"A very, very long time ago, the world was a different place. In point of fact, there were nine different worlds – when time was young and giants walked the face of Jotunheim."

Wulf interrupted. "Was that when everything began? The Beginning?"

The old man scowled at the boy. Without answering, he pulled a heavy, gold ring off the third finger of his right hand and handed it to the boy. "Where is the beginning of this?"

Wulf held the heavy object in the palm of his hand and stared at it momentarily before answering. "There is no beginning. Tis a ring. It just goes round and round."

Wotun reached over to retrieve the ring. "Twas a time I thought Gunnungagap was the beginning, but it was not so. So it is with the world. There is no beginning and no end, just points in time."

The boy was somewhat taken back at the gruff response, but curiosity won out. "I don't understand."

Eric spoke into the silence. "Wulf. I don't think we understand a lot of things about the world we live in. Please, let Wotun continue with the story."

Wulf nodded. "I'm sorry. I won't interrupt again."

The old man's eye held the boy fast for a moment, then, as he turned away, seemed to be looking into a time long past.

"When life was young, there were nine worlds that all existed at the same time. The land of men; Midgard, was one of them.

"Odin lived in the beautiful world of Asgard with his family, relatives and friends. Those that lived there were known as gods to the other worlds. Beings were known by the world they lived in. Nidavellir was known as the world of the dwarves and Alfheim the land of elves.

"As a young god, Odin craved knowledge more than anything else and was constantly in search of new information. His travels led him to Yggdrasil, the cosmic ash tree.

"The branches and roots of the primal tree spread throughout the universe, connecting all nine worlds. The center of all life and wisdom flowed from the incredibly huge base of the verdant growth.

"Mystic power enveloped the area. Visions of the nine worlds pulsated in the surrounding aura. The brilliant colors, smells and sounds of countless beings and worlds splashed the trunk and branches in a constant deluge.

"Odin knew one way of gaining wisdom was through deprivation and fasting. With the aid of blithe spirits, he tied himself to the tree and hung upon the branches without food or water for nine days and nights.

"With the passing of the days and nights, his mind reflected on all of the marvelous and terrible things he had witnessed as a young god. There could be no doubt there was good and bad in the world. The question was how to defeat evil forever.

"As death approached, he felt the molten lava of worldly secrets and arcane power flowing into his veins. In appreciation of the gift, he cried out and died. With the knowledge gained from his self-inflicted pain, death could not hold him and he returned to life. With the newfound wisdom, he freed himself from the bonds of the tree to once again walk upon the surfaces of the nine worlds.

"To commemorate the experience, he cut a long, straight branch from the Yggdrasil and made a slender, unbreakable spear handle.

"He needed a spear point to equal the shaft, so he traveled to Nidavellir, the land of dwarves. The dark elves were known throughout the nine worlds for their ability to craft fine weapons, beautiful jewelry and objects of magic.

"A dwarf named Alvis forged the spear point with the power of arcane secrets and attached it to the sacred shaft of ash. He then carved mystical runes into the sharp edges that would guide the weapon to its destination with unerring accuracy."

Wotun's eye blinked and he stopped reminiscing. Glancing back at the boys, it was as though he had forgotten anyone was listening. Coughing and blowing snot out of one nostril, he finished the story abruptly.

"Odin carried the spear with him until Ragnarok, when twas broken." Looking down, he quietly added. "Beware of wisdom lads — it brings great sorrow."

Eric studied the ancient Viking as if trying to see through the translucent veil covering the grey eye. The tale didn't sound like something the old man had made up. "Odin knew everything, didn't he?" Adding, "I mean, he had all the knowledge of the nine worlds."

The old sage shook his head, smiling slightly. "No Eric, the knowledge of all existence is like smoke; constantly changing and impossible to grasp. What is, this moment – now, no longer is."

After a brief moment of silence, Wulf couldn't keep quiet any longer. "Ragnarok. They say that's when all the gods will die." The boy looked puzzled. "You talk like it already happened."

Wotun glanced at the boy with flashes of anger and pain shooting through the iris of the flinty, slate-grey eye. "Maybe it has – and nobody realizes it."

Wulf flinched at the sudden change in the old man's demeanor and looked at Eric. The older brother swung his head, indicating it was time to leave. Turning back he said, "Thank you for the story, Wotun."

Without looking at the boys, he nodded in acknowledgement and remained silent, once again lost in thoughts of long ago.

Chapter 10

The Banishment

The little band of Vikings had moored their ships several miles south of the Oslo Fjord a week earlier before passing through a single, small village on the trek to the north.

Thorvald and the crew had been gone from Norway for over two years and the homes and village they left behind were deserted when they returned. A brief search and a lot of questions led them to the charred remains that had been their friends and families in the lowland areas of the Jaeren District of Rogaland.

Four days after leaving the massacre, they entered a peaceful little hamlet a short distance from the quiet cove sheltering their ships. Countless fjords cut into the southwestern shores of Norway and this was one of those inlets. The lone sentry recognized them from the previous visit and soon the entire town turned out to meet the newcomers.

The elders welcomed the visitors as was the custom. After the age-old greetings were exchanged, the villagers asked about the trek to the north. Many had friends and relatives living along the coast.

Thorvald broke away from the large crowd that had assembled with a few of the village elders. Once they were out of earshot, he gave the older men the news of the savage raid in the village where he found his sons.

One of the eldest members of the group nodded at the news.

"Probably the Earl of Lade, Haakon Sigurdsson. He's been marauding up and down the coast for almost a year now. Soon there will be nothing left to take from others and he will have to travel overseas to find plunder and wealth."

Life was hard and often short in this savage land. The news of barbarous acts was accepted with the same aplomb that wolf attacks and killing winter storms received.

Much to the delight of the newcomers, the town had a young man who could play the pipes and a woman harpist. Rare commodities in a village this small. Soon after the arrival of the travelers, the mead was flowing freely and the raucous laughter of men and women alike was drowning out the gentle strains of music.

Unable to hear the musicians, the young men began chanting a war ballad while stomping their feet in a dust raising rhythm. The pounding synchronization rose more than dust. The eyes of the men flashed in appreciation of the women and the faces of the women were flushed with excitement.

At the peak of the revelry, men and women started fading into the surrounding groves in pairs. Eric noticed his father disappear with a comely lass who had joined the party late. She wasn't one of the women in their group and he assumed his father met her on the first visit to the village.

The boy watched them fade into the darkness. A frown crept over his face. He resented the strange woman taking his mother's place so soon after her death. He could not yet accept the fact that life was hard and short. Time lost looking back was never regained.

Most of the men and women traveling with his father soon disappeared, either with each other or with a member of the small village.

He wrapped his arms around himself in the growing cold and noticed a dispute on the far side of the huge fire lighting up the night sky. A heavy set warrior with a pocked complexion and dark red hair was yelling at an old woman.

He couldn't understand what was said, but it seemed the man was questioning the matron about another woman's whereabouts.

The old woman finally barked something back, threw her hands in the air and walked away. The man stood glaring at her back for a moment, then grabbed a young boy racing by with a group of lads his own age. After a brief discussion between the two, Eric saw the boy point in the direction his father had disappeared.

The man stared in the direction indicated for a moment before releasing the informant. His face contorted into an ugly grimace as he grabbed a broad-axe from the cache of weapons beyond the fire and stalked off into the darkness.

Eric immediately knew he needed to warn his father of the approaching danger. He dropped the warm slice of bread he had been relishing and ran headlong through an opening in the brush surrounding the village. Breaking out into a grassy plain on the far side, he spotted a small, tree-filled glade a hundred yards to the south.

Instinctively, he knew that was where his father was and started running.

The moon gave the crests of the rolling hills a silver glow in the cool darkness while his heart hammered in his chest. He slid to one knee when the faint light on the horizon was broken by the black silhouette of the broad stranger. He only hesitated a moment before leaping to his feet and slipping into the draw behind him.

Hurrying along the bottom of a swale that paralleled the man's movements, he reached the glade a few seconds before the crunching sounds of the warrior's heavy feet followed him into the darkness of the forest.

He stopped to let his eyes adjust to the dim light within the trees and called out softy. "Father! Where are you?" Silence.

There appeared to be a trail through the little grove, which he followed, breaking into a small meadow and almost colliding with a woman who was hurriedly attaching the brooches to her woolen hangerock. The skirt and apron were twisted and grass-stained.

The woman's face was flushed with fear, or excitement, he couldn't tell which. It relaxed when she saw the intruder was just a boy.

"What are you doing out here young man? Where is your family?"

Eric was about to answer when he was struck on the shoulder with a blow that sent him sprawling. He heard the man with the battle-axe bellow at the woman.

"Gerda! I thought so! Where is he?"

The woman acted confused by the accusation. "Volnar! What are you talking about? Where is . . ."

She was unable to finish the sentence.

As Eric struggled to his feet, he heard more than saw, the impact of muscle and bone against soft flesh.

The woman didn't make a sound as she went spinning backwards. She hit the ground hard and rolled over several times before slamming into the base of a tree. A few leaves drifted down near the motionless body.

The man glared at her and growled. "Get up! I know you're not hurt. Now tell me where he's at."

He moved the axe from the right hand to his left before walking over to kick her viciously in the side.

When she didn't react, he reached down and grabbed a handful of hair, lifting her head and the upper part of her body from the ground.

"By Thor's hammer woman, if you don't . . ."

He stopped mid-sentence when a shadow stepped into the soft moonlight. The silhouette tilted its head to the side and placed both hands on the outline of hips. "You probably killed her, you stupid ox."

With a roar of rage, the brute dropped the woman, and grabbing the axe in both hands, charged the phantom outlined in the pale light.

Eric recognized the dark shadow of his father and his heart leaped into his throat when he saw the flash of silver reflections along the huge blade of the broad axe. The man's words were unintelligible as he flew across the short distance separating the two men, intent upon cutting the interloper in half.

Thorvald stood with hands on his hips as the man charged. He didn't seem surprised, or even nervous, about the attack.

He turned slightly and dropped to one knee, bracing for the collision. As the man crashed into him, Thorvald straightened, throwing the attacker over his shoulder into the vegetation beyond.

The man somehow managed to roll through the grass without losing his grip on the axe or cutting himself. Jumping to his feet in a rage, he spun around, trying to locate the object of his fury.

Eric's father held his hands up in front of him, trying to reason with the man. "Volnar! Hold on. I didn't know she was your woman and there's no point in . . ."

It was to no avail. Once again, the brooding giant charged with the grass stained blade thrown back over his shoulder. The man was in no mood for reason and somebody was going to die.

The clan leader seemed to freeze where he stood. Eric wanted to scream at his father to move, but everything happened too fast.

The attacker swung the axe in an arc that would hit his opponent just above the collar bone on the left side. Thorvald pivoted back far enough for the slicing arc of the blade to brush the front of his tunic.

In one motion, he spun away from the attacker, drawing his sword as he turned. By the time he completed the pivot, the blade was at shoulder level and moving fast.

He meant to hit the man in the back of the head with the flat of his blade, but a torn piece of Volnar's tunic snagged the sword, twisting it. The force of the swing drove the edge of the weapon into the base of the skull.

The frayed cloth tore loose as the brute crashed to the ground. Thorvald quickly sheathed his blade and knelt beside the prone body. Rolling him over, he listened for sounds of breathing and felt the chest for any sign of movement.

After a few seconds, he straightened and looked down at the dark visage reflected in the moonlight. "Hel's hound Volnar, why couldn't you just let it go?"

He exhaled quickly and walked over to the body of the woman, rubbing his chin. Just as he knelt beside her, a small shadow appeared in the periphery of his vision. Spinning and leaping to his feet, he had his sword in hand; ready for another attack, when he noticed the new assailant was merely a lad.

His heart was hammering when the boy came into view. "Eric! That was you talking with Gerda. What in Odin's name are you doing here? I might have killed you."

The boy glanced from Volnar's body to his father and then to the woman. "That man Father. Is he dead?"

"Yes he is. I only meant to knock him out, but . . ."

Shaking his head, he turned back to the woman. "We need to get Gerda back to the village. I think she's badly hurt."

He knelt down again, lifted the unconscious woman and lightly carried her back towards the town.

A few people were still awake in various states of drunkenness or exhaustion, aimlessly wandering the abandoned streets, looking for something or someone that couldn't be found.

Thorvald turned to Eric. "Go and find someone who knows something about herbs and medicine." The boy nodded and trotted toward the main part of the village.

The Viking warrior reached what he considered the center of town, resting against the town well when he saw his son and two women hurrying towards him. The women were both from the village and recognized the limp form in Thorvald's arms immediately. "Gerda! What happened?"

They looked accusingly at Thorvald but could tell from the look in his eyes that they were barking at shadows. Dismissing the question, the women told him to follow them and headed off without waiting for a response.

A couple of streets away, they turned into a large structure built of logs, brush and wattle. Inside, a long table was quickly cleared and a fire started in the fireplace.

Shortly after the snapping flames chased the cold from the room, Gerda opened her eyes and groaned. Seeing Thorvald, she smiled slightly and drifted off again.

Several hours later, the sun began pushing the cold, gray dawn over the western hills. The entire village was gathered around, or in, the lodge with Gerda and Thorvald.

Thorvald explained the accident several times and by the time the village council was in session, the story had been retold three-fold, changing a little with each telling.

"Quiet!" A village elder shouted above the noisy den in the great hall. He slammed his fist down on a table where seven men were seated and bellowed over the arguments and chatter filling the room. "Shut up and sit down!"

The noise subsided as people found seats and lowered their voices. Finally, everyone was quiet and watching the leaders of the village discussing the death of Volnar and what was to be done.

The village elder who had ordered silence was a grizzled old warrior named Gunter. He finished listening to the comments of the man on his right and turned back to the gathering in the hall. "We have heard various stories about what happened last night and some of them do not make any sense at all. We would like to hear from the stranger who is accused of killing Volnar."

Eric's father stood up in the middle of the crowd and worked his way through the mass of humanity, finally standing in front of the table of seven. "I am Thorvald Asvaldsson. I killed Volnar without malice. Twas an accident."

Gunter studied the man for a moment then nodded. "Explain what happened."

Thorvald glanced at his sons before addressing the council. "Gerda and I went to the glade south of here to be alone when Volnar showed up and attacked us. He knocked Gerda out and tried to kill me with an axe."

The Viking paused to study the reaction on the faces of the men at the table. The expressions indicated they were considering his words. Good. They hadn't already decided he was guilty of murder.

Inhaling quickly, he continued. "I have killed many men, but had no reason to kill Volnar. I only meant to knock him out with the flat of my sword. The blade twisted upon impact and killed him. That is all I can offer in my defense."

One of the younger men at the table hissed his disbelief of the statement. Gunter turned toward him. "Gorm, if you have something to say, say it."

The man turned an icy glare at Thorvald. "The stranger is

obviously a killer. Volnar was a simple farmer and a friend of mine. An experienced warrior does not 'accidentally' kill an opponent. I would rather imagine our friend here was lying in wait for poor Volnar and attacked him from behind; killing him in cold blood."

Thorvald stiffened at the accusation, returning the glare with a look that made the younger man avert his eyes.

Eric leaped up in the muttering crowd and yelled, "That's a lie. The dead man attacked my father. He was just trying to defend himself. He didn't even hit him the first time he was attacked."

A hush fell over the muttering crowd. They were angry at the death of the villager, but weren't fools and could tell from the boy's voice that the outcry was not staged in his father's behalf.

Gorm stood, raising his hands for attention. "It does not matter how Volnar died. He was going to take back what was his and this man killed him. Gerda was Volnar's wife and he had every right to attack the stranger."

Gunter spoke in a strong and controlled voice. "Sit down Gorm."

The younger man started to object and then dropped into his chair, barely able to control the anger boiling within.

The leader of the council turned to the rest of the men seated at the table. "What say you?"

One by one, the council members whispered softly to the elder spokesman and then remained quiet.

After everyone at the table gave their decision to Gunter, he addressed the gathering in a level tone that could be heard throughout the hall.

"Thorvald Asvaldsson, the council agrees you did not murder Volnar in anger, or for vengeance, but you did kill a member of this village and for that you must leave this land for a period of not less than three years. If you are seen again before that period of time, you will be killed or forced to kill in your defense. Do you accept this judgment?"

Thorvald looked at the council leader only a moment before nodding slowly in agreement. The decision was just and he would abide by it. Clasping his hands in front of him and thus acknowledging the council's wisdom, he pivoted smoothly and walked out of the huge, smoky hall.

Eric and Wulf were on his heels and although they weren't sure exactly what happened, their father was alive and wasn't going to be punished for killing the villager.

Wulf rushed in front of his father and started chattering excitedly. "They let you go Father! You're free! Aren't you happy?"

The clan leader didn't have the heart to tell his sons that banishment was a form of execution whereby nature pulled the rope or swung the axe. The distant lands to the south and east were still smoking from the last Viking raids and the inhabitants would be waiting with vengeance in their hearts. North was a vast wasteland of ice and white bears. The only course left was to sail west. West into the unknown. The chances of surviving such a trip were abysmal.

Years earlier, Thorvald's older brother had told him of a land to the west, a land of ice and terrible creatures, but habitable and some tales said there were men living there. No matter, it would be a great adventure and no one lived forever.

Pausing at the thought of a new experience, a small, resolute smile broke the craggy face as he grabbed each of his sons under an arm and increased his stride.

Chapter 11

The Voyage

The long, sleek ships cut through the rolling waves and whitecaps with an ease that astounded everyone but Scandinavians. Two of the boats were eighty feet in length and the third was over sixty feet long. A love of the sea lured the Norsemen to the far points of the world when most of Europe was still chained to the fear of dropping off the far edge of the great waters.

Thorvald stood high on the stern of the lead ship with the sting of the icy ocean's spray biting into his leathery face. The warrior gave no thought to the discomfort. Layers of ice formed on the rust-colored beard, but the man couldn't pull his eyes from the horizon. At long last he would discover for himself the myth, or reality, of the fabled lands to the West.

The northern sky was ablaze with a luminous dance of color, casting a surreal glow over the entire horizon. Beautiful Valkyries thundering through the black, swirling clouds on magnificent steeds were . . .

A shout broke into his thoughts. "Thorvald! Tis Eric. Come quickly. He is taken ill."

The warrior turned his back to the wind and looked down. Thorson, the first mate, was standing mid-ship with an icy sleet streaming from his face.

"Eric?"

The man nodded in assent.

Stepping down to the deck flooring, Thorvald glanced quickly at Thorson to see anything unsaid in the man's eyes. There was concern, but nothing more.

He nodded quickly, pulled his cloak a little closer and worked his way towards the boy. A short distance past mid-ship, he pushed his way through a group of women huddled around his eldest son.

A low growl issued from the large chest. The boy was as pale as bleached driftwood. Protected by a canopy of hides, he was covered in sweat. Thorvald's beefy hand briefly covered the wet forehead. It was warm, in spite of the biting cold.

Thorvald leaned back before turning to Thorson. "Get Wotun and bring him here." Thorson spun around and disappeared through the cluster of people.

In a matter of minutes, Thorvald could hear the muttering of the old man as they approached. "Quit yammering Thorson, I'm coming. I'm coming."

Thorvald stood as the two men approached and looked from Wotun to his son. "What's the matter with him?"

The patriarch was scowling, shoving men out of his way. He grimaced and moved closer to Eric, pushing Thorvald aside. Bending down, he took the boy's hand.

After holding the small hand for a moment, he dropped it and let out a long sigh. "Tis as I feared. Gungnir has . . . affected the boy."

Thorvald glanced from his son to the old man. "The spear? Tis truly Odin's spear they found?"

Wotun whirled around in sudden anger. "Yes! Yes it is the cursed, marvelous spear. I thought . . . hoped twas destroyed. I was wrong." Looking back at Eric, he added, "Before twas broken, a wound from the spear was always fatal. I wasn't sure if it would still the same."

Thorvald stared at the old Viking as though he had never seen him before. Searching his memory, he really didn't know that much about the ancient warrior. They had picked up survivors, strays and slaves up and down the coast of Europe and the faces blurred over time.

Wotun was the old man they found washed up on the beach of an emerald green island to the south. There were countless islands off the coast of Europe and they found him on one of the larger ones. The man was obviously a Norseman and seemed to know a great deal about medicine, runes and warfare so they welcomed him aboard.

Thorvald grasped Wotun by the shoulder and roughly turned him around. "Who are you? How do you know that broken spear was really Odin's?"

The grey eye flashed in anger at the treatment. "Tis of no matter. We must try to save the boy."

Turning to Thorson, Wotun barked, "Get the spear and bring it here."

The first mate looked to Thorvald, who nodded. "Do as he says. Tis in my quiver, hanging on the mast."

In a matter of minutes, the first mate returned, holding the quiver of arrows and broken spear.

Wotun reached over without hesitation and pulled the spear out of the quiver. The Viking warriors stepped back in surprise at the sudden hum emanating from the spear. It was vibrating as though it had been cast a great distance and slammed into a mighty oak.

The old man straightened to a height of over six feet and clenched his jaw. Watching the bent, old patriarch stand with the rigidity of youth was a surprise in itself, but seeing him calmly draw the blade across his hand until a bright red crimson flow was evident brought a deadly silence to the area.

Several warriors stepped back in awe at the faint aura pulsating from the ancient warrior. No one knew what it was they were witnessing, but every man felt the power of an age long-forgotten in that moment.

Wotun ignored the blood flowing from his palm as he reached down to pick up Eric's hand. Thorvald knew the old man was going to cut the hand of his son, but something in the white-hair's demeanor wouldn't permit him to interfere.

He watched woodenly as Wotun drew the blade across the small palm and held it so the flow of blood combined with his. After a couple of minutes, the old man released the hand of the youth, lowering it to the boy's side. Telling the men to bandage the cut, he turned and left.

Thorvald knew Wotun was trying to save his son, but he didn't understand what was going on and he definitely didn't like it.

He pulled some liquor and rags out of a nearby chest, doused a rag with the fiery liquid and gently wrapped his son's hand with it. Eric had hardly moved when Wotun cut his hand, but the burning of the alcohol caused him to groan and roll away from the pain.

Thorvald and Thorson stood quietly watching the boy until he stopped moaning and drifted off into a deep slumber. They finally looked at each other and nodded before silently returning to their duties.

The wind increased steadily, buffeting the square sails and moaning in a low wail that sent shivers up the spines of the crew. The calm surface became a stormy sea, tossing the long ships from the crest of one wave to the next. Aegir, the god of the seas, did not seem angry as much as restless. You could feel it in the air, the uncertainty, the taint of death and destruction just beyond the horizon.

Thorson barked at the crewmen to lower the sail and lash everything down. It appeared they were in for some rough weather.

Thorvald resumed his lonely vigil at the bow of the sleek vessel. He had been standing there for a few minutes when movement in his peripheral vision snapped his head around. Wotun appeared next to him, staring out across the blustery horizon.

The grey-beard was unaffected by the biting cold and icy spray as he stood besides the Viking leader and watched the white capped ridges of the rolling ocean.

Without turning his head, Thorvald spoke. "Will Eric live?"

Wotun remained silent a moment before responding. "I don't know. Much of the power in the runes has changed."

"You must know something . . . the mixing of the blood. By the gods, Wotun, talk to me!"

The old Viking whirled in anger. "'By the gods'! Mortals are such fools. Don't you realize . . ."

Catching himself, he stopped shouting and quickly turned away.

The warrior had never seen this side of the old man and was uncertain with whom he was dealing. "Don't I realize what?"

Wotun no longer seemed to see Thorvald, or even the stormy waters that faded into the horizon. "The gray wolf no longer watches the hall of the gods. Ragnarok is over. What was, is no more."

Once again a tired, bent old man, he turned and hobbled away.

Thorvald watched the man's back disappear into the cold darkness that settled over the deck. Lost in thought, he tapped the railing with his fist, realizing Wotun had just told him something very important and he didn't understand what it was.

Chapter 12

The Curse of Andvari

Morning was difficult to define, as the night morphed into day without an apparent break in between. Somewhere in the time between total darkness and the gray light of the day, it became possible to see more than a few feet and that was morning.

Eric had slept through the night, the cold sweat disappearing a few hours after Wotun shared his blood. Wulf awoke early and went to see how his older brother was doing.

Sitting beside the makeshift cot, the younger boy knew his brother needed sleep and was content to sit and watch him breath. Eric had always been his guiding star and mentor. No one knew about the uncontrollable panic Wulf felt when he found out his older brother was seriously ill.

Now everything was ok again and he smiled to himself at the thought. Leaning over to peer at his brother's face, the color was good and . . . his eyelids were moving slightly. Wulf smiled broadly. He knew Eric was dreaming, dreaming about that blond-haired girl they met back in the village of their homeland.

Eric was dreaming, but it wasn't about the blond-haired girl. He was a grown man walking through the woods with two younger men. One was a lad named Loki and the other was his younger brother, Hoenir.

Like many young men, Loki was a mischief maker. However the antics of his youth would become a terrible, dark evil by the time he was grown. The middle-aged man knew the youth would be the downfall and death of the gods. It was a strange dream.

The memories of that man were those of the god Odin. There were more vague images at the edge of his mind he couldn't quite see. The road ahead through the laughter, tragedy, battles and destruction that would eventually befall the gods of Asgard was clear. And for now it was the only road visible – there was no course but to follow it.

Loki ran ahead to look for fish or game along the inland stream

they were following and disappeared around a bend upriver. Soon
thereafter the brothers heard excited shouts.

"Odin! Hoenir! Come, see what I have killed!"

The brothers smiled at each other and continued their steady pace
until they broke into a small clearing at the base of a waterfall. Loki
was standing on the far side of a large, blue-green pool of clear water
at the base of the falls. A fair-sized animal covered with fur was lying
at his feet.

Wading through the shallow area below the pool, they could see
Loki had killed an otter. The animal was quite large; the head bashed
in with a rock Loki was still holding in his hands.

"I snuck up on it. It never saw me coming."

The young man was grinning in pride and waiting for
compliments.

Hoenir walked over and clasped him on the shoulder. "Well done
Loki! We'll feast well tonight."

They had just finished dressing the otter when the smell of wood
smoke drifted though the trees and downriver with the current of the
stream.

Hoenir noticed it first. "Smoke! That smells like the warmth of a
home fire."

Glancing over at Odin, he added. "We can't eat all of this before it
spoils, maybe we should see if they would like to share some meat . . .
and a bed?"

Odin lifted his nostrils to the air and after a moment, nodded.

"I agree. It cannot be far, or the smoke would never have reached
us."

The three men quickly found a pole to carry the otter and followed
the stream northwards, soon approaching a small hut surrounded by a
small area of cleared land. There were numerous rows of vegetables
growing in a small garden surrounded by a pole fence to keep animals
out. Smoke was curling out of the rock chimney and the faint, yellow
glow of candles was evident in the windows.

Loki ran up to the door and began banging rather loudly on the old
wooden boards.

Odin barked. "Loki! We are guests here, remember your manners."

The Viking god scowled at the youth and was about to lecture him
further when the door opened.

An elderly, kindly looking farmer opened the door and seemed
surprised and pleased at the sight of the strangers.

"Good day to you. May I be of service?"

Odin stepped forward and nodded slightly. "We are travelers from a far land and are seeking shelter for the night."

The farmer beamed at the request. "Ah yes. Please come into my house and share the warmth and small comforts."

When he stepped aside to usher them into the interior, he noticed the dead otter on the pole, lying a short distance behind the strangers. The expression on the man's face changed from a pleasant demeanor to shock, as his eyes widened in recognition of the dead animal. "Ottar!"

The man pushed Hoenir rudely aside, walked over quickly and knelt beside the bloody carcass. Running his fingers through the silky fur, Hreidmar turned glistening eyes back towards the three strangers. "You murder and butcher my son then ask for lodging? What kind of fiends are you?"

Odin stared dumbfounded at the farmer for a moment then glanced at Loki and Hoenir and finally, back to the grief torn man. "We did not know. It seemed to be an otter and nothing more."

The farmer stood slowly, trembling in anger. "Well he was more than an otter, much more. He was a *shape changer*, a good and gentle son, and the light in this old man's eyes."

Slowly wiping a bloody hand on his worn tunic, the man's features changed. Inhaling deeply, his eyes rolled backwards in his head as he straightened, extending his arms in an enveloping manner.

"You will regret your foul, careless murder."

The man began muttering an arcane incantation to the gathering storm clouds and Odin felt bands of iron encircling his arms and legs. He called upon the power in his sinews, but it was to no avail. In the blink of an eye, he was unable to move. Loki and Hoenir were also bound in the invisible coils.

This old farmer was more than he seemed. He had to be what the inhabitants of *Midgard* referred to as a magician, sorcerer or shaman. Odin wasn't afraid, but he was definitely angry.

"I told you twas an accident. Now release us before I call the gods of *Asgard* down upon you."

Hreidmar hesitated for only a moment before deciding. He was too angry to be rational. "Call them down."

Odin glared in frustration. If he called upon the other gods for help, it would be a sign of weakness. That was completely unacceptable.

The man was so angry he was taunting his prisoners, welcoming death.

The Viking god reconsidered his tactics. "Maybe that won't be necessary. We are gods from *Asgard*. Our powers are many, maybe there is someway we can make up for your loss."

The mage's eyes narrowed as he considered Odin's remark. An image of the crooked little dwarf, Andvari, came to mind. The ugly dwarf possessed incredible skills and power in the black arts. According to legend, he also had a tremendous horde of finely worked gold and jewels. The farmer knew this because he had lost two of five sons in quests for the treasure.

He circled the bound gods of *Asgard* like a snake coiling around a trapped rabbit. Tugging on a long, wrinkled nose he said, "Maybe. There is an ancient tale of a dwarf that hordes an incredible treasure. If the gold and jewels of the little man were delivered to me. I might see things differently."

Hoenir glanced at Odin. "Andvari's treasure."

Odin nodded slowly, even the gods had heard of the wealth of this dwarf. So much gold it would turn the kindest heart into a dark stone.

"Everyone has heard the tale, but no one knows where the dwarf's underground hideaway is."

A faint smile cracked the old farmer's lips. The glint of greed pushed the anger and grief aside. "I know."

For the first time, Loki spoke up. "Release me and I'll find the treasure and bring it back to you."

Odin flashed an irritated glance at the young god. The boy had promised the magician everything he wanted; there was nothing left to bargain for.

Seeing the look in the older man's eyes, Loki quickly added, "But you must free my friends and let us continue our journey unharmed."

Hreidmar looked from the youth to Odin. "If I release you, do I have your oath the boy will do as promised – or your lives are forfeit?"

Odin nodded slowly, knowing he would regret this agreement more than any other he had ever made.

The bands restraining the powerful arms dissipated and the blood rushed through the restricted veins once more. Loki was excited about a new adventure and immediately began questioning the farmer about the dwarf's whereabouts.

The magician was indeed a power to be reckoned with. He weaved his hands slowly in the air and a three-dimensional image of the waterfall where Loki killed the otter came into view. The vision moved upstream to include the clearing in which they stood. Pointing to some small figures next to the little hut, he looked from Odin to Loki. "Look closely and you can see where we are."

Loki stepped closer and his eyes flew wide. There were tiny images of four people standing outside the hut. He dropped to his knees like a boy of five and peered closely at the tiny people. "Hey that's us, isn't it?"

Twisting his head to look towards the sky above, he added, "Why can't I see us looking down?"

Hreidmar frowned at the question and looked skyward. When he realized what the young man was asking, he growled, "It doesn't work that way. Now be quiet and watch."

Slowly, the three-dimensional image moved northwards. The waterfall disappeared first and then the hut.

The image seemed to be following the thread of the stream. The four men sat in silence, watching the view move northwards. Countless bends and waterfalls passed before the flow of water moved above timberline into alpine meadows and tundra. Finally, the stream dwindled to little more than a trickle and a pristine, mountain lake came into view.

The lake looked like a thousand others the Vikings had seen in their travelers, but here the vision stopped. Hreidmar stared at the transparent image for a few moments before he finally spoke. "See that quiet bay on the west side of the lake? Watch."

Throwing a little powder that resembled ashes from a fireplace over the image caused it to waver slightly and then freeze. The shape of the lake changed slightly, leaving one inlet as a dry swale with a dark hole in the side.

The mage shook his head in satisfaction. "Nothing more than a dwarf's trick, but it took me twenty years to find it."

Odin grasped Loki's arm, as if that would somehow protect him. Giving the farmer a hard look, he glanced back at the image. "How do you know that's where the dwarf keeps his fortune?"

The image of two dead sons trying to steal the treasure came into the man's mind. Both had entered that cave less than a year apart and neither was ever seen again.

"That is not your concern. Just know and understand that is where the gold resides . . . and the dwarf."

Loki was having trouble controlling his excitement. "Well let's get on with it."

Hreidmar produced a small, leather bag and handed it to the youth. "Here, you will need this when you get to the lake. Just scatter some upon the water and the entrance to the underground caverns will become visible."

Odin wanted to tell Loki not to go, they would figure some other way of solving the dilemma. Fate, call it what you will, held his tongue and he knew there was no other course.

A great sadness fell over his countenance as he watched the enthusiasm exude from his young charge. The foundation of countless ages would crack and fall in a precipitous avalanche of death and destruction due to this simple act.

Loki hefted the little sack and saluted his comrades in parting. "Well here goes. See you in a couple of days."

The old magician smirked at the confidence in the young man. "It's a week's hard travel one way; I doubt that we will see you . . ."

He stopped short as Loki transformed into a huge falcon.

Giving a scream of excitement as he departed, the yellow eyes met Odin's for just a moment and the huge bird took flight.

The three men watched the enormous wing span disappear over the trees and fade from sight.

Hreidmar turned to Odin. "Another *shape shifter*. I did not see it. Your son is clever -- I hope he is successful."

Odin heard the man's unspoken words; 'but I doubt if he will be', and his anger flared. "He is not my son, but if there's something you're not telling us you will deeply regret it."

The farmer's eyes flashed in defiance. "You know what I know. Except I have already lost two of my sons to that soulless monster."

The missing pieces fell into place. The man was tired of sacrificing his sons for the golden horde. He was now planning on Loki's dying in another vain attempt. A life for a life.

Odin was the oldest of the *Aesir* gods and tired of the endless and futile struggle. The wisdom gained from hanging on the Yggdrasil tree unto death had given him foresight of things to come. Ragnarok, the final battle and Doom of the Gods, would come and he could finally rest, but the event was in a dim future. There were many roads to travel and much in the way of preparation that must be done.

Refusing any hospitality from the farmer, Odin and Hoenir walked a short distance away from the cottage and set up a rude campsite. They would wait for Loki's return under the stars.

The huge falcon cast a fast-moving shadow on the ground far below, causing rodents and smaller birds to dash for cover. In less than an hour, the lake came into view and the magnificent bird alighted softly at the edge of the quiet bay.

Small animals in the surrounding trees were the only ones to see the huge predator change into a man resembling the inhabitants of *Midgard.*

Loki hefted the bag of dust, trying to guess what the contents were as he approached the water's edge. He stopped a few feet from the edge of the gently lapping green water and marveled that something which seemed so real could be imaginary.

Slowly opening the sack and reaching inside, his hand recoiled at the feel of the powder within. It made his skin crawl. Loki was mischievous and always getting into things, but this stuff was just downright disgusting.

He threw a handful of the glistening powder out across the water, half expecting it to just settle to the depths. Instead, the cool, clear water completely disappeared, leaving a dry swale with a dark hole in the far side.

Attaching the little leather pouch to his belt, he headed directly towards the opening in the ground. Stopping at the entrance, he leaned forward to peer carefully into the darkened interior, trying to sense danger or a trap.

The air was cool, but he could not see anything to cause concern. He moved into the darkened interior and felt like he was crossing a threshold. It occurred to him that he had indeed changed worlds; he had crossed over from *Midgard* to *Nidavellir,* the realm of dwarves.

He had heard many tales of dwarves, but this was the first time he had actually entered their world. Many of the stories were beyond belief. According to some of the gods, the dwarves could make beautiful jewelry and terrible weapons, all with the same forge on the same day.

The tunnel's interior became quite dark a short distance from the entrance, but being the god of fire, Loki simply ignited a small flame in front of him to light the way. He smiled at the memory of discovering he could do this as a child.

The corridor appeared to be natural for the most part, a few places had been chiseled back to widen the path, but the walls were still rough and uneven. Water from underground springs began to appear on the glistening walls and then in the form of small streams that came out of the pores in the stone, running in rivulets down the rocky path.

The air became noticeably cooler as he continued the descent. The glistening walls began to reflect an amber hue in the light from the small flame preceding him.

He stopped to examine one shiny area and gasped at a three-inch wide vein of gold running up the tunnel wall, disappearing into the darkness above. Well, he knew where the dwarves got most of their gold; *Nidavellir* was laced with the precious metal.

The thought brought a frown to the young face. Andvari was supposed to have stolen the gold for his treasure horde from the Rhine Maidens. Why would there have been a need to steal with such a wealth of material so readily at hand?

He pushed the puzzling question from his mind and continued into the descending corridor.

Farther down, the tunnel widened into a myriad of caverns of various sizes. He increased the size of the flame lighting his way and noticed the glistening reflections from many of the rock walls were something other than gold or water.

Stopping to study his surroundings, he looked down and noticed the gravel at his feet was also sparking with color.

He reached down to lift a ruby the size of his thumb. Shaking his head in disbelief, he dropped the stone in a small pocket in his tunic.

The caverns were becoming numerous and larger. It was getting hard to tell where he should be going. He stopped as a multi pronged fork in the gravel trail led off in several directions from the same point of diversion.

He reached into the little pouch containing the magic dust and scattered some over the trails. Nothing changed. The different paths weren't an illusion -- he would have to decide upon one.

Loki was young and excitable, but not a fool. There were nine trails leading away from that point. Starting at the left and walking a short distance down each one, he waited for Skuld to send him a signal. The norm known as *The Decider*, had never let him down and he trusted the fate completely.

Finally, on the seventh path, he felt the oppressive, heavy threat of danger dissipate, and without testing the remaining trails, headed confidently down the steep incline.

The tunnel quickly narrowed to an arm span in width and the ceiling dropped to where he could barely walk upright.

He was beginning to wonder if he had indeed taken the wrong path when the small tunnel suddenly opened into the biggest cavern he had encountered. A small lake in the center of the cavern appeared to be a flat surface of black obsidian until the light of the fire danced across it.

The red and yellow flames were reflected in water that was impossibly clear. Walking to the edge of the pond, Loki looked down into the crystal depths. There appeared to be no bottom because of the incredible depth of the pool. The steep sides slanted downward and eventually disappeared in darkness. The light from his flame plunged into the depths with a cheery flare, but eventually gave way to the growing darkness.

Loki noticed that much of the rock in this area had been worked with hammer and chisel. There were several openings cut into the cavern wall on the far side of the little lake. He was pretty sure he must be getting close and starting to feel apprehensive for the first time. The dwarf was known throughout the nine worlds and other intruders must have tried to steal his treasure. What had happened to them?

As if in answer to his unspoken question, he noticed the white reflection of a pile of bones in the midst of scattered boulders between the pool and cavern wall. Climbing a large, sloping rock, he stopped at the edge to look down into a pile of skulls and skeletons. It looked like the remains of a frost giant, humans from *Midgard* and several fair folk.

He wiped a hand nervously across his face and for the first time, felt a little unsure. The farmer had caught them by surprise. He was on his guard now, but what was he supposed to guard against?

Walking to the edge of the water, he sat on a flat rock about two feet high and began chewing on some dried meat he had brought.

The image of a fish flashed by and Loki noticed it was a huge salmon. At first it didn't register in his restless mind how odd it was for a salmon to be swimming around in a cavern miles from the nearest sea. Then it hit him and the next time the fish flashed by, he was ready.

He tossed some of the farmer's powder over the clear water and the image of a dwarf, floundering below the surface, struggling for air, suddenly materialized.

A bent, ugly little man dragged himself up on the bank, glaring daggers at the stranger that had invaded his domain and exposed him.

"What do you want? What is the meaning of attacking me in my home?"

Loki jumped to his feet when the dwarf materialized and his mind was racing, the pile of bleached bones still fresh in his mind. "I mean no harm. I just wanted to talk to you."

The little gnome stood dripping water and studying the youth with suspicion lining his face. His eyes were darting from Loki to a faintly lit doorway in the cavern wall. "Talk about what?"

Loki glanced towards the opening. The man had just given away something. What was it?

He turned and started moving towards the doorway when the dwarf barked. "Wait! Where are you going?"

That was enough for Loki; he dashed towards the door with the dwarf in pursuit. Andvari was slower and Loki rushed into the adjoining room well ahead of the little man. The young god slid to a halt at the glittering horde within the small room. The chamber was strewn with finely worked golden objects, jewels and tools.

Something told him that the dwarf was not rushing to protect the gold; there was something else in this room. A talisman or. . .

"Get out of here! Leave now or I'll . . ."

Loki turned to see the dwarf shaking his fist in fury. The dark, little eyes were flashing to a point behind him. Whirling around, the god was looking at a work bench; a plain, wooden table with a hammer, tongs and various engraving tools.

He grabbed the hammer and tongs, spinning back towards the dwarf. Andvari's dark face turned pale, or at least a lighter shade of brown.

"Stop! What do you want? Be careful with those."

The dwarf was holding up his hands, almost pleadingly.

Loki was now in control. He held the secret of the gnome's incredible power. Something in his hands enabled the dwarf to create objects of magic and beauty that no other could equal.

The young god slowly raised the hammer, watching the eyes of the dwarf. The glare remained constant and angry. He lowered the hammer and raised the tongs as though to smash them against the rock wall of the room.

"NOOO! Demand of me what you will, but you must not destroy the tongs."

Loki allowed himself a small smile as he laid the hammer on the bench and moved slowly to where his back was to the wall of the small chamber.

"Put everything in sacks and don't try anything, I'll be watching."

Andvari glared at the young thief in silence. A faint, moaning howl emanated from the bowels of the underground labyrinth. "My . . . pets are hungry." Smiling malignantly, he added, "Tis close to feeding time."

Loki glanced nervously at the doorway. "Shut up and do as you're told."

The dwarf retrieved several large, leather sacks and began placing a lifetime of work in them. When he finished, the two sacks must have weighed close to five stones each.

He glanced at the spindly lad holding his tongs, unable to resist a taunting remark. "There ye be lad. Don't strain yourself packing all of this up a mile of steep, winding trails."

The dwarf was sure the boy wouldn't make it to the surface with more than a handful of the treasure. He would simply follow and retrieve his gold and jewels.

Loki noticed the look in the dwarf's eyes, but didn't rise to the bait. "You let me worry about getting the stuff topside. I'll leave your tongs at the entrance by the lake – if you don't follow me."

The man's eyes narrowed suspiciously, but he shook his head in agreement.

Loki was nodding in satisfaction when he noticed the heavy gold ring on the dwarf's stout, little finger.

"The gold ring, give it to me." He said, pointing at the chubby hand.

The little man's eyes flared in renewed anger. "Do not press your luck boy. Leave with what you have."

Loki raised the tongs and when it appeared he was really going to smash them into the rock wall, Andvari cried out. "Stop!"

He stalked angrily over to Loki, pulled the small, heavy ring from his finger and dropped it in the boy's hand. *By all the power of Nidavellir, I curse this ring and the owner thereof! Tis a work of evil ye do and evil shall permeate the soul of the possessor from this day forth.*

Loki's hand closed around the ring. He suddenly felt the sensation of effluent coursing through his veins and wasn't sure he was still in control of things. He slipped the ring on his finger, moved the tongs to his mouth, and morphed into a horse.

The dwarf's anger became a tangible fury as he dragged the heavy sacks over next to the horse. The loss of the ring seemed to enrage him more than losing a lifetime of work. At a nod from Loki, he tied them to each side of the animal.

It took less than an hour for the huge Percheron to reach the surface. Loki turned back into a young god, letting the heavy sacks slide to the ground. Taking the tongs from his mouth, he considered tossing them into the lake, but decided to keep his promise to the dwarf.

He dropped the tongs and changed into the giant falcon once again. Grasping the incredibly heavy sacks in talons the size of a man's fingers, the mighty bird rose into the air with apparent ease.

Flying through the crisp, clean air usually made him feel free and easy. Today, however, there seemed to be a darkness seeping into his soul that would leave an indelible stain. There was no way of knowing the darkness would grow and corrupt a mischievous but innocent heart beyond any redemption.

For the first time in his life, Loki knew greed. When he saw the dwarf's ring, he wanted it, wanted it more than anything he had ever possessed.

The little hut came into view far below, and giving a triumphant cry, the huge bird circled lower, finally coming to rest at the edge of the farmer's garden.

Two young men that Loki didn't recognize came running out of the cabin towards him. The taller of the two, and apparently the older, was hollering back over his shoulder. "Father! He's back! Come quick."

As Loki changed back into a young man, the farmer's sons slid to a halt a short distance away. Hreidmar stepped out of the cabin just as Odin and Hoenir entered the little clearing.

"Quit yelling Fafnir. I think we can all see he's back."

The youth's dirty brown hair was cascading around his face, but couldn't hide the excitement sparkling in the gray-blue eyes. His father had told him of the dwarf's fabulous horde when he was a mere lad and the story had magnified several times in his mind. "Yeah, but he's got the gold with him!"

The old magician barked again. "Well, leave it alone. That treasure belongs to me, not you . . . or Regin."

The man headed towards Loki, roughly pushing his sons aside and grabbing one of the heavy sacks. He pulled the top open and stared inside. A look of satisfied avarice spread across his face. "Well, by the hounds of Hel, you did it." Glancing up, he added in an offhand manner. "Did ja kill him?"

Loki knew the magician meant the dwarf, so he simply shook his head no.

The man let the top of the sack drop and went to the other sack.

Opening it also, the look was similar, but not quite as keen. "Well, no matter. Is this all of it?"

Remaining silent, Loki shook his head yes. He was turning away from the farmer towards Hoenir and Odin when the man spoke again. "Wait."

The Viking god stopped and looked at the mage. "What?"

The man pointed at Loki's hand. "That ring. You didn't have it when you left. Where'd you get it?"

The boy glanced down at his hand. He had momentarily forgotten the ring. He heard himself growl, "Don't press your luck shaman. Take what you have."

Hreidmar stiffened at the rude demeanor of the boy.

"I'll take what was agreed upon . . . and not a whit less. Give me the ring."

Loki was about to tell the man to go to Hel's realm when Odin grasped his arm. "Give him the ring lad. Twas the bargain made."

Glancing at the magician, the older god added. "Give him the trinket and let's be on our way."

Loki never took his eyes off of the sorcerer as he angrily pulled the ring off and threw it at the man's feet. Chuckling without humor, the farmer reached down and picked up the ring.

"It may be a 'trinket', but it's my trinket. Now, be on your way."

Loki thus passed the curse of the ring to the magician, but it was too late. The putrid rot that had started in his heart was tiny, but already starting to spread. It would be years before the transition was complete, but it started that very day.

Odin stared at the farmer a moment longer then turned to his young charge. The boy had changed somehow, and it wasn't good. He couldn't understand why the youth had raised such a fuss over a ring. He had many gold rings back in Asgard.

He reached up to muss Loki's dark, red hair and then pulled his hand back; the taint of evil had taken hold of his young friend and companion.

The ancient god glanced at Hoenir. A look of profound loss and sadness crossed his face as the image of his brother began to fade. His ability to see into the future tore at the weakening seams of his heart.

Chapter 13

The Frost Giants

Eric slept through the day and far into the next night before he finally awoke. Rubbing his face in the darkness of the cloudy, moonless night, he felt a weight across his legs. He leaned up and carefully reached down to feel the tangled mop of his little brother's hair.

He smiled in realization of the boy's devotion and spoke softly to wake the sleeping child. "Wulf. Wulf wake up."

The younger boy slowly straightened and was momentarily disoriented, until he remembered falling asleep next to Eric. Turning towards his older brother, he spoke softly into the darkness. "Eric? Are you awake?"

"Yes, I'm awake and I feel fine. Now go and find a place to lie down and rest."

Eric could barely see his younger brother moving in the darkness and edging closer to his head. He felt Wulf's hand move up his arm to his shoulder.

"I'm really glad you woke up Eric. Father has been worried and . . . well, everyone will be glad to know you're all right."

The older boy patted his brother's hand.

"Thanks Wulf. I'm fine. Now go get some sleep."

The response was a pat on his shoulder and then the soft sound of steps fading in the darkness.

Eric lay in the cold darkness enveloping the ship, staring up at the black abyss above him. The memory of the gigantic falcon, the treasure and the change in Loki, was still vivid in his mind. He tried to remember what happened after the gold was delivered to Hreidmar, but the door was closed.

Frowning at the inability to remember, he closed his eyes and the surrounding darkness gave way to another dream. It was a bright summer's day and he was staring at the pretty lass he had left behind. But she was now a grown woman.

She seemed to be asleep on a large stone covered with roses and runes. The idyllic scene was completely surrounded by a wall of fire. The flames were throwing off an intense heat and it seemed impossible for the frailty within not to be consumed.

He patted the smooth, glossy coat of his horse, knowing the animal would obey his every command. Inhaling deeply, he dug in the spurs. The fire enveloped them and breaking through the scorching barrier, he watched as the beautiful image turned to vapor and disappeared.

The leaping flames and surrounding landscape swirled in a myriad of flashing colors and were swept away by an invisible wind.

A familiar voice came from the abyss that remained. Faintly at first and then stronger. He pulled up on the reigns and listened intently.

☼☼☼

Silver shafts of light were filtering through the heavy clouds when he awoke. Blinking and rubbing the sleep from his eyes, Eric noticed a man standing over him. He jerked back with a start before realizing it was his father.

"Mornin boy. Wulf said you were feelin better."

The man waited for a reply, but Eric just shook his head up and down. The images of the night were still racing through his mind.

Pursing his lips as though in a quandary, Thorvald smiled faintly and turned to leave. "Well, in that case, why don't you come forward and get a bit of breakfast?"

Eric spoke to the retreating back. "Yes sir, I'll be right there."

He threw the tanned hides back and realized he wasn't cold this morning. The thought made him pause -- he was always cold when he woke up.

He had slept in his clothes for as far back as he could remember and last night had been no different. Brushing the dirt and some stray material he didn't recognize out of the front of his tunic, he stood up and felt the blood rush from his head.

The horizon was tilting at a weird angle so he grabbed some crates to steady himself. He stood still for a moment to bring the spinning ship to a halt and then, blowing out a quick breath, headed towards the front of the longboat.

He passed the ship's mast when the sound of raucous laughter and someone slapping a bench reached him. Walking into the area where everyone was eating, he noticed most of the ship's warriors were congregated at a makeshift table and seemed to be having a party of some sort.

Eric flashed a smile at the thought. The warriors were always having a party to celebrate one thing or another. They lived every day like it was their last and far too often, it turned out that way.

The group fell silent when he approached and for the first time, he felt like a stranger among his father's friends. These were brave men, but they were looking at him like . . . he could sense, smell the fear. These huge warriors were afraid of him.

He felt a heavy hand settle on his shoulder and flinched slightly before noticing his father was handing him a plate of steaming stew. "Here, get some of this inside you, we need to talk."

Wulf came bounding over with stew remnants streaking the front of his tunic and face. He had already eaten.

"Eric! You're up! I told father you were fine, just like you said. You still feel fine?"

He smiled at his brother's enthusiasm and mussed his hair.

"Yeah, I'm fine."

Taking the hot bowl of stew to a wooden crate a short distance away, he sat down and quietly started eating.

He glanced toward the warriors. They were now making a point of not looking in his direction and the noisy laughter became nervous whispers.

Thorvald watched his crew for a few minutes and then, with an angry glower, stalked away.

One-by-one, the rest of the men followed suit and after a few minutes, Eric and Wulf were the only ones left.

Wulf didn't seem to notice the strange behavior of the crew and was happily chattering about something he had seen earlier in the rolling waves of the ocean.

Heavy storm clouds closed in to block the shafts of sunlight and before long, an icy, gray drizzle covered the world.

Eric finished the stew and noticed his little brother was sitting quietly, bundled up in a heavy blanket, shivering.

"Are you cold Wulf?"

The younger boy stared in surprise at his brother.

"Are you serious? Of course I'm cold. It's freezing this morn." He pulled a small hand out of the blanket to point behind them. "The sail is coated in ice."

Eric rubbed his arm under the light tunic he was wearing and wondered why he wasn't feeling the cold. Even the hardened warriors were wearing furs and boots this morning.

He pushed the question aside and swung his head towards the back of the boat. "Come on, let's go back with father and see what's going on."

Wulf beamed at the invitation and waited for his brother to lead the way.

In a couple of minutes, they were mid-ship and there was no doubt it was biting cold. Ice was freezing on the railing and making it difficult to walk across the pine flooring. Their father was talking to one of the crew in hushed tones and pointing off to the west.

The boys looked in the direction indicated and could see nothing but a gray mist, extending to the limits of the world in all directions. Eric suddenly felt drawn to an unseen destiny. Unspoken, soft words were caressing his mind about fabulous lands that lay just beyond the far western horizon.

He walked woodenly to the ship's railing and gazed longingly out across the blue-green waves, looking for . . . someone, somewhere, something. Was it gone?

Wulf noticed his brother's strange behavior and became worried. "Eric? You ok?"

Eric glanced at his brother, but did not see him and returned his gaze to the water. Deep from within murky depths, something moved towards the surface. The image was little more than a blur at first, but he recognized the silhouette. Ran. The beautiful, terrifying goddess of the seas.

The woman came clearly into view just below the surface of the water and smiled when she saw the youth watching her.

Full, wet lips the color of a dark red rose parted to reveal perfect teeth, white as the first snow of winter.

Tilting her head to the side, the long, auburn-ochre tresses trailed across her shoulders and over pale breasts, flowing through the water like liquid gold. Smooth hips of flawless alabaster curved into long legs meshed in a diaphanous web.

The woman was the most exquisite creature Eric had ever seen. He could tell from the look in the deep azure eyes she wanted him to join her. An infinite variety of plants and animals, alive in an endless array of color, awaited him in her underwater kingdom.

Wulf glanced into the water where his brother was staring. It was impossible to see into the rolling waves more than a few feet and there were no fish near the surface. There was nothing to see.

The older brother seemed mesmerized, ignoring Wulf's tug on his tunic.

"Eric! What are you staring at? You ok?" Receiving no answer, the boy left in search of his father.

The eyes of the goddess moved to a point over Eric's shoulder and the expression on the flawless features changed from demure amusement to anger. Eric blinked at the sudden transition and glanced to his left.

Wotun was standing next to him, looking into the water. "Beautiful, isn't she?"

When he turned to look back into the water, the vision was gone. Stare as he would, there was nothing but the froth from the rolling waves.

He turned back to the old man at his side. "I thought she was a myth. Was that . . . is she real?"

Wotun opened his mouth to reply and then hesitated. "Well, that depends upon what you consider real."

The boy started to ask for an explanation and realized if he didn't already understand, it couldn't be explained. Nodding slowly, he returned to staring out over the water. Things were seldom what they appeared.

Without turning back towards Wotun, he spoke again. "I had a dream last night. Twas strange. I was . . ."

"In the land of Midgard with Loki and Hoenir." The old man finished the sentence.

"Yes, how did you know?"

"I see much of what you see and . . ." He let the thought hang.

Eric hesitated briefly before adding, "What happened after Loki gave the gold to Hreidmar?"

Wotun let out a long sigh, staring into the foamy waves below. "Tis a long, sad story lad. Filled with greed and betrayal, much like the human heart."

The boy remained silent, so the old man resumed.

"The treasure that Loki stole was enough to fire the desire of any man, but Hreidar's sons were definitely fruit from the tree and began coveting the golden horde.

"Before the first blazing leaf of autumn fell, Fafnir slipped into his father's room in the dead of night and buried a long blade in the old man's cold heart.

"Regin fled for his life at the sight of the blood soaked body, knowing his brother would kill him at the first opportunity.

"Fafnir immediately cut the heavy, gold ring from his father's hand and slid the crimson stained band on the third finger of his left hand. The dark stain that befouled Loki's mischievous heart now seeped into the soul of Hreidar's eldest son.

"The foul deed behind him, Fafnir spent every minute of the years that followed guarding the fabulous treasure. It became the source of his every thought and action. Time and again, a wayfaring stranger stopped at the cabin door to seek directions or shelter, only to find a knife in their ribs or feel the blinding crack of firewood against their skull.

"The young man began eating the flesh of his victims to avoid having to leave the treasure unguarded. Stories of a monster in the forest permeated the surrounding area and the horrendous tales took the form of a fire breathing dragon.

"Over time, the body of Fafnir did begin to change. The greed fueled an inner rage at imagined thefts of his precious things. The hate manifested into a grotesque beast resembling the dragon haunting people's dreams. Their worst fears had come to pass. The careless wayfarer no longer had to fear a knife in the ribs, now they were torn apart and devoured in a matter of minutes.

"Anyone lucky enough to survive an encounter with the beast spread stories of a fire-breathing dragon as big as a long-ship, burning and devouring everything in its path. The old magician's cabin was now part of a dark forest that instilled fear in the strongest of hearts.

"Regin fled to a nearby village and took up the vocation of a blacksmith. Time passed and the kindly blacksmith would simply turn away at stories of a monstrous dragon spreading terror in the darkest part of the forest. In his heart he knew it was his brother and the terrible fate that had befallen him.

"Then, one fine, spring day, a handsome young man walked into Regin's life and the smith put him to work. Forge or anvil, a blacksmith's job was backbreaking and thankless. Most people with options avoided the occupation."

Wotun paused in relating the story to glance at Eric. The boy was still watching the water. He hadn't moved. "Want me to keep going boy?"

The lad's eyes flew wide as he turned towards the old man. "Oh yes! Please Wotun. I can almost see it as you tell the story."

At that same moment, Wulf returned, without his father. "Father said to check on you and if you were still acting funny to let him know. Are you ok?"

Eric glanced at Wulf and flashed a quick smile. "I'm fine Wulf. Wotun was just telling me a story." He paused before adding, "One that I hope he finishes."

The old Viking glanced at the short newcomer and growled, "Not sure I remember the rest of the tale."

The older brother turned pleading eyes to the old man. "Please Wotun. I've got to know."

The white-hair grunted in response. "Sometimes it's better not to know things."

Eric's face dropped at the response. "Oh. Well, maybe you can finish the story some other time?"

"Never leave until tomorrow what can be done today. You might not get another chance." The old man hacked a large wad of flim into the waves below and resumed the story.

"The young blacksmith was none other than Sigurd, a Norse hero known to all. A braver man you will never find.

"Regin befriended the young man and told him of the foul murder of his father by his brother and how old age prevented him from seeking revenge that was rightfully his.

"Sigurd naturally took up the oblique challenge and, after Regin repaired Sigmund's fabulous sword, managed to slay the monstrous dragon by slitting the belly of the beast.

"He was feasting upon the dragon's heart and suddenly could understand the language of the animals, even the chirping of the birds. The creatures of the wild told Sigurd when he delivered the treasure to Regin, the old blacksmith would try and kill him.

"The trusting heart of Sigurd would not allow him to believe such an awful truth. He had taken the ring during a previous attempt to slay the dragon and given it to Regin.

"The curse of the ring quickly found its way to the old smith's heart and began the inevitable rot. Within a fortnight, the old man was plotting the murder of his young assistant and in the darkest part of the night, slipped toward the cot where Sigurd slept.

"The long, glistening blade of a bone-handled knife flashed briefly in the moonlight before it began its savage descent. Again and again, the old man slashed at the long, inert body on the bunk. Only when he stopped and turned, sucking wind, did he see the calm, blue eyes in the moonlight.

"'Regin, why?' These were the last words the assassin would ever hear as Sigurd shoved the magic sword into the assassin's chest. Silent tears streamed down the square jaw as he cleaned the blade and slid it back into the scabbard.

"Sigurd narrowly escaped an ignoble death at the treacherous hands of his friend and the fabulous treasure was now his. If only he could have seen the future, he would have known . . ."

"Is that the way it really happened?" Interrupted Wulf.

"That's what the bards of old swear to."

The tale was broken off at a cry forward.

"Land! Land on the horizon! Nor, Norwest!"

The shout from a man standing aft in the lead ship sent a ripple of excitement through the crew. The two young brothers and the old man studied the horizon intently. The ragged outline of distant cliffs came slowly into view. The land looked cold and forbidding, with a precipitous wall of rock lining the water's edge.

With a shallow draft, the longboats ran lightly in the water, but the ridges of rock stretching out from shore were sharp and just below the surface in many areas. Two men went forward to hang over the prow of the boat and watch for the deadly, underwater formations.

Looming cliffs extended out of sight to the northeast and the southwest, preventing a landing. Thorvald motioned to the southwest and the man handling the steer board threw his weight into the heavy beam, causing the ship to swing in the direction indicated.

The daylight began to wane and the cliffs receded into steep embankments, but a safe harbor eluded them. An orange glow tracking the movement of the sun passed overhead and dropped behind the landfall, leaving the ocean and her inhabitants alone in the gloomy chill of darkness.

As the night passed, so did the cloudy skies, and a glowing sliver of moon appeared to give the landscape a soft, surreal appearance. The wind died to a gentle breeze, pushing the ship along the coast at a slow, but acceptable rate. The dark landscape slid past the longboat, giving a glimpse of movement here and there, but nothing more than elusive shadows from the pale moonlight.

Low muttering from the crew followed an undercurrent of fear seeping into their veins. An ominous taint from the unknown seemed to flow outward from the shore they were following. A gray mist drifted out across the water, over the railing and through the boat. The men were courageous warriors and even delighted in the peril of battle, but this was an enemy that couldn't be seen. The crew began checking weapons and pacing the deck.

There was always a certain feeling in their gut and a taste in the air right before a battle. This was similar, but different somehow. They were entering strange territory and the countless tales of voyagers that sailed west never to be seen again were rattling their brains.

The two brothers had curled up for the night and Thorvald restlessly paced the deck. Seeing Wotun, he walked closer and grabbed some rigging to stare out across the black water.

"Looks like Eric is going to be all right."

Wotun could tell the statement was partly a question. His response was partly an answer.

"He's not going to die from the cut of the spear."

Thorvald looked at the old man and scowled. He knew the incident with the spear was not the man's fault, but somehow felt like blaming him anyway. He grunted in response and continued to stare into the semi-darkness. The faint smell of smoke twisted in the mist and drifted across the boat.

He looked towards the dark silhouette of the shoreline and noticed a break in the escarpment that could only mean one thing, an inlet or harbor. Turning towards the back of the boat, he barked, "Turn towards the land Braggia, I think I see an inlet."

Several pairs of yellow eyes watched from the dark landscape as the boat turned and headed towards shore. Their hunger satiated, they turned away from the fresh prey to head inland.

The smell of smoke was getting stronger as the Vikings sailed into the shimmering fjord. They noticed several places on the eastern bank glowing with pulses of red and yellow flames, but the area was immersed in silence. The scattered fires were a fair distance up the sloping embankment so the Vikings decided to beach their craft and spend the remainder of the night on board.

The next day broke clear and an hour before the sun pushed up from the horizon, the crew was preparing to debark.

Thorvald strapped on his sword and pulled a quiver of arrows over his head before turning towards one of the younger warriors. "Svein, you stay with the boys and keep a sharp eye. We should be back before the sun is high overhead."

Hefting the scarred shield he carried in battle, he headed for the railing.

A flash of disappointment crossed the young man's face, but he remained silent. The warrior chieftain leaped lightly overboard and waded through the cold water to shore. Soon after, a score of warriors were assembled on the beach and without looking back, headed up the grassy hill in front of them.

The stench of death was strong in the air and the warriors knew what they were going to find when they climbed the small hill separating them from the fires of the previous night. With the exception of Wulf and Eric, they had all seen it many times; the limp bodies draped over carts and lying in campfires, arrows and blood covering the corpses. Young or old, it made no difference.

They topped the knoll to see the remnants of a small village a hundred paces up the gentle slope in front of them. The mud and waddle huts had been demolished with portions of rock fireplaces still standing. Smoke curled up from mounds where the debris had been heaped up and burned.

A short distance from the edge of the village, Thorvald stopped and put up his hand. "Valdur, check it out. We'll wait here."

The middle aged Viking nodded without hesitation and continued plodding up the gentle embankment. The group learned long ago it was better to lose one man to an ambush than an entire clan.

The small cluster of warriors watched as their comrade walked into the perimeter of the village and surveyed the area in slow arcs. Finally, after meandering through the village and testing the air with his nostrils, he motioned the rest of the crew to join him.

Thorvald waved in acknowledgement and led the group the remaining distance to the village.

Shortly before reaching Valdur, the leader stopped and stared at the grisly remnants of what had been a human being. The clothes were gone and most of the flesh had been torn away. The left arm and most of the right leg were missing. The arm hadn't been cut off, but torn away, as evidenced by the long, ragged shreds of flesh still clinging to the torso.

He was staring at the corpse when Valdur walked back to him. "I've never seen anything like it. It's like this all over the village. Something tore these people apart and most of the fleshy parts are . . . gone."

The Viking leader stared at his second mate a moment before slowly nodding. "Any tracks?" Valdur swung his head in the direction of a large, still smoldering pile of debris. "Over here."

Various members of the crew began wandering around the morbid scene, looking for survivors or anything of value.

The two men stopped near the indicated pile and Valdur pointed to imprints in the soft soil. "Don't know what it is. It almost looks human, but it's not shaped right and too big for a man."

Thorvald knelt down and brushed some loose grass from the indentation. "Looks like the footprint of some huge primate."

He glanced up at Valdur. The other man raised an eyebrow and stepped into the indentation. He was a large man and his foot only covered half of the print.

"Tis evil, whatever else it may be. I feel it in my bones."

Valdur stepped out of the imprint and waved his arm in a sweeping motion. "There are footprints like this all over the place. Either there were a lot of these creatures or one that was very busy . . . and hungry."

The clan chieftain stood slowly, staring at the huge impression and shaking his head. "I've never seen anything like it."

He looked around for Thorson, his first mate, and catching his eye, motioned him over. The huge Viking had a hand on the hilt of his sword as he approached. "What do you make of this?"

Thorvald's eyes were sweeping the surrounding area. "It's something we've never encountered before. Whatever it is, it's big and mean." Pausing briefly, he added, "And apparently hard to kill. I haven't seen anything but dead villagers."

He took a couple of steps to the left and kneeled again, next to another print. It wasn't as large as the first, but this one definitely wasn't human.

Thorvald stretched his right hand open and laid it over the indentation. The outline was larger than his hand – the paw print of a carnivore.

Thorson moved next to him and glanced down. "Wolf?"

The clan leader lifted his hand. "You ever see a wolf print that large?"

"No. That thing must be close to five feet at the shoulder."

Thorvald brushed some stray grass and food out of his beard as his gaze swept the village. His eyes passed what he was looking for and returned.

"Wotun! Over here."

The old man was studying another set of tracks in the middle of the village and looked up when he heard his name. He grasped the bent, wooden staff he used as a cane and slowly walked over to where the two Vikings were standing.

"What do you want?"

Thorvald pointed at the tracks. "Ever see anything like that? Or this?"

Wotun didn't look down, but continued to stare at Thorvald. "No, but I . . ." He stopped mid-sentence, evidently changing his mind about what he was going to say.

"But what?"

"But nothing. We should leave this accursed place quickly and never look back."

There was no fear in the old man's eyes, but the voice seemed to come from the abyss of time, a thousand generations of life and death. "There are things of this world that must run their course and it is best to steer clear until they do."

Thorson spoke up. "Wotun. You're not making any sense. Something killed and butchered these people. Don't you want to know what it is?"

The old patriarch had turned to leave, but stopped and spoke back over his shoulder. "No. Certain death and utter despair lie down that path." Saying nothing more, he shuffled away toward the ocean and the ship.

Thorvald looked at Thorson and shrugged. Wotun was probably right; they should just leave. Anyway, there didn't appear to be much left worth fighting for.

Having made up his mind, he inhaled to call the warriors to head back to the ship.

A piercing scream broke the morning stillness. The shriek sounded like that of a woman enveloped in terror. It hit the looming cliffs and ricocheted down the valley through the ravaged village like the wail of a *Valkyrie*.

The Vikings stopped in their tracks and looked upwards. High above them on a rocky rampart stood a huge, hairy beast outlined in the light blue of the sky above. Throwing its head back in a howl that resembled insane laughter, it stepped to the edge of the cliff, swinging a woman in one massive paw.

The animal thrust her out over the 200 foot vertical drop and another piercing shriek reverberated up the river's gorge and back again. The scream shattered when he suddenly released his grip – then grabbed her with the other hand. The woman went limp in the huge paw. She had passed out, or was dead.

The hairy brute studied his plaything for a moment and after shaking the supple torso, tossed her aside and disappeared behind the granite rampart.

Everyone standing in the devastated village continued to stare in the direction of the monstrous apparition, spellbound.

Finally, Wotun spoke barely above a whisper. "By all that's sacred Loki, what have you done?"

Thorvald heard the word 'Loki' and it was enough to bring him spinning around. "What was that? What did you say?"

Wotun's eye flashed in anger. "I said we need to get away from this place as fast as we can. Do you believe me now?"

Thorvald tried to stare the old man down, but failed. "Run if you want. I'm going to see if that woman is still alive."

The greybeard whirled away in frustration, snarling as he stalked away. "Bah. Vanity and pride flow from your mouth. You do not know the woman and she is probably dead. But you risk all, just so you can be right."

Thorvald glared at the old man's receding back. The clan leader was impulsive, but no fool. He carefully considered what the aged warrior said. He knew Wotun was probably right about the woman being dead, but what did he mean when he said 'you risk all'?

He knew Wotun was right, he should take the crew and head back to the ship. Instead, he heard himself raising his voice to no one in particular. "I am going after the woman. Stay or come as you will."

To a man, the warriors quietly walked over and stood next to him.

"We cannot all go. Some must remain to guard the ships."

In the next few minutes, Thorvald picked a score of his best men before turning his gaze to the looming cliffs.

He glanced at Wotun. "This may be a trap, but we need women and she might still be alive. I will not stand in judgment if any man changes his mind about going."

The group remained silent. Thorvald nodded acceptance, absently reaching down to feel the hilt of his sword before turning toward the rocky cliffs.

When they reached the bottom of the vertical rock face, the Vikings were amazed the animal had apparently climbed it while holding the woman.

Working along the base of the cliffs, they found a wedge-shaped crevice filled with brush and ragged breaks in the rock to serve as hand holds. The climbing was arduous, dangerous and slow. The cleft was so narrow that if one man fell, he would take all of those below him to their deaths.

By the time they reached the top, Thorvald was wondering if this was indeed a fool's errand. They had lost most of the day in the ascent.

Helping the last man reach the top, the leader stood and looked over the vista below. It was a truly beautiful harbor, extending up the inlet for close to a mile, with rolling grass glades and trees on both sides of the channel.

Far below, he could make out the tiny image of Wotun, sitting on a rock at the edge of the village, apparently lost in thought.

He looked to the left and the right. The animal had been around a hundred paces to the north. That was where the woman should be.

Thorvald unhooked his shield and strapped it on his left arm. He then pulled his sword and started moving along the top of the soaring escarpment. Invisible from below, the ragged edge of a dense forest paralleled the cliff about thirty yards back from the vertical drop.

The warriors followed in single file, walking quietly and alert to every sound. Long ago, they had learned that survival often depended upon the ability to sense danger and fight with unreasoning ferocity when confronted.

A deadly silence enveloped the entire area. Even the ubiquitous chirping of birds was absent. The heavy, quick breaths of men attempting to breathe steadily and listen intently, became discernable.

Part of a woman's tunic became visible at the base of some brush near a salient point directly in front of them. Thorvald raised his hand and silently pointed at the ragged cloth. A small area of ivory hued skin appeared as they moved closer.

The sound of steel sliding against leather and brass whispered through the surrounding trees as the men drew their weapons and began to spread out in an arc around the woman.

Several sets of silent, yellow eyes watched the warriors from the darkness provided by the surrounding trees. Thorvald could feel their presence and it made his skin crawl.

When he reached the woman, he turned his back towards her, facing the forest. Unconsciously tapping his shield lightly with his sword, he backed to within a few feet of the woman and stopped.

The rest of his men formed a protective arc around him and the prone body, facing outwards towards the thick spruce and fir.

Thorvald slid his sword in its sheath and turned toward the woman.

She was lying on her side with a crimson stain that trailed from the long reddish-gold hair down the side of her cheek. Her face was sallow and she didn't appear to be breathing.

The chieftain knelt beside her and laid a hand on her side. It was rising and falling ever so slightly. He let out a quick breath, unsure if he was relieved or disappointed. If she had been dead, they could have made a hasty retreat, having done their duty. Now, it would be foolish to have started the quest and not finish.

He laid his shield down and gently rolled her over. The upper portion of her tunic had been torn away and her chest was streaked with bloody claw marks. She groaned at the touch and her eyelids fluttered.

The woman stopped blinking and slowly opened her eyes as Thorvald pushed a mass of dirty, unruly hair back from her face. The dark green eyes were glazed and she began muttering incoherently. "No . . . please, no more. Just kill me, please."

Thorvald gently placed a large, rough hand on the side of her face. "It's ok. They're gone. You're safe now."

The women's eyes fixed on the rugged visage behind the voice for a moment before becoming vacant again. Rolling upward, the whites of her eyes dominated the pale face as it fell backward.

Thorvald pulled his hand back, wiping the blood on a leather jerkin and studying the woman momentarily. Standing to face his men, he felt guilty for having gotten them into this situation.

"She's alive, but in bad shape. I don't think we can get her down the cliff before it gets dark."

The men looked at each other in silence. Every man in the group knew what the statement meant. They probably wouldn't survive the night if they remained and there was no question about them staying. Dying in a glorious battle was the most any Viking could hope for. Their worst fear was to lose courage in the face of an enemy or die a 'straw death' in bed.

One grizzled old warrior, who had already survived far too many campaigns, slid his sword home and growled. "Fair enough. Did anyone bring something to eat?"

The decision made, the men seemed to relax somewhat, waiting for the inevitable attack. A small fire was started a short distance from the woman and some dried strips of stringy, tough meat passed around. It would be a dry camp since there were no springs or seepages in the area.

There were twenty men in the group and they took turns standing guard in teams of five, changing every couple of hours.

The sliver of moon from the previous night had vanished and the creatures of the night moved in the total darkness of a cloud filled sky. The tiny campfire produced the only light and sound in the vicinity of the Vikings as the interminable night wore on.

Soft, grey light from an invisible sun began to permeate their surroundings and for the first time, a faint glimmer of hope, or disappointment, began to ripple through the men. Maybe the creatures had their fill of human flesh and left the area for good.

The old warrior that had asked about the food the previous evening was in the last group of five sentries and getting restless. "Gunnar, you got any more of that dried ox left?"

A tall, hawk-faced man with several white lines running down the left side of his face glanced at the old warrior.

"Thor's hammer Halvdan, I told you last night that was all I had and there weren't no more."

Halvdan pursed his lips. He was hungry. There was enough light to see the edge of the woods now. He was fairly certain if the man-eaters were going to attack, they would have done so by now.

He glanced back at Gunnar. "Bet there's some rabbits in those trees."

His stomach growled as he stared into the cold shadows between the tree trunks. He had just made up his mind to find some breakfast when a howling nightmare came charging out of the brush to the left of him.

The 'thing' was well over seven feet high and covered with hair, but resembled a man. Halvdan let out a bellow in answer, pulling his sword and charging the animal. Ducking below a haymaker swing by the animal, he flashed the heavy blade towards the torso and connected just below the rib cage.

He saw a two foot gash open up in the beast's middle and snarled in satisfaction as he withdrew. The animal bellowed in pain and rage, grabbing at the entrails spilling out. Mortally wounded, but far from dead, the beast watched as Halvdan circled to the left, looking for another opportunity when two arrows thudded into the hairy hide.

Halvdan realized the rest of the warriors were joining the fight just as a monstrous paw grabbed his arm in a bone-breaking grip and lifted him from the ground. Unable to free himself, he growled in frustration as a second beast twisted him around face-to-face. The putrid stench of the animal's breath blasted into his face as it roared in fury.

Ragged, broken teeth resembling an old cross-cut saw filled the animal's mouth and Halvdan thought the creature was going to bite his head off. Instead, he felt his shoulder wrenched out of the socket as the beast slammed him to the ground and savagely hurled him towards the woods. He hit and rolled into the base of a tree, with his left arm twisted behind him.

The small camp turned into a war zone in a matter of seconds and men were screaming in the throes of battle. The monstrous brute that threw Halvdan into the trees was joined by another creature that seemed to be a female.

The first attacker had dropped to its knees and seemed to be focused on keeping its guts in and little else. The last two ignored their wounded comrade and charged the camp. Several warriors were sinking arrows into the monsters at an incredible rate, but it seemed to be just making them more insane with rage.

Thorvald had his rune covered sword in one hand and a large battle axe in the other. Throwing his head back with a guttural roar that was as wild as that of the attacking beasts, he charged the larger of the two. The animals resembled huge pin-cushions with the splay of arrows sticking out of them.

The hairy fiend reached for the battle axe as it descended towards its head. Thorvald felt the axe slam to a stop like it had hit a tree when the animal grabbed it. Trying to pull back, he was jerked off his feet towards the open, slavering jaws.

Relishing the rush of adrenaline, the Viking brought the broadsword forward in a savage lunge. He felt it hit solid in the middle of the animal's torso and landing on his feet, shoved it home.

The creature stopped, temporarily stunned by the unusual feeling. It slowly looked down at the hilt of the sword, dropped the axe and stared at Thorvald for an explanation. It was obvious the beast had never been seriously injured and wasn't sure how to deal with the situation.

The huge animal arched its back and released a wail that rocked the canyon walls on the far side of the inlet. Still staring at Thorvald, it reached down to grip the hilt of the sword.

Everyone stopped in the middle of the battle and watched the giant sink to its knees. Panting, with arrows drawn, the warriors stared as the creature pulled the blade partway out, staring at it for a moment and then falling forward in a crashing heap.

The female froze when its companion fell. It stared at the huge, hairy body lying face down in front of Thorvald and then to the first animal to attack. The beast was now sitting, but still holding its entrails. Tilting her head slightly to the side, the female spoke to the fatally wounded creature.

"Hagggghhh?"

The animal holding its guts responded without looking up. "Baakkiissh. Kuuucknef."

Exhaling a long breath, it leaned over and fell, letting the bloody intestines spill upon the grass.

The remaining beast watched as the gutted monster let out a last shuddering breath and stopped moving. Even the warriors remained motionless, watching the eerie exchange. The animals had been communicating, talking. It made them more human somehow.

Thorvald reached down to grab the axe and looked at the huge female. Rage and fear flashed through the huge, black eyes before she whirled and charged for the trees.

Three more arrows struck her in the back before she disappeared, but the men didn't pursue. The strange encounter and verbal exchange between the 'man-beasts' had swept away the berserker boil of blood.

The warriors had started gathering arrows and checking on Halvdan when a woman's voice broke the quiet mutterings.

"They are dead?"

Thorvald swung around in surprise to see the woman sitting up, leaning against the rock she had been lying next to. She was obviously weak and terrified, but seemed lucid and was speaking clearly.

The leader walked over and watched her for a moment before responding. "Yes they are dead. Do you know who, or what they are?"

The woman spit on the grass next to her. "They are pure evil. An abomination to this world. They live in the snow far to the north, but come down to kill and . . . eat."

She glanced towards the forest. "They travel with wolves as big as ponies. What they do not want, the wolves get."

If the men had not seen the tracks in the village, they would have thought the statement was the rambling of a madwoman, but the wolves must be huge to leave tracks bigger than a man's hand.

The Viking reached down to gently squeeze the woman's shoulder. "Everything is going to be ok. But we need to get you down from here."

She nodded, but remained silent as he turned back to the slain creatures.

Thorvald managed to wrestle his sword loose from under the giant 'snowman' and wiped the blade on the shaggy fur before shoving it back in the sheath.

When he turned to survey the damage, he noticed three men sitting on Halvdan, trying to get his dislocated arm back in place. A discernable pop signaled their success and the color momentarily drained from the Viking's dark visage.

Grunting in satisfaction, Thorvald turned back to the woman. "Can you walk?"

She glanced up while trying to tie the torn garment back together. "Yes."

The curt answer was matched by quick, angry movements of the small hands. Thorvald knew this was an attempt to divert her mind from the previous night. The effort proved unsuccessful.

Viking women were incredibly hard and not prone to showing emotion, but the woman had lost her family, her friends and everything that had been her life in the last twenty four hours. The pain was making it hard to breath.

She stopped struggling with an obstinate strip of cloth and sucked in a ragged gasp. "Ohhh Freyja . . ."

The memory of the attack pushed into her mind and she stared vacantly ahead as the carnage began to unfold . . .

The monsters were stories from her childhood, but real, and far more terrifying. Many of the men had grabbed weapons but froze in terror at the sight of the aberrations. The animals were tearing people apart and howling in a gleeful frenzy. Arrows seemed to have little effect on the thick hides. The villagers that did fight were killed immediately with a savagery that was unimaginable. The animals were lifting people completely off the ground and biting arms, legs and even heads from the bodies.

She felt something smack the side of her head and the pain blurred the vision in front of her eyes. There was a man standing in front of her, a stranger.

"You must not think about it. It will drive you insane."

Thorvald grasped her by both shoulders and stared intently into her eyes. "Get up and get moving. Those beasts may come back. There will be time for grieving later."

The woman blinked several times as he hauled her to her feet. Nodding slowly, the glaze left her eyes to be replaced with a look that glistened with pain. Glancing absently around her to ensure she wasn't leaving anything behind, she turned and started walking woodenly along the top of the escarpment.

They reached the crevice in the rocky wall shortly thereafter, but it was late in the day before they completed the descent to the base of the cliffs.

Tired and bloody, they returned to the boat just as the fading warmth provided by the yellow streaks of the late summer sun dropped below the horizon.

The boys were huddled around a small fire at the water's edge with Svein, Wotun and the women of the clan. Eric and Wulf ran to greet their father, vying for his attention. The Viking leader hefted the younger brother and put his arm around Eric. The older boy noticed a strange smell in the group as they walked the short distance back to the fire. It was an odor he had never encountered before.

"Father, you're all bloody. What is that awful smell?"

The man set Wulf down and glanced at the rescued woman before responding.

"There were strange animals up there. They attacked the woman's village and . . . we encountered three and killed two."

Eric could tell his father had left out a great deal and did not care to discuss it further. He glanced over at the woman and felt a pang of sympathy. She must have lost everything, everyone. He found himself walking over and asking if she was hungry.

For the first time since they had found her, she actually seemed to focus on something. Smiling faintly at the boy, she pushed some auburn hair back from his face and nodded. Her eyes glistened with unshed tears as the young man turned away to get her some food.

She had found a jutting rock to sit on by the time Eric returned with a steaming bowl of stew. Handing her the wooden vessel, he flashed a timid smile over the rim.

"Here, it's pretty good. I think it's the only thing Alve knows how to cook, but it's not too bad."

The woman made a futile attempt to wipe the dirt and blood from her hands before accepting the stew. "Thank you. How are you called?"

The boy straightened up, slightly self-conscious, before answering. "Eric, Eric Thorvaldsson."

She reached out to muss the red hair. "They should call you Eric the Red."

Eric smiled broadly. He liked this woman, beneath the blood and dirt, she was really quite pretty. "May I ask how you are called?"

The woman had a spoonful of stew halfway to her mouth when she stopped. She slowly lowered the spoon and realized the boy was the first person to ask what her name was. "Freyhild. I am called Freyhild."

He drew back slightly at the name and the woman noticed the sudden change in demeanor. "What is it lad?"

"Nothing, it's just that my mother's name is . . . was Thjodhild."

The woman paused, uncertain how to respond. "I see. You lost your mother?"

"Yes, just a few weeks ago."

A small fire ignited in the liquid, green orbs when she finally spoke again. "Life is hard child. Like iron on the anvil, we are beaten down again and again, to see if we will succumb, or harden to the trials of living."

Eric smiled ever so slightly, nodding that he understood, before turning away and disappearing into the darkness.

The woman sat watching the boy walk away and for the first time, she felt like she could endure. She would survive. Once again, the spoonful of stew moved towards her mouth.

Thorvald awoke in the middle of the night, added some dry driftwood to the embers of the dying fire and sat watching the stars move across the black canvas of *Valhalla*. As a boy, he had heard hundreds of stories about the Viking berserkers of old, the warrior maidens called *Valkyries* and the glory of dying in battle – to be reborn in the majestic, spear lined halls of Odin's golden citadel.

As a young man, he had been sure he would die a glorious death in battle and live as a warrior in the Viking heaven. In *Valhalla*, you slept with a beautiful woman every night, ate a hearty breakfast and charged into some marvelous combat. Whether you lived or died mattered not; by nightfall, you were healthy and whole again, back in the halls of *Valhalla* with a host of warrior brethren; where the mead flowed freely and the ox or goat meat was always hot and fresh from the spit.

He picked up a few more pieces of driftwood, smiled grimly at the memories and tossed the wood onto the fire. Everything was different when you were young. Anything was possible and easy to believe. He glanced over at his sleeping boys. When he was younger, he always seemed to have the answers. Now there were more forks in the road and far less certainty about the path ahead.

A cold breeze moved through the camp to ruffle loose strands of hair and tease the flames of the crackling fire. Thorvald looked upward again and turned a fur collar against the cold.

The next morning metamorphosed from a cold, crisp blackness to a colder grey dawn with scudding clouds and a biting wind. Tiny bits of snow were clinging to the faces of the men, melting in the fog of their breaths to trickle down through the heavy beards, forming shimmering icicles at the tips.

A faint, whining moan emanated from the upper canyon, bemoaning the approach of winter and forecasting the coming storm. Winter would come early to this land and judging from the heavy spruce and hardy vegetation, it would be hard to survive on this strange island.

Men were beginning to stir and the women were busy preparing the customary stew and meat for breakfast. A dozen campfires sprang to life and soon the inaudible mutterings and hushed conversations of morning could be heard up and down the sandy stretch of beach.

The unspoken questions were beginning to move from fire to fire. "What now? Are we going to stay here? Are those things going to come back?"

Thorvald tossed another chunk of driftwood into the fire and stood up. He had made his decision. He thought about it half the night and still wasn't sure about the correct course of action, but one thing was for certain, they couldn't stay here.

Chapter 14

New Horizons

Thorson walked up to Thorvald and paused as if testing the water before he spoke. "Have you decided?"

Thorvald looked at his first mate steadily for a moment and then responded. "Yes. I think it would be unwise to remain here. Winter is closing in and we may not survive if we stay."

The first mate studied the older man. It would be a hard winter, but both men knew that was not the reason for leaving. Neither man mentioned the beasts that had attacked the village.

"I'll give the order; we can set sail in two hours."

He started to leave and then turned back to the clan chieftain. "What's our heading?"

Thorvald stared into the dying fire, trying to see into the future. The fire cracked and snapped, but said nothing more.

"If we sail south or east, there will be no welcome for us, or our women. We cannot sail north." He let the unspoken words hang in silence.

There were at least three versions of what lay west of where they were; the first was you would encounter more land; the second, you would sail in a circle and somehow wind up back in Norway; the third and most likely, was that at some point you would drop off into a vast darkness that was the realm of demons.

The Viking leader felt they had no choice. Letting out a long breath, he pointed towards the horizon. "West, we sail west."

Thorson nodded and spun on his heel, heading back towards the cluster of campfires. In the distance, Thorvald could hear him barking orders to get things aboard ship and ready to leave.

By mid-morning, the square sails were filled with a strong westerly wind. The oars pulled in and dropped in their slots.

A long row of personalized shields lined the ship's railing on both sides. The heavy, bull-hide covered ovals were a testament to the battles the warriors survived. Leather strips and bright braids of cloth intertwined with mystic runes were burnt into the taunt coverings.

The prows of both ships were adorned with the fierce replica of a dragon's head. Although nobody in the clan had ever seen a real dragon, everyone knew they existed. The only dispute was over what they actually looked like.

The crewmen turned to the never ending tasks of repairing the rigging, sharpening weapons and cleaning. A restless wind curled through the heavy sail, carrying the distant, moaning howl of monstrous wolves, hungry once again.

By late afternoon, they were hours away from the ragged ramparts surrounding the abominable island and the only thing visible in all directions was the ocean. The white caps crested the grey-green depths, skipping along the top of the wave for a brief moment and then sliding down the lee side in a foamy froth to vanish and reappear with the next surge.

The days wore on with a monotonous repetition. Eric's dreams about strange places and events continued. The nightly adventures were sometimes marvelous and often terrifying. Odysseys so real he would wake up in a cold sweat, heart pounding and gasping for breath.

If anyone asked, he would tell them he had a nightmare about the burning of his village, but strange as it seemed, that was the one thing he hadn't dreamt about.

The moon had grown to a full circle when a cry from the helmsman in the first boat drifted back across the water. "Land! Land ahead!"

Everyone rushed to the front of the long crafts to see what lay in store. To a man, their hearts were hammering in their chests. The legends about nine different worlds, frost giants, monstrous serpents and blood-thirsty demons were in every man's mind. How many tales were the fabrications of an intoxicated mind and how many were based upon fact?

Who was to say there weren't creatures more fearsome than the abominable creatures they had encountered on the last island? They had seen the footprints of wolves that were impossibly huge. Everyone had heard fabulous tales and terrifying stories of the lands to the west, but no one on the ship knew for certain what lay ahead.

When they reached the coastline of the strange landmass, the shore extended northeast and southwest. Turning to port, they followed the coast most of the day before a yawning inlet came into view. They headed inward, still following the shoreline, now leading northwest. The estuary was a mile wide in many places.

By morning of the following day, they had sailed up the inlet to where the channel was not much more than two hundred yards wide. The river came from the northwest as it narrowed. Lush vegetation and trees lined the shore in places.

The southern bank was free of snow and bright green in the sunlight. One of the crew noticed a whitetail buck leap to its feet at the sight of the strange thing in the water. Switching its tail nervously, it turned away and disappeared into the surrounding foliage.

"Deer! There was a deer!"

Several more crew members rushed to the port side of the boat to stare at the tree line in wistful hunger.

Dried fish and salted pork grew wearisome when they were still edible. After turning rancid, it made you wish you had never eaten it. The thought of some fresh venison made every mouth on the boat water.

A short distance up the river, a broad expanse of sand and grass stretched off to the southwest. The ships beached side by side and within an hour, there were several fires going. Shortly thereafter, everyone cheered when two Vikings came walking back into camp, dragging the light-brown carcass of a young buck.

The animal was hung on a stout pole and quickly skinned. The fat and flesh clinging to the hide were scraped away before stretching it out to dry. Long, crimson strips of meat were carved from the loins and hind quarters and carefully placed on green saplings over the fire.

The hiss of grease dripping into the fires was accompanied by the smell of fresh venison roasting over crackling flames.

Thorvald motioned to a couple of men as they watched the meat cook. He leaned over to mutter something in the first man's ear and then allowed himself a smile as they disappeared toward the boats. It wasn't long before they returned with two small kegs of ale, amusement and anticipation dancing on their faces.

By the time darkness fell over the new land, the men and women had cleaned the venison to the bone and found a third barrel of ale. The chanting and war songs were gaining momentum when an argument between two crew members broke out.

Bjarne had finished the last of the ale and decided to tell Halvdan he had the face of a pig. Halvdan wasn't sure if he was offended or not.

"A handsome pig or an ugly one?"

Bjarne looked thoughtful for a moment.

"I'm not sure, what's the difference?"

Halvdan drew back at the question. "What's the difference? You mean you can't tell the difference between a hog with square shoulders, a fine, arched back with long loins . . . and a fat, stubby, malformed swine?"

Bjarne grinned at the outburst. "Well why didn't you say so? You have the face of a fat, stubby, malformed swine."

Ripples of laughter swept through the little camp as Halvdan glared at Bjarne. He wiped a beefy paw across his mouth, pulled his sword free and staggered over to stand in front of the other man.

Bjarne had to make two attempts to get to his feet, but when he finally managed, was ready for battle. Almost. His sword seemed to be stuck in the scabbard. He raised a hand to indicate he wanted Halvdan to wait until he got his weapon free. Unperturbed, he began pulling at the sword in earnest.

Halvdan watched the struggle for a few minutes and becoming impatient, decided Bjarne needed some help. He slid his sword back in its sheath, stepped next to his comrade and shoved Bjarne's hands out of the way. Spitting some foreign material from his mouth, Halvdan reared back on the sword, spinning Bjarne around in the attempt.

The two Vikings got their feet tangled as they twisted around and went down with a bellowing roar into the campfire. The furs they were wearing immediately became engulfed in flames as the men rolled away to clamber to their feet and make a dash for the water.

For a brief moment, the beach was lit up as the two poorly made torches charged into the shallow surf. Smoke from extinguished flames rolled back towards the camp amidst gales of laughter.

Both men struggled to their feet, realizing the water was barely above freezing and sloshed back towards shore. Apparently they had forgotten what got them into that situation as they plodded back up the beach towards camp, laughing and shoving each other.

The burns were minor and quickly taken care of before the last of the fires was doused and everyone turned in for the night.

Thorvald was up before daybreak as usual. He had been walking the beach by the light of the stars and a sliver of moon, trying to get a feel for this new land. The tingle of magic was here, but it didn't contain the dark undercurrents permeating the last island.

The beach was lit with a million reflections from the gentle waves. The silver and gold radiance from the moon and stars hitting countless undulations along the surf were deflected inland, to go skittering across the grains of sand. The tiny facets of the particles glowed iridescent when the flickering light danced across them.

Feeling eyes on his back, Thorvald placed a hand on the hilt of his sword and turned slowly, as though he was just changing directions. He could barely see the outline of a man against the dark backdrop of trees. He recognized the bent, slow moving silhouette.

"Wotun. Good morn. What brings you out before the sun?"

The shadow of the man maintained the slow, steady pace towards the clan leader until they were face to face.

"Morn Thorvald. I came to talk to you."

The two men turned side by side and resumed a leisurely walk along the beach. Thorvald kept looking straight ahead. "What's on your mind?"

Wotun was also looking ahead, but seeing far into the past.

"The last island we landed on. I think I know what those creatures were."

"Figured you did."

"Legend tells of a battle called Ragnarok. As you know, it is to be the doom of the gods. The gods of Asgard and frost giants of old will meet in a terrible battle to the death."

Wotun paused and when Thorvald remained silent, he continued. "I am sure you have heard the tales of the treacherous Loki."

The way the old man said 'treacherous' brought Thorvald to a halt. He turned slowly towards Wotun.

"Those monsters. Where did they come from?"

Wotun stared into nothingness. "Whether you believe what I am about to tell you matters not. The stories of old are not of what is to be, but tell of what has already happened."

The old man paused as though gathering his thoughts. "The tales have been handed down through the generations and much distortion has taken place, but an element of truth threads through each telling."

Once again he stopped, but his mind's eye was looking far into the past. "The battle of Ragnarok was real. Many of the legends surrounding it are mere fabrication, but some are true."

He pulled on the long, white beard and let out a sad sigh of resignation. "For a long time, I was never sure. Now I am."

Looking back at Thorvald, his eye came into focus. "Not everyone died in that battle. There was white and black magic everywhere. The air was crackling with the fragrance, and the stench."

Turning away, the grey orb lost its focus and traveled back through the centuries.

"Some frost giants were much like the gods in those days. The giants were towering brutes, most dumber than a rock, but many were smart, strong and handsome. Some of the giantesses were beautiful. The world was a different place, but I believe that island was once a place called Jortunheim. I thought they all died at Ragnarok. The last thing I remember . . ."

The quiet reminiscing of the old man was interrupted by the sounds of men shouting in the distance.

Both Vikings turned in the direction of the noise to see several men and two women break out of the trees a short distance down the beach. A score of other men were chasing them and soon had the small group surrounded on the beach.

One of the cornered men rushed into the water and quickly climbed back out. There were five men with the women and it looked like three had knives. The resistance was short lived. In a matter of seconds, two of the men carrying knives were lying on the beach with blood flowing freely from multiple wounds.

The remaining three men and two women were roughly pushed to their knees. It appeared the captors were simply going to cut their throats when Thorvald hollered, "Hold on."

The men surrounding the captives whirled around to face the new threat. Short and stout, they were covered with the white fur of the huge bear of the North. Some had slashes of color on their faces or arms.

Seeing two strange men, one of them obviously very old, approaching them with such nonchalance was disquieting to the natives and for a moment, their captives were forgotten.

A dozen of the men circled around to where they were between the two strangers and their prisoners. They quickly decided it was a trick, or a trap, two men would not attack twenty – unless they were crazy.

One of the taller warriors barked a command and a handful of the natives charged the newcomers. Thorvald swore as he pulled his sword free. Why couldn't people just discuss things?

Fifteen of the warriors remained with the captives and watched the brief encounter in disbelief. The taller of the two strangers decapitated the first man with an effortless pivot and swing. The old man dispatched two of their best warriors with an ease that was close to contempt.

Thorvald had hardly broken stride in the 'fight', sliding the bloody sword back in its scabbard with a finesse that came from countless repetitions.

The natives took one look at the trail of carnage behind the towering monster that was striding towards them and, forgetting their prisoners, made a dash for the trees.

The three men and two women remained on their knees, too terrified to move. The fate that awaited them at the hands of the other natives was something they could understand. What these strange giants would do to them was unimaginable.

As Thorvald approached them, they began chanting something in a language the Vikings did not understand. The clan leader walked around to stand in front of the oldest of the men and looked down at him.

"Stand up."

Middle aged, the man was obviously terrified. He glanced up at Thorvald and quickly looked down again. He stopped chanting, fidgeting with his hands nervously.

Thorvald dropped to one knee and clasped the man on the shoulder. "We are not going to harm you. You do not need to be afraid."

The man didn't understand the words, but he understood the tone and gesture. Slowly raising his head, he watched as Thorvald stood and took a couple of steps back.

The huge warrior motioned him to stand and he did so. The Viking flashed a relaxed smile and swung his head toward the kneeling natives. The older native quickly shook his head and said something to the others over his shoulder.

They looked at each other and slowly stood; casting nervous glances at the two towering giants. If they weren't going to kill them, why did they stop the others? You didn't interfere with another tribe's business unless you wanted something.

The three men and two women kept their eyes down as they edged away from the Vikings. Thorvald and Wotun stood watching them until they were about ten feet away.

One of the women glanced up and, spinning on the ball of her foot, dashed away down the beach. The rest of the natives froze, waiting to see how their captors would react.

When neither foreigner moved, they all turned and ran like the hounds of Hel were on their heels.

Thorvald glanced at Wotun and shrugged. "Looks like we're not going to get a 'thanks', much less an invite to supper. Shall we head back?"

The old man scowled and without replying, turned and started walking up the beach, back towards their encampment.

By the time they returned to the ships, most of the clan was up and about in the cold, grey dawn. A few fires were going and the quiet mutterings of numerous conversations could be heard above the faint chirping of birds and rhythm of the tide.

The two boys came running out to meet their father. Thorvald smiled in spite of himself. He had only spent a few years with the boys as small children and yet they acted like he had been doting on them all their lives. That was the way of it with children. If a parent showed them affection, they belonged to that person, heart and soul.

Packing Wulf and mussing Eric's hair, he walked over to where Freyhild was preparing breakfast. Fresh fish, salt pork and spring water were served with a shy smile. Thorvald and the woman exchanged glances as the boys dove into their food. The look in her eyes told him she was considering him for a mate.

She turned away from the Viking leader, taking her plate to sit by the boys.

" Good morn Eric, Wulf. How are you boys?"

Wulf's bright face popped up with a broad smile. His chin was streaked with breakfast grease.

"Real good, ma'am. Thank you."

She looked over at Eric's red mop of hair. He slowly raised his head and wiped grease from his face with the sleeve of his shirt.

"Mornin Freyhild. I am well, thank you."

The woman's smile faded when she noticed the drawn face and tired eyes. The boy appeared to be exhausted and the sun was barely up. She glanced over at Thorvald. He was telling the story of the encounter with the natives to some of the crew. When he finished, everyone laughed and more stories began.

It was obvious the boy had said nothing to his father and the chances of him telling her anything were slim.

"Are you feeling all right Eric?"

The lad quickly looked up and turned away before answering.

"Ahh, yes ma'am. I'm fine."

Freyhild ate a few more bites and stood up. She moved closer to Eric and ran long, slender fingers through the unruly mop of hair. After studying him for a moment she gave him a motherly smile and walked away.

Wulf watched his brother as he talked around a mouthful of food. "She's pretty. I like her."

Eric frowned at his little brother. "You like every girl that feeds you."

"I do not. Besides, she's not a girl," said Wulf, somewhat offended.

"You're right." Eric flashed a quick smile. "She's not a girl. And I like her too."

He watched as she stopped a moment to say something to his father. Thorvald spoke briefly with the woman and looked pointedly at Eric. The look of concern on his father's face made him think he might be in trouble, and for a minute he was wondering if he had upset Freyhild somehow.

But she was smiling when she left and did not seem angry. No, it was something else. He watched his father stand and approach the two of them. The brothers moved apart a little, allowing their father to sit between them.

Thorvald was picking his teeth with a sharpened twig and working up to saying something. The boys remained quiet, finishing their breakfast in silence. Finally, their father spoke. "How would you boys like to go hunting today? We need meat and it looks like there is quite a bit of game hereabouts."

Wulf jumped up and started chattering like a squirrel. "You mean it father? That would be great. We'd love to go hunting, wouldn't we Eric! We talk about it all the time. We used to pretend . . ."

Thorvald held up a hand. "Whoa, hold on there Wulf. I'll take that as a yes from you. How bout you Eric?"

For the first time, Thorvald noticed that his older son did look drawn and tired. The boy smiled slowly. "Yes, I would like that."

The man nodded, patting each of his sons on their knees. "Then it's settled, we leave as soon as you finish breakfast."

Wulf resumed his chattering. "I'm done. See, my plates clean. I'll get the bows and arrows. Will we need knives? Of course we will. I'll get us some knives too."

Eyes flashing with excitement, he rushed off in the direction Freyhild had taken.

Thorvald glanced over at Eric and quickly looked away. "Are you all right son?"

The boy looked at his father for a moment and then slowly dropped his eyes. "I don't know. You know the nightmare I keep having . . . about our village burning?"

The man pursed his lips, watching his son. "Yes. Are you still having that dream?"

Eric picked up a small piece of driftwood, broke it, and dropped the pieces. "I've never had a dream about our village. They're dreams that don't make any sense."

He brushed his hands off on his breeches. "They're weird dreams, about the gods Odin and Loki, dwarves and . . . beautiful, terrifying places."

Thorvald rose to his feet. Angry and frustrated, he had no answers for his son. His eyes found Wotun and glared angrily at the arched back. He knew it wasn't the old man's fault. Somehow he felt responsible, but wasn't sure why. He had left the boys alone too much.

Turning towards Eric, he placed a huge hand on the small shoulder. "Give it some time son. These things have a way of working themselves out."

He tried to lighten the tone in his voice and changed the subject. "Now, what say we grab a bow and go kill something? I think that brother of yours may leave without us if we don't get a move on."

Eric flashed a real smile at his father and nodded in understanding. "You're probably right. I'm ready."

He stood up and picked up the plates he and Wulf had been eating from, before adding, "I'll be fine father. Like you say, it will all work out."

Chapter 15

The Ice Castle

Heading up a gently sloping trail that paralleled a clear stream, Eric did feel a little better. Telling someone about the dreams seemed to help. He had experienced a wide variety of dreams and nightmares in his life, but these were different somehow. It was almost as though he was transported to a time and place far removed from the world he knew. That was the problem – the nightly sojourns were unlike anything he had ever encountered and impossible to describe.

Thorvald told Wulf to stay close to him as he led the boys uphill, following a clear, cold creek. They came to a fork in the steam and decided Eric would follow the channel to the right and Thorvald and Wulf would go to the left.

The older brother had spent much of his life in the woods and felt comfortable in going alone. However, he had never killed a deer before and was excited at the possibility. After practicing countless hours, he was a good shot and the bow he carried was far better than any other he had previously used.

Climbing steadily for a couple of hours, he broke into a large meadow surrounding a small, pristine lake. The setting was absolutely beautiful. Ragged, snow capped mountains forming a backdrop for the placid waters were reflected in the glistening surface.

His heart skipped a beat when he saw a small buck with its head down on the far side of the lake. The animal had come down for water in the mid-morning quiet. A gentle breeze moved through and rustled the tall grass at the lakes' edge. The caressing wind was pushing gently against his face. That was good; his scent would not be carried to the deer.

Crouching down and working back into the timber, he turned to the left and broke into a dog trot as soon as the cover of the trees concealed his movements. The ground was still moist from the mornings dew and he moved with a practiced grace in complete silence.

In less than ten minutes, he was directly behind and slightly above the deer. He realized the wind was now moving from him towards the animal and quickly backtracked a short distance. The buck lifted its head abruptly and turned to look into the woods.

Suddenly nervous, the animal turned to walk along the bank a short distance, continually glancing into the woods. Finally, satisfied the danger had passed, he began nibbling on the tender shoots growing along the lake's edge.

Time passed and the long, beige ears picked up the sounds of a distant human voice. Flicking them in agitation, the white-tail turned and headed back into the woods.

The hunter remained crouched in silence, waiting for close to an hour. The patience finally paid off. The three-point buck passed within ten paces of the concealed bowman, carefully picking its way, testing the air and listening intently.

Eric's heart was pounding so hard it was difficult to breathe, much less hold the bow steady. Positioned on one knee, the tip of the bow barely cleared the ground as he pulled it to a full draw.

Sensing the boy's presence, the deer froze. The huge, brown eyes were sweeping the area, but the head remained motionless. By the time it heard the twang of the bow, it was too late. The animal leaped at the impact, fleeing into the dense timber.

Eric knew he was supposed to sit still and give the animal time to lie down and bleed out, but he was so excited he raced after it. The scattered streaks of blood in the grass turned onto a game trail a short distance from the lake.

Fifty paces down the wooded path, it dropped off a steep embankment into a ravine. He rushed down the slope, hooking his foot on a ground vine to go tumbling head over heels.

Lights flashed in his eyes and a searing pain shot through the back of his head. He rolled to a stop and lay flat on his back for a few minutes until the spinning stopped. Rising up on one elbow, he rubbed his nose with the back of his hand as the surroundings came back into focus.

He stood and wiped the mud from his hands. Picking up his bow, he retrieved the scattered arrows, placed them back in the quiver and checked his knife. Chiding himself for acting like a child, he sat down and started sharpening the blade of the bone handled weapon.

After waiting about half an hour, he told himself if it was a good shot the deer would be dead by now. He climbed the other side of the ravine and there, about twenty yards farther down the trail, lay the buck.

He allowed himself a small smile of triumph as he approached the carcass. Kneeling beside the animal, he took out his knife and was about to cut the throat when he heard a voice behind him.

"You must thank the deer for its life."

He jumped at the sound and spun around with the knife in his hand. The knuckles were white around the bone handle in his fist. He froze as his mouth dropped open. Standing in front of him was the most beautiful woman he had ever seen.

A soft shimmer in the air surrounded her. Eric's heart had leaped into his throat and he was having trouble getting in back down.

"Who . . . who are you? Where did you come from?"

The woman's lips formed a beatific smile. "We . . . I am a guardian of the wild rivers and woodland creatures. In my homeland, we were sisters of the Rhine Maidens."

Eric stared at the woman, slowly closing his mouth and swallowing. As far back as he could remember he had heard incredible tales of the Rhine Maidens. Some stories told of horrendous creatures that lived in the rivers in the countries south of their homeland. The terrible creatures would drag children to their death if they dared to venture near the stream. Others told of beautiful, gentle fairies living in the glistening streams during the long, cold months of winter and roaming through the forests in summer.

The youth noticed the gossamer gown was transparent and he flushed with embarrassment. He had seen women and girls without their clothes on before, but never one so beautiful and . . . His mind went blank as he searched for words that weren't there.

Once again, she smiled. "You should finish your task."

Blinking at the statement, he turned woodenly back to the deer. "Thank you for . . . providing us with food."

It sounded silly talking to a dead animal, but somehow he knew the deer had heard and acknowledged the gratitude.

In a daze, he cut through the hide just below the head and a crimson flow gushed forth. He cupped his hand for a little of the blood and bringing it to his mouth, gulped it down. It was warm and tasted slightly salty. Somewhere in the inner recesses of his mind, he realized he had been blooded with his first kill.

He wiped his mouth with his sleeve and turned to see if the woman was still there. She was, and did not seem disturbed at the timeless ritual. He stood up, trying to think of something to say.

The beautiful vision glanced at the bloody knife and then to his face. Her brows lowered into a frown and he suddenly felt she disapproved of his actions.

"We're supposed to drink the blood of our first kill. I did not think . . ."

He stopped when she shook her head. "No it is not that. You have hurt your head. It's bleeding."

Reaching up with his free hand, he felt the sticky wetness on the side of his head. He was so excited he hadn't noticed. "Oh. I fell chasing the deer. I must have hit my head."

The enchantress stepped closer and pushed some damp hair out of the way. The touch of her hand was a completely new experience. He wanted to tell her not to take her hand away, but realized it would sound childish.

The fairy maiden froze momentarily at the contact and then carefully continued to move the hair back for a better look. "You are not what you seem lad. The blood of the old gods flows in your veins. How is this possible?"

"I . . . don't know. We . . . my people come from a place far across the sea. I'm a stranger in your land."

The woman started to say something, but changed her mind. Instead, she reached down and gently grasped his wrist, sliding her palm against his. He felt a jolt and everything disappeared in a swirl of warm colors.

When the spinning stopped and his vision cleared, he was standing in the midst of an exquisite garden. A gay profusion of flowers lined crystalline pools and equestrian statues. The expansive lawns had been manicured with loving and experienced hands.

The stone paved walkway led to a towering, magnificent castle. He was still holding the woman's hand and began wondering if he had died and been taken to *Valhalla.*

Stories of the Viking heaven told of towering walls made of golden spears and vaulted ceilings constructed from the countless shields of brave warriors. Combatants lucky enough to be swooped up from the battlefield among the glorious slain would live on until the final battle of Ragnarok.

The citadel appeared to be made of glass, or ice. It was incredibly beautiful. Glistening spires extended into the low hanging clouds and a rainbow of colors flashed from every facet of the structure.

The woman watched him briefly and smiled knowingly. "Do you like it?"

Eric pulled his eyes from the castle to the maiden. "I've never seen anything like it. It's the most beautiful thing I have ever seen." He reached up and felt the dried blood on the side of his head. "Am I dead?"

His chaperon blinked in surprise. "No. Why would you think that?"

He shrugged and waved his hands in a sweeping gesture. "Where are we? Is this *Valhalla*?"

The enchanting woman laughed lightly. "Oh my goodness! No, this is . . . well, long ago it would have been known as *Alfheim*."

Eric looked back at the castle. *Alfheim*. The home of the light elves and fairies; a magical land that existed only in the sagas of bards and the minds of children.

Looking back towards the marvelous structure, he noticed another woman walking towards them. Tall and slender, power emanated from her that could be felt even at a distance. She was surrounded by the soft glow that comes from candles and walked with the feline grace that only women possess.

The woman holding Eric's hand gave a quick bob in the form of a curtsey and addressed the other woman as she approached. "Groa, I encountered this young man in the woods – he was hurt."

The newcomer studied him for a moment before responding. "You have done well Rosvet. I imagine you have already discovered the lad is not what he seems."

She reached over to place her hand under his chin and lifted it to where he was looking into her eyes. The orbs were a piercing azure. He noticed a sapphire sparkle deep within for just a moment, and then she spoke again.

"He reminds me of Orvandil when he was this age."

Rosvet glanced quickly at the other woman and then looked away. Orvandil was Groa's eldest son; kidnapped by frost giants as a young man and never seen again. Not knowing how to respond, Rosvet said, "I think the cut on his head is the only hurt."

Groa looked at Rosvet for a moment and then mysteriously produced a small cup of liquid which she offered to Eric. "This is a light mead made from Idun's fruits. It tastes good and will heal your wound."

Eric felt he could trust the women and drank the fluid without hesitation. The throbbing pain in his head slowed and disappeared. When he felt his scalp, he could detect a slightly raised line that had been the gash in his head.

He lowered his hand and turned slightly towards Rosvet. "Idun's fruit?"

The woman gave him a smile that reached his very core and replied, "Ah, Freyja's apples. They are truly a marvelous fruit. They keep you young, as well as healing wounds."

Rosvet released his hand and pushed the heavy mop of hair back from his face. "It appears your head is almost as good as new. Would you like to have a look around before you return?"

Eric's eyes swept the area before nodding. "Yes. I would like that very much."

Flanked by Groa and Rosvet, he started toward the massive front doors of the castle. Tiny figures flitted by, causing Eric to stop and stare. "Fairies . . . are those fairies?"

The women stopped at the same time, laughing lightly. Groa spoke first. "That is what they were called in *Midgard* . . . what used to be *Midgard*. We refer to them as nature's rhapsody."

Looking towards a small cluster of the tiny beings, Groa called softly. "Feejar! Have you a minute?"

In response to the call, one of the delicate creatures flew directly towards them. Groa turned her hand so the palm was up and opened it. The fairy landed lightly and curtseyed. The long hair and curves made it clear she was a woman -- her miniscule features were well defined and quite lovely.

A tiny smile lit up the glowing face and she spoke with a voice not unlike the ringing of a small bell. "Yes mistress. You called?"

"I have a young man here I would like you to meet." She waited until Feejar turned to face the boy.

"This is Eric, a lad from a land far away."

A small voice in Eric's head asked him how Groa knew where he was from, but he never took his eyes from the tiny fairy.

The delicate creature bobbed her head in greeting and extended a dainty hand. Eric blinked and realized she was offering to shake hands with him. He reached over carefully to touch the impossibly small digits and almost jumped back when he felt a normal hand clasp his, in a warm and friendly grasp.

When he felt the grip release, he stepped back slightly, unable to keep from staring at the small, beautiful apparition.

"Your wings are the most beautiful things I've ever seen."

"Yes, it is with sadness we lose them at summer's end."

"You lose your wings?"

"Yes."

"How do you fly?"

A tinkling sound from the sprite indicated she thought the comment humorous. "Humans still think fairies need wings to fly. That is, those who believe in us. If that were true, we would be in sorry shape each winter."

She straightened a few errant folds in her diaphanous gown and ran her hands over her butt, glancing back over her shoulder in a manner that was all female.

"All fairies, men and women, shed their wings each fall with the first snowflake and grow them back when the first bud of spring opens."

It appeared the tiny woman was going to say nothing more, so Groa added, "In spring, summer and fall, the land is dressed in its finest and so it is with nature's rhapsody."

Feejar glanced at Groa and at some unspoken signal, flashed a parting smile and flitted away.

Eric stood spellbound as the myriad of sparks clustered momentarily and then vanished into the surrounding vegetation.

"No one will ever believe this. I'm not sure I do."

For the first time, the two women grew serious and after exchanging glances, the older woman placed a hand on Eric's shoulder. "What I am about to tell you will be hard to understand, but you must try."

The change in the woman's tone brought Eric out of his reverie and he turned a solemn face to her. "I'm listening."

She walked over to sit on a nearby bench and motioned Eric and Rosvet to join her.

After they were seated comfortably, she drew in a deep breath and began. "You're coming here is not an accident. The path you follow may lead to great deeds and even glory. This sounds exciting, but men of honor and valor travel in the company of terrible hardship and sorrow. I wish it were not so, but that is the way of life. It has always been and always will be."

Pausing, she reached over and patted Eric gently on the knee. "As you travel on your life's quest, there will be times when you feel you cannot continue. The urge to share your burden with someone, anyone will be tremendous, but it is a journey you must take alone.

"That is all I can tell you for now. Come, there is someone I want you to meet."

She stood and glanced at Rosvet. "There are three . . . women that live in the heart of the castle. I think it is time you met them."

Rosvet gasped slightly and her wide eyes were questioning the wisdom of Groa's decision, but she remained silent. She wrung her hands nervously and began to fidget. "I better check on the garden and see . . ."

The sentence was left unfinished as her eyes returned to those of Groa's. "I'll take the boy back when you're . . . when he is ready."

Groa nodded in dismissal and Rosvet quickly walked away. The older woman then turned and headed towards the castle, calling over her shoulder. "Come."

Eric leapt to his feet and rushed to catch up. His heart was racing -- he was somewhat frightened, and irritated by the fact he wasn't sure what he was scared of. He caught up with the woman, but still had to hurry to keep up with her long, purposeful strides.

When they reached the steps of the palace, he stopped briefly to reach out and touch the glistening surface. It was not ice. At least it did not seem to be cold or slick. It did not resemble the material that made glass trinkets either. He could not identify the substance. Groa noticed him stop and drew to a halt as the boy touched the wall.

"You have never seen that material before, and will probably never see it again. This is the only place it exists."

He looked up at her. "What is it?"

Groa frowned at the question. "I'm not sure I can explain."

She moved back down to the step the boy was on and thought for a moment before answering. "You are familiar with the cold burn of ice?"

When Eric nodded in ascent, she resumed her explanation. "Well, everything in nature has a good and bad aspect; light and dark, kind and cruel, happy and sad. The winters of Midgard were cold, dark, long and frightening. The season of snow and ice provided only death to the weak or careless.

"Mankind saw winter as the taker of life, cruel and unforgiving. The other side of winter consists of an incredible beauty, peace and renewal."

She reached over and placed a hand on the boy's shoulder. "We see what we are looking for. Far too often the things that make us happy; the sunshine on our face, the fruit of life, or a child's smile, go unnoticed. We only see what our eyes have focused on. There is nothing else in life at that moment in time. Life is composed of moments.

"This fasthold is the embodiment of the beauty in winter. The glistening snow, sparkling springs and warmth within the deep snows." The woman paused and looked backwards into a long forgotten past. "As winter holds the promise of spring and rebirth, this citadel holds the good and beauty of a time long past, in hopes that someday, evil will fade and we can return to the glory of a forgotten age."

Eric nodded slowly. He was fairly sure he understood. This . . . realm was a frozen moment in time representing all the good that had been lost through the folly of gods and men.

Looking around him, he soaked in the vista. "All of this. Is it just in my mind?"

Groa smiled. "That is a very good question. No, it really exists, but you are getting the idea. You are learning to think with your senses, as well as your mind."

They started up the steps again. Eric's mind was whirling with the concepts that had just been placed before him. Like an iceberg, a small portion of life was easy to see and understand, but the important things, the real mass, was hidden from view.

The massive, towering doors leading into the castle were intricately carved with woodland creatures, gods and countless runes. Eric could feel a powerful aura created by the doors as he passed. An incredible amount of magic had been instilled in the portal and it seemed neither bad nor good, but timeless.

Inside, the main hall was vast, brightly lit with a natural light that permeated the interior, providing warmth similar to the sun's rays. He felt small and insignificant following Groa across the barren expanse of glistening floor. In the distance, a tall rectangular door was outlined in the far wall. That was where they were heading.

Exiting through the portal, he noticed there were numerous hallways leading from the doorway and Groa took the first hall to the left. She checked to see that her charge was still in tow, nodded her approval, and headed down the corridor.

Less than thirty paces down the hallway, she stopped at the head of a stairway, leading down to the right. She cast a nervous glance down the stairwell and turned back towards Eric. "From this point on, you must not speak. Touch nothing except the floor. Is this understood?"

"Yes." Eric swallowed, nodding his head.

Groa studied him for a moment as though she were having second thoughts. Uncertainty lined her face as she slowly turned away. "Very well. Stay close to me and remember – absolute silence."

Eric felt a shiver run up his spine as they started the descent. He told himself his imagination was getting the better of him and to stay calm.

The light changed from a warm yellow to a soft chaos of colors as they descended deeper into the bowels of the castle. The riot of hues in the far northern skies came to mind as he tried to reason the source of the colorful illumination.

A strange smell drifted past and his skin began to crawl, reminding him of walking through the burned-out village of his childhood. He was trying to identify the odor when a low, wailing moan found its way to his eardrums. He reached up to touch Groa on the sleeve. She stopped and turned towards him.

The look in her eyes said it all; 'Be silent and follow me'.

He realized the older woman was not frightened, but concerned. Concerned about him. He looked inward, wondering if he was in mortal danger. His father had once told him that only a madman, or a fool, never knew fear.

These thoughts were tumbling through his mind when they reached the bottom of the stairs. Groa stopped and reached back to gently touch his arm. He stood motionless as her hand slid down to take his hand.

There were three doorways leading from the landing and for a moment, Groa seemed uncertain of which to use. Finally, letting out a long breath, she glanced at Eric and walked through the middle portal.

They entered an incongruous room, filled with cobwebs and crude toys. An antiquated spinning wheel sat in the middle of the room, covered with dust. A huge fireplace was dimly lit by a small fire in the center of the cavernous opening. Directly above the fire, a large, bronze caldron was suspended from an ornate iron arm. Arcane runes, encased with black soot, covered the bulging sides.

Remnants of gigantic tree roots were visible here and there in the walls of the chamber. Burnt to charcoal, the tentacles had been lifeless for countless generation and Eric felt a strange pang of loss at the sight.

A woman's voice emanated from a darkened corner of the room.

"I see you have brought us a visitor Groa. To what do we owe this . . . honor?"

Groa turned towards the sound, trying to see into the darkness.

"I have a young man I wanted you to meet Verdandi. You and your sisters." She paused before adding, "But then you already knew that."

The darkness in the corner evaporated to reveal three women in various positions, watching the visitors. The woman on the left was sitting in a chair and appeared to be ancient, even antediluvian. Standing next to her was a woman about Groa's age, mature, neither young nor old. The last was little more than a child. The slender figure giving way to the blossom of womanhood.

Groa addressed the two additional women by name. "Urd, Skuld, it is good to see you again. I hope you are well."

Urd, the Old One, glared at the woman and then at the boy. Exhaling through her teeth in a hiss, she looked down at the fragile scrolls in her lap before speaking.

"The blood of the old gods flows in that boy. Many and varied are the threads that lead to and from his body. I know why he is here, but the trail ahead is not mine to see."

Groa looked towards Skuld. The youngest Norn's eyes were glazed over, revealing nothing. The Norns were known as the fates when Thor, Odin and the frost giants walked the nine worlds. Now, they were the tattered remnants of a glorious age long past. But the arcane power still residing in the three small, frail frames was unfathomable.

Once again, Groa spoke. "Skuld, the boy is a mystery. Can you tell where his future lay?"

At first, there was no response from the young woman; she remained standing at a distance with the opaque gaze locked on infinity.

After a moment, she turned slowly and moved towards the boy, but Verdandi gently took her younger sister by the arm, holding her back.

"Wait. Let me see who the young man is, and where he is now, before we determine his destiny."

Skuld stopped. The response neither subservient nor defiant.

The middle aged fate walked over to Eric, placed her hand on the side of his neck and held it there briefly. After a moment, she dropped her hand and studied the boy.

"Strange. Tis almost as though . . ."

She turned to look at Groa and frowned. "Urd is right. The boy's blood is tinged with that of a god long dead. Where did you find him?"

The aged fairy didn't turn away from the challenging stare. "I told you Verdandi, the boy is an enigma. Rosvet found him hurt in the forest and brought him here to heal his wound. That is all I know."

Verdandi held Groa's eyes for a moment and then turned to her sister. "Skuld, come here please."

The girl slowly raised her head and opened lidded orbs to look at her sister. The eyes within were streaked with a myriad of colors that seemed to recede into an abyss.

"As you wish."

She walked over to stand next to the boy. They were about the same height, but the girl appeared to be slightly older. She reached down and grasped Eric's hand and held it briefly.

The Viking youth felt a strange sensation flowing into his arm and back out again. His arm tingled slightly when she released it and he unconsciously began rubbing it.

The girl stared at him for a moment with a questioning look on her face and then turned to Verdandi.

"A young man with a glorious and tragic destiny stands before you. Hard and bloody is the trail he is destined to follow. The next few years will provide the training ground for the mighty quest of discovery that lay ahead.

"The hammer of Thor will fall to his seed. The footsteps of the greatest of the gods he will follow. But the darkness that was Loki will inflict a wound of evil from which there is no recovery."

She looked steadily at Eric before closing her eyes and turning away, saying nothing more.

Verdandi glanced at the boy and then to Groa. "Tis as I thought. The young man could be our salvation, or death knell. Our future lies in his hands."

Making the statement seemed to irritate the Norn and she turned away abruptly before throwing back over her shoulder. "We have answered your questions, now leave."

Groa opened her mouth to speak, but after a moment, closed it and took Eric by the hand. Verdandi's last comment had her mind reeling. The fate of the world lay in the hands of the Norns. How could their future lie in the hands of a small boy?

She was heading for the door when the youngest fate spoke again.

"Wait."

They stopped and the Skuld moved next to Eric. She grasped his wrist and placed a small object in his hand. He glanced down and in his palm rested a tiny dragon. The talisman was attached to a finely wrought chain, so he placed it around his neck.

He looked up at the girl, but she had already turned away and was walking back to join her sisters.

"Thank you Skuld, but what is it for?"

Without turning around, she answered. "The dragon is a sacred symbol of the old beliefs." She stopped and turned. "What do you wish it to be?"

The boy stared in silence as the dimly lit corner of the room returned to darkness. Groa let out a long sigh and once more started for the door with her charge in tow.

A thousand questions were flashing through Eric's head as they headed out of the castle. What had Skuld meant by a 'hard and bloody trail'? She said something about Thor's hammer . . . and the evil of Loki?

He was about to ask Groa if she understood the strange premonitions when Rosvet showed up out of nowhere.

The two women exchanged greetings and Rosvet asked if Eric had met the fates. Groa quipped, in the form of an answer, that no, actually the fates had met Eric and didn't seem pleased with the encounter. When Rosvet frowned and started to ask for an explanation, Groa extended the boy's hand to the other woman.

"Later, right now we need to get our charge back where he belongs."

Rosvet closed her mouth and reached for Eric's hand. He felt the soft, warm touch and collapsed into the warmth of summer's darkness.

Carl James

Chapter 16

The Cycle of Seasons

"Eric! Eric wake up."

His father's voice drifted to him from a distance. He looked through the mist and tried to get his eyes open. A fuzzy image of Thorvald came into view. His mind was tumbling around trying to figure out where he was and why his father was staring down at him.

He groaned as a rush of memories from shooting the deer and falling down the ravine poured through his mind.

"Ohhh, I must have hit my head. It hurts something awful."

Struggling to a sitting position, he noticed Wulf and his father were both kneeling beside him with worried expressions on their faces.

Wulf began to chatter. "You ok Eric? We thought you might be dead. There's blood all over the ground. You must have really hit hard. Why were you running? Did you fall? How long . . . ?"

Thorvald held up a hand to interrupt. "Wulf! Hold on a minute. Let him catch his breath."

The younger boy became quiet, but the worried look in his eyes did not change. He reached over to put a hand on Eric's shoulder as a way to tell him he didn't know what was wrong, but everything was going to be all right.

Eric scrubbed a hand over his face and blinked before speaking. "I . . . I'm ok. I just fell and hit my head." Reaching up to gingerly touch the side of his scalp he felt a small ridge under the hair with some dried blood, but no wound. His fingers were tinged with a dull, dusty crimson when he looked at them. He glanced down the trail in the direction the buck had been going.

"I shot a deer and . . ."

Thorvald interrupted. "A deer! Where? Did you kill it?"

Eric looked around, trying to remember if he had killed the buck. He seemed to remember . . . wait, he had gotten up and found the deer. That mysterious woman appeared and . . . nothing was making any sense.

"I'm not sure. I thought I killed it. As a matter of fact, I started to dress it out when . . ."

He stopped and looked around the bottom of the little ravine. Reaching up, he felt the slight ridge on his head again and frowned.

His father noticed the look. "What? Did you remember something?"

Eric forced a slight smile. "I had a strange dream after I fell and hit my head. But I'm pretty sure I did shoot a deer. It should be a short way down this trail."

Thorvald helped him to his feet and Wulf picked up his bow. The older brother dusted himself off and accepted the quiver of arrows from Wulf. Adjusting the quiver on his back, he started up the incline.

They quickly topped the far side of the little ravine and another twenty paces led them to the carcass of the deer. Thorvald cried out in surprise and pride at the discovery. "There it is! Well done boy!"

The pats of congratulation and compliments stopped suddenly when they reached the deer. The broken stub of an arrow was protruding from the animal's side, but that wasn't what caused the sudden change in Thorvald's demeanor. The animal's throat had been cut, leaving a coagulating pool of blood underneath.

Holding up his hand in alarm, he motioned for the boys to be quiet and quickly drew his sword. "Somebody has already been here. They cut the deer's throat."

Listening intently to the silence, the only sounds were coming from a few birds and the hushed breathing of the hunters.

Eric reached up to his chest and felt a small object under the leather jerkin. His heart began to pound as he remembered Skuld and the silver dragon. His dream had been real. Somehow, he had traveled to the glorious realm of the fairies.

He glanced over at his father and voices began arguing furiously in his mind. 'You better tell him what happened!'

'Yeah, right. Tell him a magic fairy swooped me up to a place that doesn't exist. He would laugh out loud unless he thought I was serious. Then he would think I had lost my mind."

'You have the talisman.'

'I could have gotten that anywhere. It proves nothing.'

Exhaling quickly, he decided to let the matter go unresolved for now. He needed time to sort things out. There had to be some rational explanation for what happened – or irrational, if that were the case.

Thorvald stood frozen with sword in hand, testing the breeze and listening intently. He hadn't lived this long by being careless.

Finally satisfied that whoever had come upon the deer was no longer in the vicinity, he let out a long breath and sheathed his sword. He flashed a smile at Wulf and winked at Eric. "What say we get this critter dressed out and back to camp?"

The boys helped their father gut the animal and remove the head. There was no point in carrying anything they couldn't eat or wear. The deer was hoisted onto Thorvald's back and the trio started back towards the coast.

In a couple of hours, the camp's western sentry called out their arrival and soon after most of the clan gathered around the returning hunters. Little was said until Thorvald announced the kill belonged to Eric, his first blooding.

Thorson clapped a huge hand on the boy's shoulder with a 'well done lad'. Several of the young girls in the crowd eyed Eric with a new appreciation. The young man had the makings of a good provider.

The clan needed little in the way of an excuse for a celebration and this was definitely a reason to celebrate. The mead flowed freely late into the night and the entire venison had been consumed before the moon began its ascent.

Time passed and the clan discovered another small village inhabited by Norsemen on the southwestern edge of the huge island. The southern part of the land mass held the best pasture and they learned the place had been named 'Iceland' by a Floki Vilgerdason some thirty years previously.

Floki had found the island known hitherto as 'Gardarsholm' only to lose his livestock and entire family in the cruel winter that followed. He returned to Norway with tales of a frozen land of ice to the west, calling it Iceland.

Shortly thereafter, two foster brothers, Ingolf Arnason and Leif Hrodmarsson took a ship to investigate the tale. Finding good pasture and open land, they returned four years later with their families, slaves and livestock to establish the first settlement.

Two decades later and a year after the incident with the deer Thorvald walked up to Freyhild and bluntly told her he wanted her for a wife. She shook her head at the scowl that accompanied the request and replied, "Well, it took you long enough."

Then with a twinkle in her eye that the man would come to love, she added, "Besides all the good men are already taken."

Thorvald stared at her for a moment, shook his head in agreement with her statement and then realized she was teasing him.

The small clan built huts surrounded by an earthen berm and in three seasons, an additional twenty boats with immigrants from their homeland arrived to expand the little village into a respectable hamlet. The years passed and the two brothers grew into men a day at a time.

Another four snows came and went. The village now had hogs, sheep and oxen wandering past the huts, in and out of the surrounding fields. The hunting was good, the winters had not been extremely hard and there had been no attacks from abominable snow men or the natives known as *skraelings*. It was getting downright boring.

But change is the only thing that remains constant and one beautiful fall day, late in September, the world came crashing down. Eric had earned quite a reputation as a hunter and worked hard to maintain the image. It not only produced the desired response from the young women of the village; it helped keep the larders stocked with fresh meat.

Thorvald and Wulf had left early that morning with several other men from the village in search of game. The deer population had been virtually decimated. There were foxes, mink and a wide variety of rats, mice, ducks and geese, but the villagers were becoming more and more dependent upon domestic stock for sustenance.

Eric was sliding an iron spear point over a fine grained stone, sharpening the foot-long blade, when his vision started to blur. His head felt strange, not a headache, but difficult to ignore. He reached up to rub his temple. The image of the hut in front of him began to waver in the mid-day sun. Trying to focus only increased the swirling image and when it finally cleared, he was staring down a woodland trail in the forest to the west of the village. He blinked, but the scene remained as clear as if he were actually standing on the trail.

Thorvald came striding through the trees, barking something in laughter over his shoulder. The image shifted slightly and Wulf appeared a short distance behind his father, with a large buck across the young shoulders.

He smiled at the scene. Wulf was fifteen and big for his age. Incredibly gentle and strong, he was proving to be a good companion, whether on the hunt or doing grueling, backbreaking work. The lad was also a good influence on his father, taking away much of the bitter hardness that had darkened his soul.

Harald, Alve, Snorrack and Gulev were strung out along the trail behind Wulf and his father, carrying another deer and several more smiles. The light banter stopped at the sound of bear cubs a short distance away. The Vikings had not seen any bear on the island for several years and it took them a moment to identify the noise.

From the sounds, the cubs were only playing; growling in mock battle. The young bears posed no threat to the hunters, but the mother would not be far away.

Throwing a hand up, Thorvald motioned for the men to back up – quietly. They had only taken a few steps when Gulev cried out in response to the guttural roar of a full-grown tundra grizzly. What the bear was doing on this remote island, they would never know, but they were between the sow and her cubs and she wasn't going to give them a chance to get out of the way.

Gulev screamed in agony as the huge bear ripped open the front of him. The remaining men dropped the deer carcasses and leapt in defense of their comrade. Given time to think, they would have realized the man was already dead. They needed to look to their own safety, but the rage of revenge was upon them and they charged the shaggy beast.

Alve managed to sink his spear half an arms length into the side of the beast, but a downward swipe of the massive paw left a bloody skull where his face had been. Harald and Snorrack were stabbing into the heavy fur repeatedly with eight inch hunting knives. The roars of pain and rage from the carnivore gave evidence of the damage inflicted.

A backward swipe from the old sow sent Snorrack rolling head over heels into the surrounding brush and the other front leg grabbed Harald in a bone-crushing hug. Dropping to all fours, the bear rolled back lips to expose ivory stubs the size of a man's thumb and clamped down on Harald's neck. The sound of bones breaking and flesh being torn apart was followed by a scream cut short.

The bear threw up a bloody snout when a searing pain shot through its gut. Spinning in fury at the new pain, she threw a huge paw at the boy standing by her side. Wulf had buried his sword to the hilt and the wound would be mortal, given time. The lad ducked the savage swipe, but she caught him with a backward swing and lunged towards the fallen body.

Everything happened incredibly fast. A massive forepaw landed on Wulf's chest and he threw up his arm in front of the jaws as they flashed towards his face. The bite from the bloody jaws never came.

Thorvald lunged at the bear as it dropped towards his son. Pulling his knife free in mid-air, he knew he wouldn't survive, but it was better than dying in bed and he smiled at the thought.

The old sow was huge, but Thorvald was close to two-fifty and still solid. The collision resulted in a spinning brawl between Viking and bear as they rolled down the steep embankment. Both combatants were roaring in rage as the sound continued into the dense foliage below the trail.

Wulf struggled to his feet and gasped in pain. The huge grizzly must have broken several of his ribs because the pain was nauseating. His sword was gone, but a spear head with two feet of splintered shaft was lying near Alve, so he grabbed it and biting down against the pain, followed the trail of destruction down the hill.

Rushing down the steep hillside, the young warrior lost his footing and hurtled face first into the broken vegetation. He crashed into the base of a tree, unaware that distant eyes were watching intently. Gasping in pain, he tried to rise again. Waves of excruciating agony shot through his mind and the surrounding leaves dissolved in a myriad of colors before fading into darkness.

Eric was still staring straight ahead when an old man's voice broke the trance. "So it has come to pass, you see what I see."

He blinked and the trees vanished, to be replaced by an old, white haired man standing in front of him. He nodded slowly, feeling panic rising from deep in his chest. "Are they dead?"

Wotun shook his head. "I do not know, but what is done, is done."

Eric glanced at the ground, his mind swirling. Inhaling deeply, he jumped to his feet. "Braggia! Magnus! To me! The hunters need our help!"

Rushing into the adjoining hut, he grabbed his sword and almost knocked Freyhild flat in his haste.

"Eric! What is it? What was that about the hunters? Are Thorvald and Wulf all right?"

The woman had become the young man's second mother and he addressed her as such. "They have been hurt mother; I must go to them at once."

The woman's mouth dropped open and slowly closed as Eric rushed across the open ground of the village. Two other men ran to catch up with him as he dove into the trees surrounding the cleared fields.

She turned away and noticed Wotun watching her. When their eyes met, the old man's eye dropped with a slight shake of his head. With that simple gesture he tore her world apart. She knew she had lost the man who made life worth living.

Unable to swallow, she clutched her stomach and began to wander aimlessly. Several other women approached her questioningly and then quietly moved away.

Meanwhile, trying to keep up with Eric proved futile for the two young men who had responded to his summons. They staggered to a stop on the side of a distant ridge to lean against the trees, gasping for breath. By the time they resumed the chase, Eric reached the scene of the sow's enraged attack.

Snorrack had managed to sit upright, but was spitting blood and swaying back and forth. Seeing Eric, he frowned in a daze and slowly looked around him. Alve and Gulev were both lying in contorted positions in the blood splattered shrubs.

Eric quickly checked the chests of both men and glanced back at Snorrack, shaking his head. The huge bear had broken Alve's neck with the swipe that removed half his face.

The young clan leader stood up and swept the surrounding trees, searching for his father and brother. The entire area was torn asunder with blood smeared leaves and broken brush everywhere you looked. A trail of crushed oak and debris led off to the south over the steep hillside.

He threw a quick questioning glance at Snorrack, nodding towards the trail of carnage. Snorrack lifted his hands in a confused gesture, indicating he didn't know where the missing hunters were. Eric nodded quickly and dropped off the little plateau.

Thirty paces down the rugged incline, he saw Wulf lying face down at the base of a tree amidst the lush, torn vegetation. He wasn't moving.

His heart leaped into his throat, making it difficult to breathe. He slid to a stop a short distance above his brother and carefully worked his way down the rest of the way to avoid further injury to the prone body.

He gently laid a hand on his brother's back but his heart was hammering so hard he couldn't feel any movement at first. Then he discerned a slight movement.

His breathing steadied, concentrating on the gentle rise and fall under his hand – Wulf was still alive.

Hearing a noise just above him, Eric spun around as his sword leapt into his hand. Braggia and Magnus came to a sliding stop, falling on their backsides in a hasty attempt to put on the brakes. "Eric! It's us!"

The young Viking slowly lowered his blade. His chest was heaving as he replaced the sword. "Braggia, Magnus. Good, you're here."

He nodded towards his brother. "Wulf, he's hurt . . . badly, I think."

Glancing down at the torn brush below, he turned back toward his comrades. "Thorvald must be down there somewhere. I have to find him."

Braggia quickly stood. "Go Eric, we will tend to Wulf. Go. Find your father."

Eric knew the men would care for his brother and said nothing, but shook his head in gratitude. Spinning quickly, he flew down the path of destruction as though it were a well worn trail.

Fifty paces down the hillside the ground disappeared over the edge of a cliff. He grabbed some young saplings to avoid tumbling off the edge and hit hard, but stopped.

In his heart he already knew, but this meant he could no longer deny it. His father was dead.

He crawled to the edge of the precipice and peered over. Far below, he could see the broken body of the man he had loved since he was a small child, lying next to the biggest bear he had ever seen.

A deep swallow lodged in his throat and refused to move, he backed away from the scene as it began to blur into a glistening image. Moving uphill a short distance from the cliff, he concentrated on getting his breathing steady and his mind to stop tumbling.

After the searing pain began to subside, he let out a long, shuddering sigh and slowly stood. Glancing left and right he started working along the edge of the dangerous drop.

Sixty paces west a deep crevice in the cliff allowed Eric to work his way to the base. It seemed an eternity to the young warrior by the time he approached the stream flowing along the canyon bottom.

He raced upstream along the boulder strewn bank, reaching the body just as the sun dipped below the ragged, green horizon.

Kneeling beside the craggy face, he gently lifted his father's head, brushing the grass and leaves from the grey streaked beard.

He let out a long sigh and wiped blood from a deep gash in the cheek. "Well father, twas a good death. I just wish . . ."

A rustling sound nearby brought the quiet lament to a sudden halt.

Without looking around, he slowly lowered Thorvald's head and moved his hand toward the hilt of his sword. Spinning to his feet, the sword was in his hand and flashing with the last rays of the day.

There, less than ten paces away were the intruders. The two cubs had found their way down into the canyon and were hesitantly approaching the body of their mother. The pathetic nudging and coaxing by the cubs produced no results and they finally plopped down beside the body and curled up, waiting for the sow to awaken.

Eric looked away from the heart wrenching sight and slid the sword back home. A faint, keening wail reached his ears as he turned back toward the prone, lifeless form. He froze.

Listening intently, he heard it again, only much closer and louder.

He looked upwards and noticed what appeared to be a ball of azure fire hurtling towards them. Reaching for his sword again, his mind began to spin when he heard his father speak. "It's all right Eric. She comes for me."

He whipped around at the voice and saw a translucent image of Thorvald standing over the body of his father. The man was smiling and watching the streak of iridescence flashing downward.

"Stay true to all that is right son." He said, without taking his eyes from the approaching vision.

Eric looked back in the direction of the maelstrom and threw up his hand against the brilliant light.

In the span of three heartbeats, the manifestation of an incredibly beautiful woman, mounted on a glistening black station, materialized next to his father. Wearing the trappings of a warrior with long, flowing hair, she held a spear at the end of a slender arm wrapped with the horse's reins. Her free arm reached around the dead warrior and pulled him into the midst of the fiery image.

The horse was massive, with a heaving chest and eyes the color of a smoldering campfire -- the woman was the personification of war itself.

She flashed a smile at him that was both fierce and proud. The *Valkyrie* was claiming a jewel among the stones of the world and she knew it. A brief, furious whirlwind whipped the surrounding brush, and with the crackle of a small thunderstorm, they were gone.

Eric stood spellbound, staring at a point in the sky where the apparition vanished. Finally, he allowed a small smile to chase across his face before turning back to the earthly remains of his father.

Reaching down to pick the body up, he heard a call from high above. He looked up and saw the silhouettes of several men from the village at the rim of the cliff above. He motioned for them to move west towards the crevice in the rock wall and sat down to wait.

The moon was high in the night sky by the time the dead and wounded were transported back to the hamlet. Freyhild moved woodenly towards the litter carried by Eric and Braggia. Muscles were flexing beneath the drawn cheeks as she reached out to touch the warrior she had come to love so dearly. Silent tears slid down her face as she walked the remaining distance with her hand on the dead man's arm.

For the first time in a dozen moons, a ship was filled with dead warriors and set ablaze in the outgoing tide. The entire village stood at the shore, watching the reddish orange blaze leap higher and higher, splashing a riot of color across the foaming surf.

The night gave way to morning and the soft glow of a crimson dawn crept upward into a pale, pastel blue sky. A lone figure stood silent sentry on the quiet beach.

Eric had been walking for hours, watching the darkness fade as the sun began its daily ascent when he felt, more than saw, a movement over his shoulder. Turning to see who was approaching, he noticed the linen wrapped ribcage before he found Wulf's face.

"Good morn Wulf. How are your hurts?"

The younger brother placed a hand on Eric's shoulder and smiled sadly. "Tis a bother, nothing more."

The brothers found the bleached remnants of a tree trunk that had washed ashore and sat in silence for some time before Wulf finally spoke again.

"I shall miss him sorely."

Eric smiled faintly without looking at his brother.

"Aye. It took many a year to realize he was not just another man."

Wulf nodded with his eyes fixed on the horizon and remained silent. Pulling up his hood, the morning breeze seemed to have turned a little colder as a sign of things to come.

The bright colors of autumn began to fade and the lush green grass turned a dusty brown. The leaves of gold and crimson began to lose their grip on the branches that gave them life. Summer was gone and the crisp feeling of fall was in the air. The game trails were covered with a thick carpet of red, brown and gold when a small boy on the beach cried. "Ships! There are ships coming!"

Newcomers were a rare event and within minutes everyone in the village rushed to the shore to see what banner was streaming from the mast. The flags were solid white with no apparent markings and the shields lining the railings were inverted. Signs of peace, or a trick?

With few spoken words, the women began pulling the children from the water's edge and shooing them towards the huts. The men slid their swords a short distance from the sheaths and let them fall back in place. If the newcomers wanted a fight, they wouldn't be disappointed.

When the boats were within hailing distance, the men lining the shore began to notice there were few men standing along the railings. The vessels appeared to be manned by women and children.

If it was a trick, it was a stupid ploy. Warriors left the women and children behind when they went on a raid. They didn't put them in harm's way if it could be avoided.

A few of the men from the village waded into the surf to catch ropes that were cast ashore and in less than half an hour, five ships were beached side-by-side in the lapping waves.

It was no trick; when everyone was ashore, there were close to sixty women, almost a hundred children and less than twenty men. They were the remnants of the village that Eric and his father had been banished from so many years earlier.

The struggle for good land in the Scandinavian countries had intensified and spread. Erik Segersall had defeated Svein Forkbeard of the Danes and then moved against his western neighbor, Olaf Tryggvason.

The only thing that had saved them was an advance warning of the ravaging horde. The men of the village knew there would be little precious time before the attack, so they loaded their women and children on the few available, moored craft and sent them away to safety.

The savage cries and screams of victor and victim could be heard long after the village was no longer in sight of the fleeing survivors. The heart wrenching sounds finally faded with the last rays of day. The first night aboard the ships was long and quiet.

A few old men, forced to board with the women, provided the necessary navigation. By now, anyone familiar with the sea knew they could follow their latitude by keeping the northern stars at the same height above the horizon.

The men of Eric's village were pleased with the arrival of so many women and the survivors of the ravaged town were thankful to be alive.

The bonfires were banked high and the mead began to flow freely before the sun was completely down. The men and women from sixteen to sixty were flirting and getting to know each other. Everyone knew the harsh reality; today and maybe tomorrow, that might be all there is.

Eric had walked down to the beach when the boats first arrived to ensure they posed no danger. Satisfied that the arrival of the newcomers was a good omen, he left and returned to his hut.

After Thorvald's death, the villagers looked to his son for guidance and he worked hard at meeting their needs, but his heart wasn't in it. As a matter of fact, there didn't seem to be anything that interested the young man any longer.

The moon was a rune covered silver platter, high in the star splattered heavens, when he finally left his hut to wander through the revelry. Many of the warriors were stumbling drunk and deep in their cups, but harmless for the most part. He had been worried that the sudden influx of women might result in a flurry of fights, but thus far all he had heard was a lot of guffaws and squeals of laughter.

He smiled slightly at the lighthearted jesting and couples walking arm-in-arm. Shoving large hands into the pockets of his tunic, he steered away from the fires and liquor to the quiet of a secluded cove.

Climbing a small hill, he located a jutting rock and sat down. The glowing moon and starlight ignited a billion tiny points of light across the bay and seemed to reflect a promise of better days to come.

"Hello."

The soft sound in the night startled him. The voice was that of a young woman.

"What do you want?"

The question came out as a harsh bark and the maiden was taken back. Softening his tone, he added, "I'm sorry. You startled me. What do you need?"

The lass stepped closer, looked him in the eyes and smiled. "There really is a fountain of youth, somewhere far to the south."

Eric started to respond before his mind had processed the statement. He slowly closed his mouth as a look of confusion crossed his face. The statement made no sense. No sense at . . .

The expression on his face changed from confusion to recognition and a smile. The first smile to grace the hard lined face for almost a year.

"Thorhild?"

The young woman's face lit up the entire area when she smiled.

"Yes Eric it's me. I heard you were here and have been looking for you ever since we landed. I had just about given up when I saw you wander by."

She paused and the smile left her face. "I hope you don't mind that I followed. I wanted to talk to you."

Eric stepped down from the rock, wanting to wrap his arms around her, but stood a short distance away.

"No, I don't mind. As a matter of fact . . . I'm glad you came."

After a brief, awkward silence, he turned back towards the rock. "Would you like to sit down?"

She placed a small hand on his shoulder and quickly stepped up onto the rocky perch.

He gently grasped the pale hand and smiled at the long, slender fingers. They appeared delicate, but were strong. He could think of nothing to say that wouldn't sound dumb, so he remained silent.

She patted a spot on the rock beside her, so he climbed up and sat down. For a long while they sat in silence until he finally spoke.

"You said you wanted to talk to me?"

She smiled somewhat shyly. "I saw you and I just had to talk to you." Again the smile faded. "Someone told me your father . . . is it true?"

The faint smile on his face sagged at the statement and he looked away. He had always discussed his father's death in a matter of fact tone – a grown man didn't display emotions.

The crystalline eyes that held him fast made it hard to speak in the cold, indifferent tone he was accustomed to. "Yes . . . it's true."

She remained silent, the azure orbs glistening in the moonlight. "I'm truly sorry Eric. I know how close you were."

Her eyes were dancing with the reflected starlight from the bay when she reached over to place a hand on his knee. A look of uncertainty passed over her face and remained until he reached down and wrapped his huge paw around the small digits.

The hours passed in complete quiet as they sat hand-in-hand, watching the day dawn slightly gray and turn to a ruddy glow. A couple of hours before daybreak, Thorhild had leaned over against Eric's shoulder and began breathing steadily.

He could have sat there for days and ignored the cramping muscles, but knew his kinsmen would be starting to worry if he didn't return soon after daybreak.

Shifting slightly, he spoke softly into Thorhild's ear. "The sun is coming up."

She started slightly at the words as memories of the night slid past her eyes. Brushing a hand across her face, she smiled. "Oh goodness, stars in Valhallah. I must have fallen asleep. I'm sorry."

He pushed some stray hair back from her face. "Tis no matter." He released her hand and stretched before adding, "But we best return to the village."

Hopping down from the rock, he extended his hand to help her. Arm-in-arm, they walked back to the hamlet in a blissful silence.

The days grew short and there was a bite in the wind. Winter was coming. The warriors were hunting and fishing every day, providing wives and daughters with meat for the long nights of bitter cold and the short, gray days ahead. The beach was covered with racks of drying fish and smoke huts filled with jerky.

Thorhild moved in with Eric and the village shaman blessed the union amidst gay revelry. The transformation in the young clan leader was obvious and good for the entire village. He was up early, working for the good of all, laughing with the children, helping young and old alike.

Within a few months, Thorhild was expecting and her husband was seldom seen without a broad smile on his face. For the first time in a very long while, the winds were fair for the young Viking.

Wulf had also found a mate among the refugees and built a new hut before the winter snows began to fall. It was an unusual match, Wulf was well over six feet three inches and she stood about five feet two.

Fate stepped in to bring the young couple together. Wulf's bride-to-be; a lass named Geijee, had fallen out of the boat upon arrival and couldn't swim. The cold water was only about five feet deep, but the pounding surf made it impossible to stand.

At that instant, Wulf was carrying supplies up the beach less than twenty paces away. He heard a squawk and the sounds of someone thrashing in the water.

Dropping the crate he was packing, he rushed into the surf to see slender arms thrashing the choppy surface.

Wulf couldn't swim either, but gave it no thought as he dove into the foaming waves in the direction of the arms. He struggled to the surface and realized he could stand. Pushing a wet mop of hair out of his eyes, he began working his way through the pounding surf.

By the time he was up to his neck, he took a deep breath and dropped below the surface to try and see the girl. It came as quite a shock when small hands grabbed hold of him and began climbing. He stood upright; having trouble breathing due to the soggy mass that had wrapped itself around his head.

Trying to remain calm, breathe and unwrap himself from the death grip, he spoke to the young woman. "It's ok . . . I've got you."

He turned to where he could see her face and smiled broadly. "Or in this case, I think you've got me."

The terrified eyes were staring at him, but not seeing. He continued to watch her with a reassuring look on his face, speaking calmly and quietly.

After a few moments, the glazed look began to fade and the eyelids blinked. She slowly focused on Wulf and, if possible, the ruddy completion glowed even more.

"Oh my, I'm sorry . . . I thought . . . I couldn't breathe, twas . . . you're very handsome."

Gasping, she couldn't believe what her mouth had just uttered.

"Oh goodness. No . . . I didn't mean . . ."

She stopped and looked as though she had avoided drowning, but would now die of embarrassment.

Wulf waded back to bank, lowering her as he walked. When he was a few steps from shore, he took her by the waist and set her down. He had forgotten all about the cold water.

She stood, with one hand clinging tightly to his tunic. He started to pat her on the head when he noticed the clinging wrap was not on a child, but a young woman. He felt a slight flush in his face when he noticed she was definitely a woman.

Now it was Wulf's turn to blink and stutter. "I . . . you're . . . what I mean is . . . I thought."

She had stopped and was staring at her rescuer, wondering what come over him. "Are you all right?"

Wulf turned away, shaking his head. Women didn't usually affect him this way. Taking a deep breath, he turned back toward her. "Yeah, I'm ok, just a little light headed for a moment, that's all."

Glancing around, everyone seemed to be going about their work as though nothing had happened. He looked back at Geijee. "Where are your people? Your mother and father?"

The expression on the girl's face changed from excitement to grief. Her eyes dropped and she turned away. "My mother died when I was small. My father stayed behind to . . ."

She still couldn't bring herself to say the word. As long as she didn't say it, maybe there was still hope her father was alive.

Wulf had seen the expression enough to know the answer. "I'm sorry. Do you have any other relatives?"

The girl remained with her back to him, but shook her head no.

"I have friends, I'll be ok."

Wulf spoke as she started to move up the beach.

"Wait."

She stopped and looked back. He waded ashore and took her hand. "There's someone I want you to meet."

He introduced her to his adopted mother, Freyhild, and the two became immediate friends. Time went by and eventually, Geijee moved from Freyhild's hut into Wulf's.

Winter came all too soon, spreading a cold, glistening blanket over the sleeping landscape. An icy, northern wind blew the snow into drifts high as a man standing on a horse. A few trails were cut into the surrounding woods for hunting, gathering firewood and to get away for a little while.

The long nights went on without end, approaching mid-winter -- a time the countries to the south celebrated something called the Christ's Mass. A few of the Vikings had heard of the religion of the southern lands, but the ways of Odin, Thor and Frey still ran strong in their veins.

Thorhild was heavy with child when the winter solstice came, but making daily trips into the woods to gather firewood remained a necessary chore.

It was just another gray, cold winter's day when Geijee threw a laughing smile over her shoulder at Wulf and headed to Eric's hut. Thorhild met her a few paces in front of the house and gave her sister-in-law a quick, awkward embrace around her bulging stomach. Beaming with happiness, they headed up the gentle slope through the deep snow banks. Geijee was not yet pregnant, but there was plenty of time.

Arm in arm, neither woman saw the broad, wavering shadow that followed.

All of the firewood close to the village had been consumed, so they found themselves a long way from the hamlet before dead branches began to appear.

Chattering about what they would do when spring came, both women had collected a fair-sized armload of wood when a strange voice broke the pleasant interlude.

"Morn ladies."

Geijee squeaked and dropped her load of firewood.

Thorhild inhaled sharply and turned her armful of dry branches to see who it was. She recognized the man, but didn't know his name. He had arrived with Geijee's group, but had remained aloof and withdrawn from the rest of the clan.

Geijee put a hand to her chest. "Tord. You scared me. What are you doing out here?"

The man eyed her through lidded eyes and spit into the clean snow. "Felt like some company and decided you would do just fine."

Thorhild dropped her load of wood. "I think you better go back to the village."

The man glanced in Thorhild's direction. "I wasn't talking to you – Thorhild is it? I recommend you go back alone. Geijee and I won't be long."

He moved towards Geijee as Thorhild reached down and grabbed a heavy, short chunk of wood. The man continued to ignore her and in a matter of seconds, had the struggling Geijee down on the packed snow. She was screaming and clawing at his face, but it wasn't slowing him down.

Laughing, he tore her tunic just as a crashing pain flashed in the back of his head.

He fell face down on the young woman, but pushed himself up to his knees and felt the back of his head. His hand came away streaked with blood. "Thor's hammer woman. What's the matter with you?"

"Get off of her!" Thorhild attempted to shove him away from Geijee, but he roughly backhanded her. She went sprawling into a snow bank, crying out in pain. Leaping to his feet, he took a couple of quick strides towards her. "Hel's daughter! I told you to stay out of this."

He kicked her violently in the side as she rolled off the mound of snow. Thorhild screamed in pain and drew her knees up to her swollen belly. The brute shook his head with satisfaction and started to turn when Geijee leaped on his back and began clawing his face like a wild woman.

"Odin curse you woman! By the gods you're going to regret that."

Grabbing a long mass of light brown hair, he jerked the girl over his shoulder, throwing her into the snow. Placing a foot on her stomach, he started to punch her when he felt an iron manacle on his wrist.

Jerking loose, he spun around, standing face to face with Eric. The clan leader's voice was calm and deadly. "If you caused serious hurt to either of these women, you will die."

Tord knew Eric was leader in the village and had a reputation for being dangerous, but he was furious and the voice of warning in the back of his mind fell of deaf ears. "To Hel with you!"

Jerking a long broadsword from his scabbard, he grabbed the handle with both beefy fists, and swung downward towards the neck of the intruder.

Eric's blade seemed to appear in his hand of its own accord and moved effortlessly to deflect the killing blow. The man almost stumbled and fell, having put all his weight into the swing. Eric pivoted smoothly, stepping back.

"Put the sword away and the village elders will judge you. Raise it again and I will kill you."

The man roared in an insane rage and charged. Once again, he missed the target of his anger, but felt an odd sensation in his chest. He had charged completely past Eric and was turning around slowly, looking down at the hilt protruding from his tunic.

He gave Eric a bewildered look. "You kilt me."

Dropping to his knees, he blew a bloody froth through the heavy beard and fell face forward in the snow.

Not bothering with a backward glance, Eric rushed to Thorhild's side. She was curled up tightly, making small, moaning sounds.

He felt a soft touch on his shoulder and glanced upward. It was Geijee. "He kicked her."

Eric nodded. "We must get her back to the village."

He lifted her as gently as possible, but she gave another groan and passed out. Eric felt the warm flow of blood against his arm as he lifted her and the first fear he had known for a very long time hammered in his heart.

Geijee looked at Eric as he turned towards home. "How did you know we were in trouble? I thought we were all alone."

Without glancing back at Geijee, he answered. "I saw you. I just couldn't get here in time."

She glanced in the direction of the village. They would have to walk for several minutes before the smoke from the huts became visible. She didn't understand how he could have seen them, but asked no further questions and hurried to catch up.

Wulf was walking out of the village by the time they reached the outskirts of the hamlet and broke into a run through the deep snow when he saw them.

"Eric! What happened?" He quickly took in the scene and turned to break trail the remaining distance back to their homes.

The faint light provide by a false day was completely gone by the time Geijee walked out of the hut that evening and approached the hunched figure outside. "She's going to be all right Eric. She lost a lot of blood, but Tyrkir says she will live."

Eric glanced up at the pallid, tired face. Lines of fatigue and concern stretched out from the blue orbs.

"The baby. Is the baby all right?"

Geijee's face wrenched into a vision of agony and the tears she had been holding back broke forth in a torrent.

"I'm sorry Eric. I am so sorry."

She dropped to her knees and grabbed him, unable to control the flood of emotions.

Eric held her gently and told her everything would be ok and not to cry. He kept saying it was all right as he felt his heart ripped from his chest.

A long shadow from the cracking fire fell across his feet and he glanced up. Wulf had not left his side and was now looking down at his brother and wife. Eric had not seen his younger brother cry since he was a child, but the gray-blue eyes were glistening with unshed tears. Unable to speak, he gave Wulf a shrug indicating he would accept whatever life gave.

Wulf reached down and placed a large, gentle hand on Geijee's shoulder. She started slightly at the touch and looked up. Upon seeing her husband, she leaped into his arms and muffled her cries in his shoulder. After holding her for a moment, he turned and led her away.

Eric sat and watched until they were out of sight, then stood and brushed imaginary snow off his trousers. Letting out a long breath to get his composure, he ducked under the hide covering the hut's entrance and stepped into the dim, smoky interior.

Freyhild was kneeling near Thorhild's cot on the far side of the room and she turned at the sound. She had been holding Thorhild's hand, but gently placed it on the edge of the cot and stood. Saying nothing, she quietly left the hut.

The smell of blood was still strong in the room as Eric walked around the little fire in the middle. He leaned over and brushed a few strands of loose hair away from Thorhild's moist face. The eyes didn't open and he knew she was exhausted, but breathing steadily. Dropping to the floor, he placed the small hand in his and leaned against the cot.

He felt the dragon talisman underneath the heavy tunic, and the memories of the ice castle and three fates began to assuage the pain in his chest. What was it Skuld said before giving him the tiny icon? 'The footsteps of the greatest of the gods he will follow. But the darkness that was Loki will inflict a wound of evil from which there is no recovery.'

The crackling of a small fire in the hearth drew his attention to the carefree flames. He was so tired he felt his eyelids droop as his mind slid towards a dark, quiet abyss. Leaning over against the cot, the vision of the glowing coals faded.

☼☼☼

Heat from the huge fireplace warmed a large portion of the floor, casting a pleasant glow across the smooth slabs of paving. Odin held his hands toward the glowing embers and sighed. The beginning of the end. It started so long ago, but today would be a terrible milestone in the tragic journey.

He turned as a huge Viking strode across the broad expanse of glistening tiles. Heavy brows furrowed as the man approached the throne of Hlidskialf. A large, calloused hand rested on the hilt of the sword at his side.

"Tis the spawn of evil itself I tell you." Heimdall's large hands swept away from him in a disgusting gesture. "Did you know of this?"

"Know of what?" Odin moved from the fireplace to the massive chair of his throne room.

"Loki and Angerboda."

"The giantess?"

"Yes."

"The union has produced . . ."

Stopping mid-sentence, Heimdall was as angry as Odin had ever seen him.

"Produced what?"

"Come."

A short while later found the two gods moving through an assembly of gods and goddesses, standing at the entrance to a birthing room. Pushing his way through the crowd, Odin stepped into the room and drew back.

The giantess was asleep in a large bed and at her feet curled a large snake, a girl child and a wolf. Still wet from their introduction to the world of Asgard, the newborns turned towards the towering stranger in their midst, cowering in fear.

Odin's breath was coming in short, rapid pulses. The visions; forewarnings of Ragnarok. No longer something in the future – the premonitions were here.

Too many mistakes – they had allowed evil to exist and grow far too long. There was no way to go back. Gaining control of his emotions, he spoke in a low, deadly voice. "Kill them. Kill them all."

"Odin. NO!"

It was Loki. The pleading face reminded him of the laughing lad he had known in their youth. "There are but helpless children. Only a heartless barbarian would kill them."

The god-of-gods looked at the circle of faces – family and friends, all looking at him with horror in their eyes. Once again, fate was turning him in a direction that led to destruction. Unable to resist, he heard himself say, "The girl will reside on the throne of the netherworld, the snake is to be cast into the coldest waters of the north and the wolf must be caged."

A look of relief passed over Loki's face. "Thank you Odin. You will not regret your kindness."

"I already do."

Feeling older than he had ever felt before, Odin left the chamber, unable to believe what was happening.

In accordance with the orders of the supreme god, Hel was sent to reign over the cowards, thieves and scum of the underworld. Jormungand was cast into the sea, but rather than perish from the cold, the serpent grew into a leviathan that would haunt the dreams of sailors in the ages to come.

Fenris grew at a rate unparalleled in the world of wolves and soon amazed even the gods with his strength. Odin realized the day would come when the massive, iron cage would no longer be sufficient to confine the animal and summoned Tyr to discuss it.

"The wolf is surpassing our worst fears Tyr; the cage will not hold him for more than a few months."

"Aye, tis as though a dark power feeds the beast. His strength is unlike any I have ever seen."

"We must find a way to bind him with unbreakable fetters."

"The beast breaks chains as though they were hemp." Tyr's eyes were darting back and forth. "Chains that would hold that animal would have to be . . ."

He paused not wanting to say the words.

"Magic." Odin said them for him.

"Aye."

Standing, the supreme god stared at the god of war a moment before speaking. "Summon Hermod, I will send him to the dark dwarves to find such a chain."

Two days hence, the messenger was standing before Odin, holding what appeared to be a handful of thread. He stepped down from the throne and ran his fingers into the spidery web. "What is this? I sent you to get bonds that would hold the fiercest beast we know. This . . . would not hold a leaf in the wind."

"Try to break it my lord."

Odin scowled and grabbed a handful of the thread into his beefy paws and pulled, not taking his eyes from Hermod. The glare turned quizzical and then a look of surprise crossed the grizzled visage."

"By the mead of Kvasir, the threads are unbreakable!" Releasing the web, he grasped Hermod by the shoulder. "Well done! Now we have but to bind Fenris in this material."

The wolf was filled with the cunning of hate and every attempt by the gods to approach the beast was quickly thwarted. Finally Heimdall suggested they challenge the animal to a contest of strength; the gods would find a material so strong the carnivore would be unable to break it.

Fenris, sure of his strength, accepted the challenge and broke ropes, cables and chains with ease, delighting in the sport. When Tyr approached the monstrous canine with the tiny threads, the wolf suspected treachery and refused to allow his binding. After hours of fruitless coaxing and reassurances, Tyr finally told him it was not a trick and he would place his hand in Fenris' mouth as a symbol of trust.

The beast agreed and, loosely holding Tyr's hand in his jaws, watched as the gods wrapped him in the gossamer mesh. Feeling the powerful magic in the tiny threads, he snapped the rows of ivory fangs shut, ripping off the hand of the god of war. Roaring in fury, he twisted and spun around in an attempt to free himself of the web.

Exhausted, and bound in the unbreakable fetters, Fenris howled with a rage that would never be satiated until . . . the huge, yellow eyes found Odin. The unspoken communication that flowed between the two would haunt the dreams of the god in the decades to follow.

The mightiest of the gods returned to the throne room and once more stood before the glowing pile of embers in the huge hearth. Another wrong turn, but there seemed to be no other choice. Dragging up a small chair, he pulled off his heavy, leather boots and called for a mug of ale.

The jug of mead appeared and he took a large swig, not tasting the smooth, mellow liquid. His foresight was almost the equivalent of his memory and it was tearing him apart. There was no way to change the past, but there had to be some way to change the future.

The reddish-yellow glow faded as his head slumped forward. Warmth from the fire went unheeded.

☼☼☼

Eric awoke suddenly and looked around him. He was sitting on the dirt floor of their hut, leaning against the cot Thorhild was resting on.

The present came rushing back. Their baby. Gone. Life was hard and often unfair to the point of being cruel.

Straightening up, he moved carefully so as not to waken Thorhild, but realized she was already awake, watching him.

"We will try again. We have time."

She was so incredibly strong. He nodded and took her hand. Somehow, that seemed to make everything bearable. They would make it another day.

"I will get some broth."

The days passed but the dream refused to leave him alone. Night after night, the monstrous canine returned. He finally went in search of Wotun. The old man was splitting wood near his hut and lowered a battered axe to his side as Eric approached.

"Good morn Wotun."

"Morn Eric."

The old man seemed at the verge of death, and unchanged from twenty years ago. Eric picked up a piece of cordwood and placed it on the chopping block. He reached over to retrieve the axe and split the chunk of wood. "Tis a hard winter we're seeing."

The story of the fight and Thorhild's loss of the baby had spread through the village before daybreak and Wotun had received the news without comment.

Through the years, a special bond had formed between the wizened old Viking and the young clan leader. Wotun had long ago come to believe he was no longer capable of feelings, but the hushed story brought a pang of anguish to the worn, tired heart. Memories of Ubbe returned to salt the wound.

He reached over to pat Eric on the shoulder, taking the axe from his hand. "Come, let us share a warm drink. There is something on your mind."

The old relic terrified the children of the village, but Eric had long ago lost any fear of the man. "That would be good. Thank you."

After sitting in silence for a period, holding cups of warm mead in their hands, Eric finally spoke. "I've been having the same dream every night. It was like the ones I had as a lad on the ship -- remember when we were coming from the old land?"

Wotun's countenance turned downward into a grimace, not angry but deep concern. "I had hoped we were done with those. What was the dream about?"

Eric related as much of the dream as he could remember and found Wotun filling in some of the blank spaces. When he finished, he knew the old shaman knew what was behind the dream.

"Why would the dreams be returning now and what do they mean?"

Wotun stood and turned away before answering. "I have long lived in fear of this day. I understand, but cannot explain what is happening, or why. It would be like describing a garden of flowers to a blind man or a vulture infested battlefield to a small child."

The old man turned to face Eric, his eye flashing with intensity. "There is one thing that you must understand. Whatever happens in your dreams is somehow happening to you."

The force in the old man's voice cut to the core of Eric's consciousness. The sage was telling him that the dreams were more than nightly voyages; they were part of his life, this life.

He reached up and felt the small dragon under his tunic. There were so many things in this world he did not understand.

"Your words strike home old man, but it seems I am not in control of much of my life."

The intense look on Wotun's face softened as he reached over to pat the broad shoulder. "The beginning of wisdom is the realization that much of what we know as fact has no basis in truth. In many ways, we are like leaves in a current, subject to quiet eddies and raging forces we cannot understand, much less control."

The man paused, as if reflecting inward. "The price of knowledge and pride is heavy beyond comprehension. Wisdom begets regret and one follows the other as night follows day."

Eric studied the patriarch before nodding slowly. He stood up and glanced at the small fire in the blackened, stone fireplace. "Thank you Wotun. I should be return . . ."

A cry from the beach brought them both up short. "Ships afar! There are sails on the horizon!"

The entire village turned out to see the newcomers, be they friend or foe. Spring was still in the distance and few travelers ventured abroad in the cruel, lashing currents of winter.

The ship's bow was lined with people in strange clothing. A few of the old timers recognized the garb of people from the south. There were only two ships and from the looks of the occupants, they were not warriors.

The appearance of a number of children at the prow removed all doubt. These people were not looking for pillage or plunder; they were looking for a haven.

The men of the village were soon hauling on the heavy ropes from the boats, dragging them up the sandy incline to where the keel refused to go any farther. The ship's draught was deeper than the Viking longboat and much of the afternoon was spent in carting goods and people through the shallow water to the sandy beach.

One middle-aged man seemed to be treated with substantial deference by a majority of the seafarers. Clothed completely in black robes, the man never smiled and looked at the welcoming committee much as a farmer might inspect a plow horse.

Isleifur Gissurarson was a holy man from the south, spreading the teachings of a man dead almost a thousand years. Shortly after the boats were unloaded and the newcomers clustered around him, he removed the large, black hat and raised his voice above the scattered conversations.

"Oh Lord, hear our prayers."

A hush fell over the cluster of people and even the Vikings became silent. The men among the newcomers removed their hats and the villagers looked at each other, wondering if they were supposed to do likewise.

The black robed visitor raised a hand over the crowd. "God, grant me the strength and wisdom to bring these lost souls into your fold.

Help me guide them to your safe haven."

The man dropped his hand, and amidst murmured 'amens', turned and headed up the beach.

Eric approached the apparent leader of the new arrivals and extended his hand in greeting. "Welcome to our village. I am called Eric, the leader of the Asvaldsson clan and this hamlet."

The man extended his hand with the palm down, waiting expectantly. Eric grabbed the extended hand in a firm grasp and gave the traditional two or three quick shakes before releasing it.

The priest's eyes flinched at the strength in the grip, but quickly recovered. "I am Isleifur Gissurarson, you may call me father."

The clan leader bristled slightly at the statement. "My father is dead."

The man did not seem disturbed, or even surprised by the strong reaction. "I represent the Church of the Almighty God, the Father of all, and therefore all people are rightly considered our children. If you are a child of God, you will address me as father."

The muscles under Eric's jaw flexed. "I bow knee to Odin, Allfather of Norsemen, and no other." The hard, blue eyes held the soft, grey eyes of the priest fast. "I call upon Thor and Freyr when the need arises."

The grey eyes dropped. "I am not your enemy young man. I come only to spread the light and hope that comes from One greater than us all."

"No god is greater than Odin!"

Eric was about the grab the man and shake him when he felt a firm hand on his shoulder. Whirling at the touch, he was face to face with Wotun.

"Let it be Eric. This man is just the first of many, bringing a flood you cannot withstand."

Something in the old man's voice hit home and the anger was suddenly gone. The world was changing and there was nothing he could do about it. Without so much as a backward glance at the priest, Eric turned and headed back to his hut.

Throwing back the heavy hide covering the hut's entrance, he noticed Thorhild sitting on the edge of her cot. He forced a smile and walked across the small room to sit at her side.

"The new arrivals have a man with them that says he's the messenger of some all powerful god. He reminds me of the Irish monks we met last year, but more self-important. I started to braid the offensive oaf when Wotun stopped me."

Thorhild placed a hand on his knee, but remained silent. She knew he would speak what was really on his mind, given time.

Eric placed his hand on top of his wife's. "There's something about the man . . . he seems so sure . . ."

The statement was interrupted by the rapping of a stick on the lodge pole entrance to the hut.

"Eric. Tis the village elders; we need to talk to you."

"I'll be right out."

Patting Thorhild on the knee, he stood and strode out of the hut. Just outside was a gathering of about a dozen men, most of whom were the oldest members of the small village.

"Bjarne. What can I do for you?"

Bjarne Herjufsson was a highly respected member of the community and kept to himself for the most part. The man was getting on in years and had many times related a story about fabulous lands to the west he had encountered while sailing in his youth.

"Tis the matter of Tord's death. Were it up to me . . ." He let the thought hang a moment before adding, "Well, his kin will not let the matter rest."

Eric placed huge hands on his hips. "Well, out with it Bjarne. What's to be done?"

The man glanced at the men surrounding him. "There's to be an Althing. Your fate will be decided there."

Eric's mind flashed back almost two decades when he had heard a group of men telling his father the same thing. If it were not for Thorhild, he really wouldn't care.

Two days later the village assembled for the traditional gathering and formal declarations that would result. Tradition required the law speaker to cite one-third of the laws of the land at each gathering.

Although it took longer, the results were the same his father had heard some twenty years earlier in Norway. Eric Thorvaldsen was to be banished for a period of no less than three years. It was not justice, but it was the law. The Icelanders knew without law there was nothing but chaos.

Wotun sat quietly in the back of the lodge and listened to the proceedings and when the decision was delivered, stood up and left the huge hall.

He felt responsible for the young man in so many ways, but had learned ages past that the fates were independent of all. Eric was a strong and fierce Viking. He was honest to a fault and served others well. The old man was very proud of him.

The thought brought him up short. He chuckled quietly, pride -- that had been their undoing ages ago. The gods of old had indeed been a proud lot. He dropped the cover to his hut and added a little wood to the fire. It would be good to see summer come.

The quiet reminiscing was broken by a tapping at his door. Thinking it was Eric, he barked. "Well come in, don't stand out there like some frightened child."

The voice that came back was not Eric's. "I am not a frightened child Wotun, but wish to speak to you."

The old man hesitated. The voice sounded familiar, but it wasn't anyone he knew. Then it hit him. The holy man from the south. But why would the man want to see him?

"Come in," was the gruff response.

The man entered the dim interior and straightened to his full height. Less than six feet tall, he still invoked a quiet awe in most circles. However, in Wotun's domain, he was simply a man.

"Speak your mind and be gone."

The priest inhaled deeply and let it out slowly, as though carefully considering his words. "I have been sent . . . I wanted to talk to you about . . . your past."

The tone in the man's words brought Wotun up short. The man knew something. Something that terrified and yet intrigued him at the same time.

"My past is my business. No others."

"I know you are . . . much older than people realize. I know, believe, you have secrets and knowledge that many would kill for, or flee from."

Wotun stood. The man was either fishing or . . . was it possible this God of his could know of his real identity?

"You waste my time shaman. State your business."

The priest flinched slightly. He licked dry lips and quickly hurried on.

"If you are who some believe you are, you should have been dead generations ago. For some reason, you have been held back from . . . death, as those who have preceded you. Whatever you hold to be true, believe this, the God I serve is truly all powerful. There is nothing that lies beyond His comprehension, or ability.

"If you tire of this world and are unable to leave, call upon Him and He will help."

The old Viking stared into the solemn grey eyes. "You speak of something no one can understand. Do not offer that which cannot be delivered."

Isleifur's face softened. "You have answered my question. There is nothing more I can say. If you are to change your . . . future, you must go to the Lord."

Wotun crossed his arms, turning his back. "Bah, begone and bother me no more."

He waited in silence for a response and when none came, turned back. The room was empty. A low growl emanated from his throat. The priest truly believed what he was saying. It was unsettling.

The next few days were spent in preparation for Eric's departure. The clan leader would have to leave Thorhild behind. A score of loyal followers would accompany him, but it was agreed Wulf would stay with the women and do what he could.

The ships were finally ready but Eric knew he needed to confer with Wotun before they left. There was something he had to know. He dropped the lead rope onto the sand and headed up the beach toward the lone hut. It would be hard to bid the old man farewell. The ancient reprobate was like a second father to him.

Wotun turned upon hearing a rap at the hut's entrance. He smiled at the familiar knock. "Come in Eric."

Eric ducked his head entering the small hut and walked over to embrace the grizzled, old grey beard. "I know you have no use for sentiment, but I shall miss you sorely."

Wotun smiled slightly, a strange decoration on the craggy face. "As long as the sentiment is not misplaced, I can tolerate it."

"I needed to speak with you before I left." Eric ran a calloused hand over a bushy, rust colored beard. "My dream about Loki and Angrboda . . . and Fenris. Do you know how it truly ends? Are the bards of old right?" He stared at the old man with desperation in his eyes. "Does Loki die?"

The smile quickly vanished. "Of course he dies. Everyone dies. Even gods" Wotun exhaled quickly. "I'm sorry. I didn't mean to growl at you. I would tell you to forget about it, but I know that's not possible." He paused briefly and then hurried on. "But knowing the rest . . ."

He let the sentence hang.

"Sit and I will tell you of the death of Loki."

Eric moved some hides from a small bench and sat down as Wotun shuffled across the room and stirred something in a large, black pot hanging over the fire.

He still had his back to Eric when he began the story.

☼☼☼

"Twas as though the end of summer were signifying the end of the golden era. A time of honor, valor and great deeds was drawing to a close.

"The offspring of Loki and Angrboda had grown to enormous proportions and power, feeding upon the growing evil in the world. Hel was confined to the realm of the underworld, Jormungand to the vastness of the seas and Fenris was still bound with the unbreakable fetters, but nothing lasts forever.

"Loki was still free to spread the evil that had taken his heart as a youth. Time and again, he perpetrated the foulest deeds, only to make amends and gain forgiveness.

"He even left Angrboda and married a good woman named Sigyn, but twas to no avail. The evil within him had taken control of his every thought and deed.

"The gods had banished the 'evil one' from their midst, but still tolerated his existence. As long as he wasn't in their sight, they decided he could do no harm. Another grievous mistake.

"The final blow came when Aegir, the ancient god of the sea, invited the host of Asgard to a great feast. We gladly accepted and were enjoying the fruits of boon companionship when the 'deceiver' walked in uninvited and unwelcome into our midst.

"Casting insults and derision to all present, Loki spewed venom like the most poisonous of snakes. Unable to tolerate the inexcusable behavior longer, we threw him from the great hall, forbidding his return.

"He not only returned, but with a vengeance. Slaying Aegir's favorite servant, he attacked Sif, beloved of Thor, and slandered the memory of Balder.

"Fleeing before he could be caught, he knew his life would be forfeit if ever captured by the gods. But his deceit and trickery were not sufficient to forever elude the fury of those he had once called friends.

"Many of the gods wanted to cleave his head from his shoulders when he was finally imprisoned. But I decided he was to be bound as his offspring Fenris. Side-by-side, the manifestation of evil and the most fearsome beast in the world, were confined to the lowest reaches of the dark caverns of Svart-alfa-heim.

"A poisonous serpent was suspended over the face of Loki, dripping venom upon his face. The punishment was to remind him of the evil he spread throughout Asgard. If not for the tender caring of Sigyn, I think the torment would have been unbearable.

"There he remained until the Fimbul winter and the battle of Ragnarok. One of my . . . Odin's last memories is seeing Heimdall and Loki battling to the death – both on their knees, covered in blood and still trading mortal wounds. No one, mortal or god, could have survived those final sword thrusts."

Wotun stopped as though remembering where he was. Running a ragged sleeve through a greasy mustache, he glanced at Eric.

"The gods of Asgard died that day lad. It marked the end of an age of swords, axes and wolves. Twas as inevitable as the rising and setting of the sun."

"But . . . you survived."

"Nay. Tis not Odin that stands before you, but a sad reminder of a proud and glorious era. The gods and goddesses of that time are gone forever."

"It is possible that a . . . remnant of Loki survived?"

"That, lad, is a thought that has haunted my dreams since the day I walked from the glaciers of the north."

End of Book 1

Excerpt from Book 2

Silence covered the crew like snow on a flower. Heavy, cold snow.

Eric stood and walked towards the head of the stairwell. His legs were so tired they were trembling. Stopping at the top, he stared down into the darkness. Someone, or something, had extinguished the few torches lighting the lower level.

*"**Cooommme doowwwnnn.**"*

The words were barely recognizable, but he knew the meaning. It was a challenge – a challenge meant for him alone.

When he started down the stairs, his men moved to follow, but he turned and motioned them back. This was something he had to do alone.

Satisfied they understood, he headed down the cold, stone paved steps. Upon reaching the bottom, the smell of smoke swept over him like a veil of spider webs. Flickers of red and yellow from an unseen fire danced up the corners of the walls. A strange, wavering light emanated from some source a short distance down the hallway leading off to the left.

His hand slowly moved to the hilt of his sword. The cold, polished iron gave him reassurance as he stared at the glowing apparition in the black corridor. The soft sound of metal sliding against leather filled the silent chamber. "Well, I'm here. Are you the leader, or just a spokesperson for the real power?"

The inhuman chuckle that emanated from the darkness sent a shiver up the Viking's spine. "So, you wake me, destroy my servants and throw insults – without even knowing who I am. Such arrogance I have not seen since . . ."

The specter left the sentence unfinished, moving in total silence toward Eric. The eidolon stopped about ten paces away and stood in quiet reflection, studying the defiant human with an idle curiosity.

"My rest has been undisturbed for a thousand years." A faint, red aura pulsated around the apparition. "You do not have the appearance of one who can no longer think clearly. Why would you provoke one who can easily kill you without mercy or regret?"

Eric bristled at the casual dismissal and reached under his jerkin to grasp the small, iron dragon. "I suppose you didn't know about the abominations that filled your dungeons and their captives. Good people who simply want to raise their families in peace and safety."

"Good people who . . ." The apparition snarled in disgust. "Good,

bad – words of Midgard mortals, nothing more. You cannot comprehend the mind of a god. Do not try."

Even though the thing standing in front of him looked in every aspect to be a man, he knew it was not human. In some circles he would even be considered handsome. There was something familiar about the face . . .

The thought was shattered when the man drew a gleaming sword and turned it back and forth as though studying it. "Curious instrument. I seldom had need of it . . . in times past. Cunning and stealth always served me well in those days."

He drew in a deep breath and turned to the Viking as though he had temporarily forgotten he was there. "Ah yes, I have no use for the human fodder you referred to, but I did need my servants, and for that you must pay."

Reflexes honed through battle were the only thing that saved Eric from the first lightning strike. Faster than the eye could follow, the demon attacked, his flashing sword moving with the speed of a striking snake. Sparks from the ringing swords filled the small chamber and soon the sound of the Viking sucking wind accompanied the clanging of metal.

Eric's blade creased the apparition and not only revealed a tiny crimson line, it brought about a profound change in the creature's demeanor. The sneer disappeared and the taunting stopped. "You're no ordinary mortal! What magic do you conceal?"

Suddenly there was an uncertainty in the demon's carriage that wasn't there before. Deflecting blow after blow from the Viking, he began looking around the room as though searching for something. "Odin? Are you here? Show yourself!"